About the author

Born in 1963 to Jamaican parents living in Brixton, Alex Wheatle spent most of his childhood in a Surrey children's home. He returned to Brixton in 1977 where he founded the Crucial Rocker sound system and performed his own songs and lyrics under the name of Yardman Irie. He spent a short stint in prison following the Brixton uprising of 1981. Following his release from prison he continued to write poems and lyrics and became known as the *Brixtonbard*.

His first novel, *Brixton Rock* (Arcadia Books), was published to critical acclaim in 1999. Five more novels, *East Of Acre Lane, The Seven Sisters, Island Songs, Checkers* and *The Dirty South* followed, all highly praised. His books are on school reading lists and Alex takes part in Black History Month every year, while working with English PEN and the Children's Discovery Centre to promote reading.

He teaches in various places, including Lambeth College, holds workshops in prisons and is frequently invited to schools to speak to students, inspiring in them, with his own story, a passion for literature. A UK Film Council-backed film of *East of Acre Lane* is in the making. He appears regularly on BBC1's *The One Show* and on radio. In the autumn of 2010 he wrote and performed his own one-man autobiographical show for Tara Arts, *Uprising*, and took the performance on tour in 2011 and 2012. He was also part of the creative team (and starred in a cameo role) in the short film production *Tiny*, in 2012, which warns young people about the dangers of joining gangs.

Alex was awarded an MBE for services to literature in 2008. He lives with his family in South London and has just completed a new novel about a young white teenage girl being adopted by a black foster family.

Brenton Brown

Alex Wheatle

ARCADIA BOOKS

Arcadia Books Ltd
139 Highlever Road
London W10 6PH

www.arcadiabooks.co.uk

First published in Great Britain by Arcadia Books 2011
This B format edition published 2013

A catalogue record for this book is available from the British Library.

ISBN 978-1-908129-86-4

Typeset in Garamond by MacGuru Ltd
Printed and bound by CPI Group (UK) Ltd, Croydon CR0 4YY

Arcadia Books supports English PEN *www.englishpen.org* and The
Book Trade Charity *http://booktradecharity.wordpress.com*

Arcadia Books distributors are as follows:

in the UK and elsewhere in Europe:
Macmillan Distribution Ltd
Brunel Road
Houndmills
Basingstoke
Hants RG21 6XS

in the USA and Canada:
Dufour Editions
PO Box 7
Chester Springs
PA 19425

in Australia/New Zealand:
NewSouth Books
University of New South Wales
Sydney NSW 2052

in South Africa:
Jacana Media (Pty) Ltd
PO Box 291784
Melville 2109
Johannesburg

Brenton Brown

I curve my body to compete with the bends in your life.

You ask me to sit on top of the barbed wire fence that surrounds us.

When darkness descends, we'll use the echoes bulging like toads in our throats to build an orange road.

We'll walk that blurry eyed. At the end, before you leave I'll warn you, that my tongue will pierce through the tear in your chest like a cheated pink flag.

Irenosen Okojie

Chapter 1

Termination

South London, February 2002

THE SEX WAS GOOD, Brenton thought, but it failed to match the intensity of making love with his half-sister. Of all the women he had slept with in those twenty-odd years since he and Juliet had their brief but passionate affair, no woman had ever got close. And in those quiet morning hours, when a partner was gently snoring, curving her shape into his, Brenton would feign sleep. He would think of Juliet. Always Juliet.

Rising out of bed, Brenton could hear the ugly sound of the water gurgling through the pipes from the bathroom. He made a quick mental note to deal with the problem later as he pulled on a pair of boxers he found on the floor. Then he heard his girlfriend, Lesley, brushing her teeth with her battery-operated toothbrush. The noise irritated him so he switched on the mini-stereo beside his bed and inserted a CD. Carolyn Catlin's *Peaceful Woman* sopranoed out from the small speakers and Brenton started to nod his head, his mind filling with long-ago blues dances and parties. His memories morphed into making love to Juliet.

He didn't bother to smooth the bedsheet. Instead he simply flattened and spread the duvet. The Gong stared intensely at him from a framed poster hanging on the wall opposite the bed. Shelves fixed to the sidewalls were filled with reggae CDs and DIY books. In the corner of the room stood a desktop computer that Brenton rarely used and next to this was a pair of black leather slippers that had seen better days.

It was a good night. He had taken Lesley to a revival session at the Ritzy in central Brixton and the DJs had spun some serious lovers' rock tunes that had the forty-somethings pining for a lost time. Lesley had yet to reach forty but she could grind and crub with the best of them. They returned to Brenton's flat just off Brixton Hill where they shared a couple of spliffs and a bottle of wine before making love on the sofa and in the bedroom. But now Brenton wanted to tell her it was over.

He acknowledged the Gong with a slight nod before taking in a deep breath. He then pulled out a towel from the top of his wardrobe and stepped to the bathroom.

Wearing a black bra and black panties, Lesley accepted the towel from Brenton, smiled and kissed him on his left cheek. She was humming along to the music in the bedroom before she filled her mouth with water to gargle. Brenton half-grinned and wiped off the spittle of toothpaste that was now on his face. 'We have to talk,' he said.

Lesley spat out the water. 'Oh?' she said. 'About what?'

'T'ings.'

'T'ings?' Lesley repeated, her toothbrush poised two inches away from her mouth. She tried to read Brenton's face. 'Your mum? You want me to go to the hospital with you today?'

Brenton eyed her, appreciating her toned legs and fit backside. Her breasts were kinda small, he thought, but they looked nice and round in a clingy T-shirt. For a woman of thirty-seven she was pretty enough and intelligent too. She didn't mind him watching football if she came around on a Saturday evening and he didn't have to step to some stush wine bar and greet and smile with her permed and weaved-up friends. So why was he thinking of breaking up with her?

'Get dressed first,' Brenton said finally.

'No,' said Lesley, now rinsing her toothbrush under the cold tap. The horrible gurgling sound started again. 'You know I hate suspense. Tell me now.'

Putting down the toothbrush, Lesley placed her arms around Brenton's neck and kissed him on the cheek. She always wondered about the nasty-looking scar that was four inches long and shaped like a slim S. It was just beneath his right jaw but she learned not to ask about Brenton's past. He would get defensive and evasive.

'How was she yesterday?' Lesley asked, her expression full of concern.

'Not good.'

'She'll pull through. Don't fret, man.'

'She won't,' Brenton said flatly. 'It's just a matter of time till we get the bad news.'

He returned to the bedroom where he picked up the clothes he had been wearing the night before. On one side of his double bed was a rosewood-coloured bedside cabinet. Half covered in shadow was a framed picture of his half-sister Juliet and Brenton's niece, Breanna. Brenton was also Breanna's father. The snapshot was taken on Breanna's eighteenth birthday and now she was only days away from reaching twenty-one. Next to this was another framed photo of Brenton's mother, Cynthia. The picture was taken in the sixties and it reminded Brenton where Juliet got her perfect looks. Cynthia's beehive hairstyle, sleeveless dress and long white gloves made Brenton think of Diana Ross and the Supremes in their heyday. And now Cynthia lay in a hospital bed, her forehead heavily lined and her eyes full of dreams that were never fulfilled and loaded with hurts that were impossible to mend. After seeing her yesterday, Brenton told himself that he would never have *that* haunted look on his deathbed. No, he thought. I'd rather go out with a bang. Fuck all that waiting to die in a hospital.

Driving Lesley to her flat in Norbury, Brenton kept his gaze on the road and said little on the journey. Lesley glanced at him every now and then, sensing something was wrong. Johnny

Osbourne's *Ice Cream Love* boomed out from the cranked-up car stereo. 'You're very quiet,' she said. 'Are you gonna come in when we reach? Rachel and Leon should be home soon if their dad drops them off on time.'

'No, I won't,' answered Brenton, his eyes still fixed on the road ahead. 'I'm going to the hospital as soon as I drop you off.'

'You sure you don't want me to come with you? I can call the kids' dad and tell him not to drop them off till later?'

'No,' said Brenton. 'In fact … t'ings are not working out. I need a break.'

Her mouth open, Lesley was too stunned to reply. Instead, she glared at Brenton but his eyes were on the road. His square jaw was still and his almost-bald head still had red blemishes from his last visit to the barber's. 'But, but …' Lesley managed.

Brenton's mobile phone vibrated. He flicked it open, ignoring Lesley's blazing stare. 'Hi, Juliet … Oh no … Another heart attack … Just now? … No, wait till I reach …Yes, I wanna see her before they take her down. I'm in my car … Yes, I'm alright … We were expecting it … OK, I'll be there soon … Juliet … Sorry.'

Lesley placed her hand upon Brenton's arm but he kept his eyes fixed straight ahead. He finished the call and replaced his phone inside his jeans pocket.

'She gone?' Lesley asked delicately.

Brenton nodded.

'You sure you don't want me to come with you?'

'Sure.'

'Call me if …'

'Yes, if I need anything I'll give you a ding. Now, I have to make my movements 'cos Juliet's saying they won't leave her in the ward for too long.'

As Brenton walked through the corridors of King's College

hospital in Camberwell he wondered about all the personal stories the walls in the building had seen and heard. The joy of birth, a football career abruptly halted because of a busted knee, the expression on a patient's face when they have just been informed that they have incurable cancer, the worry etched on a mother's face as she watches her teenager being wheeled into theatre following a stabbing. While I was growing up I never saw Mum with a worried look when I hurt my knee or broke my arm, he thought. I hate her for that. How am I supposed to react now that she's dead?

Arriving at the ward Brenton saw that his mother's bed was ringed with a blue curtain. He slowed his walk as he approached and before entering he paused and took a deep breath. He could smell Juliet's deodorant. Composing himself, Brenton entered the curtained chamber and his gaze found Juliet first. She was sitting quietly beside the bed, head bowed. She was wearing jeans and an oversize pullover and she looked desperately tired. Her mother's right hand was between her hands and she was gently caressing it, a half-hearted attempt to keep it warm. Brenton then looked at his mother. She seemed at peace, regal almost. The lines in her forehead didn't seem so deep and the stress lines that crossed her eyebrows seemed to have disappeared. The calmness of her expression masked the incredible drama of her life and Brenton felt that although he was staring at his mother, she wasn't there. He didn't feel any fear, just a feeling of mystery, as if he was peering at something that wasn't quite real. He switched his glance to Juliet and she raised her head.

'I knew it was coming but it's still not easy to accept,' she said. 'She just closed her eyes and let go.'

Finding words hard to come by, Brenton walked slowly over to Juliet. He spread his arms just a little but Juliet saw the invitation. She stood up and comforted herself in Brenton's embrace, the top of her dreadlocked head nestling under Brenton's chin.

She squeezed tight as Brenton closed his eyes, a sense of warmth and belonging filling his body. They hadn't hugged for over twenty years but to Brenton it felt natural and right. This is how they were meant to be, he thought.

They remained in their clinch, tears now falling from Juliet's eyes, until a nurse interrupted them.

'Er, sorry to interrupt, Mr and Mrs Hylton,' the nurse said. 'Hospital policy is to move the deceased to the mortuary as quickly as possible.'

'This is *not* my husband,' replied Juliet, quickly removing her arms from Brenton. 'This is my brother, Brenton.'

'Sorry,' said the nurse. 'As I was saying we need to take your mother's body to the mortuary. There will be a post-mortem because your mother passed away whilst in hospital. I'm very sorry.'

'I understand,' said Juliet. She glanced at Brenton and he nodded.

Chapter 2
The Wake

FOR BRENTON THE DIGNITY of the funeral service and much of the day was ruined by a JCB earth-digger creating a hole in the frosted February ground. It whirred and it clunked and its mud-splattered exterior was so out of sync with mourners wearing black suits, black coats and black hats. When they finally lowered Brenton's mother into the ground, it wasn't the coffin that Brenton was looking at. He was watching Juliet being supported by her husband, Clayton. Brenton wanted to catch Juliet's attention. A glance would have been enough just to acknowledge what they had once shared and what was still secret. Clayton's right arm was around Juliet's waist and he was being so protective of her, showing everyone how much he cared. He was wearing a tailor-made black suit and a black camel-wool coat that Brenton had to admit looked good on him. His black brogues seemed much more appropriate than Brenton's dull black slip-ons. Fuck him, Brenton thought.

To Juliet's left was Breanna. She was dressed in a short black coat, long black skirt and black boots and her gaze was distracted by other mourners, as if she was wondering who most of them were. Brenton thought she had his eyes but Juliet had told everybody that Breanna got her eyes from her grandmother. Another fucking cover-up, Brenton said to himself. She looks like *me*. Why can't no one else see it? She's old enough to know the truth, Brenton convinced himself. I'm sick and tired of this fucked-up lie! Breanna's *my* daughter. Not *his* or anybody else's. Mum took our secret to the grave. Fuck if I will.

7

Two hours later mourners gathered at Juliet's home between West Norwood and Streatham. Guests were sipping wine and spirits, eating curried goat and rice and reminiscing about Juliet's mother. Ray Charles, Ms Massey's favourite singer, was singing about Georgia as Breanna and her parents played the perfect hosts. Brenton was brooding in a corner, only exchanging the odd word with other guests when approached. What could he add to everyone's memories? He can't say to them that his birth and existence caused his mother the most anguish in her life. Guests might shake his hand and offer their condolences but he felt they didn't really mean it.

Brenton spent most of his time looking at framed photographs of Breanna that were resting on an expensive-looking redwood coffee table. He reflected on the first time he had set eyes on his mother and how much he had hated her back then. Once he got to know her he realised she was just an ordinary woman who had made bad choices and mistakes like everyone else. He grew to respect her but he never loved her. He wanted to understand Juliet's loss but he couldn't. He wanted to offer her words of comfort but he didn't know what to say. He looked at the floor in frustration.

The tiled wooden flooring throughout the house was Brenton's work and so were the fitted cupboards in the kitchen. Brenton wanted to punch Clayton when he offered him a bonus for his handiwork. 'No, it's all sweet,' Brenton said, declining the offer. 'Juliet's my sister, innit.' What he really wanted to say was 'You really think I done this shit for you? Take your raas money and fuck off out of Juliet's life. She's always been sweet on me, not you.'

Looking up, Brenton spotted Juliet approaching him with a can of cold beer. Brenton instinctively smiled as she moved closer to him. 'You alright, Brenton? You've been very quiet.'

'Yes,' Brenton replied, accepting the beer and opening it immediately. 'Just thinking about Mum.'

'So am I,' Juliet nodded. 'You know, it didn't seem real until they lowered her coffin into the grave.'

'Didn't seem real for me either.'

'I thought Clayton said some wonderful things about Mum at the service. Didn't you? He'd been working on it for the last two days. You should've stood up and said something.'

Taking in a deep breath as he always did when anger was growing in him, Brenton said, 'You know me. Don't like chatting in front of a whole heap of people. And yeah. Clayton said a few nice t'ings about Mum. I'll thank him for that later.' Like fuck I will, Brenton thought to himself.

'You sure you don't want anything to eat?' asked Juliet.

'Not yet,' replied Brenton. 'But we need to talk.'

'About what?'

'About t'ings.'

'You mean Mum's will?' Juliet guessed. 'It'll be sorted out in the next week or so.'

'*No*,' Brenton snapped, just keeping his voice in check. 'Not the will. Breanna.'

Juliet glanced around her to check if anyone was listening. She then walked to the kitchen and Brenton followed her, sipping his beer. Opening a back door that led to a patio, Juliet sat down on a white plastic chair that was set around a white table. Plant pots were spaced neatly on the patio but the life within them was cold, withered and dry. The garden was tidy and the lawn was trim. Everything in their life is so fucking ordered, Brenton thought to himself. His skin pimpled in the cold February air but it didn't seem to bother Juliet. Clayton glanced at the siblings through a kitchen window. Brenton thought he looked suspicious, like he knew something. Nah, he concluded. He would've said something years ago. Can't a brother have a quiet word with his sister without that prick always checking on us?

'Brenton, I thought we decided to leave it,' Juliet started, her tone angry. 'She's happy. You want to spoil that?'

'She deserves to know the truth.'

'Brenton, I haven't got time for this today. We've already had this argument.'

'And you always get your own way.'

'No,' Juliet argued. 'You want *your* way. Never mind the fact that if Breanna finds out it could destroy her life.'

'You mean it would destroy your life,' Brenton countered. 'Life's all sweet for you, innit. Mrs Deputy Leader of Lambeth Council. Wife of Clayton Hylton. Mr Fucking Perfect who brings home nuff money from his banking job. The man who orders a fucking tailored suit when his mum-in-law dies. What will he buy if I suddenly keel over? A fucking remembrance ring? I know you don't love him.'

For a moment Juliet could not utter a word, as if Brenton's last words had knotted her tongue. She glared at him and saw the endless anger and pain in his eyes. She wanted to hug him. She wanted to hold his face in her hands. But she knew she couldn't. 'Grow up, Brenton,' she snapped before she stood up and prepared to leave.

'That's just your way, innit,' Brenton argued, still trying to check his temper. 'Walking off when the truth hits. Go on then, walk off.'

Juliet stood her ground for a long moment with her eyes blazing. She then sat down again. 'Whether I love him or not is not your business,' she countered.

'It is my business if he's playing daddy with my daughter,' Brenton argued.

'Look, Brenton, I haven't got time for this. Why are you bringing this up again anyway? I'm getting tired of this. There are guests to be taken care of. And since Clayton's been in my life he *is* a father to Breanna. That's the way it's been and that's the way it is. *Deal* with it.'

'Guests can look after themselves, they know where the food and drink is. That's why most of them come anyway.'

'Always cynical,' accused Juliet.

'Always naïve,' retorted Brenton. 'You know what? Go back to your fucking guests. I'm gonna stay out here, drink my drink and fuck off home.'

'You do that!'

Juliet marched off into the kitchen and fake-smiled at the guests who were milling around there. Clayton, sipping a glass of wine, approached his wife. 'Everything alright?' he asked. 'Seems like you and your brother arguing again.'

'Oh, it's nothing,' smiled Juliet.

'What's it about?' Clayton wanted to know.

'Oh, it's just that Brenton feels left out of things,' explained Juliet. 'He's complaining that we organised everything and he feels that we should have let him contribute more to the funeral arrangements and all that.'

'OK,' nodded Clayton, glancing at Brenton through the window once more. 'Is he alright out there? It's freezing.'

'You know my brother,' smiled Juliet. 'He hates crowds. He'll be back inside in a minute.'

'Maybe I should go …'

'No, Clayton. Leave him. He'll be OK. Let's get back to the front room, people must be wondering where we are.'

Lighting a cigarette, Brenton pulled on it hard. He felt the adrenaline rushing through him and after his first exhalation he shouted, 'Fuck it!' He finished his beer, left the empty can on the trimmed lawn and returned to the house. He ignored guests' condolences and made his way to the front door. There he saw Breanna with her boyfriend.

'Going already, uncle?' Breanna queried.

Brenton looked over Breanna's boyfriend before answering. He was wearing a black polo jumper and black jeans that were dropping off his waist. His black trainers looked like the bastard offspring of seventies platform shoes and he owned a number one clipper haircut. Brenton didn't like him.

'Not feeling too well,' Brenton finally replied. 'Gonna step home and rest up.'

'It's been a mad day,' Breanna said. 'So many people I've never met. Don't think I've ever cried so much.'

'Yeah, it has been a mad day,' nodded Brenton.

'Oh, this is Malakai,' Breanna introduced.

'What's gwarnin'?' Malakai offered his right hand.

Brenton scanned Malakai's face again before accepting the handshake with a vice-like grip. 'Good to meet you.'

Not showing the pain he was feeling, Malakai said, 'Good to meet you too.'

Turning to Breanna, Brenton said, 'I'll catch up with you later.'

'OK, uncle.'

Chapter 3
The Ugly Truth

STEPPING TO HIS CAR, Brenton turned around to see if Juliet had come to see him off. She hadn't. Kissing his teeth, Brenton switched on the ignition and he had to turn it twice before the engine started. He turned up the heating and switched on the windscreen wipers to help clear the frosted glass. Junior Murvin's *Cool Out Son* falsettoed from the car stereo. He checked his mobile phone before pulling away and saw that he had three messages from Lesley. He didn't bother to read them. Instead he called his friend, Floyd.

'What's happening, bredren?' Floyd greeted. 'Ain't you at your mum's funeral?'

'I was but I'm chipping home early.'

'Why?'

'Can't take the shit anymore.'

'What shit?'

'Juliet and her attitude on the Breanna t'ing.'

'That again?'

'Yeah. It's doing my head in. Can you come around?'

'Sharon's got me slapping on new paint in the hallway. Been making excuses since Christmas but she went Homebase yesterday and bought some bitch brushes. She left them in the front seat of my car.'

'Can't you take a break?'

'Alright then, but you're coming back to my yard to help me finish it.'

'No, I ain't. Every time I come to your yard Sharon finds me something to do. Last time she got me putting a new lock on the back door.'

'You haven't stepped into my yard for over six months.'

Brenton thought about it. 'OK, deal. Oh, bring some bush with you.'

'Why do you always assume I've got bush?'

'Have you got bush or haven't you?'

'Er, yeah I have but that's not the point.'

'Bring the raas bush then!'

'Alright, no need to go all cuckoo on me. I'll be around in about an hour. Gotta fling away my BO and paint and t'ing.'

Pulling away, Brenton heard his mobile bleep again. It was another message from Lesley and he kissed his teeth once more.

There was a knock on Brenton's front door when he was in the middle of eating a microwave casserole. He took the carton with him as he opened the door.

'Yes, volcano,' Floyd greeted. 'How's t'ings?'

Brenton noticed an oval-shaped spot of paint above Floyd's left eyebrow. His hair was recently cut and his beard neatly trimmed. He'd only put on a few pounds since he was eighteen and there was still a fresh look in his eyes. 'As I said,' Brenton started. 'Hasn't been a good day. Or to be more blatant it's been a fucked-up day.'

'Funerals ain't supposed to be good days, unless they're burying Maggie T'atcher's bones.'

Taking a seat around the small, varnished teak dinner table in Brenton's lounge, Floyd searched his pockets and came out with a bag of high-grade weed and cigarette papers. He took out his box of cigarettes and paused to look around the room. He hadn't been in Brenton's place for a while. The brown and cream paintwork was applied expertly and it complemented the two black two-seater sofas. There was a smart-looking glass cabinet at one end of the room which housed small framed photographs of

Juliet, Breanna, Brenton's mother and Floyd himself when he was nineteen. There was also Brenton's carpentry and joinery graduation certificate, wine and whisky glasses that were a Christmas present from Juliet and a large souvenir mug from Amsterdam that Brenton had bought on a boys' weekend trip. The television in the corner of the room was modest but the carved, oval-shaped rosewood frame that held a portrait of Bob Marley dominated the room. It was made by Brenton's own hand and he liked the look of guests admiring it. Brenton switched on his mini-stereo and turned down the volume on Jacob Miller's *I'm a Natty*. He sat down opposite Floyd.

'How's Sharon?' Brenton began, pushing his carton of food away and picking up the cigarette papers.

'Oh, you know how she is, man. Always stressed out from her job. You know how social services stay these days. Risk assessment this and risk assessment that. Fill in this form and that and her team of social workers always fucking up t'ings and taking nuff time off sick.'

'Gregory and Linval?'

'They'll be alright if Sharon stops spoiling dem too much. She still cleans and washes up after dem. They have friends around till Lord knows what time and they stink out the yard with their skunk. I keep telling them that man put nuff chemical and t'ing in there, but do they listen? No, they fucking won't. Sharon says I'm being a hypocrite 'cos that's what we used to do in our fresh days. But that skunk is fucked-up lab shit. Anyway, they're only allowed to smoke it in their room now.'

'Yeah, I hear you,' nodded Brenton as he began building his spliff. 'But Sharon's right. We used to do that shit in the hostel, didn't have to worry 'bout parents.'

'Only Mr Lewis.'

'And I still reckon the man used to take a draw too.'

'Nah.'

'Not in front of us,' said Brenton. 'On the sneak, like how dem teachers, judges and dem kinda people draw on it. I wonder whatever happened to Mr Lewis?'

'I bet he ain't working in Lambeth,' replied Floyd. 'He came from the wilderness so he's probably gone back there. Dem kinda people always have trouble working in the inner cities. If I was a social worker I wouldn't work in Lambeth. Fuck that. Don't know how Sharon tolerates it. Keep telling her she should move but she ain't listening.'

'Lewis. Maybe he's working in Redhill or somewhere?'

'True t'ing,' nodded Floyd. 'But you didn't ask me to come to your yard to chat 'bout old Mr Lewis and how Gregory and Linval are smoking out my yard like they're Red Indians sending out nuff message and t'ing.'

'Yeah, you're right.'

'So what is it, bredren?'

'Juliet and me had another argument.'

'In front of everybody at the funeral? Man! You pick your moments.'

'No, not in front of everybody. What you take me for?'

'You ain't called the stepping volcano for nothing. What happened?'

'I just told her that I think Breanna is old enough to know the truth. That I'm her daddy.'

'And you decided to bring that up at your mother's funeral?'

Arsoning his joint, Brenton inhaled on it deeply as he fixed his gaze on his long-time friend. He blew the smoke over Floyd's head. 'Breanna's old enough, man.'

Floyd took a little longer to wrap his spliff. He made sure it was smooth and straight before he put it into his mouth. He lit it with an expensive lighter and took a leisurely toke. He exhaled through his nose. 'You expect me to give you my opinion on this, right?'

'Yeah.'

'My feelings on this haven't changed from the last time. Breanna will *never* be old enough to hear that you're her real daddy. It will fuck up her head, make her go cuckoo. I mean, say for instance that Elton John arrives at your yard with a strange smile and he's saying that he's your real daddy? How would you feel about that fucked-up situation?'

'Wouldn't mind his money. But Elton John is not my fucking uncle.'

'Try and put yourself in Breanna's boots,' reasoned Floyd. 'She thinks you're her uncle, right.'

'But I am her uncle.'

'Yeah, you are, but you're her daddy too. It's a big raas leap to find out that your uncle who came around now and again to do a little carpentry work in your yard, ate out of your pot when he couldn't be bothered to microwave anyt'ing, and who bought you some nice shit for Christmas and birthdays is your daddy too.'

'All families are fucked up these days,' countered Brenton.

'But yours don't have to be.'

'There's this so-called family who live behind me with this woman who's got four kids and the man she's living with ain't the daddy for none of dem but he's a daddy for another five with three different woman. I was there on a Sunday once with all the various mothers turning up to drop off their children and the daddies turning up to see their children. I haven't been so confused since Breanna was showing me how to do invoices on my computer.'

'Other people and other families are not important,' stressed Floyd.

'So it's not important that Breanna don't know the truth?'

'OK, Brenton. Say you have it your way and the whole damn world get to know the truth about you being Breanna's daddy.

Who's gonna benefit? Juliet won't, Clayton won't and Breanna won't.'

'Yes she will,' argued Brenton. 'We get on really well. She comes around sometimes even when I'm not expecting her. She talks about boyfriend troubles and t'ings with her career.'

'But she's coming to see you as an uncle. You don't know how she's gonna react if she knows that you're her daddy.'

'It'll be sweet.'

'No, it won't be fucking sweet!' shouted Floyd, losing his patience. 'It'll be like some dirty, ghetto-arsed tramp with nuff spots on his tongue spitting in your sweet hot milo. There'll be serious repercussions.'

'She'll be alright with it.'

'No, she won't! What's the blasted point of you asking for my opinion on something and you never listen what I'm telling you?'

'Why you always on Juliet and Clayton's side?' yelled Brenton.

'What?' queried Floyd. 'I ain't on no one's side, apart from Breanna's.'

'Yes, you fucking are,' Brenton continued shouting. 'Every time I talk about this situation you side with that pussyhole Clayton and Juliet.'

'Brenton, you're chatting fuckeries.'

'It's true!'

'You're paranoid,' accused Floyd.

'Fuck you!'

'Oh, that's sweet. You ask me to come around to your yard, I bring some nice weed and all I get is a fuck-you. What do you say when you invite women over for a booty call? Give them a banana and tell dem to fuck themselves?'

'For just one minute can you drop your sarcastic chat?' Brenton began to breathe heavy. 'Or I'll drop it for you.'

'What? And if I don't you gonna lick me now? Grow up, man.'

In a fit of temper Brenton threw his half-eaten carton of food to the floor. Floyd took a mighty toke of his spliff and blew the smoke towards the ceiling. Rising out of his chair, Brenton kicked the carton before disappearing into the kitchen to get something to clean the mess. Five minutes later he parked himself opposite Floyd, his face stern and his eyes blazing. 'You can erupt all you like,' Floyd said. 'But I ain't changing my mind about this.'

'Fucking know all!' Brenton fired. 'I don't know why I asked you to come around. You never support me anymore. Not like you used to.'

'Oh, so now you're trying to lick me with emotional black-mail. And you think 'cos I'm a bredren I have to agree with anyt'ing you do and say? Fuck that! So if you're gonna have a tantrum 'bout it then drop it somewhere out of my eyesight.'

Relighting his spliff, Floyd returned Brenton's intense stare. Brenton hoovered his joint and only when he had finished it did he speak again. 'Every time I see her and him it just pains me, you know. Makes me vex.'

'But you must have got used to it by now. It's been a long time since Clayton and Juliet first got together.'

'Time don't ease nothing,' said Brenton.

Floyd studied Brenton's eyes. 'You sure this is all about Breanna?'

'What you mean?'

'What you said. Seeing them together makes you erupt. You still jealous of Clayton?'

'Why would I be jealous of that pussyhole?'

Floyd tipped his ash in the ashtray. He took another pull from his spliff, his eyes fixed on Brenton. 'Why? 'Cos he's with Juliet and you're not. You never got over it.'

'That's fuckery,' Brenton countered.

'Brenton? Who you think you're chatting to? I ain't no dumb

social worker from the seventies. I ain't no mate who you work with. I've heard how many times you get vex after you've seen or visited Clayton and Juliet. You rant about something else, complaining that Breanna should know who her real daddy is and t'ing. But the t'ing that makes your lava spew is seeing Clayton and Juliet together. Am I right or am I right?'

Watching Brenton get to his feet, Floyd thought his friend's eyes had some kind of gas rings behind them because they were so intense. He took another drag and tried not to appear intimidated. Brenton went to the kitchen and Floyd heard him getting something from the fridge. He returned with two cans of soft drinks. 'Don't drink lager too tough these days,' Brenton said.

'Nor do I,' replied Floyd.

Downing half of his drink in one gulp, Brenton slammed his can on the table and gazed at Floyd once again. Floyd felt he was being penetrated by lasers. 'You're right,' Brenton finally admitted. 'Don't know how to stop.'

'Stop what?' Floyd asked, his tone softer. 'Stop losing that bitch temper of yours?'

'*No!*'

'Then stop what?'

'Wanting her. Don't know how to stop wanting her.'

Brenton dipped his head. He took out one of the cigarette papers and crushed it into a small ball. He then rolled it between his right thumb and forefinger. 'Feeling won't go away,' Brenton admitted, now examining the tiny paper ball. 'Don't know what to do about it.'

Opening his can, Floyd took a short gulp. He then stood up, re-lit his spliff and walked towards the mini-stereo. He turned up the bass a notch. Yellowman's *Morning Ride* toasted from the speakers. 'My Uncle Herbie told me once that we can't choose who we love,' said Floyd. 'He had this gay cousin.'

'You're comparing me to your uncle's gay cousin?'

'No, it ain't like that. It's just that he can't help who he loves and wants and nor can you. That's the way it is.'

'But what do I do?' asked Brenton again.

Floyd thought about it. He returned to his chair and took in another leisurely toke. 'I think you two are living too close,' he said. 'Must be kinda hard you seeing Juliet all the time. Bumping into her in the supermarket, seeing her in a traffic jam and t'ing. You even did her fucking flooring. You need to get away from her. Ain't good for your mental health, bredren. Seriously.'

'What? Move out of south London?'

'Not just move out of south London. Move out of London full stop. Even move out of the country. Start somewhere else fresh. Get Juliet out of your head for once and for all.'

'Ain't that too drastic?'

'No. Brenton, you been pining for her for over twenty years.'

'It's been that long?'

'Breanna's gonna be twenty-one soon, innit. Can't you count? Where the fuck did you learn maths?'

'Fuck you!'

'What about Lesley?' Floyd asked. 'Ain't t'ings going good with her? I thought she looked alright. She's quite serviceable and t'ing for a girl of her age. And she ain't no damn fool. She's working and t'ing and me and Sharon were thinking that she might be the one for you.'

'She ain't the one,' replied Brenton.

'Why?'

''Cos she ain't.'

'What's wrong with her?'

'Nothing.'

'Then why can't you make a go of t'ings with her?'

Brenton thought about it. He was about to give Floyd a bullshit answer but glancing at him he knew he didn't have to lie to him. The Mighty Diamonds' *Identity* pleaded from the speakers. Brenton halved a cigarette and began constructing a new spliff. "Cos she ain't Juliet,' he finally answered.

'Man! You still got it bad. You can't go on like this, bredren.'

'I know.'

'Then do something about it. Start afresh, somewhere new.'

Brenton licked a cigarette paper. 'It's so fucking hard,' he said. 'When you hate someone you have it out with them. It might end up in a fight or some mad slanging match but it comes to some kinda end. But when you really … like someone, it doesn't stop. You can't stop liking them. That feeling I had for her… It …'

Sprinkling the cannabis into the joint, Brenton closed his eyes as if he was reliving some painful memory. He almost grimaced before he spoke again. 'It never faded.'

For a long moment the two friends just looked at each other, acknowledging their shared history and their secrets. Finally, Floyd stood up, walked over to Brenton and playfully punched him on his left shoulder. 'Start afresh,' he said. 'But before you do, you're following me to my yard and helping me to finish that damn hallway. Bring your tools too; Sharon might want you to fix something.'

'I knew it,' Brenton laughed. 'Knew it!'

Chapter 4

Frustration

COLLECTING THE GLASSES and the paper plates from the lounge, Clayton brought them to the kitchen where he dropped the plates into a black rubbish bag and put the glasses on the side of the sink where Juliet was washing up. The washing machine had reached its spin cycle and the sound and vibration of it almost drowned out Alexander O'Neal. White blinds covered the windows and outside the night had brought with it a deep frost. The smell of curried goat and roasted mackerel still lingered and it blended with the overproof rum and brandy that emitted from countless paper cups. The Bob Marley clock, a birthday gift from Brenton to Juliet, fixed to the wall above the fridge, had just turned eleven o'clock.

'This is the last of it,' said Clayton, his sleeves rolled up but still wearing a black tie. He put his arms around Juliet's waist and kissed her on her neck but she continued washing up.

'I'm tired, Clayton,' she said. 'Where's Breanna? She promised to give us a hand.'

'She went to see Malakai out to the bus stop.'

'Did you get a chance to talk to him?'

'Malakai? We had a brief conversation. He seems OK but he could've given more thought to the clothes he was wearing. Last time I checked we weren't hosting a hip-hop night.'

'Oh, he's young,' said Juliet. 'He probably doesn't even own a suit or a tie. Why should he?'

Switching on the kettle, Clayton sat down at the kitchen table. 'Respect. That's why he should. Coming into the place with his backside out of the door! He knew he was attending a funeral. Or at least the wake of a funeral.'

'Mum wouldn't have minded.'

Standing up again, Clayton took out a mug from a cupboard and brought down the coffee jar. He scooped a heaped teaspoonful of granules as he admired Juliet's figure. Not quite as slender as when he first blessed his eyes on her but she looked incredible for a woman of forty. Her legs were still toned and her backside moved provocatively whenever he walked behind her. Her breasts were generous but it was her big, round eyes set in a milk chocolate face which was framed by shoulder-length dreadlocks that still enchanted him. He could look at her all day. Even if it was simply watching her apply make-up or walk up the stairs.

Pouring boiled water into his mug, Clayton took his seat at the kitchen table again. He blew on his black coffee as he watched Juliet drying her hands. 'What was all that with Brenton?' he asked.

'Oh, I think he found the whole day upsetting,' answered Juliet, putting glasses away in a cupboard.

'He didn't seem too upset. He was coping OK ... until he spoke to you.'

'He thought that I left him out of things,' replied Juliet, deciding not to face her husband. 'I mean, we did pretty much organise everything ourselves.'

Clayton watched Juliet's every move like a juror studying the accused. 'I thought he would've wanted us to arrange everything. I mean, he was never really close to your mum, was he? Not as close as you were to her. And he hardly knew any of her friends.'

'They *were* close,' Juliet insisted, at last turning around and meeting Clayton's eyes. 'They had a strange relationship. Sometimes stressed and awkward. But they needed each other.'

'But he never really forgave her for abandoning him as a baby? Did he?'

'Yes, he did. Brenton made his peace with her.'

'It didn't look like that to me.'

Taking out a mint-flavoured bag of herbal tea, Juliet placed it in a mug and poured hot water over it. As her back was turned to Clayton she closed her eyes and inhaled deeply through her nose. She breathed out softly and tried to compose herself. She then joined Clayton at the kitchen table; hard-dough bread-crumbs were still on its surface. She sipped her tea and held the mug with both hands in front of her face. 'You didn't see them together when they showed affection for each other,' she said. 'They were very private.'

'If they were so lovey-dovey with each other, as you call it, then how comes when we used to visit and Brenton was there, she was always upset when he left? I've heard how cruel he can be. He called her a whore once even in my presence. I felt like saying something.'

'That wouldn't have been a good idea.'

'Why not? Why did he continually abuse her like that? She was always saying sorry to him but it was never enough. What did he want her to do? Flail herself with a metal chain and spiked ball?'

'No need to be flippant, Clayton.'

'Don't know why he kept on seeing her? And I don't know why she kept opening the door to him.'

'He had to see her. To find out his identity. And she had to learn how damaged he was and understand the consequences of what she did. She knew that and that's why she put up with his shouting and upsets. And he *didn't* continually abuse her.'

'She didn't deserve any of it. He was always upsetting her. He always played on her nerves with his flashes of temper. If you ask me *he* only added to her stresses and ...'

'OK, Clayton!' Juliet interrupted. 'That's enough.'

She took another sip of tea and momentarily closed her eyes.

When she opened them again the tiredness had been replaced by anger. 'Mum's gone! And whatever stresses she had were the result of things that happened a long time ago. Long before Brenton turned up. She was always a sick woman.'

Looking at his mug of coffee, Clayton picked it up and took a sip. He wiped his lips with the back of his left hand and met his wife's stern gaze. 'So you're still going to give him everything?'

'Yes I am,' Juliet answered. 'He deserves it.'

'Not from what I've seen.'

'Oh for God's sake, Clayton!' Juliet suddenly lost her temper. She almost dropped her mug onto the table and it spilled over. 'Brenton spent his childhood in a fucking children's home! Do you know how that makes me feel? I grew up with photos of me filling up my mum's bedroom? My mum taking me to dancing lessons. Taking me for a day out at Littlehampton. Mum leaving work to collect me from nursery school because I had a head-ache. Have you any idea how fucking guilty that makes me feel? He was institutionalised. Physically abused. Damaged. It's a wonder that he made something out of his life.'

'Why you always have to feel guilty over Brenton?' argued Clayton. 'He was never your responsibility. It wasn't you who abandoned him. It was your mother and whoever his *white* father was. Can't you for once understand that, Juliet? Your mum was *meant* to take you to dancing lessons and for days out to the seaside. She was *meant* to pick you up from junior school if you were ill. That's what mothers do.'

'Mothers *don't* abandon their babies!' Juliet raised her voice. For a short second there was hatred in her eyes and her hands shook. She closed her eyes again, trying to control her breathing.

'But it's not your job to make up for that!' Clayton countered, frustration showing on his face. 'You don't have to take on your mother's wrongs.'

Picking up her mug, Juliet stood, went to the sink and rinsed it under the hot tap. 'I haven't got time for this tonight, Clayton. I'm tired, I'm missing my mother and I'm chairing a committee meeting first thing in the morning.'

'So I have no say on what your mother leaves in her will and who should get all the money?'

'I've made up my mind,' affirmed Juliet. She gripped a tea towel in her right hand and for a short second she wanted it to be Clayton's throat. 'Everything that she has left for me I will give to him. We've gone through this and I don't want to talk about it anymore.'

'She was your mother too!' Clayton persisted. 'And your best friend. When she needed someone to look after her she didn't call Brenton. You did all the caring so you deserve the bigger chunk of what she's left.'

'Clayton! My mind is made up. I'm over and done with it. Please drop it.'

Opening the door of the washing machine, Juliet pulled out the clothes and placed them in a basket. She carried the basket upstairs to the bathroom where she hung the clothes on a washing line suspended high above the bath. When she was done, she closed the bathroom door, walked towards the mirror that was fixed above the sink and studied her reflection. The lines were increasing around her eyes, flecks of grey were just about visible at the roots of her locks and the strain of the secret she had held for so long showed itself in two short deep lines between her eyebrows. Her head then dropped. 'Oh, Brenton,' she whispered. 'Won't you ever heal?' Her eyes closed and she supported herself with her two hands resting on the sides of the sink. She breathed in deeply, composed herself and made her way to her bedroom. She sat down on her bed and looked around her room.

The dressing table in front of her was stocked with framed photographs of Breanna in her schooldays. There was shyness and a vulnerability about her poses, Juliet thought. On her side of the bed there was an open bedside cabinet that was full of romantic novels. Next to this was a pink armchair that had three heart-shaped cushions resting on it. A shelf on the wall housed her CDs of Janet Kay, Carroll Thompson, Roberta Flack, Anita Baker, Mary J Blige and other R&B female vocalists. The walls in the room were painted something between yellow and beige and had framed sketches of laughing boys hanging from them; one was of a black boy on his bike doing a paper round. Clayton's side of the room had similar furnishings but instead of romantic novels he had books about finance and investments. Last Friday's *Financial Times* was still on the floor next to his wardrobe. Juliet heard Clayton climbing the stairs; she reckoned he was as tired as she was because his footfalls seemed so heavy. He came inside the room and paused as he undid his tie and loosened the top button of his shirt.

'I'm sorry,' he said. 'It's been a long day.'

'Yes, it has,' Juliet nodded.

Taking off his shirt, Clayton kissed Juliet on the forehead. She didn't respond. Instead, she just remained seated, too tired to move. Eventually, she returned to the bathroom to brush her teeth. Again, she looked in the mirror as if it might solve all her problems. 'Brenton,' she whispered.

When Juliet returned to her room she noticed that the lights were dimmed. Clayton was in bed; he had already taken out his clothes for the morning and they were neatly folded on his armchair. Juliet undressed and put on her negligee; she felt Clayton's eyes watching her every move. She switched off her bedside light and climbed into bed. She closed her eyes and she could hear Clayton reading over some papers and tapping on his calculator. She wondered what Brenton was doing and hoped he wasn't too mad with her.

Twenty minutes later, Clayton switched off his light and Juliet heard him place his reading glasses in their case. Clayton snuggled up behind Juliet and after a while she felt his left hand over her right breast. He began to kiss her neck. 'I'm really tired, Clayton.'

Without a word, Clayton rolled over onto his stomach, placed his arms above his head and settled down to sleep. Juliet could only think of Brenton.

Chapter 5

Turning the Tables

THE WAILING SOULS' *Things and Time* filled the room. Wearing boxer shorts and a Jimi Hendrix T-shirt, Brenton slipped into bed. He lay on his back with his hands interlocked behind his head. In his mind he went over the day's events and regretted his anger at Juliet. He thought about Floyd's suggestion of starting somewhere afresh. Where would he go? He liked Jamaica, especially the steep green hills and the lush vegetation. He could imagine living in one of those lofty houses overlooking Kingston and its harbour and he could never forget the sounds of cocks crowing to herald in the morning. He enjoyed the reggae music blasting out from everywhere and the open-air dances. But Jamaica was too distant. Too far from his friends. Too far from Juliet. Besides, he knew little of his family there. Mum did introduce him to aunts, uncles and cousins but they seemed to be more interested in what was in his suitcase than meeting a new relation. Maybe Spain? Brenton thought. Nah, fuck that. Not after their racist football supporters abused all the black players in the England team.

Old Mr Lewis was always going on about visiting other countries, Brenton recalled. After Mr Lewis graduated from university he backpacked around Europe and South America. On cold winter evenings at the hostel Brenton remembered the social worker telling stories of how he climbed step pyramids in Mexico, watched ships entering the Panama Canal, drank yards of beer in Munich and hitched rides on sailing boats in Lake Geneva. 'No raas claat yodeling boatman is gonna give a black man a free ride on Lake Geneva,' Floyd had remarked. 'They'll probably arrest him for trying to steal fish. And all that short leather trousers and lederhosen fuckery is a battyman t'ing.' Brenton laughed at the memory.

'I learned more from travelling than I ever did at university,' Lewis once said.

Lewis was the only social worker he ever gave time to. The rest of them were social wankers.

Brenton's eyes were now closed and images were forming in his mind. He could see himself at thirteen years of age. He was playing football in a field within the grounds of the children's home. T-shirts were used as goalposts and Brenton's friends played with a heavy lace-up ball that was a birthday gift to one of the boys. It was a hot day and the grass had just been cut. Girls were playing hopscotch on the road and boys went by on skateboards. A hay fever sufferer sneezed in the distance and three teenagers were watching the football from the branches of an oak tree. Seven guys were playing with another in goal. If you scored three times then you would take over between the posts. Brenton had hit two goals and was determined to add another when someone walked onto the field of play. It was a white guy wearing a corduroy jacket, a Jethro Tull T-shirt and tight-fitting jeans. He had long brown hair and a hippy moustache. 'Brenton!' he called.

The football game continued, Brenton going close with a right-foot thunderbolt. The goalkeeper frowned when he realised that to retrieve the ball he had to negotiate stinging nettles. The other players argued about some incident on the pitch. They pushed and shoved each other.

'Brenton,' the man called again.

Turning around, Brenton looked at the man. 'For fuck's sake,' he said. 'What do you want? Can't you see I'm in a middle of a game?'

The man walked closer. He smiled nervously and his hands were in his pockets. 'I'm your new social worker,' he said. 'I came yesterday but you were out. Can you see me now?'

'Why?'

'So we can get to know each other.'

'I don't want to get to know no one.' Brenton studied the social worker. 'Especially if they're dressed like you. You look like a fucking bummer.'

'I've come all the way from my office in Brixton, Brenton,' said the social worker, his calm now rattled. 'And I came yesterday too. Can't we just have a chat for half an hour or so?'

Ignoring the stifled giggles of his mates, Brenton thought about it. 'You got a car?'

'Er, yeah,' the social worker nodded. 'It's parked over there.'

Pointing to an orange Volkswagen Beetle that was parked outside Brenton's house, the social worker smiled again. 'It just about got me here.'

Not responding to the joke, Brenton offered, 'If you drive me to the nearest Wimpy and buy me a Knickerbocker Glory I'll talk with ya.'

'Deal,' smiled the social worker.

'But you have to wait for me to finish my game,' added Brenton.

Sitting on the grass, the social worker had to wait another twenty minutes or so until Brenton scored his third goal. Brenton then bade goodbye to his mates, slung his T-shirt over his left shoulder and walked towards the social worker. Sweat was dripping off his face. 'My name's Phillip,' the social worker introduced himself. 'Phillip Lawson.' He offered his right hand but Brenton looked at it as if it was caked in slug vomit.

Walking towards Phillip's car, Brenton waved a final farewell to his mates. Phillip opened the passenger door but Brenton climbed into the back. 'So how long are you gonna be my social worker?' Brenton asked. 'A month? Three weeks? A week? Two days? A fucking hour?'

'I think you'll have to put up with me for a bit longer than a month,' Phillip replied.

It took Phillip over half an hour to drive and pull up outside the Wimpy restaurant in Croydon. Brenton went inside with his T-shirt still draped over his left shoulder, his grass-stained cut-down jeans and a pair of battered Dunlop trainers; two toes were visible and he wasn't wearing any socks. He settled into a seat and bad-eyed anybody who stared at him.

'Now, what is it you want again, Brenton?' Phillip asked.

'A Knickerbocker Glory.'

'Don't you want any burgers and chips before it?'

'No, I want a Knickerbocker Glory with everything in it. Make sure it's got the cherry on top like in that picture on the menu. And all the hundreds and thousands sprinkled all over it.'

'Not a problem, not a problem. I'll just go and order it.'

Phillip went to order the food and Brenton slouched into his chair. 'What a fucking wanker,' he whispered. 'Fucking tosspot.'

Ten minutes later, Brenton was enjoying strawberries, chocolate-and-raspberry ice cream, meringue, wafers, sliced almond nuts, whipped cream, strawberry syrup, hundreds and thousands and a glacé cherry in a very tall glass. He wished he had a camera to take a picture of it so he could show his mates.

'Enjoying your treat?' Phillip asked, nibbling on a cheeseburger and fries and dabbing his mouth with a napkin.

'Yeah,' Brenton replied, his eyes transfixed on what he was eating. 'First time I've had one of these. Always dreamed of it. My mate Rodney had one when his uncle took him out three weeks ago. He really wound me up about it, fucking cunt! Showing off he was. I felt like shoving my shoes up his cakehole.'

Phillip smiled and took another bite. 'It's obvious you love football but can you tell me more about yourself? How you're getting on in your household? School? Any problems you are going through?'

Brenton looked up. His spoon was poised over his tall glass. 'Why should I fucking tell you?'

Phillip smiled awkwardly. 'Because I'm your new social worker.'

'But I don't fucking know you.'

'This is why I have come and why I have taken you out for this treat, Brenton. To get to know you.'

'I just come with ya 'cos I wanted a Knickerbocker Glory.'

'You're not being very cooperative, Brenton.'

'Fuck you!' Brenton spat. A slither of ice cream landed on Phillip's chin. He wiped it off with his napkin. Brenton continued, 'I have never seen you in my life and you expect me to talk to you like we're mates? And answer all your nosey questions? Fuck that!'

Checking to see if Brenton's raised voice had disturbed anyone, Phillip lowered his tone into a whisper. 'Perhaps I was going a bit fast. Of course you should have the chance to get to know me before we discuss other things.'

Scooping every last drop out of the tall glass, Brenton nodded. He then emitted a satisfying sigh and leaned back into his seat. 'I should ask you questions. You people always do the asking.'

'Ask me questions?' Phillip chuckled. He looked at Brenton and saw that he was serious. He fidgeted in his seat. 'OK, go ahead.'

There was a pause as Brenton thought about it.

'Where did you grow up?' Brenton finally asked.

'Er, Guildford.'

'Rich people live there?'

'Not sure about rich but people do OK there.'

'You got a nice mum and dad? Did they give you pocket money and stuff? Did you get Chopper bikes and Subbuteo games for

Christmas? Father fucking Christmas treat you alright? He was a right cunt to me.'

'Er, I didn't get any football games for Christmas but one year I received a bike. I suppose I was very fortunate. I have wonderful parents.'

'Got any brothers and sisters? Cousins? Uncles and aunts visiting?'

'One brother, two sisters,' Phillip answered, knowing after studying Brenton's file that he had no family whatsoever that was in touch with him or the social services. 'And there are a few cousins I don't see much of. I have one aunt who, as far as I'm concerned, visits too much.'

Placing his spoon into the glass, Brenton leant closer to Phillip. His gaze was hard and unwavering. 'Did your mum and dad hit you from the age of five with wooden hairbrushes and a belt?'

'No, not at all.'

'Did they lock you up in your outhouse 'cos you were crying too much? 'Cos you wet the bed? Or just 'cos they wanted to get rid of ya?'

'We, we didn't have an outhouse,' stuttered Phillip. 'We had a shed in our back garden.'

'Did they shove a pissed bedsheet in your mouth 'cos you wet your bed?'

Phillip grimaced. 'No. Why are you asking this?'

'Did your parents ever get a psychiatrist to talk with ya and did that psychiatrist ask you to take off your clothes?'

'N … No.'

'Did they tell you that you was an animal, a jungle bunny, golliwog, nig nog and a nigger and that you should be glad for any bit of food you ate?'

'Brenton, Brenton. Why are you asking these questions?'

'To get to know you. And so far I've worked out you had it alright. Can I have a Coca-Cola?'

'Er, yes, of course. I'll go and ask for it.'

Phillip stood up and let out a sigh. It was a relief to get away from Brenton's laser-like eyes. He ordered a strong coffee for himself. He returned to his seat to find Brenton's eyes boring into him once more. He had seen scores of children in orphanages since he became a social worker but he couldn't remember if he had met a boy with such rage in his eyes. Finishing half of his glass in one gulp, Brenton belched, wiped his lips with the back of his right hand and addressed Phillip once more. 'What did you do after school?' he asked.

Stirring his coffee more than necessary, Phillip answered, 'I eventually went to university to study sociology. I studied at Oxford.'

'Oxford? Their football team is shit.'

'I suppose they are.'

'What's social bology?'

'You mean sociology. It can cover many things but I was interested in examining working-class and middle-class lifestyles and why it's so difficult for the working class to progress.'

'What's working class?'

'Erm, people who live in poverty, people who have no choice but to work for a living. People who are unable to leave anything substantial for their children. People who don't own land, that kind of thing.'

'I used to own a tree,' Brenton said. 'In the orchard. An apple tree. It had a branch that I could sleep on. I used to pick the apples off the tree for apple crumbles. If any of my mates climbed it I'd beat them up 'cos it's my tree. *My* fucking tree. I used to like sitting in it. Everyone knows it's my fucking tree. So, if I still owned that tree would it make me middle class?'

'Er, not quite.'

'So I'm working class?'

'Well, you're Brenton Brown but, yes, you would be described as working class.'

'So if I'm really working class that means I know more about it than you.'

'Er, not quite.'

'But I live it. You don't fucking live it. I only get paper-round money, I don't own no fucking land, I was beat up a lot when I was younger and if I ever get out of that fucking place I'll have to work so I can buy my apples and Knickerbocker Glorys. I reckon that makes me an expert in social bology or whatever you call it. Posh people like you should be asking me questions about it instead of reading all those books. That's all bollocks.'

'Yes, maybe we should ask you questions. It's why I wanted to be a social worker. Because I wanted to make a difference directly. To work at the coal-face as they say.'

What a fucking tosspot, Brenton thought.

'You got a girlfriend?' Brenton asked suddenly, his gaze unrelenting.

'Er, yes.'

'What's her name?'

'Caroline.'

'Does she hug you?'

Sipping his coffee, Phillip felt his cheeks warming. He thought about his answer carefully. 'At times she embraces me to display her affection for me.'

'What? Fuck me! You do speak funny sometimes. Like in that programme *Upstairs Downstairs*. You speak like the upstairs people. Your parents *are* rich, aren't they?'

'Not quite.'

'You had enough money to buy me a Knickerbocker Glory.'

Phillip laughed, his tension eased for just a moment. 'In time when you find a girlfriend she'll embrace you too.'

'Did your mum hug ya?' Brenton wanted to know. 'Did she kiss you on the cheek before you went to school like in those stupid family films and did she fix your tie? Did she wash you in a bath?'

'Er, yes. She did all of those things.'

'Of course if I had a mum I'd be way too old for all that bollocks.'

Phillip chuckled again, warming to his charge.

'And do you kiss your girlfriend?'

Studying Brenton, Phillip couldn't find a hint of a juvenile grin or any evidence that he was playing about. He wanted to be honest in his reply. 'Yes, we kiss at times. Again, to show our affection for each other. That's what happens when you're in a loving relationship.'

'Have you sucked her tits? Did you put your finger up her pussy? It's the middle one, right? Have you fucked her?'

Almost choking on his coffee, Phillip cleared his throat. 'I don't think that's appropriate, Brenton.'

'What does appropriate mean?'

Opening his eyes and shaking his head to rid his mind of the memories, Brenton heard the sweet tones of Sugar Minott's *Show Me That You Love Me Girl*. He climbed out of bed, switched off the mini-stereo and lay back down once more. 'What a fucking tosspot,' he chuckled.

Chapter 6

Political Opportunity

HER THREE-INCH HEELS ECHOING off the spiral stone steps that led from the council chamber, Juliet sighed, glad that the Children and Young People's services committee meeting was over. She had suggested to high-ranking social workers, youth leaders and others in attendance that young people who had left social services care at the age of eighteen should have additional help from the council to help them adapt to life on their own. Too many young people who had left care had ended up in prison, on drugs or in mental institutions, Juliet had added, and it's the council's duty to halt that trend. She received warm applause and nods of agreement but others had asked how much funding would be required to set up a network mentor scheme to help vulnerable young adults. No matter how good the idea, Juliet thought, it would always come down to money. The London Borough of Lambeth couldn't afford such great initiatives, Juliet frowned again, but they could spare the odd hundred grand a year to pay the chief executive.

'Mrs Hylton! Mrs Hylton!' somebody shouted above her.

Juliet stopped at the foot of the stairs and saw Councillor Reynolds hurrying down the steps towards her. Reynolds was wearing an Italian-made suit and Juliet could almost see her reflection in his black shoes. His blood-red tie was nearly choking him and she recoiled ever so slightly at the smell of his P Diddy aftershave. God forbid he ever makes it to Prime Minister, she thought to herself. She half-smiled a greeting.

'Have you heard?' Reynolds asked in a low voice, his eyes shifting here and there as if he was passing on state secrets.

'Heard what?'

'Mrs Crowey, our dear Member of Parliament.'

'What about her?' Juliet asked, not liking the way Mr Reynolds always talked to her breasts. But she chose not to rebuke him because he was short.

'She's standing down at the next election.'

'She is?'

'Yes, she's just made a statement. Now she can fuck off to the shires where her heart really belongs and campaign for tally-ho riders and mad dogs to rip up foxes again.'

Juliet didn't laugh at Mr Reynolds' attempt at humour. Instead, remembering she had a lunch appointment to make, she set off walking at a brisk pace along a corridor towards the Town Hall reception. Mr Reynolds paused for a moment, appreciating Juliet's elegant stride. He soon caught up with her. 'Let me guess, she said she wanted to spend more time with her family,' Juliet remarked.

'That's a laugh,' Mr Reynolds chuckled. 'Everyone knows her old man is screwing away from home and her daughter hates her.'

'That's a bit harsh, Tom.'

'It's true though. Remember last year when her daughter turned up to her surgery meeting?'

Juliet tried to suppress a smile.

'She sat opposite her mother and said her problem was she couldn't remember what her mother looked like. Soooo embarrassing. That taught her to stop appearing on Sky News all the time reviewing right-wing newspapers and making an arse of herself on *Question Time*.'

'I for one wish her well,' Juliet replied, wondering why Tom always tried to talk like a teenager when he was with her. He's thirty-two for God's sake, she thought. Act like it! 'She served her constituents for a long time,' she added.

'You sound like our all-great and powerful leader, Juliet. That's what his official line will say. His scriptwriters are probably working on it now. They won't say she was a pain in the backside to the Labour Party and opposed the government every chance she had, the old crow.'

'They're not going to say that, are they? And I'm sure he can write his own political eulogies, Tom.'

'Can he? He doesn't even sign Christmas cards any more without consulting the Spin Boy Three. God, Juliet, you're beginning to sound like them. You'll go far. You just got to work on that smile of yours.'

Juliet's face broke out into a grin and then she laughed out loud. 'Oh Lord! Lick me if I talk like them again.' She immediately regretted saying her last sentence.

Tom deliberated for a short second, thinking of something that gave him great pleasure and then he pulled on Juliet's left arm. He stopped walking and faced her, admiring her beauty for a moment before adopting his serious face once more. 'We all want you to go for it,' he said. 'It'll be sooo cool. You've got a lot of support in the Town Hall, the local rank and file membership and beyond. And you sent Breanna to a normal comprehensive! You'll walk it. First black Member of Parliament representing the Brixton area? The media will love it. Well, not all the media but the *Guardian* and *Independent* will be coming over all sweaty and turned on at the thought of it.'

'Tom!'

'I can see the 1981 riot footage on Sky News now,' Tom went on, ignoring Juliet's disapproval. 'You'll have features in *The Sunday Times* magazine about your memories of the Brixton riots and how you wanted to make a difference for the young and marginalised in the area. And you are better looking than that, yes sir, yes, three bags full sir, do anything to get a cabinet job bitch MP from east London, even if it pisses off ninety-nine per cent of her constituents. How do you say her name? Shluna Keane? A right bitch. You won't be as media-slutty as that patronising cow in north London either. Damn! That woman will turn up on *Big Brother* soon. They should put her out to grass.'

'That's below the belt, Tom.'

Not hearing Juliet or wanting to hear her, Tom kept up his flow. 'When you're on the scene the media will lose interest in all of those so-called black women MPs. They're going to love you though. You're the real deal. And because of that, even though our great and powerful leader hates working-class people like you and me, he'll have to give you a decent job. Who knows? Within a few years you might be Secretary to the Treasury or something? After that Home Secretary. You'll have to play your cards right though, work on that smile. Also that sad look needs polishing for when you're talking about police pay and when social services neglect another murdered child that was on their list.'

'Tom, can you stop planning my political life for a second.'

'And later on Prime Minister!' Tom continued. 'First Labour woman Prime Minister. And you're black so you might make it onto *Time* magazine.'

'Maybe you should make the Spin Boy Three the Spin Boy Four,' replied Juliet, going through a doorway that led to the lobby of the Town Hall. 'You definitely got the imagination to be a spin doctor. I don't even know if I want to be an MP. I'll have to talk it through with my family.'

'Knowing Clayton he'll support you all the way. He'll be so proud.'

Yes he would be, Juliet thought. Too bloody proud.

'Where're you going to lunch?' Tom asked. 'We need to talk about strategy. By the way, my offer still remains.'

Juliet remembered why Tom spoke like he did to her. He

really didn't have any other black friends apart from her and maybe he thought that you have to sound hip if you were talking to a black mate. He knew black people alright, but not to visit or to go out for a drink with, or to have lunch with. He only knew the black people who made up his particular ward and they only ever complained to him about their high council taxes, damp walls, blocked toilets, the queue at the post office and wild dogs crapping on their streets. They also whispered about his lack of height.

'What offer, Tom?'

'My offer to be your campaign manager. It'll be sooo cool working together.'

'Campaign manager?' He must be out of his crazy fucking mind if he thinks he's working as my campaign manager, she thought. 'That's a long way off, Tom. Election isn't for another two or three years. And like I said I haven't even made up my mind if I should run for it.'

'But you still have to prepare and have a strategy in case you do,' argued Tom, stepping ahead of Juliet to open the door for her. 'Trust me, the starting gun has been fired already and all kinds of ambitious Labourites will be sniffing around, especially those poshed-up bastards from the Islington set. Don't want one of those smiley bastards parachuted in with their Chelsea scarves, their Islington dinner invites and body language experts. This is one of the safest Labour seats in the country and you have to make sure you get it. And we don't want someone like Crowey, who is a Tory grandee in disguise.'

'Thanks for your support, Tom, but I can't strategise this lunchtime because I'm meeting a friend.'

'Another colleague?'

'No, Tom, just a friend.'

'Anyone I know?'

'No, Tom.'

'OK, enjoy your lunch then,' Tom said, the tone of his voice disappointed. 'We'll do lunch soon, yeah? We'll strategise then.'

'OK, Tom, maybe when I haven't got so much on.'

'Cool.'

Tom watched Juliet walk down the steps of the Town Hall before disappearing inside. Making her way along Brixton High Street, Juliet felt a harsh breeze slap across her cheeks. She tightened the belt of her coat and made a mental note to buy Breanna a birthday card. She heard an argument coming from the newsagent's and the cheap noodle restaurant she passed was as busy as ever. Someone was selling international calling cards outside Red Records and some Christian guy was sermonising outside Brixton underground with a loudspeaker. A normal Brixton day, Juliet said to herself.

Opposite the tube station was a walkway that led to the SW9 bar. Juliet checked her watch – twenty past one. She took a deep breath and went inside. Slouched on a sofa with too many cushions and nursing a strong coffee was Tessa, Juliet's friend. She raised her hand on seeing Juliet. 'Jules! Over here! What's a matter with you? You blind?'

Juliet smiled and took a chair opposite Tessa. 'And you're *late*,' Tessa added.

'Sorry, Tess, meeting ran a bit late.'

'So what's this all about then?' asked Tessa, flicking her auburn hair out of her eyes. 'You only saw me yesterday at your mum's funeral?'

'Oh and how are you too,' snapped Juliet, glancing over the menu.

'Excuse me for asking! You are touchy today. I usually get summoned by you every three months or so. So what is it? The mayor tripped over his robes? Lambeth can no longer afford the free sugar in the Town Hall canteen? Someone dumped a truckload of parking tickets in your office? Clayton still not adventurous enough for you?'

'Tess!'

A young Mediterranean waiter came over and asked the women for their order.

'I'll have the lamb burger, salad and fries,' said Juliet. 'And a glass of cranberry juice, please.'

'I'll have the quarter pounder and fries,' ordered Tessa. 'And another coffee. Don't make it as frothy as the last one. Thanks.'

Scribbling down the order, the waiter moved away and Tessa took a peek at his behind. 'Then what is it?' she asked again.

'Why do you think there is an *it*? Can't I want to see you just to catch up? Didn't really have a chance to chat yesterday because of the other guests.'

'Oh stop giving me the twaddle, Juliet,' Tessa sniped. 'When I left last night I could see you were stressed out about something. And it had nothing to do with your mum dying. You have mourned for that already.'

'Not sure if I have,' replied Juliet staring into space. 'It was quite something watching her coffin being lowered into the ground.'

'Yes it was,' nodded Tessa.

'How's the kids?' asked Juliet.

'Niall's decided to stay on to the sixth form and I've renamed Candice Miss Glamorous. She's still only twelve but she wants to dress like she's eighteen with all the make-up and stuff. You know what I mean? They both miss their dad but they'll get used to it. He was supposed to come last Friday evening for them but did he? So fucking unreliable he is.'

'I had the same trouble with Breanna and the make-up,' said Juliet. 'They're all the same. So much pressure on young girls to look adult these days. It isn't any surprise when you see pop videos. The divorce must be shit for your kids though.'

'You're right about that,' nodded Tessa. 'But they seem to be coping. They would cope better if their skint-arse dad would

45

turn up when he says so. He was probably fucking that new young girl of his. *Tramp!* No time for his kids anymore.'

The waiter returned with a coffee for Tessa and a cranberry juice for Juliet. Tessa inspected the coffee. 'That's a bit better,' she smiled. The waiter returned the smile.

'How is my goddaughter Breanna?' asked Tessa.

'She's doing really well at her accountants' place. Did I tell you she started off as an intern and after six months they decided to give her a job?'

'Yes, you did. You kept going on about it like she became the US President or something. What have you got planned for her birthday?'

'A car.'

'A car! When I reached twenty-one all I got was a gold-plated necklace from East Street market and a bottle of Pink Lady from my nan. You spoil her too much, Jules.'

'You're only twenty-one once.'

'Have you told Brenton you're buying her a car?'

'No. I don't have to tell Brenton everything we're doing for Breanna. Clayton is picking the car up tomorrow. He's sorting everything out, insurance and tax.' Juliet paused and sipped her cranberry juice. She stared at the floor and for just a short second her expression revealed a deep anxiety.

'So that's *it*,' guessed Tessa. 'Brenton! I noticed you two going outside to the garden for a chat. I thought to myself, what's a matter with them two? It was freezing out there.'

'We needed some privacy.'

'Then why didn't you go upstairs?'

Juliet sipped her cranberry juice again. She met Tessa's eyes and there was a knowing pause. 'What is it, Jules?'

Juliet paused for a moment, taking in a long breath. 'He wants Breanna to know he's her father.'

'You told him no, right?'

'Yes, but …'

'There ain't no buts, Jules. It's a no-no with two big Ns. You can't ever let Breanna know.'

'You should've seen his face,' Juliet said, staring blankly over Tessa's right shoulder. 'He was so upset. It's been shit for him watching Breanna grow up with another dad.'

Tessa placed her coffee down on the table and grabbed Juliet's wrists. 'You can't weaken! How's it going to look after all these years? You told her that you got pregnant after a fumble at a drunken party and that you can't remember who the dad was. Breanna's learned to accept that. So has Clayton. Don't mess it up now 'cos you feel sorry for Brenton. Don't fall for the *oh it's shit for me* line. In that children's home didn't they beat him up all the time and weren't he fiddled with?'

'He wasn't fiddled with, Tess.'

'Whatever, *don't* let him have his way on this one. Protect Breanna.'

'Maybe she will handle it?'

'*No!* Jules. What you thinking? Breanna will never trust anything you say to her again. And as for Clayton, well, it'll certainly knock you off that virginal perch he's had you on since you got together with him.'

'Clayton hasn't had me on a virginal perch!'

'Yes he has. Sometimes listening to him I get the feeling he thinks you're the Virgin Mary reincarnated. The last time you invited me to one of your Town Hall dos we was watching you make a speech and he said, "Doesn't she make Halle Berry look like a zombie in a Michael Jackson video. She's beautiful." I nearly threw up.'

'Stop it, Tess!'

'It's true! The way he doesn't like to talk about who Breanna's father is or even discuss the issue. It's as if he thinks you had some kind of divine conception and you never had sex before you met him.'

47

'You're being ridiculous, Tess.'

'No I'm not. Look how long it took you guys to have sex after you met. Seven months.'

'It was five months.'

'That's just as bad. What was the matter with him? I still think he's got a fruity streak going through him.'

'He's not gay, Tess.'

'But he might be bi though. Think about all those business trips he goes on. Maybe he goes up Hampstead Heath for a bit of dogging? Or whatever people call it these days. And he seems at home with all your gay political mates.'

'I haven't got any gay political mates.'

'Yes, you have. That midget one. What's his name? Tom. That's it. He's definitely sooo gay.'

'No he's not.'

'Yes he is! He's as gay as that *Top Gun* film.'

'Tom's not gay. He flirts with me all the time.'

'Yeah, to make it look like he's straight. He's over-compensating. If he ever had his way with you he'd take one look at your naked body, throw up and start crying for mummy.'

'Trust me, he likes his women.'

'If you say so, Jules. Anyway, Clayton seems to like being around men like Tom.'

'He just likes being around shakers and movers.'

'Yeah, men who shake and move their arse.'

'Tess!'

'Five months,' Tessa took a slurp of her coffee. 'How old were you when you met? Twenty-three, weren't it? If I was twenty-three and my guy didn't make a move on me I would've thought there's something wrong.'

'Clayton's shy,' said Juliet. 'He was traditional, respectful and polite. He came from a church family.'

'And boring,' added Tessa. 'You went from one extreme to the other. You might've known Brenton in the biblical sense and when you first told me I couldn't believe it but at least he weren't boring. What was it? Weren't you tearing off each other's clothes on the fourth or fifth time you met?'

'The fifth,' Juliet remembered.

'He didn't place you on any pedestal,' said Tessa. 'Going by what you told me it was just raw, animal sex. I could do with some of that right now. Since the divorce I've had to resort to all things that buzz. I do miss that part of being married.'

'Your lamb burger, Miss, and your quarter pounder, Miss,' the waiter said, placing the plates on the table. 'I hope it is to your liking, yes?'

'I'm sure it is,' nodded Juliet, trying to kill her embarrassment.

'Thanks,' giggled Tessa, picking up her knife and fork.

The waiter moved away and Tessa dropped her tone. 'As I said you went from one extreme to another.'

'Mum really liked him,' said Juliet. 'They got on really well.'

'You don't marry somebody all because your mum likes them! Your mum didn't have to fuck him so why does she have to like him? I still say you marrying Clayton was a guilt thing.'

'No it wasn't!'

'Yes it was! You felt so guilty after the Brenton thing that you tried to make up for it and make your mum feel better by going for boring, safe Clayton. It would have been more exciting in the bedroom if you married a dead castrated pope.'

'Stop taking the piss, Tess. Clayton's alright.'

'Hmm? Only alright?'

'He's dependable, never let me down.'

'Dependable? My fucking hoover is dependable! So is my hot-water tap and my Duracell batteries! The thing I keep in my knickers' drawer never lets me down either. Jules, not once have you ever told me that you want to rush home and shag his arse off. Not once! And by the way if it was a contest of arses then

49

Brenton wins hands down; he's still very fit. How long have you been with Clayton now?'

'Seventeen years.'

'And in those seventeen years you have never told me what he's like in bed or if he satisfies you.'

'Tess!'

'You told me about Brenton though. In fact you told me in such detail I thought I was shagging him myself.'

'Enough!'

'You are touchy about this,' remarked Tessa, jawing her quarter pounder. 'I think you still have feelings for him. Admit it.'

'Of course I do. He's my brother.'

'I'm talking about biblical feelings.'

'That's ridiculous. It happened a long time ago.'

'Jules, it's me you're talking to. Not one of your Town Hall la-di-da mates.'

'What are you buying Breanna for her twenty-first?' Juliet suddenly changed the subject.

Tessa offered Juliet an accusing stare. She took a big bite of her quarter pounder and chased it with a gulp of coffee. 'You think you are so crafty changing the subject, but I'm going to talk this out with you one day. Breanna? If you're getting a car for her then I s'pose I'll get her something for the car. Maybe a toolkit, jump leads and stuff. Something like that. It's not good for a woman to be stranded. She should know something about starting the damn thing if it breaks down.'

'That'll be nice.'

'She's my goddaughter,' said Tessa. 'And if you go telling her that Brenton is her real dad then I'll take that flashy handbag of yours and clout you with it.'

Laughing, Juliet replied, 'Don't worry, it won't come to that.'

'It better not!'

'By the way, how you coping financially?'

'Graham's already said I can keep the house. He's moved in with his young slut. I've put away a bit and I've got a feature film coming up.'

'Who's in it?'

'No one you know, Jules. But I'll be doing their make-up. Shoot should last about five weeks and fuck if I'm gonna let the taxman know.'

'So you're alright for now?'

'You know me, Jules. I'm a survivor. Fuck all men … apart from the hard-arsed ones … hang on a sec, you think you're so crafty changing the subject. *Don't* you give in to Brenton. *Never* tell Breanna the whole, dirty biblical details.'

'I won't,' said Juliet. 'I promise.'

Chapter 7
Insecurity

'MAYBE THAT NEW PLACE in Clapham Common,' said Breanna on her mobile.

'Nah,' came the reply. 'The guys in there are too dry. Too many of them are wastemen.'

'But you got a man,' returned Breanna.

'No harm in looking though, is there.'

'I suppose so.'

'When you gonna introduce me to Malakai?'

'*Never!* Don't trust you.'

'Screw you!'

'Screw you too.'

'No, seriously. When.'

'You might see him tomorrow night if we can decide on a bar or club to go to. In fact, I'm just about to go to Nando's. Meeting Jazz there. Malakai's linking me there too.'

'So you're letting Jazz see Malakai before me? That is bad-mind! Mind they don't leave the table together.'

'Jazz ain't like that.'

'Ain't she? I'd meet you there if I didn't have to cook tonight. Mum's late from work and my two brothers don't know where the kitchen is. I'll see you tomorrow then.'

'OK, tomorrow, Joanna. And when you see Malakai keep your eyes to yourself.'

'Don't worry, Breanna. He's probably ugly anyway. And if he ain't you better keep Jazz's flirting on lock.'

'You joker. See ya.'

Breanna snapped her mobile closed and opened her wardrobe. She considered changing her clothes but couldn't be bothered. Instead she cleaned her face with a wet wipe, sprayed her neck and wrists with fragrance and then pondered over her shoe collection. She decided to pull on her cream Ugg boots over her black Adidas tracksuit bottoms and her green waterproof body-warmer over her grey hoodie.

She left her house and made her way to the bus stop near West Norwood train station. It was a cold evening and she cursed herself for forgetting her gloves. She checked her watch. Seven fifteen. She hoped Malakai wouldn't be late. She hoped Jazz liked him; Jazz didn't like the last guy she dated and they didn't last long. God! she thought. There's her worrying about what Jazz would think about her new man but Gran is dead! Bree, you're a dog-heart!

It didn't seem real looking into her coffin, Breanna recalled. At least that haunted look in her eyes was gone. She wondered what lay behind it. She'd always had it in mind to ask Gran what troubled her over the years but never got around to it. No. That ain't true, Breanna reconsidered. I was just too scared to ask. Maybe it was just regrets? Or was it living on her own for so long? Mum's face is beginning to look like Gran's. She's starting to develop that same tormented expression. It was there at odd times when she was reading one of her books or when she was watching one of her romantic mini-series DVDs. From a warm smile her expression could change into a sad look in the space of a blink. She's still so much better looking than me though.

She wondered if Mum ever thought it was a mistake marrying Dad. After all, she pondered, I'm not his. How many men take on women with kids? Maybe because Mum was so good looking it didn't matter to him that she was a single mother. But their body language is messed up. They sit apart watching television. They never kiss in front of me, not even a goodbye kiss when one of them is leaving for work. Man! Their generation's weird. Malakai and me won't go on like that if we last that long.

Uncle Brenton's got a chance of a long relationship with Lesley, Breanna thought. She's alright. He can be intense sometimes but you can have a laugh with him; can't have a giggle with Dad. Uncle Brenton should settle down with Lesley. It's obvious she really loves him but her two kids are spoilt. Maybe that's what's holding Uncle Brenton back. Wonder what he and Mum were arguing about in the garden?

A 68 bus screeching to a halt stopped Breanna's thoughts. She had to stand on her journey to Brockwell Park and longed for the day when she could afford a car. She caught the 37 from the park to Brixton and as she passed the Town Hall she guessed her mum was still working there. She wondered if her place of work would be Westminster one day. You're too damn ambitious, Mum, she said to herself.

Nando's restaurant was opposite Brixton Academy; some band Breanna had never heard of was playing there next weekend. Across the road a bus driver was refusing to proceed because a passenger didn't want to pay his fare. A toddler was playing up in his buggy at the bus stop and his mother was trying to calm him with chicken nuggets. Breanna kissed her teeth.

Breanna found Jazz sitting in a corner of the restaurant. There were some uppity young blacks there too who wouldn't be seen dead in a McDonald's or Kentucky, she reckoned, but they couldn't afford much more than a Nando's. She didn't like the place but Jazz loved it, especially as it was located in the centre of Brixton.

'What's up, sis?' Breanna greeted. She kissed Jazz on her left cheek and gave her a hug.

'What's up, girl?' Jazz returned. 'So where is he?'

Breanna sat down. She picked up a menu. 'He'll be here any minute,' she said. 'He better be here.'

'What you having?' asked Jazz.

'The usual. Rice, leg of chicken and roasted corn.'

'And let me guess,' continued Jazz. 'A cheesecake to take home.'

'You know me too good.'

'You know it, girl.'

'Have you ordered?' asked Breanna.

'Just my drink.'

'Then let's order.'

The two girls made their way to the kitchen counter. Just as they were giving their orders to the waitress, Malakai and a friend arrived. Breanna turned round, spotted Malakai and smiled as wide as a Joker in a *Batman* film. She hugged him tight and kissed him on his left cheek. His jeans were barely covering his backside and Breanna spotted he was wearing dark blue boxers.

'This is Sean,' Malakai introduced. 'He asked if he could come and link us. He's well hungry.'

'No problem,' said Breanna. 'This is Jazz. One of my best friends.'

Sean's eyes lingered on Jazz's heart-shaped, caramel-coloured face. Then his gaze dropped a little to her chest. 'My bredren's girlfriend has pretty friends,' he charmed.

Jazz blushed.

'You know it,' continued Sean. He turned to Breanna. 'And I'm sorry about losing your gran.'

'That's alright … So you're going around the place calling me your girlfriend?' Breanna laughed turning to Malakai. 'I *better* be the only one. I know how you guys stay. You have links here, there and everywhere.'

Guilt struck Breanna again. Should she be laughing a day after Gran got buried? she asked herself. Gran would have wanted me to carry on, she convinced herself. To live my life.

'How many times do I have to say I'm not into that?' pleaded Malakai.

Ten minutes later they all settled down to eating various portions of chicken, fries, rice and roasted corn. Napkins littered their table. Breanna sipped wine and the others drank lemonade and cola. Breanna noticed that Jazz was quieter than usual.

'So, Malakai,' said Sean. 'Breanna already invite you round to her gates. Bredren, seems like t'ings are getting serious. You only linked a few weeks ago.'

'Not that serious,' replied Malakai.

Breanna gave Malakai a playful punch.

'It was at the reception after the funeral,' continued Malakai. 'Breanna asked me to reach and pay my respects. I met her family. Her Uncle Brenton and everybody.'

'Uncle Brenton?' repeated Sean.

Jazz and Breanna paused their eating. 'You know my uncle?' asked Breanna.

'His name rings a bell,' said Sean. 'Can't be that many Brentons around. Not with a name like that. Think my mum might know him.'

'Oh lordy Lord,' laughed Jazz. 'Your mum didn't go out with my girl's uncle, did she?'

Everyone laughed except Sean. He smiled politely. Breanna guessed there was some kind of connection or hidden history behind that smile.

'No, it was nothing like that,' Sean finally answered. 'I think they just knew each other back in the day. Friends maybe? It ain't no biggie.'

'Lordy Lord!' exclaimed Jazz. 'That's a relief.'

'What do you mean that's a relief?' challenged Breanna. 'What's wrong with going out with my uncle?'

'He is a bit … scary,' answered Jazz. 'With those eyes of his. Whenever I see him he always looks like he's planning to eat somebody 'cos someone put shit in his best Nikes or something. And that scar on his neck. Ugh!'

Sean stilled as if suddenly frozen.

'He's just quiet and shy,' countered Breanna. 'When you get to know him he can be really funny. Wasn't you there, Jazz, when he told us when he was a yout' he used to go out on street looking for cigarette butts. And he used to t'ief milk and bread from a milk float.'

'He sounds crazy to me,' said Jazz. 'But I s'pose everyone's got a mad relative somewhere.'

'He's not crazy,' argued Breanna. 'He had a hard-knock life.'

'Maybe he got too many knocks on his head?' laughed Jazz.

'Them old-school days were rough though,' added Malakai. 'My mum told me her older brother had to get the paraffin bottle before he went to school. When he reached school he stank out the classroom with his paraffin fumes all on his uniform. Brothers would chase him down in the playground with boxes of matches. Old-school times weren't easy. Believe.'

From a small name-brand rucksack that was draped over his chair, Malakai took out a gift-wrapped box. He placed it on the table and grinned widely. 'I dunno if Brenton searched the streets of Bricky for cigarette butts but I thought he was cool,' he said. 'He was about the only one out of the older ones who took time chatting to me at the wake. Anyway, Bree. This is for your birthday. Hope you like it.'

Cleaning her fingers with a napkin, Breanna wasted no time unwrapping the box.

'Ain't you supposed to wait until the day of your birthday,' protested Jazz. 'You're so fast, girl.'

The box contained a bottle of perfume. 'Is it the real t'ing?' asked Breanna, checking the labels. 'Not a fake from Nine Elms market or East Street?'

'What you take me for?' protested Malakai. 'Course it's the

real t'ing. When I come buying presents for *my* girl I come proper. You understand.'

Leaning over the table, Breanna cradled Malakai's cheeks with her hands and kissed him on the mouth. 'Thanks, choc.'

'I told you she'd like that,' said Sean. 'Man can't go wrong when he buys his girl a proper perfume. Chicks love that.'

'You two better behave yourself,' warned Jazz. 'I ain't getting fling out 'cos of you two getting it on. I still wanna get my cheesecake.'

'What's with the choc?' Sean wanted to know.

'That's my nickname for Malakai,' explained Breanna. 'Don't you think his complexion is like milk chocolate?'

Jazz picked up the bottle of perfume and she inspected it like a Z-list celeb studying an article about themselves in a tabloid. 'Mind my girl don't lick your complexion off,' she joked.

After everyone bought a cheesecake to take away, Sean walked with Jazz and Malakai stepped with Breanna. He had his right arm around her shoulders and they soon lagged twenty yards or so behind the others.

'So your dad is not your real dad?' Malakai said.

'No,' answered Breanna. 'Him and Mum got together when I was about two years old or something.

'Do you know your real dad?'

'No. Mum said it was one of those t'ings. You know. A one-night stand kinda t'ing.'

'Your mum? A one-night stand? She seems so …? What you call it? Don't be offended but a little bit … stush.'

'Yeah, so everyone says,' said Breanna.

'She must have an idea who your dad is. Haven't you ever asked her about it?'

'Yeah I did. Nuff times. But I gave up after a while. She's sticking to her story.'

'What story?'

'Back in the day she went to some party. Someone made some hash cakes. The chronic was burning. Everyone had a proper buzz on, drinks were flowing and Mum ended up in a bedroom with some guy. She was so out of it she doesn't remember who she was with or what happened. Two months or so later she found out she was pregnant with me.'

'And you believe that?'

They were passing under the bridge in Brixton High Street. A train rattled overhead. A sudden gust disturbed debris alongside the kerb. Breanna secured the top button of her body-warmer. She paused and looked at Malakai. 'No. I never believed it,' she finally answered. 'But if Mum wants me to believe her story then I will. I don't want to dig deeper 'cos the truth might be something a lot worse. I think she was raped.'

'*Raped!*'

'It's a mad guess but it would explain a lot,' reasoned Breanna. 'You should see photos of Mum when she was young. She was beautiful. Still is. Even now I see men much younger than her step up to her. I wish I got all of her looks.'

'You're beautiful too,' said Malakai.

'Sometimes Mum's so sad,' resumed Breanna, ignoring Malakai's compliment. 'So was Gran. You know when someone's smiling but you can still see their pain? Them two were like that. Mum's still like that. It's like they knew something but they won't tell me 'cos they know it would hurt me.'

'Their generation went through a lot,' said Malakai. 'My mum's kinda sad too. She split up from Dad when I was about five. She's had about four boyfriends since then but all of them let her down. She's always cussing about black men and when she does I feel kinda bad. I'm a grown-up black man now. I'm twenty-three. Makes me wonder if one day I'll make a good dad.'

'Do you still see your dad?'

'Now and again. He lives in Crystal Palace with some white

girl. Younger than him. They got a six-year-old daughter. Precious is her name. My baby sister. Mum don't like me calling
Precious my sister. So I don't tell Mum when I visit her.'

'It's good that you see her though.'

Stopping at the bus stop outside Brixton market, they caught
up with Jazz and Sean. The cold air couldn't quite quench the
smell of rotting vegetables, spoilt fruit and stale fish. No one was
paying any attention to the ranter with a microphone outside
Brixton tube station. Close to him was a tall rasta selling incense
sticks; he wasn't getting much trade.

'I think you should ask your mum about your real dad,' said
Malakai. 'You're a big woman now. Twenty-one tomorrow. What
she told you about your real dad don't sound right. Ask her again
but be polite about it. Be understanding. Ask in a mature way.'

'I will,' replied Breanna.

'We'll wait until your bus comes,' offered Malakai.

Breanna kissed Malakai again and she snuggled up to him
while waiting for her bus. Jazz was exchanging phone numbers
with Sean and by the time they had finished their bus had arrived.

'Don't be late tomorrow!' said Breanna.

'I won't,' replied Malakai. 'Get on the bus!'

Malakai and Sean watched them step up to the top deck. They
both waved as the bus pulled away.

'Man! You work fast,' said Malakai. 'Did you get her number?'

'She asked for my number first, bredren,' Sean replied.

'Do you really know Breanna's Uncle Brenton?'

'I don't know him. My mum does. Did you see the scar on
his neck?'

'Yeah. Looks ugly, man. It's like brown jelly or somet'ing.
Wouldn't like to touch it.'

'Then it's him,' Sean confirmed. 'My mum definitely knows
him.'

Half an hour later Sean reached his fourth-floor flat in the

Lilford estate off Coldharbour Lane. There was scaffolding surrounding the blocks to help the construction workers replace old windows. Eek-A-Mouse's *Virgin Girl* singjayed out from a second-floor flat. Sean heard two dogs barking as he climbed the stairs. Entering the flat he glanced at the yellowing paintwork in the hallway. He wiped his feet on the tatty mat on the imitation wood-panelled floor. He found his mother in the cramped kitchen washing up mugs and dishes. She was listening to a radio phone-in programme; a caller wanted to know what to do after discovering that her boyfriend had made seventeen calls to a girl she didn't know on his mobile in the last two days. Sean sat down at the small kitchen table. Without turning around his mother said, 'There is chicken in the oven for you. Wash up after yourself. I'm tired of getting up in the morning and seeing the sink full up. And if you have any friends around tonight tell them to keep it quiet … Fling him out, you damn idiot! What's wrong wid you? He's fucking another bitch! Lord Jesus! You get pure foolish woman 'pon de radio.'

'Already eaten, Mum,' answered Sean. 'Went Nando's with Malakai.'

'Why you never tell me? That food better not waste! You can have it for your lunch tomorrow.'

'Yeah, Mum. I will.'

'And you'd better be careful out there on street. You shouldn't be going to a place like Nando's. I don't want no damn phone call telling me somet'ing happen to you.'

'Mum! What do you expect me to do? Sit in the flat all day? You keep telling me I get on your nerves.'

'Those bad breed boys might be still looking for you.'

'Most of them are inside. And the rest of the crew who aren't doing time are pussies …'

'Don't use that language in my yard!'

'They won't do me nothing, Mum. It's been over two years now.'

'There's still nuff bad feeling around. Maybe we shoulda take up the police offer to relocate?'

'What? Be driven out of our ends by those puss ...'

'*Don't* use that word in my yard!'

'Look, Mum. I'm not involved in that life anymore. I'm trying my best to walk good as you say. I'm ignoring all the crap that's on road.'

'Where have you been today anyway? You'd better be looking for work. I can't run this place by myself. I need help.'

'I was this afternoon. Then I bump into Malakai and I followed him Nando's. You'd never guess who his girlfriend's uncle is?'

'Eddie Murphy? Stevie Wonder? Bob Marley? The raas claat Cream Puff Man in *Ghostbusters*? What kinda stupid blasted question is that? How am I supposed to know?'

'Brenton Brown.'

Sean's mother, Venetia, stopped washing the dishes. She stilled for two seconds before turning around to face her son. 'Brenton Brown?'

'Yeah. The same Brenton Brown who you've been telling me all my days that mash up your life.'

'That was the past,' said Venetia. 'A long time ago. I don't want you doing anything stupid.'

'Don't do nothing stupid? You're the one who kept saying everything was his fault. You know, with my paps.'

'Stay away from him, Sean,' Venetia warned, pointing a finger. 'He's a dangerous man. Crazy, so some people say.'

'I ain't gonna be afraid of him. I just wanna meet him. See what all the fuss is about mad Brenton Brown.'

'I'm warning you, Sean. *Stay* away from him.'

Rising to his feet, Sean offered his mother a contemptuous glare before disappearing into the lounge. He switched on his Playstation. He turned up the volume. His thumbs and fingers were a blur as he played a violent game where he had to kill as many characters as possible before reaching the next level.

'Don't think you're playing that damn somet'ing all night!' Venetia yelled. 'I want to watch my news in fifteen minutes. And turn it down! What you take this for? You think you inna disco?'

Sean kissed his teeth and kept on killing characters on the screen. Venetia returned to her washing-up. 'Brenton Brown,' she whispered. 'You fucker. You wreck my life.'

Chapter 8

Renewal

TAKING OFF HIS HARD HAT, Brenton walked into the kitchen of the house he was renovating. Dustsheets were on the floor and the smell of paint attacked his nostrils. A white guy with a measuring tape and a pencil was marking something on the kitchen wall. Brenton watched him for a few seconds before admiring once again the new kitchen cupboards he had fitted. A naked bulb illuminated the undercoat on the ceiling. A bruised, dusty radio with a coat hanger acting as an aerial was playing Spandau Ballet's *Gold*. 'Daniel, try and finish up by tomorrow morning, yeah,' pressed Brenton.

'Should do so, Bren.'

'The lady of the place been on my case all day,' revealed Brenton. 'Wanted to turn off my mobile. I told her ages ago that we should finish her flat by the end of this week. But nah. Her parents are coming down from wherever tomorrow afternoon and she wants to show off her new flat all decorated and t'ing.'

'Just got to put the second coat on and tidy up the corner of the ceiling then I'm done.'

'Good,' said Brenton, examining the paintwork of the ceiling. 'I'm stepping now 'cos it's my niece's birthday today. You're alright to lock up, aren't you?'

'Yeah, no probs.'

'And remember to put the lids back on the paint cans and sweep up when you finish. That fussy bitch might decide to come round later on and have a look at what we've done today. I don't want her loading off to me in the morning.'

'Alright, Bren. I get it. You told me five times today already.'

'OK, Daniel. Sorry about the grief I've given you today but that woman really gets on my tits.'

'Tomorrow, Bren.'

'Try and make it for seven in the morning, Daniel. Let's finish this job and get the fuck out of here. I've got a job in Barnes I want to start.'

'Barnes? Where's Barnes?'

'The other side of Putney,' Brenton answered. 'We got another conversion to do, making three flats out of a three-storey house. Should keep us going till Easter. The man who asked me for a quote drives one of them new Jags so I'm gonna jack up my price.'

'Overtime?'

'Yes, Daniel, they'll be overtime if you want it.'

Taking off his overalls before stepping out of the building, Brenton wondered if he should've made more of an effort to buy Breanna a present. He had been busy with work but was that a reasonable excuse? Dunno what to buy her anyway, he shrugged. She's got the latest mobile, iPod and all that fuckery. And no way am I gonna dare buy her clothes. Fuck that. Hope she's happy with two hundred pounds. Was it too much for an uncle to give to his niece? Nah. She's twenty-one. It's a milestone. And I'm the only uncle or aunt she's got. Maybe I should give her more? Make it a round figure. Five hundred pounds. Maybe not. Don't want to give Breanna more money than what Juliet and Clayton might spend on her. Fuck Clayton. Maybe I should give Juliet a call to find out what they're buying her? Haven't spoken to her since the funeral. It'll be nice to put that argument behind us.

Before getting into his car, Brenton took out his mobile and thumbed down to Juliet's number. He paused. He stared at her number. He visualised her face. A deep longing stirred in him. He checked his thoughts. Nah, she's probably busy with all that

Lambeth Council shit. She might still be mad with me. Still gotta buy Breanna a card. I bet Clayton buys her a card and does some writing in it that is well over the top. *To my darling dearest sweet daughter on her most special day.* Fuck Clayton. Breanna *ain't* your daughter.

Climbing into his car, he switched on the ignition and Little John's *Smoke Ganga Hard* exhaled from the stereo. From Pimlico it took him half an hour to reach his home off Brixton Hill. He stopped off at the Nubian culture shop where he bought Breanna's card. Once he reached home he washed his hands before writing in the card, *To Breanna, Love Uncle Brenton.* He dreamed of one day signing a card, *Love Dad.*

Deciding against a shower, Brenton took a leisurely bath and felt good that all the dust, grime and dirt from his day was washed away. Daniel better sweep up when he's finished, he thought. Should I call him? Nah. He's already said I've been stressing out too much this week.

Once he had pulled fresh clothes on he inserted Breanna's card and two hundred pounds into an envelope. He felt good and smiled in anticipation. He wrote Breanna's name on the envelope and underlined it with a flourish. For a moment he wished he had a better writing hand. Like Juliet's. Her writing is so neat, so elegant. There was a knock at the door and he went to open it

Standing perfectly still in a black trench coat with both hands on her hips was Lesley. Something was erupting in her eyes and Brenton noticed the solid look of her jawline. Her lips seemed that bit thinner than the last time he'd seen her. Oh shit! he thought. I haven't called her back. Oh fuck! 'Come in,' he said.

'So you can talk?' snapped Lesley. She marched in and sat down at the dinner table. She placed her designer handbag on the table and folded her arms once more. She didn't unbutton her coat and she looked out of the window as if she was waiting for some kind of apology. 'Forgotten how to use your mobile?'

Taking his time closing the door, Brenton cautiously joined Lesley at the table. He carefully pulled out a chair as if any noise he made would ratchet up her obvious anger. He struggled to come up with a greeting.

'Why haven't you returned any of my calls or texts?' asked Lesley. She was still staring out the window. 'And don't give me no rubbish about your battery playing up.'

'Just … busy, you know.'

'What do you mean you're just fucking busy?'

Brenton had never heard Lesley swear before. Well, maybe the odd *shit* but she only said it if she dropped and smashed a glass while drying up or something. 'I've been stressed lately.'

'You've been stressed lately? Ahhh. Poor you. Life been a bit too much for you these past few weeks, has it? *Rubbish!*'

'It has with my mum dying and t'ing.'

'*Rubbish* again. You're using that as an excuse and you're insulting my intelligence.'

'I'm not.'

'I can't ever remember you expressing any undying devotion to your mum so don't give me this grieving *oh my god my mum just died* rubbish.'

'It did hit me hard. Sometimes you don't appreciate somet'ing till it's gone.'

'If you're gonna chat rubbish in my ears then I might as well leave.' Lesley stood up from her chair and hooked her handbag over her left shoulder.

'It's not just Mum,' Brenton explained. 'It's work as well. Been stressful lately.'

Sitting back down again, Lesley offered Brenton a hard stare. He looked away as if guilt slapped his face. He rested his eyes on the framed sketch of a resilient rasta boy that was hanging from a wall. 'My son was sick the other day,' Lesley stated. 'Usually I would call my mum to look after him but she's sick as well.

There's a flu bug going around. It's that time of year. I've already taken enough days from work and I know I'm beginning to piss off my boss although he's been polite about it.'

'Sorry to hear,' offered Brenton.

'Sorry to hear? When I come home I'm tired but I have to sort out dinner and make sure my kids do their homework. Then I have to deal with bills that I haven't opened for days. Then I have to remember to call Mum or otherwise she'll accuse me of not caring. If I'm lucky I might get time to cool out with a glass of Baileys about ten o'clock and watch *CSI: Miami*. But I don't get that luxury 'cos there's always something to do in my house like cleaning, sorting out the kids' clothes and stuff. I really look forward to the weekend, when I've got time for myself, time to see you. Then I get a call from that wort'less father of my kids saying he can't take them at the weekend because he's working or something; what he really means is that he's taking his new woman on the fucking Eurostar to Paris. After all that shit, I still find time to call you. If your phone's off then I send you a text.'

'I know,' Brenton nodded. 'Sorry.'

'Sorry? So when I'm stressed out and feeling emotional I still wanna be in touch with you. A nice conversation after a tiring day would be nice, you know, with my so-called man. You know? Give me a bit of understanding. A boost. But oh no! Not from you. You can't answer my *fucking* call or text 'cos you're too *stressed*. You're nothing but a selfish, me-me-me piece of shit.'

'It's not that I meant to disrespect you …'

'Oh so that makes it alright? For what? Two or so years I've been trying to make it with you. I ignored how little you put into our relationship. I ignored that it took you months to introduce me to your precious family. I overlooked you being rude to my friends; Cerise thinks you're a mental case by the way. I even put up with you not inviting me back to your place for the first three months. Jesus! I thought you was fucking around.'

'Look, Lesley. Let me explain.'

'No! You listen to me.'

'I admit I've been off-key lately.'

'Is that what you call it? Off fucking key? When you haven't got the decency to return any of my calls? You know what? I don't deserve this. You're the worst kind of man. A fucking shit!'

'Lesley, you need to calm down.'

'Don't fucking patronise me! After everything I've done to make our relationship work, what did you say to me in the car? *T'ings are not working out. I need a break.* The way you said it was so casual. Like I was a stereo or something that didn't work anymore. Don't you respect anyone's feelings? Are you even capable of considering someone's feelings? Is it all about you and only you?'

'I have nuff respect for you.'

'No you don't,' accused Lesley. She glared at him. 'You're a cold-hearted piece of shit. You used your mother's situation to try and break up with me.'

'That ain't true,' argued Brenton. He looked away, unable to face Lesley's contemptuous glare. She laughed.

'Like I said, you're the worst kind of man. Maybe you're not the kind that sleeps around but at least you know where you stand with those men. No, you're the type that can't commit. You allow women into your life but only up to a point. You allow women to start loving you but there's a limit. You can't let them get too close. Oh no. Guys like you are too precious for that. You never let them get too intimate. And when I say intimate I don't mean making love.'

'Two years is a long relationship,' said Brenton. 'Don't that mean something?'

'Not in your case it don't. As soon as I managed to get close to you, get to know your family and stuff, you say you need a raas claat break. It was only three months ago your sister invited us to her place for that dinner party. I thought, OK, we're really tight now.'

Brenton bowed his head.

'Your sister joked that we should get married,' resumed Lesley. 'You remember? Everyone had a giggle about it but *not* you! We're not even thinking about it, you said. We don't even live together you said. *You* humiliated me in your sister's house. But even that I put up with. Be patient I said to myself. He'll come around. Like *fuck* you would!'

'Did I ever say we was gonna get married? Did I?'

'No, you didn't. But where were you expecting us to go in our relationship? Carry on meeting every Saturday night, go out somewhere and then have sex? You really think that's all I wanted? You really think I'm the kind of woman who would just settle for that? Was I some kind of sexual relief after your *stressed-out* week of work? Am I just a little notch better than a fucking blow-up doll?'

'No, course not.'

Needing to escape Lesley's biting glare, Brenton went to the kitchen. He stood at the sink and bowed his head. *Fuck!* he screamed in his head. I've really fucked up. 'Can I get you a drink?'

'*No!*'

'Do you want a biscuit or something? Got some custard creams. Apple?'

'*No!*'

Returning to the dinner table with a cold beer in his hand, he faced Lesley again. 'What can I say? I'm sorry.'

'Sorry for what?' Lesley countered. 'Sorry for letting me get close to you? Sorry that I developed real feelings for you? Sorry you met me? What are you running away from? What did you expect to happen when you have a relationship with someone for two years or so? Or in our case an *alleged* relationship.'

'I … I had a fucked-up childhood,' admitted Brenton. Maybe I should tell her all about it? he considered. She might be sympathetic. Don't tell her everything though.

'Yeah,' Lesley nodded. 'I know. You had a bad childhood. Breanna told me you were in a home. You think my childhood was any better?' 'Cos I was the oldest my mom beat the living shit out of me when things went wrong in our house. If Dad came home drunk and shouted at her I would get it in the neck in the morning. On some mornings I got it all over my fucking body. I spent my eleventh birthday in some battered woman's home. The crazy thing about it was that Mum was in there for Dad battering her but the social workers never even realised she was beating the living shit out of me!'

'Sorry,' Brenton managed. He didn't know where to look.

'My dad beat me up on my sixteenth birthday,' Lesley continued. 'For putting on make-up, and you know what's funny? If my dad won on the horses he'd take his winnings and go and see prostitutes. After all that my mum still went back to him. So don't come to me with no *fucking* violin tissue story wanting my pity. I don't want no man of mine crying about *his sad life in a children's home* while he's in his forties.'

'I didn't know you had it so rough,' said Brenton.

'You didn't want to know. You never asked. It was just about you and when I asked about your past you told me you didn't want to discuss it! So you lived in a home. Do you wanna hear a fucking violin concerto? Do I have to buy extra towels to dry your tears? So fucking what! At least you got three meals a day. Where I grew up everyone had a sob story but you know what? Most get over it and don't wallow in self-pity. They move on.'

'You don't understand,' said Brenton, his voice now almost in a whisper.

'Don't understand? I understand this. I don't allow my past to affect my present. I can't afford to. I've got two kids to raise and I don't want to raise them full of my shit and baggage. What are you? You're very weak. You ain't no man. You're not a man at all. You can't deal with your past, you can't commit to anybody. You're a fucking emotional cripple. *I can't discuss my past!* Boo fucking hoo! I'm not gonna waste my time with someone as emotionally weak as you. Grief! They say you're the stronger sex!'

Brenton closed his eyes. He opened them ten seconds later. He glanced at Lesley. 'You finished?'

'Just about.'

Sipping his beer, Brenton glanced at the image of the boy rasta once again. Lesley rose from her seat and went to the bathroom to collect her toothbrush. She then quick-stepped into the bedroom to pick up some spare underwear that she had left in Brenton's chest of drawers. She put them in her handbag, and returning to the lounge she regarded Brenton once more. She shook her head. 'In a way I feel sorry for you,' she said. 'Because you are so selfish you can't recognise a good thing when it enters your life. You'll probably end up alone, old and miserable, still trying to work out your issues … Don't *ever* contact me again.' She walked towards the door. 'Oh, I almost forgot.'

Taking out a gift-wrapped box Lesley placed it on the dinner table. She offered Brenton one last glare before slamming the door behind her. Brenton felt the vibration from the door frame. He took a generous gulp of his beer, closed his eyes and bowed his head again. He didn't move for the next twenty minutes.

Rising from his chair, he picked up the gift-wrapped box and guessed it was an expensive bottle of perfume. He looked at the tag. *Happy Birthday, Breanna. From Uncle Brenton and Lesley* it read. He sat back down and thought about what Lesley had said. Was he uncaring? Was he selfish? He did take her for granted. He didn't want her to meet Juliet or Mum. He had never been comfortable introducing his girlfriends to Juliet. Mum was pleasant to Lesley on the two occasions they met. Why didn't he suffer when Mum passed away? He had long accepted her reasons for giving him up. They had got on reasonably well. Once they were reunited she had always treated him well. Why did he always insist on talking about the past with her instead of enjoying her company? He knew she was sick. When she had passed there was no sense of deep loss. No tears. He didn't suffer that same crushing feeling as when Juliet told him their relationship had to end over twenty years ago. Since then other women had come into his life. Some lasted a few months, some a few weeks. He didn't regret breaking up with any of them. Then there was Lesley. She was perfect for him. Intelligent and considerate. A fantastic mother. Independent and sexy. Why couldn't he love her? If he did he would run out of his flat pleading with her to take him back. He didn't like her calling him an emotional cripple but he didn't feel devastated. Just annoyed. No, something a bit stronger than annoyed. Maybe that trauma with Juliet was so deep he could never recover from it. Can't move on even though it's twenty-odd years. Or is that an excuse? Perhaps Lesley's right. I'm just a selfish me-me-me piece of shit.

On his way to Juliet's house Brenton didn't have the will to turn on the car stereo. Am I this bad a person, he kept asking himself. Maybe with my selfish ways I fucked up Juliet's life too? What am I doing insisting that I should be named as Breanna's father? Gotta drop that shit even though it will pain me for the rest of my days.

He pulled up opposite Juliet's home and remained in the car for the next ten minutes. He needed to compose himself. With a deep sigh he made his way over to the house and pressed the doorbell. Breanna's gifts were in his other hand and he almost dropped the envelope. The door opened to reveal Breanna. She was as happy as he had ever seen her. Would she still be smiling if the truth came out? Brenton asked himself. She might hate me.

73

'Happy birthday, Breanna,' Brenton smiled, handing her the presents.

'Thanks, Uncle Brenton.'

She read the tags.

'Where's Lesley?'

'Er, she ain't coming,' stuttered Brenton walking into the hallway.

'Tell her thanks from me,' insisted Breanna.

'Yeah, of course.'

Don't contact me ever again echoed inside Brenton's head. He visualised Lesley disappearing out of his flat. Breanna led him to the lounge. There were birthday cards on display on the large teak coffee table. Brenton glanced at the largest one. It was from Clayton and Juliet and there was a long handwritten message inside. It wasn't Juliet's writing. Fuck Clayton, Brenton screamed in his head.

Sitting together on a three-seater leather sofa were Juliet and Clayton. Clayton was dressed in a suit minus the jacket. He had loosened his tie and was nursing a brandy from a special wide glass that he used only for drinking brandy. He caught Brenton with a suspicious sideways glance but he quickly changed his expression to a smile. *Fuck* Clayton, Brenton repeated in his mind.

Smartly attired in a blue skirt suit, Juliet was sipping a glass of champagne. Wearing dark tights she was flexing her toes. She glanced at Brenton cautiously. 'Can I get you a drink?' she offered.

'No, thanks,' declined Brenton, still standing by the lounge door. 'I had a beer at home and I can't stay for long.'

Picking up a set of car keys from the coffee table, Breanna turned to Brenton and said, 'You'll never guess what my parents have bought me for my birthday.'

'Breanna!' rebuked Juliet. 'Where's your manners! Open your uncle's card and gift.'

'I got a car,' Breanna blurted out. She showcased her enamel and Brenton thought she might have a pleasure overload.

'*Breanna!*' Juliet scolded once more.

'It's a Renault Clio,' Breanna went on, ignoring her mother. 'Sky blue. Even the insurance is paid.'

Clayton sipped from his brandy. There was a quarter grin developing from his eyes. Juliet glared at Breanna but she was still oblivious of her. 'Do you wanna see it, uncle?'

'Er, in a minute,' said Brenton.

'He's brought you presents,' interrupted Juliet. 'Open them, Breanna.'

'It can wait,' said Brenton.

'Open them *now*,' insisted Juliet.

Doing what she was told, Breanna opened the box first and it revealed an expensive perfume. 'That's the second perfume I've got. Malakai bought me perfume too.'

Clayton rolled his eyes. Breanna opened the envelope and her eyes lit up when she saw the two hundred pounds in cash. She threw her arms around Brenton. 'Thanks so much, uncle. I'm so lucky to have you.'

'Maybe you can spend it on stuff for the car,' Brenton suggested. 'Car stereo, jump leads, furry dice, nice car seats. What do kids have in their cars these days? Little Jamaican boxing gloves? That kinda stuff.'

'She's got jump leads already,' said Clayton.

Fuck Clayton, Brenton wanted to roar.

'You're not staying?' asked Clayton. 'Breanna will only be twenty-one once. There's some cake as well. Have a drink with us. You can leave your car here and we'll call you a cab when you're ready to leave.'

'Friends are coming around later,' added Juliet. 'And the cake is chocolate.'

'Er, I'll stay for some chocolate cake,' said Brenton. 'But I can't stay for long.'

Taking an armchair Brenton was drawn by all Breanna's

birthday cards. He recalled her past birthdays and it was the same. Gifts and cards all over the place. I didn't get shit for my birthdays when I was growing up, he reflected. Lesley would laugh if she heard me say that. *You're an emotional cripple, chained to the past. You can't move on.* She's probably right but I didn't make me, circumstances made me. Breanna's so lucky though. And a little bit spoilt. If I was allowed to be her dad I wouldn't buy her no raas car. Clayton's mum probably spoilt him. I bet he wore Farah trousers to school. Fuck him.

'So how's business?' Clayton asked.

'So-so,' Brenton answered, jolted out of his thoughts. 'I'm surviving.'

'The housing market is very strong,' said Clayton. 'And should stay that way for quite a while. I should imagine you'll be very busy.'

'I'm just going to sit in my car again,' said Breanna, still excited. 'Might go for a drive around the block. Come and have a look, uncle.'

'I'll be out in a minute,' said Brenton. 'Let me eat my cake first.'

'Have you thought about designing your own website to promote your business?' asked Clayton. He sipped his brandy again and regarded Brenton in a friendly, helpful way. Fuck him, thought Brenton. Hate it when he goes on all nice and t'ing. 'Er, not really had time to think about it,' he finally replied.

'If you like I can give you a few contacts in that field,' said Clayton. 'I know a few people who design websites for businesses.'

I bet you fucking do, thought Brenton.

'It's a bit of an investment but you would reach far more potential customers if you advertised yourself on the internet and it would be a great idea to have a satisfied-client page with comments.

'Yeah, I suppose so,' said Brenton. *Where's Juliet with the fucking cake?* his inner voice screamed.

'Word of mouth is the thing in your business,' said Clayton. He poured himself some more brandy. He swirled it before taking another sip. He loosened his tie a bit more. 'Have you ever thought about buying your own property, doing a conversion into flats and then selling it on? It's very lucrative.'

'No I haven't,' replied Brenton. He wished he now had a drink. Juliet returned with a generous slice of cake on a plate. She gave it to Brenton and he ate it as if it might explode if he didn't finish it in the next sixty seconds.

'Do you want another slice?' offered Juliet.

'No thanks.'

'Brenton and I were just discussing ways of improving his business,' mentioned Clayton.

Putting the plate down on the coffee table, Brenton stood up. 'I suppose I'd better have a look at Breanna's new car. Back in a sec.'

'I'll get you another slice of cake while you're out,' said Juliet.

Relieved to get out of the house, Brenton found Breanna and her new car parked just a few yards up the road. She was texting someone on her mobile and didn't even see Brenton climb into the passenger seat. 'This is nice,' said Brenton.

'It is,' nodded Breanna. 'Can't believe it. Mum's always gone on about how lucky I am and I have to learn about working for anything I want and she goes out and buys me a car for my birthday.'

'You're only twenty-one once,' said Brenton.

'And they got it in my favourite colour.'

'I didn't know your favourite colour was sky-blue. That's the same as your mum's.'

'Don't you notice anything, uncle? My bedroom is decorated in baby-blue and when it's summer I always dress in baby-blue tops and accessories.'

I would notice stuff like that if I was allowed to be your dad, thought Brenton.

'You going out celebrating tonight?' asked Brenton.

'Yeah. Not taking the car though. We still haven't decided where to go yet. Might go to this bar in Clapham Common.'

'Who you going with?'

'Oh, the usual crowd ... and Malakai.'

'So you two serious?'

'It's getting that way,' Breanna blushed.

'Remember what I said. If a guy's really serious he'll stay around even if he's not getting any sex in the first few weeks or months in a relationship. You understand?'

'Yes, uncle. You're not gonna lecture me about this on my birthday, are you?'

'No, just be careful. Don't give it up too easily for him. You're twenty-one now so it's not all about the sex. At Malakai's age they basically just want sex but if they're made to wait for it they'll learn to respect you. That's what you should be thinking now. Serious. And if he gets peckish and goes somewhere else to satisfy his cravings then dash him to the rough part of the kerb. Understand?'

'Yes, uncle. Don't worry, I don't let man take advantage of me. I know what I'm doing. I'm twenty-one now!'

'You have a good time, yeah.'

'I will. Thanks again.'

'No problem. I'm going back in now. I'll see you soon. You coming in?'

'Not yet. I'm gonna drive around the block.'

Smiling, Brenton climbed out of the car as Breanna turned the ignition. He watched her very carefully check her wing and rear mirrors before pulling away. He returned to the house and as he re-entered the lounge he noticed that Juliet had already wrapped another slice of cake in kitchen foil.

'For tomorrow,' she said smiling.

Not bothering to sit down, Brenton said, 'Thanks. I'll have it when I get back from work.'

'Going already?' asked Clayton.

'Yeah. Gotta do some paperwork and prepare stuff for tomorrow.'

'We appreciate you coming around,' said Clayton standing up. He walked three paces towards Brenton and shook his hand warmly. Brenton made sure his grip was tighter than Clayton's. Fuck him! he yelled in his mind once more.

'I'll see you to the door,' offered Juliet.

She followed Brenton into the hallway. Before opening the front door, Brenton turned around. He gazed at Juliet. For just a moment his expression softened and became vulnerable. Longing was evident in his eyes.

'You OK?' asked Juliet.

'Yeah. I'm fine.'

'You look a bit … kind of pale.'

'How can I look pale, Juliet? I'm brown.'

'Sometimes people have a delayed kind of reaction to bereavement. We all react differently. I cried my tears at the hospital.'

'Yeah, it's hitting me now,' Brenton said.

'I'll let you know when we can go and see the solicitor. He said about two weeks.'

'OK, I'll be there.'

'Look after yourself, Brenton.'

'I will.'

'Oh, one sec.'

'What is it, Juliet?'

'I'm having a dinner party for a couple of Mum's old friends soon. It'll be nice if you were there.'

'I dunno,' Brenton answered. 'I'm very busy. Starting a job in Barnes soon.'

'I haven't set a date yet. It'll be on a Sunday.'

'I'll see how it goes,' said Brenton. 'But I'm not promising anything.'

'As I said it'll be nice if you can make it.'

I hate Juliet's dinner parties, Brenton thought. But she's really being nice. And she didn't make an issue of me arguing with her about Breanna at the wake. She never holds grudges. Not like me. And the chocolate cake was fucking delicious.

'I'll try my best,' he said. 'Bye, Juliet.'

'Bye, Brenton. Wrap up warm when you're working. Looks like you're coming down with something.'

'I'm fine. See ya.'

Juliet didn't go back inside until Brenton pulled away in his car. She raised one arm to bid farewell and Brenton replied with a toot of his horn. What's a matter with me? he rebuked himself. Why didn't I just say no? I hate Juliet's dinner parties. Why can I still not say no to her?

Chapter 9

The Question

LOOKING AT HERSELF in the bathroom mirror, Juliet noticed a grey hair on her fringe. She plucked it out, looked at it and threw it in the sink. She ran the cold tap and watched the rogue strand disappear. She then splashed water over her face and studied herself in the mirror once again. Those lines around my eyes are getting deeper, she concluded. So much for black don't crack. Getting greyer. My looks are fading. Got to deal with it. Better wash and dye my hair again this weekend, she decided.

She checked the temperature gauge and clock that hung from the bathroom wall. One forty-five in the morning. Nineteen degrees centigrade. Breanna hadn't arrived home yet. Hope she's behaving herself, Juliet said to herself. Lord! Why can't I sleep? I'm so tired. I thought making love to Clayton would've helped. Can I call it making love? We just have sex these days if I'm honest. Tessa would laugh at that. I'm sure she's never fucked three times a night and screamed down her bedroom no matter what she used to say. I wonder how many other couples just drift along having obligation sex. There must be millions of couples out there who have been together for years and years but they don't screw in the lounge, in the kitchen or on the stairs like they used to. Or they can't be bothered with the oral thing or screwing more than once a night. And then people say it's so nice that you're still together with your husband or wife. Brenton would call it a load of fuckery. Do we do it just because our wife or husband is lying there? How are you supposed to maintain passion when you've been with someone for so long? Lord!

I know precisely where Clayton is going to put his hand, kiss me and what position we will make love. He touches me like I might break. Why can't he be more ... more mannish. And he does it all without saying a word to me. But he spends so much time just staring at me. He makes me feel like I'm some kind of expensive painting. At least he still wants me in his own way I suppose. Not like some of those women at the Town Hall. Christ! How can they be so open about their men staying up as late as possible drinking until they crash out? Don't they realise that people know that's all about avoiding sex with their partner? At least Clayton's not like that. Why can't I want him as much as he wants me? Christ! I don't even kiss him on his cheek before he leaves for work like I used to do. I wonder if he's noticed? The older I get the more I understand why people have affairs. To catch that old excitement again. *Brenton.* Mustn't tell Tessa that. She'll go on at me forever.

Juliet washed her hands and dried them on a towel. Jesus! she thought. Do I really want to be an MP? Can't imagine what the *Daily Mail* or *Evening Standard* would do to me if they ever found out who Breanna's father really is. Lord! They'd be so deliriously happy they got that scoop they'd probably invite me to their Christmas party and airbrush a pic of me for their front pages.

She made her way back to the bedroom. Clayton was sleeping. No snoring, Juliet noted. He always sleeps better after sex. She sat down at the foot of the bed. Brenton, she repeated in her mind. He looks like he's coming down with something. I keep telling him to wrap up when he's at work in the winter months. He was feeling it today. I should've told him about Breanna's car. Lord! Those eyes. If someone ever does a scan of my brain they will see Brenton's eyes. He still wants me. After all this time. I just know it. I feel it. Wonder why Lesley wasn't with him today? Maybe she couldn't get someone to mind her kids. I wonder if Brenton wants to get deeply involved with someone who's already got kids. And she seemed a bit needy when I met her. Maybe I should say something to him. Tell him to be careful. She looks good for her age though but Brenton could get someone younger if he wanted to. No, better not say anything. Wanted to hug him today. Who are you kidding, Jules? I want to hug him every time I see him. But can't. Hope he's alright. Even if by a miracle we did live together, after twenty years we might end up like me and Clayton. Having obligation, grey-hair sex where no one bumps no heads, the sheets stay on the mattress, no one falls out of bed and we never fuck in the lounge or in the kitchen. Christ, Jules. You're a miserable negative cow sometimes. Stop doing this to yourself.

Standing up, she picked up her dressing gown that was on a chair near her side of the bed, put it on and made her way downstairs. Once in the kitchen she poured some water in the kettle, took out a bag of her favourite strawberry and mango herbal tea and sat down at the kitchen table. Brenton. Why can't I get you out of my mind? Kylie Minogue's *I Just Can't Get You Outta My Head* popped into the part of her brain that memorised music.

A minute later, the kettle boiled and Juliet poured the water into a Paris souvenir mug. She let it brew for another two minutes. Brenton. What are we going to do? She heard a key rattling in the front door lock. Funny how that kind of noise sounds louder at night, she thought. She sensed Breanna walking through the hallway and wondered if she'd notice the light on in the kitchen. She did.

Crashing onto a chair opposite her, Juliet could smell the drink on her daughter's breath. 'You enjoyed yourself,' stated Juliet. 'How did you get home?'

'Taxi,' Breanna answered. 'It's taking Malakai home now.'

'So where did you go?' asked Juliet, sipping her herbal tea.

'Some new bar in Clapham Common. Can't remember its

name. Drinks were a bit pricey but the music was slammin'. We had a good time.'

'Before you go to bed don't forget to take your make-up off. It won't do your skin any favours if you sleep with it on.'

'So you keep saying, Mum. Stop fussing. It's not like I'm shooting an ad for Clearasil in the morning. They'd never ask me anyway – not good looking enough. What you doing up anyway? Checking what time I get in?'

'No, no. As if? No, just couldn't sleep. And stop this rubbish about not being good looking enough.'

'It's true. Most of my friends are better looking than me … Why can't you sleep?'

'Oh, this and that. Still thinking if I want to put up with the hassle of being an MP.'

'Mum, can you make me a coffee?'

'Last time I looked you had a pair of hands and a pair of feet.'

'Yeah, but I'm not sure if my brain's still there.'

'Hmm,' Juliet replied. 'Maybe it drowned in vodka?'

'Funny.'

Grabbing another mug, Juliet added a generous spoon of coffee and three teaspoonfuls of brown sugar. Breanna, blinking away her tiredness, watched her every move. She didn't speak again until the coffee was placed in front of her. 'Mum,' she said.

'What is it?'

'I wanna ask you something. Don't flip.'

Picking up her mug of tea, Juliet took a sip. 'What is it? Don't be flipped by what? You better not be pregnant.'

'I am *not* pregnant, Mum. What do you take me for?'

'Then what is it?'

Breanna paused. She avoided her mother's gaze.

'Who's my dad?'

'Excuse me?'

'Who's my dad? I'm twenty-one now. You don't have to hide anything from me.'

'I'm not hiding anything from you.'

'Oh come on, Mum. You went to a party, you got high on something and then you had sex with some guy that you don't remember?'

'Yeah, *that* was it. These things happen. I wasn't always an angel.'

Juliet half-smiled but Breanna wasn't buying it.

'Things don't just happen to you,' Breanna said. 'Gran always said you were sensible. She said she never saw you drunk or even smoke a cigarette.'

Placing her mug on the table, Juliet took in a deep breath. Under the table she clasped her hands together to stop them shaking. She composed herself and returned Breanna's accusing glare. 'My mother didn't know everything about me. I wasn't exactly the Virgin Mary.'

'Come on, Mum,' Breanna pressed, forgetting about her coffee. 'Your story is just … unlikely. Why can't you trust me enough to tell me what really happened? Was it bad?'

'Are you calling me a *liar*?' Juliet raised her voice. 'What's done is done. It's in the past! Why are you bringing this up?'

'Because you're not being honest!' Breanna shouted. 'And you want to be an MP? You can't even be straight with me let alone any voter out there.'

I wish she would stop looking at me like that, Juliet thought. Why is she bringing this up? What brought this on? *Don't* shout, Jules. Stay calm. Don't be so defensive.

Juliet picked up her tea again and took another sip. Her eyes never left her daughter. 'I wasn't the perfect girl that my mother thought I was,' she said calmly. 'I was curious about drugs, drink and sex just like anyone else. I was sneaking out going to blues dances and pyjama parties when I was fifteen. At the same age

I had two guys on the go. Boys … always liked me and they invited me to parties and … places.'

'That doesn't mean that you have no idea who you're having sex with.'

'*Breanna!*'

'It's true. You went to a party, right? People usually go to a party with friends. So whoever this guy was, someone else must've known who he was.'

'Maybe they did. But *I didn't.*'

'So once you became pregnant didn't you try and find out? It wouldn't be rocket science trying to find out who followed you up into a bedroom and had sex with you. At least you must know what he looks like?'

'I didn't know what I was doing.'

Not liking the taste of her herbal tea anymore, Juliet stood up and poured it down the sink. She closed her eyes and drew in a long breath. She then stared out into the darkness of the back garden. 'As I've told you before I can't remember anything. I was fully charged, as we used to say in those days.'

Approaching her mother, Breanna's mouth was only a few inches away from Juliet's right ear. 'So you're telling me that you didn't even realise that some guy was … inside you?'

'I *don't* remember, Breanna! What do you want from me?'

'The truth might be helpful.'

'I've told you the truth. Are you calling your own mother a liar?'

Backing away a step, Breanna primed her tongue. Juliet dared to turn around and she saw Breanna's eyes gas-ringed with anger. She could see Brenton in her glare. Uncompromising, fierce eyes.

'*YES!*' Breanna raged. 'You've been lying to me all my life. *Who is my father?*'

'I don't know!'

'I *don't* believe you!'

'I'm your mother!'

'So you say. I'm starting to wonder if that's true.'

'Oh you're being ridiculous.'

'Am I?'

'I think you had a bit too much to drink this evening. Why don't you go to bed and we'll forget about this?'

'*No!* I will not forget about it. *Who's* my real dad?'

About to answer, Juliet noticed a shadow behind the frosted-glass kitchen door. She wondered how long Clayton had been standing there. She watched him enter the kitchen. Breanna folded her arms. She was breathing heavily. Juliet stood up and went to switch the kettle on once more.

'What's going on?' asked Clayton. He was dressed in a black silk dressing gown with a yellow dragon imprinted on the back; Juliet always thought it looked ridiculous. 'I could hear you two from upstairs. You might as well go out to the street and carry on because I'm not sure if they heard you in Uffington Road.'

Glancing at her daughter, Juliet said nothing.

Breanna dipped her head and failed to acknowledge Clayton despite him glaring at her. She suddenly stood up and announced, 'I'm going to bed.' She brushed passed an outraged Clayton and Juliet could hear her stomping up the stairs and then her bedroom door slamming.

'What was all that about?' Clayton asked.

'She wanted to know about her father,' Juliet answered.

'I'm her father,' insisted Clayton. 'She has only known me as her father.'

'She's curious.'

'Too curious,' said Clayton. He poured himself a glass of water and drank it in one go. 'Some birthday.'

'What do you mean some birthday?'

'I help buy her a brand new car for her birthday and at the end of it she wants to know about her *real* father. That's the respect I get in this house.'

'You feel hard done by?' Juliet asked.

'Yes, I do.'

'*I'm* the one she's calling a liar,' Juliet raised her voice. 'I'm the one she hates right now.'

'Maybe the emotion of the day caught up with her?' suggested Clayton. He opened the fridge, took out a carton of apple juice and found his favourite whisky glass in a cupboard. He downed his drink in one go. 'But no emotion is an excuse for shouting at her mother. Maybe we should take the car keys away from her until she apologises.'

'That's ridiculous.'

'She needs to learn respect.'

'The car was a birthday gift,' insisted Juliet. 'She's twenty-one now. We can't punish her like she's twelve.'

'Maybe if we did punish her when she was twelve she wouldn't be so spoilt now.'

'And that's my fault, is it?'

'It's not my fault that I was out there working all the hours I could to put a decent roof over our heads. I didn't have the quality time with Breanna that you did.'

Meeting Clayton's stern gaze, Juliet nodded in acknowledgement. She stood up and got herself another bag of herbal tea. She didn't bother switching the kettle on again and instead poured its lukewarm contents into her mug. She felt Clayton's eyes watching her every move and making love only an hour ago now seemed as if it was a year.

'You coming to bed?' asked Clayton. 'We'll all be in a better mood in the morning.'

'Not yet,' replied Juliet, poking her tea bag with a teaspoon. 'I'll be up in a minute.'

'I'm going up,' said Clayton. 'You should speak to Breanna in the morning and make sure she apologises.'

'She had a bit too much to drink.'

'That's no excuse.'

'I just want to forget about it.'

Clayton shook his head before he left. Juliet took another sip of tea and opened a packet of chocolate biscuits. She enjoyed the sensation of chocolate melting over her tongue and wondered why she had made a New Year resolution to stop eating chocolate. She finished her snack and thought of Brenton. Always Brenton.

Chapter 10

Seeing the Whales with Jonah

TWO THIRTY A.M. Unable to sleep, Brenton climbed out of bed and built a spliff. His eyes felt heavy and he had developed a sniff. He switched on his stereo and Frankie Paul's *Worries in the Dance* played on a low volume. Rolling his joint carefully, he reflected on the day's events. He sniffed again. They bought Breanna a car! he raged inside. I felt like a fucking pauper with my card and two hundred notes. Why didn't Juliet tell me she was buying a car? Why should she tell me? Why can't I deal with that? Clayton. He looked so happy with himself. Fuck him. I wanted to disappear. Vanish. Couldn't get out of their place quick enough. Not gonna go there for a while. Fuck it.

Finished with wrapping his spliff, he lit it and pulled on it hard. He winced as he suffered a bit of discomfort in his throat. He exhaled through his nose and made smoke rings with his mouth. He felt as if a miniature heavy metal guitarist was strumming away beneath his forehead. Hate heavy metal, his inner voice yelled. Shit. No paracetemol or aspirin. Fuck it. Wish I could escape this shit of a life. Wish I could escape my feelings for Juliet and Breanna. It's not easy to let go. Fuck! My head hurts. Maybe Floyd's right. Maybe I need to make a move. Can't take this shit. Can't take Clayton. Him playing daddy. Maybe I should just bust him up and accept the prison term. At least in there I know I can't have Juliet.

He toked again. The smoke corkscrewed towards the ceiling. Need to give it another coat of paint before too long, he promised himself. He drifted back in time. Late-night smoking sessions in the social services hostel where he had first met Floyd when he was only sixteen. He could hear the dominoes being slammed on the table during a raucous game. He could hear Dennis Brown thumping out of the boom box or what Floyd called the Brixton suitcase. *Three Meals A Day! No rent to pay, only the boss is getting pay, no wife to obey. Sitting in a two by four, looking through an iron doooor! Whoooaaa I could never get used to the smell! I'm talking 'bout detention, detention. Oh a whoaaa!*

He remembered searching his road for cigarette butts. Never could roll a decent spliff, he laughed at himself. Even now. Eating corn beef and soggy rice for Christmas dinner. Watching a grainy black and white James Bond on TV on Christmas Day. Getting fucked on Special Brew and Tennent's beer. Eyeing up girls in tight two-tone skirts and crimplene blouses. Buying a two-pound draw of weed from a dealer who walked through the aisles of the Ace late-night cinema. He felt the abrasions, bruises, blows, cuts and stabbings from the street fights he had in his youth. Was that really me? he asked himself. I could have died. Shit. Why was I so reckless? He fingered the scar on his neck. A stark image of his former nemesis Terry Flynn grew large in his mind. Brixton tube station. The ticket barriers. The escalator. The fight. Flynn's arm being ripped off by a train. The blood. Maybe I should've let the train kill me rather than kill you, he concluded. My life's been shit since that day. I survived *that* home. Just about stayed alive in Brixton. Juliet broke me completely. Don't think I'll ever recover from that. The future ain't bright or fucking orange for people like me. No woman, no children that I can call my own. The women I have relationships with end up hating me. People like me don't have happy endings. Fuck! I'll just get old and die a fucked-up miserable bastard with a reggae album full of issues. They might as well bury me in a Soferno B speaker box and fling it down one of them old mines they tried to keep open back in the day. Poor miners. Arthur fucking Scargill and his fucked-up baseball hat; them t'ings never look good on old white people. Fights with the police. Maggie 'Iron Heart' Thatcher. State burial? Yeah, they should give her a state burial, he decided. But make sure she's alive when they fucking do it!

His thoughts drifted further back in time. To when he was seven years old. Living in *that* home.

Pinewood Hills Children's Home Village, November 1970

He was sitting on the crisp, damp grass in his school uniform. Alone. It was early November. All shades of purple, brown and red leaves skirted the field. A hobby bird glided majestically over his head. He felt no wind. Someone was playing football in the distance and he could just about hear the shouts of *goal* whenever someone scored. He could smell the bark of the nearby trees and the forming dew. An orange sun was dipping beyond the big houses in the west. Beyond that the hills shadowed the horizon. Red night shepherds' delight, Brenton remembered. He couldn't recall who told him that phrase. It was probably Father Holman.

A gathering chill was in the air. He knew he should have been home. It was dinnertime. Roast beef, cabbage, carrots and roast potatoes. That was alright. He wouldn't get in trouble for leaving anything on his plate. Think about the starving children in Africa, she would say. The Biafrans and the Pygmies aren't as lucky as you, she would add. You could have been one of those poor mites. They would give their skinny little arms for a Sunday roast. Be grateful for what you get! Rhubarb for dessert, he remembered. Hate rhubarb almost as much as her, he thought. He knew that even if he went home now he would get a beating. He hated *that* belt. He would get a whipping if he was at home anyway for not eating the rhubarb. If child Jesus was sitting at his dinner table and He didn't like rhubarb would she beat Him too? Why can't they make apple crumble every day? Maybe that's why boys of his age and up to eleven were told to wear shorts. So they could feel the full pain of the belt. Got to escape, he decided. He'd better get a move on. Be like Steve McQueen in that film. One day I'm gonna learn to ride a motorbike and when I do I'm gonna run her over. Squash her like those round flat pieces of shit in the cow field. Squash her head until blood comes out of her nose.

He jogged out of the meadow and started down the road towards the back gate of the children's home. He saw some boys collecting wood from a glade for bonfire night. He quickened his pace and by the time he went through the back gate he was sprinting. He rested for a minute, his muddied hands on his knees. He felt his heart pumping. He kept checking behind. She's really gonna beat me now and then she'll probably lock me up in the outhouse for ten years, he reckoned. Out of breath but gotta keep on moving.

Now walking on an affluent street with semi-detached houses, he wondered how often the kids who lived in these homes got their beatings. Maybe every day like he did? Or because they got mums and dads maybe every other day? I wouldn't mind that, he thought. You get hits from the belt but tomorrow you can look forward to a no-beating day. Yeah, I wouldn't mind that at all. That'd be cool. Maybe 'cos they got mums and dads they only get beatings from the hand? That'd be easy peasy. I'd do whatever I wanted if that's all you get from mums and dads. I'd be nicking from the staff cake-tin every night.

He came to the end of the road. He checked behind. He half expected to see her with the belt in her hand. No one following. He let out a sigh. This was easier than I thought, he said to himself. I should have done this before. He looked over his shoulder again. Father Holman will be glad to see me, he anticipated. He likes kids. Kids belong in God's house. Yeah, that's what he said. Jesus loves children. He said that too. He told off those horrible apostles because they were stopping the children coming to Jesus. He even told off Saint Peter. Let them come to me He said. Saint Peter had to get out of the way. Saint Peter's an idiot anyway. Why did he ask to get crucified upside down? What an idiot! That must've hurt more than getting crucified the right way up. All his blood would've trickled over his face.

I'm gonna live in God's house, he decided. No way will she dare to take me away from God's house. Father Holman called it the Kingdom of Heaven. Hope they got a football pitch in the Kingdom of Heaven and lots of Angel Delight pudding and apple crumble. Maybe there you only get beatings once a week. I wonder who gives out the beatings? Can't be Jesus. No, He likes children. Maybe Moses. He's got a bit of a temper. He went a bit mad with all those people when he came down from that mountain. When I finish playing football I'll ask the angel Gabriel for a ride on his back. He can take me all over heaven. He can take me to see strong Samson. I'd like to see Mary. She can tell me who my mum is and introduce me to all my great-grandparents and all that. And I don't care what she says. They don't live in a jungle. Then I'll ask Jonah if he can take me fishing and for a look at the whales. I wonder if whales are up there in heaven. Yeah, why not? God must have some gigantic swimming pool for them. Dolphins too. And sea horses. But no sharks or octopussies. Or snakes. Maybe all the Mars bars are free in heaven. Yeah, it's gonna be brilliant.

Twenty minutes later he reached the Catholic Church of Our Lady of the Annunciation. It was now dark. He walked along the curved driveway and passed a fir tree on the green. He looked up to the tower at the left of the building. It had three slim windows and he wondered what it was like inside there. The doors of the church were closed. God's house, he thought. It was very quiet apart from the murmur of traffic on the main road. He looked at the church again and wondered how long it took God to build it with those red bricks. Maybe it took him a day and an extra day to colour in the stained windows. It looks pretty. Maybe he could ask Father Christmas for a colouring book of stained church windows. Then again Santa hadn't given me the football or the Subbuteo game I wanted last year. Doesn't Santa know I go to church? I'll tell Father Holman. He can tell Father Christmas that I deserve presents this year 'cos I've been to church every Sunday and Sunday school.

There was a noticeboard fixed onto the front of the building. Brenton walked up to it. The church autumn fair was advertised. There was going to be a tombola and a fancy dress competition. If I was allowed to enter I'd go as the Artful Dodger from that *Oliver Twist* film, he decided. Yeah, that should win it. He looked a bit dirty in that film, so with my brown skin I could be him. I could pretend my brown skin is dirt. That's what she says anyway. Yeah, I could win it. There was also a coconut shy, arts and crafts and a beat-the-goalie contest. I'd like to enter that, he thought. I'd win that. Wonder what the prize is gonna be? Maybe a chocolate bar? Or a sixpence? Or even a Brazil football kit with number ten on the back. Pele's shirt. Who knows? Maybe even a football. But she won't let me go. No way. But Father Holman will. It's God's autumn fair after all. Not hers.

Next door to the church was the church hall. There were no lights on in the building but Brenton approached it. He looked through a window. Maybe God don't like anyone inside the place apart from when they have Sunday school, he guessed. When I live in God's house I'm not going to Sunday school. I wouldn't have to. Father Holman can teach me during the week. Don't like the other boys at Sunday school. One day the devil will have them for dinner with his Brussels sprouts. He'll flatten them like pastry, put them in the oven, put brown sauce on their heads and gobble them up like their gingerbread men. Yeah, eat them slowly. Crumb by crumb.

Mustn't think that, he rebuked himself. Father Holman won't be happy but I can't help it. How am I supposed to show them my other cheek? Why can't Moses come down from heaven and hit them with that concrete thing that God wrote His rules on? Why can't Jonah's whale come down from heaven and swallow them? Or Samson can crush all their jaw bones so they can't call me names any more. Maybe Joshua can come down and beat them up with his rod. When I grow bigger I'm gonna beat them all up and pray to Jesus to tell Him sorry before I go to sleep. I'll tell Him it won't happen again.

Beyond the church hall was the priest's house. Brenton slowly walked towards it and half-expected to hear angels singing. A double red door was situated in the centre of the residence and Brenton looked at it for a long time. He felt his heartbeat up-tempo. The front garden was small and he felt disappointed that there wasn't a pond there with fish swimming in it. If there was a pond Father Holman could fish them out with a net and make more fish and bread, he imagined.

Hesitantly, he started up the pathway to the double doors. It was a big house for just Father Holman to live in, he thought. At least he'd have room for me. Maybe I'll have my own bedroom? Yeah.

He knocked the brass knocker seven times and retreated three paces. He held his hands together behind his back and his mouth was open. God's house! he thought again.

A light illuminated a window to his right. Brenton smiled. He tried to remember all his good manners. He wiped the grass stains off his left cheek.

The door opened to reveal a tall man with a white beard. He was wearing a long black cloak that reached down to his black shiny shoes. His white collar was too tight around his reddened neck. He had a wart on his left ear and a few tufts of wispy white hair. His sharp blue eyes moistened in the chill of the night. He looked down at Brenton and the lines in his forehead seemed to have doubled. 'And what are we doing here on a school night?' asked Father Holman. 'Isn't it your tea time?'

'I missed it on purpose,' stuttered Brenton.

'Your guardian Miss Hills will be wondering where you are. She'll be worried. And you don't want people who care for you to be worried, do you?'

Brenton thought about it. 'I wanna live here!'

'Er, you have a nice home, Brenton. And ...'

'This is God's house, isn't it? Kind of anyway. God's house is the church so you're really living in God's outhouse.'

'I suppose it is. You better come in. I need to sit you down and talk to you. Explain a few things.'

'Thanks, Father Holman. I'll be really good. I'll do all the chores. I'll collect the coal, scrub your steps, do all the hoovering, washing-up and brush all your shoes. I'll even go out in the summer and jump in the stinging nettle bushes to pick you the best berries.'

Pushing the door further open, Father Holman ushered Brenton inside. Before he entered, Brenton wiped his feet many times on a brown bristled mat. He even bent down and wiped his hands on it. The hallway was decorated in red embossed wallpaper, and images of the cross, the Virgin Mary, Jesus and the twelve disciples stared down at him. He heard a ticking clock from an unseen room and his feet sank into a deep beige-coloured carpet. Lamps were fixed to the walls. Brenton was disappointed they weren't candles and he still expected to hear angels singing. He had an urge to tread very carefully and slowly and he felt God's eyes watching him. He was led to a kitchen and he sat down on a wooden stool that was next to a wooden table. There were oranges, pears and apples in a glass bowl. The apples and pears looked so much better than the ones he picked from the children's home orchard, he reckoned. He licked his lips.

Observing his surroundings, Brenton noticed prayers and the words of Jesus covering the walls. God's kitchen, he thought. There was a carved figure of Christ dying on the cross above the door frame. He died for me, Brenton remembered Father Holman saying to him. Maybe He wouldn't have died for me if He knew about what she would do to me. But I'm glad He didn't die like stupid Saint Peter. Meanwhile Father Holman had taken out a scone from a cake tin and placed it on a plate. He cut it in half and smiled at Brenton. 'Would you like jam or butter on your scone?' he offered.

'Jam please.'

Father Holman opened a cupboard and took out a jam jar.

'Can I have two, please?' Brenton asked.

Smiling in reply, Father Holman sliced another scone in half and spread jam on it. 'Would you like a drink? I've run out of Coca-Cola but I have some lemonade and Tizer left.'

'Tizer please,' Brenton replied excitedly. This is brilliant, he thought. I only get fizzy drinks when it's Christmas. I'm gonna love living here. When it's my birthday I might get a chocolate cake with candles on it. Father Holman might take me shopping to get my own clothes. Wouldn't have to wear hand-me-downs all the time. Maybe he'll let me stay up after eight o'clock?

Placing his drink and scones in front of him, Brenton downed half the glass in one go and then almost ate one scone in one bite.

'Take your time,' said Father Holman.

'Oops! Sorry,' apologised Brenton. 'I forgot to say grace.'

'That is not …'

Before Father Holman could finish his sentence, Brenton had already closed his eyes and placed his palms together. His mouth was still full of scone and jam. 'Dear Jesus, may I be grateful for what I get tonight. I'll be a good boy for Father Holman. Amen.'

Crumbs fell onto the table.

Chuckling, Father Holman placed a kettle on the stove. 'Now, lad,' he said. 'You shouldn't really be here, should you? You have a good home. You have good people looking after you.'

Brenton continued eating. He finished his drink. It all tasted so good. 'I've come to live here, Father. In God's house. I'll be on my best behaviour every day. You said Jesus loves children. He told off the disciples 'cos they wouldn't let the children go to Him.'

'It's splendid that you're paying attention, Brenton. One day you'll be an excellent Bible student.'

'She don't like children,' Brenton resumed after a pause. 'She hates us. She don't like us bothering her. She always says we're bothering her. She hates me the worst. She said she can't stand the sight of me. Sometimes she tells me to go back to the jungle.'

'I'm sure that's not true, Brenton. Miss Hills has a lot on her plate. I imagine she's always busy.'

'She's not busy. We do her work.'

'She cooks and cleans, doesn't she?'

'She cooks,' Brenton admitted. 'But we do everything else. Getting the coal is making me cough.'

'Do you want some more Tizer?'

'Yes please, Father.'

Father Holman filled Brenton's glass. As he drank it he noticed Father Holman was no longer smiling. Brenton guessed he was thinking about something. He didn't know what. Maybe he is thinking that he has no pyjamas for me. Maybe he doesn't have a bed made up for me. He might be wondering what I eat for breakfast. Hope he's got Sugar Puffs and Weetabix. Don't want lumpy porridge or a boiled egg with stupid soldiers. That's for babies.

'Would you like another scone?' Father Holman asked.

'Yes please, Father.'

Hastily slicing the scone in half, Father Holman spread jam

on it and placed it on Brenton's plate. The kettle boiled and Brenton watched Father Holman make himself a cup of tea. He added one teaspoon of sugar and he didn't stir it as madly as she did, Brenton observed. His hand was calm and steady. Not like hers.

'I have to go to my study and do a bit of paperwork,' said Father Holman, sipping his tea.

He's got a strange look on his face, Brenton watched. Like he's happy to see me but something else has upset him. Maybe he has to scrub the church floor tonight before he goes to bed?

'Please stay in the kitchen and help yourself to more Tizer if you want it.' Father Holman added.

'Thank you, Father.'

'Stay where you are and I'll be back shortly.'

Finishing his scones and drink, Brenton waited patiently. He looked at the silver-coloured kettle. Never had tea, he suddenly realised. Wonder what it tastes like? Why do adults prefer it to lemonade or Tizer? Should I make myself a cup? It'll show how grown up I am. No, I'd better not. I'd better ask permission.

Ten minutes passed. Twenty minutes passed. He remained in his chair. He was now staring at the fruit. The pears looked delicious, he thought. He licked his lips. Where's Father Holman? He wondered. Better not take a pear, he warned himself. But they look so ripe. Better than the ones in the wonky orchard. Father Holman can't eat all those pears on his own. Maybe he gives some to the poor and the hungry Biafrans and Pygmies in the African jungle. If they all live in the jungle then how comes Tarzan never gets hungry or skinny? I'll ask Father Holman.

Another fifteen minutes passed. He poured himself another drink. He wanted to use the toilet but Father Holman told him to stay where he was. He gazed at a pear that was sitting on top of the pile of fruit. He had to have it, he decided. He looked at the kitchen door. The handle wasn't turning. He heard no footsteps. Suddenly, he reached out a hand and grabbed the pear. He turned it around in his hand to examine it and without further hesitation sank his teeth into it. The flesh was soft, juicy and delicious. He took another bite. He enjoyed the sensation of the pear going down his throat. He munched again. He heard something. Was that the front door? He panicked. Footsteps. Father Holman's footsteps. Should he go and look? No, he was told to stay where he was. He concentrated his ears. He felt a slight draught of wind. Footsteps again, he sensed. More than one pair of feet. Father Holman's talking to someone. They were coming towards the kitchen. Oh, Jesus! Where's the bin? He spun around on his stool. There it was in the corner of the kitchen. He ran over to it and dropped the half-eaten pear inside it. He returned to the stool. He wiped his face with the sleeve of his school pullover. The door opened.

Father Holman appeared first. Brenton's heart was racing. She came in behind him. Miss Hills. Brenton cowered in his seat. His stool scraped backwards. She was wearing her best light blue coat, Brenton noted. The one she wore to church. She had her stupid yellow woolly hat on and her red mittened gloves. Her brown hair was squashed into a round bun and Brenton dreamed of kicking it one day. She had her glasses on. She was staring at him but she had happy cheeks. She was wearing her tight black trousers and Brenton wondered how they kept the fat from her legs from spilling out.

'There you are!' Miss Hills hailed. 'I've been worried sick about you. I went down to the school, I asked your classmates. Thank goodness I've found you safe and sound.'

Deciding not to say anything, Brenton gazed at Father Holman. Please don't let her take me, he prayed inside. Please, please. I wanna stay here. In God's outhouse.

'His teacher said he was upset because he got a few arithmetic questions wrong,' Miss Hills turned to Father Holman. 'But she never expected him to take off. I'm always telling him that all we expect from school is his best.'

'Now you didn't tell me that,' Father Holman said turning to Brenton. 'Miss Hills is right. We only expect you to do your best. You're half-caste so we don't expect you to be the top of the class. Just try your best. Jesus would like that.'

Jesus wouldn't like to go home with her, Brenton thought.

'Thank you for keeping him, Father,' said Miss Hills. 'I hope you only gave him one scone. We don't want to spoil him and have him boasting to the other children.'

Father Holman made way for Miss Hills to leave the kitchen. Brenton remained on his stool. He stared at Father Holman, pleading with his eyes. 'Come along, Brenton,' snapped Miss Hills. 'I'm behind with my work. Don't you want your cocoa tonight?'

Brenton refused to answer. Cocoa? he wondered. She never gives me cocoa. She just makes it for her staff. He continued to stare at Father Holman. The priest looked away. Finally, Brenton moved off his stool. His head was down as he walked out of the kitchen and the house. A jeep was waiting for him on the street. He recognised Uncle Georgie. Hate him, he wanted to shout out. He lets her do what she likes. He's always helping her.

'Bye, Father,' Miss Hills said cheerily. 'We'll see you Sunday and I'm sure Brenton will be on his best behaviour.'

Brenton was about to climb into the back of the jeep. 'Aren't you saying goodbye to Father Holman, Brenton?' rebuked Miss Hills. 'Remember your manners.'

Brenton paused. He took a long hard look at Father Holman but said nothing. I ain't saying bye to you, he decided. You're not like Jesus. You're just like the apostles. You're stupid like Saint Peter. You're turning me away. Jesus won't be happy. Maybe you should crucify yourself upside down and I hope they bang those metal things into your hands and feet.

'I'm sure he's tired,' smiled Miss Hills.

'I'm sure he is,' replied Father Holman. For a short second he had a doubtful look on his face but it quickly passed. He raised his right arm and waved. Brenton ignored him. He climbed into the jeep and sat behind the driver. He could smell dried mud and old grass. Georgie did not look behind or acknowledge Brenton.

Brenton heard the back door of the jeep slam shut. He closed his eyes and jolted as Georgie pulled away. Miss Hills sat opposite Brenton. She stared at him for a while. Brenton watched her take her mittens off. She rubbed her hands together. 'You have embarrassed me,' she said. 'When we get home you're going straight to bed.'

Expecting a beating at any moment, Brenton pushed himself into the corner and looked at the floor of the jeep. He glanced up and found Miss Hills still glaring at him. She's really gonna beat me, he thought. She's mad. Never seen her that mad before. She might kill. I'm not gonna go in the house. I'm gonna stay in the jeep.

Ten minutes later the jeep pulled up outside Brenton's home. He remained in the corner as Miss Hills opened the back door. 'Get out,' she said.

Brenton didn't move.

'Did you hear what I said? I have work to do and so does Uncle Georgie. Now *get out!*'

Turning away from Miss Hills, Brenton bowed his head and closed his eyes. He covered his face with his arms. He could hear Miss Hills approaching him. She grabbed his arm and yanked him off his seat. '*Noooo,*' he screamed.

He wrenched his arm away and scrambled back to the corner in the jeep. He curled himself into a ball.

'George,' Miss Hills called. 'I need a hand.'

A few seconds later Brenton felt big hands over his body

pulling him out of the jeep. His head hit the floor and his knees hit the side of the vehicle. '*Noooo!*'

'Shut up!' Miss Hills yelled as she slapped him about the face. '*Noooo!*'

Brenton fought as much as his strength allowed but he felt his body being carried out into the road. He screamed as loudly as he could but Miss Hills put her hand over his mouth and stifled him.

'Take him to the outhouse,' Miss Hills ordered. 'I'm not having him like that in the house. Like an animal he is. Like a bloody animal.'

Wriggling as much as he could, Brenton didn't have the strength to escape the clutches of Miss Hills and Uncle Georgie. They took him around to the back of the house where a short pathway led to the outhouse. Georgie fumbled for a key in his trouser pockets.

'Hurry up!' Miss Hills demanded, looking around.

Georgie opened the door. Brenton fought again. He kicked wildly. He punched Georgie in the face and he let go of Brenton's arms. Brenton's head dropped onto the doorstep and he screamed again.

'Hold onto him,' Miss Hills demanded. 'Get him in.'

Brenton felt his body being shoved and pushed and he was launched into the outhouse. He got up off the floor and heard the key being turned in the lock. He looked through the chessboard-sized, wire-meshed window.

'When he's calmed down we'll bring him out,' Miss Hills said. 'But I'm not having him in the house screaming to high heaven. He'll wake the saints! By the patience of sweet Mary!'

Sitting cross-legged on the concrete floor, Brenton noticed his clothes were covered with dust and grime. He ran his right thumb over the floor and it collected a film of dirt. He could smell oil and rubber from a corner full of forgotten bike frames and trolleys. He stood up and pressed the light switch near the door but it didn't work. Maybe that's a good thing, he decided. Don't like the look of cobwebs.

He felt cold and damp. He rubbed his hands together and looked out of the window opposite the door. He spotted an old dartboard resting in the corner of the windowsill and he imagined Miss Hills' head in the middle of it. He gazed out of the window again and he could make out the stars. He tried to get closer but broken plant pots, biscuit tins full of nuts, bolts and screws and a discarded pram hampered him. He leant forward to see what he could of the night sky. Yeah, he thought. One day I'm gonna ride on the angel Gabriel's back. And Jonah will take me to see the whales.

A week later Brenton was standing in a field. He was wearing his school uniform and it was dark. He couldn't see any stars and all he could hear was the breeze disturbing the trees. He was clutching two plastic bags in his right hand. Gonna get him back, he said to himself. *Hate* Father Holman. Hope he gets crucified upside down and it really hurts. He's going to hell. And I don't care if *she* beats me again. And I'm not scared of the out-house anymore. I'm gonna do it.

He sprinted out of the field and approached the back gate. Before he left the children's home grounds he walked along a mud path that ran parallel to a tall fence and when he came to bushes he stopped. He looked around and listened. She'll know where I'm going but I don't care, he thought. He noticed a star appear in the sky and he smiled. He climbed onto the fence, peeped over the other side and jumped down. He then walked out of the bushes and checked the road and the fields. Satisfied that no one was near, he returned to the undergrowth. He then pulled down his trousers and pants and placed the plastic bags directly beneath him. He had been saving himself from doing a number two all day and now he could do it. When he had finished he wiped his backside with toilet paper that he had stolen from the school toilets. He then pulled up his pants and trousers and carefully picked up the plastic bags that now had his own excrement inside. He held the bag away from his body as he made his way through the gate at the back of the children's home.

He slowly walked up the path that led to the double red doors. He knelt down and then pushed the plastic bag through the letter box. He flinched and recoiled at the smell. As it landed with a soft thud on the tiled floor, Brenton smiled. He stood there for two minutes, wondering what Father Holman would do when he saw it. He then retreated, took out three stones from his pockets and hurled them at the bay windows to the right of the double doors. The first stone missed the window but the next two found their mark. The shattering of the glass sounded to Brenton as if the biggest building in the world was tumbling down. He turned and ran as hard as he could.

Two hours later he was back inside the outhouse. He felt his bruised face and rubbed his swollen left eye. The blood that had oozed from his right knee had solidified. He tried the door but it was locked. He tried hard not to cry. 'Where's my mum?' he whispered to himself. He felt a cold draught. He sat down with his back against the wall and pushed his knees against his chest. He thought of the archangel Gabriel and Jonah. 'Yeah,' he said to himself. 'One day. One day I'll see the whales with Jonah.'

Chapter 11
A Nursing Hand

WITH SWEAT RUNNING DOWN his left cheek, Brenton felt the soreness of his throat and the pounding inside his head. He had the weird sensation of his head feeling heavy while the rest of his body felt light. Something cold and wet was placed on his forehead and it sobered him up a little. Am I dreaming? Am I hallucinating? He was exhausted and wondered if he had slept. He hated that space between slumber and insomnia and he made a mental note to visit his doctor and persuade her to give him something to help him sleep. He slowly opened his eyes and in that nanosecond before they focused he saw an indistinct figure looming over him. He shut his eyes and reopened them. He saw Juliet. He smiled. She was dabbing his forehead with a damp flannel. Feels so good, he thought. It was even better that she was looking after him. Her sleeves were rolled up and he could smell the anti-bacterial hand wash from her hands. She was wearing white pearls around her neck, or at least he thought they were pearls. She had her efficient, concerned face on. Just like Mum, he thought. He suddenly came to the realisation that he had hardly ever seen Mum smile. Not even on those days when we did get on, he recalled. Not even on those evenings when she used to put a little rum in our tea and talk about the chancers and players she flirted with in her young days in Jamaica. Maybe her life was more fucked up than my own? What's it all about? What was God's purpose for her life? When she can't even fucking smile. Even I can smile ... sometimes ... when I'm with Juliet. No, not just Juliet. Floyd makes me laugh. He wouldn't approve of all this Juliet-coming-around-to-look-after-me shit. He'd tell me to get my sad backside to the doctor or down to the chemist. Still, it's nice to be looked after.

'How?' Brenton stuttered finally. 'How did you get in?'

'You have a bad memory,' Juliet smiled. She was picking up the dirty clothes from the bedroom floor. 'You gave me a key. Remember? You gave me a spare one for safekeeping when you first moved in. I tried to call you yesterday. No answer. So I thought I'd better come around. I saw the light on but you weren't answering the front door.'

'And you found me as sick as anything.'

'You had a fever.'

She's got her efficient, nursey face on again, Brenton noted.

'You'll be alright,' she said. 'A bit of rest. Now you're awake I have to take your temperature just in case you have a real fever instead of man fever.'

'What day is it?' Brenton wanted to know.

'Tuesday,' Juliet answered. 'It's just gone half past eight and I haven't been home yet from the Town Hall. I put some dirty clothes in the washing machine. You need a new drum for it. It's making a hell of a noise.'

Hope she didn't see the shit in the kitchen, Brenton fretted.

'And how can you leave your kitchen in such a state?' Juliet nagged. 'Dirty plates, bits of food in the sink, floor needs mopping. Didn't Mum teach you anything when she came around here or are you just friggin' lazy?'

Mum didn't teach me a lot, Brenton thought. She wouldn't nag at all. She would just start clearing up the place without me saying anything. She was good that way. Spoilt me big time. Then she'd make us cups of tea and nice it up with a drop of rum. I miss those teas. Miss her coming around. Never used to be sure if I was over the limit when I drove her home. *Fuck my days!* I wonder if Clayton gets nagged like this? Probably not.

Wanker. I bet if he has a pizza at two in the morning he probably gets his gloves on to Mr Sheen the fucking oven after he's eaten. Fuck him.

Brenton watched Juliet rummage around in her handbag. He didn't recognise the brand but he bet it was expensive. 'Where is it?' Juliet asked herself.

She took out her brush, her two mobile phones and a purse that was almost the same size as the handbag. Brenton noticed all the credit cards in her purse. I wonder how much money Clayton's on, he thought.

'Here it is,' she smiled.

She had a slim case in her hand. She took out a thermometer from it, checked her watch and placed it inside Brenton's mouth. Brenton recognised it. It was Mum's.

'It's sterile,' Juliet added.

Brenton studied her. Can't stop wanting her, he admitted to himself. She hasn't changed a damn t'ing since I first saw her. Hold on. Maybe a little. Her breasts are bigger. Why does she have to be my half-sister? Why is she here? She's looking after me, just like Mum did once when I was sick. It's weird. She's got the same style and the same expression. Can't stop wanting her. What the fuck is wrong with me?

She pulled the thermometer out of his mouth, and Brenton watched her as she read his temperature. He imagined her in various states of undress, in her trousers and blouse, in her underwear, naked. He lifted his head and lunged for Juliet kissing her on the mouth. For half a second she did not pull away. Brenton could taste some kind of lip seal and her breath was fresh. He guessed she had just chewed on some peppermint gum or something. He could smell her deodorant and the wax she greased her hair with. He closed his eyes and placed his right hand on Juliet's left shoulder. His nose rubbed against her cheek and he could detect some kind of foundation on its surface. It smelt good.

'Don't do that, Brenton,' Juliet rebuked. She pulled herself away before disappearing into the kitchen.

Why did I do that? Brenton questioned himself. I'm too fucking lusty. She's gonna step now and I could do with some company. *Shit!* What's a matter with me? Why can't I control myself? Then again. It's just a kiss. It's not like I used my tongue or anything. Brothers kiss their sisters, don't they? Yeah, they do. To show their appreciation. I was just showing my appreciation 'cos she's looking after me. But brothers don't kiss like you, you fucking weirdo.

Juliet returned. Brenton sat up in the bed and checked her expression. He expected a cussing. He avoided her gaze, but she seemed normal.

He watched her sit on the bed. She picked up the thermometer that was now on a pillow. 'I'm just going to rinse this.'

Brenton nodded as she disappeared into the kitchen. She returned two minutes later. She had her serious face on, Brenton noted.

'Oh, by the way,' Juliet said. 'There were messages on your phone.'

Oh no, Brenton fretted. Must be Lesley cussing off my behind again. 'Yeah?' he answered. 'Who?'

'Daniel,' Juliet answered. 'I rang him back. I told him you are sick. He wanted to know if you want him to get to a job in Barnes and start preparation.'

'Oh yeah. Jeez and crime. I forgot about that. I was supposed to start that job Monday.'

Why isn't she cussing me? Brenton thought. Why isn't she vex? Why is she carrying on as if nothing happened? I'd rather she cuss me out so I know what she's thinking.

'Don't worry,' smiled Juliet. 'I told Daniel to get himself up there. You just get better.'

'Thanks.'

'By the way, your temperature is ninety-nine, a tiny bit over normal. So we can tell the priest to remove himself from the door. I don't know. *Men.* They have a little cough and blow their noses and then they collapse into their beds for the rest of the month.'

'Think I was worse than that,' replied Brenton, injured. 'My temperature was probably higher yesterday when you weren't here.'

'Hmm.'

Sitting down on the bed, Juliet made sure she was out of range for any lunging kiss. 'I … I'm surprised,' she stuttered. 'That Lesley's not here or hasn't been around?'

Brenton began, but paused as he tried to find the words. 'We broke up,' he said eventually.

Standing again, Juliet folded her arms and turned her back on Brenton. She gazed aimlessly out the bedroom window. Brenton wondered what she was thinking. He admired her shape. She spoke again a few minutes later. 'What happened?'

'I … I didn't want her,' Brenton admitted.

'I really thought she was *the* one,' said Juliet, still peering out the window. 'She looked after you, she's intelligent, she looked good for her age, and you had plenty in common with her.'

'I didn't want her.'

Juliet didn't respond.

'I … I still want you,' Brenton confessed.

Juliet turned around. Her arms were still folded. Brenton couldn't detect any emotion in her expression. She fixed her gaze on him. He was unnerved. Maybe she'll cuss me now, he guessed.

'You can't think of me like that,' she said. 'You mustn't. It has to stop, Brenton.'

Every word she uttered felt like a breezeblock weighing down on his chest.

'How do you think it makes me feel that every time you break up with a woman you call my name? I still think you should get counselling.'

'I don't need counselling.'

'You do, Brenton. Not just about me but all you went through in that home. A counsellor will help you …'

'I *don't* need fucking counselling! I ain't mental. Is that what you're trying to say? You trying to say that 'cos I want you I'm a nutcase?'

'No, I'm not saying that.'

'Yes, you are.'

'You think I'm gonna spill my guts about me and you to some fucking stranger? Fuck that!'

'It will help, Brenton.' Juliet sat on the bed and placed her hands on Brenton's shoulders. 'Look at you! You're still hurting.'

'I'm not fucking hurting,' argued Brenton, shrugging off Juliet's hands. 'I just, I just want …'

'What you can't have,' Juliet cut in. 'You're quite a catch. You've got your own business, you've kept your looks, you've dated plenty women. Don't you think there's a problem that you haven't got close to any of them?'

'They weren't right for me. None of them could give me the same … the same vibe like I had with …'

'So all of them weren't right for you? Did you give them any chance to become right for you?'

'Oh for fuck's sake, Juliet! Stop analysing everyt'ing. Are you a fucking agony aunt now?'

'I'm trying to help you see where you're going wrong. None of them have the same vibe like you had with me? Do you hear yourself? Brenton, what we had is history. Finished. You need … counselling so that you can stop comparing all women to me. You *have* to stop that. Also you need to deal with your child-hood issues. Over the years I've done the best I can but you were traumatised as a child, treated appallingly …'

'I don't fucking need to deal with my childhood issues, right. I ain't mental. I've done alright. Got myself a trade and a little business. Bought this place but you just love to put me down. *I need to get counselling to help with my childhood issues!* I'm a fucking man for God's sake. Not some fucking pussy who can't deal with life. I'm alright. Nothing the fuck is wrong with me. My life is good. The only thing missing is you.'

'I'm married, Brenton,' said Juliet, now becoming visibly upset. 'There can never be a me and you. Not in that sense. I'm with Clayton.'

'FUCK CLAYTON! Don't mention his raas name!'

'He's my husband! DEAL WITH IT!'

'NOOO! He ain't my fucking husband and he ain't my brother.'

'If you want me in your life you *have* to accept him.'

'I ain't accepting *shit*.'

'Oh, that's very grown up of you! You going to have your sulk now, Brenton? 'Cos you can't get what you want.'

'Don't fucking talk down to me!'

'I should have made you come with me to discuss the GSA issue with the counsellor a few years back,' Juliet said. 'You should've come.'

'GSA! CSA! Fuck SA! I don't even remember what it means!'

'You *know* what it means, Brenton. Genetic Sexual Attraction. It would have helped you to under–'

'No it wouldn't! It's all bollocks! All fuckery!'

'I'm really getting sick and tired of you shouting and swearing at me. You're not a teenager. You're a grown man, for God's sake!'

Brenton was about to say something but the words wouldn't come out. He breathed heavily for a few minutes.

'I *know* you still have feelings for me,' Brenton finally countered. 'More feelings for me than you have for that lame pussy Clayton.'

'He's my *husband* and you have no right to talk about him in that way,' stressed Juliet. 'It was *my* choice and how we conduct our marriage has nothing to do with you.'

'But you still have feelings for me. Look me in the eye and swear that you don't.'

Brenton noticed that Juliet's bottom lip was trembling. He remembered it always did that when she was really vexed. Her eyes were boring into him and he wondered if he had gone too far. You and your fucking temper, Brenton Brown, he rebuked himself. Why you have to keep swearing so much? You fucking idiot. You can take the man out of the ghetto but you can't take the ghetto out ...

'Of course I have feelings for you,' said Juliet after a pause, interrupting Brenton's thoughts. 'You're my brother.'

She stood up, fixed Brenton with an angry glare and then went to the kitchen. Brenton heard a cupboard door opening and a tap being run. He shook his head. Juliet returned with a glass of water. She glared at Brenton once more, drank half of the glass and put it down on a bedside cabinet. 'Look after yourself, Brenton,' she said calmly. 'It's important you keep the kitchen clean when you're sick. I'll call you tomorrow to see how you are.'

Brenton sat up in bed watching Juliet leave the room. As she went through the door she didn't look back. He lay back down. '*Shit!*'

As soon as she closed Brenton's front door, Juliet paused and took a deep breath. She closed her eyes, trying to compose herself. She then checked her make-up and hair with a small mirror from her handbag and walked down the two flights of stairs out of Brenton's block. She climbed into her car and turned the ignition key. She paused again. She checked herself in the rear-view mirror. She closed her eyes. '*Brenton*,' she uttered. She threw her handbag onto the passenger seat, and kicked the car above the pedals. 'Arrrggghhhhh!'

After ten minutes of aching pain in her right big toe, Juliet just about composed herself. She gripped the steering wheel tight, indicated and pulled away.

Chapter 12
First Time

MYA'S *AFTER THE RAIN* trilled from Breanna's new car stereo. Sitting in the passenger seat, Malakai was nodding. Checking herself in the rear-view mirror, Breanna pulled up and parked outside her house. With her hands still tense on the steering wheel she looked at her boyfriend. 'I hate this deceit, Malakai, lying to my boss and my mum.'

'How else are we gonna get *our* time?' asked Malakai. 'And you told me since you started at your place you've never taken a sickie. Everyone gets sick sometime.'

'Yeah but they don't lie about it.'

'Bree, if you're having second thoughts about this then you can drop me back to my yard and you can still go to work half-day … I can wait.'

Breanna thought about it. She stared through the windscreen with her hands still holding onto the steering wheel. It was an overcast day with the promise of rain in the skies. A white-haired woman wearing sunglasses was crossing the road with a white Labrador. Breanna glanced at Malakai whom she thought seemed too relaxed. She then pressed a button on the car stereo and the music stopped. She looked at him once more before opening the car door. 'Come on.'

She climbed out of the car and made her way to her front door. Spots of rain dampened her hair. Malakai watched her before he got out of the car. Breanna was turning the key into the lock when he reached her. 'You sure your mum and paps are at work?'

'Yeah, I watched them leave this morning. Stop fretting, man. My paps ain't laying in wait with an axe.'

Malakai scanned the hallway before crossing the threshold. Breanna led him to the kitchen. She opened a drinks cabinet and took out a bottle of Baileys. 'What do you want?' she asked.

'Er, don't mind. Whisky, rum or vodka and Coke. Thanks.'

Grabbing a bottle of Appleton Special rum, she poured it into a whisky glass and filled it with four cubes of ice before topping it up with Coca-Cola. 'This is pap's,' grinned Breanna. 'He never notices. But if I trouble even a capful of my mum's wine she'll kill me.'

'I didn't want the ice,' laughed Malakai.

'Well take it out and fling it in the sink if you don't want it,' snapped Breanna.

'Just joking! Why you getting so touchy?'

'I'm not getting touchy. Sorry I didn't ask you if you wanted ice. It's not a biggie for fuck's sake.'

'Alright, Bree. Seems like you need a next ice cube in your drink!'

Breanna kissed her teeth before leading Malakai into the lounge. They both sat on the black leather sofa. Breanna watched Malakai admiring the framed family photographs hanging from the walls. Suspended from a wall above the sofa was a framed picture of Martin Luther King. There was a mini-stereo on a shelf. Within a glass wall cabinet were crystal champagne glasses, two crystal decanters and flower-patterned china plates. Resting on a solid redwood coffee table were framed photographs of Breanna at various ages. Malakai settled his gaze on a photo of Breanna, aged eleven, in her school uniform complete with hat. She was sticking her tongue out at whoever took the picture.

'Hated school,' she said.

'You wore a *hat*?'

'Let's not go into it.'

'What school was that then?' Malakai pressed.

'One that had a strict uniform policy. Didn't really mind but they wouldn't even let us wear earrings … what school did you go to?'

'Charles Edward Brooke. In between Camberwell and Bricky. Started there with Sean. He was always getting into … teachers there were well happy if you just got entered for any GCSEs.'

'How's it going with the plumbing training?'

'Alright, you know,' Malakai sipped his rum. He gently shook the glass before he took another sip. 'Can be a nasty job though. We were learning yesterday how to unblock toilets. I think I could unblock my own shit, maybe even my mum's shit but other people's? Not sure if I can do that, Bree, blatantly. My older brother has done some fucked-up nasty shits in his day when he was living at home and I wouldn't unblock any of them monsters, blatantly!'

'You'll have to do it when you're a pro,' giggled Breanna. 'Stick with it, man. A plumber my paps knows charges fifty sheets just to look at a job before he does anything.'

'I know. Trust me, I ain't gonna mess this up.'

'So you met Sean at school. You was gonna say he's always inna trouble?'

Malakai took his time in answering and took a generous sip of his rum before he did so. 'Yeah … you could say that. He had a lot of … shit at home to deal with, blatantly. It's just him and his mum. I don't know who his paps is.'

'What kinda shit?' Breanna wanted to know, ignoring her drink.

'You know … the same old road t'ing, walking with brothers man ain't s'posed to walk with. That kinda t'ing. Doing t'ings you ain't s'posed to do. Terrorising peeps and shit.'

'Like who or what?' Breanna pressed.

Malakai gave Breanna a cautious glance before he continued. 'This is between me and you, right.'

'Course.'

Placing his glass down by his feet, Malakai turned to face Breanna. 'While we were in Year Nine Sean had some issues with his mum. He left his yard. For a while he slept on my couch but my mum didn't like him burning spliff late at night and stinking up her front room. To say sorry Sean even bought some incense sticks for her but she weren't listening. She fling him out.'

'If that was my dad he would've probably dragged him to the police station,' Breanna chuckled.

Malakai didn't laugh. He continued. 'He left my yard and started to walk with the P.I.K.'

'P.I.K? What does that stand for? Who are they?'

'Poverty Inspired Kids. A crew that started from Angel Town estate.'

'Wait a sec,' thought Breanna. 'I've heard Mum talk about them once. Weren't they involved with that …'

'Yep. The murder of that thirteen-year-old boy in Flaxman Sports Centre.'

Breanna leant back into the sofa. She stared straight ahead. 'Shit!'

Malakai took another gulp. 'Sean got messed up in all that.'

'You're joking.'

'I ain't joking, Bree. He didn't do the shanking though. He thought they were just gonna rough him up, slap him up and shit. It was all over some girl this boy was s'posed to have dissed. Sean didn't expect the yout' to get shanked, blatantly.'

Breanna nodded, her expression serious.

'It was all over the news and shit,' continued Malakai.

'I know,' said Breanna. 'I remember now, Mum sent the boy's mum her condolences. She asked if she could do anything to help. Mum's like that. She's always getting involved with other people's business but she ignores what's going on in her own home.'

'Sean was going on all weird and messed up.'

'What happened?' Breanna pressed.

'We saw some news conference with the boy's older sister. She was all crying and shit, begging anyone with information to step forward. We were watching it at my yard and Sean left my room to take a piss. He took some long time so I got up to find out what happened to him.'

'And?'

'... he was sitting on my stairs, just staring into space. Something was messed up. I asked him if he knew who shanked the boy. For the longest time he didn't answer and then he nodded.'

'What did you do? Go to the police?'

'We had this argument,' Malakai admitted. 'I was saying to him that he's gotta say somet'ing. Even if it was an anonymous phone call. Sean was saying he wasn't no snitch and if he did say somet'ing he would get shanked. We were firing off on each other, we almost bruk out in a fight. I left his yard cursing him. I ran back up to him and started to chant Buju's *Murderer* in his face. You know the tune, right? *Murderer, blood upon ya shoulder, kill I today you cannot kill I ...*'

'Yeah, yeah, I know the tune,' nodded Breanna. 'Uncle Brenton is a big Buju fan ...what happened after that?'

'Can't this wait for another time?' protested Malakai. 'I kinda come here for another reason. You know. And you *asked* me to reach.'

'Just finish off, man. What happened after you chanted *Murderer* in his face?'

Malakai shook his head. 'Sean *t'umped* me! Blatantly! Then ran back inside his yard. He wouldn't come out so I had to walk home. But I was switching. *Mad.* I felt like going to the police station myself. When I got home I was gonna tell my mum.'

'What stopped you?'

'To be honest, Bree, I was kinda afraid. Blatantly! I have to admit that. I was thinking that the P.I.K. crew would come looking for me. I was thinking about what might happen to my mum, my sis and my older brother. While all this was going on I could hardly look into my mum's face … she thought I was sick.'

Leaning in closer to Malakai, she kissed him on the cheek and gave him a hug. He responded by kissing her on her neck. His left hand slipped under her beige crewneck sweater. Kicking off his trainers, he placed his right leg over her left thigh.

'Hold on, man!' Breanna protested, pulling herself away. 'Hold on … what went down after your mum thought you were sick?'

Malakai continued to kiss Breanna on her forehead down to her cheeks and finally on her mouth. His left hand was trying to unclip her bra.

'Malakai!'

'Alright! Man! You invite me around here and now you're changing your mind.'

'I'm not changing my mind … tell me what happened with the Sean, P.I.K. crew situation. Did Sean confess to his mum?'

'No … But after he t'ump me I was trying to call him. I was leaving messages on his voicemail saying I was gonna bruk him up when I see him. He didn't answer for a week. Then he came around my yard. He was all quiet and shit, not his usual self.'

'And?'

'He told me what happened. It was over stupidness. The boy was only running up his mout' and boasting at school that he was going out with this girl. He was even saying that he fucked her and shit. The girl get upset now, she tells her man who happens to be Nasher, one of the P.I.K. crew. So the boy was set up. He was only s'posed to be beaten up, you know, as a warning t'ing. But Nasher took out his blade and shank the boy. It turned out that sometime before the shanking the P.I.K. crew was jacking somebody and Nasher froze. The rest of the crew was all taking the piss outta him. They were calling him a pussy and chicken and t'ing. Peer pressure, blatantly!'

'*Shit!*'

'After Sean told me what happened he made an anonymous call to the police. Nasher, Sean and everyone else messed up in the whole shit was arrested in a dawn raid the next day. 'Cos Sean helped the police he got time taken off his sentence. He went to some secret prison for three years. Most of the others got life. Some went to Feltham, some started their sentences in Ashfield, some country place near Bristol.'

Breanna drew in a long breath.

'You can't spill this, Bree, blatantly.'

'I won't Malakai. What do you take me for?'

'Anyway, Sean and his mum were offered a new life, new names, everyt'ing. They offered to set them up somewhere far.'

'And they turned it down?'

'Yep,' answered Malakai, taking another sip of rum. 'Sean wanted to go. He was fucked off with Bricky and south London. He wanted to go to America but they weren't gonna pay for that shit. They offered places only in the UK. But his mum didn't wanna go anywhere. She said she ain't going nowhere where white people look at you weird, where only one bus comes once an hour and where the people chat some strange fucked-up accent.'

'But the guys who did it are all still inside, right?'

'Yeah, but they know Sean snitched.'

'Shit!'

'Exactly.'

Breanna finally took a sip of her Baileys. When she gulped it down, Malakai took the glass from her, placed it on the floor and started to kiss her on the forehead, her cheeks and then her neck.

'Malakai!'

'Yes, Bree.'

'Not here … stop it! You got a condom, right?'

'Course. Man is prepared.'

Malakai's right hand slipped beneath the front of Breanna's jeans. Breanna closed her eyes, enjoying the sensation of it all.

'*Not here!*' she protested as Malakai fumbled with the zip of her jeans. 'Get off, you maniac!'

Breanna shoved Malakai off her and ran laughing out of the room and up the stairs. Malakai regained his footing and set off in pursuit, knocking over Breanna's glass of Baileys on his way. He reached Breanna's bedroom door but it was locked.

'Stop fucking about, Bree, let me in.'

'Not until you control that boner I just felt,' chuckled Breanna.

'What do you expect? At least your man's in working order, innit.'

'You kissed my forehead and I felt it.'

'Take it as a compliment, Bree.'

'I'm *not* letting you in.'

'For fuck's sake, Bree! This was *your* idea. You know what, stay in your room! I'm going downstairs and I'm gonna trouble your mum's wine before I step home, blatantly!'

The door opened. Breanna yanked Malakai's right arm and pulled him inside. Before he knew what was going on Breanna kissed him. She then pulled away and locked the door. Malakai looked at the leopard-print blanket covering the double bed. There was a menagerie of cuddly tiger cubs, leopard cubs and cheetah cubs resting on the bed. Malakai couldn't count the number of beauty products on the dressing table. Stuck with Blu-Tack to the walls were posters of Omar Epps, Tupac Shakur and Tyrese. He pulled Breanna to him and kissed her. They fell onto the bed.

'Careful,' Breanna said softly. 'I want this to mean something … you got a condom, right?'

'Course, Bree … man prepared.'

'Is this your first time?'

'Er, not really.'

'So who was she? For your first time?'

'Bree!'

'Sorry.'

They resumed kissing and Malakai began to take off Breanna's clothes. She sprung up in just her bra and knickers and pulled the curtains closed. She then dived under her bed covers, her fingers gripping the duvet. Malakai joined her and caressed her forehead and cheeks. 'Don't worry,' he said. 'We're gonna be doing this for untold years.'

Chapter 13
The Half That's Never Been Told

OPENING A COLD BOTTLE of mineral water, Brenton drank half of it in one gulp. He looked towards the changing rooms of the leisure centre once again but still no sign of Floyd. A boy sitting in the corner was examining the contents of his nose on his right index finger as his tracksuit-wearing mother was ordering tea and chocolate muffins. Her hair was still wet from showering. Brenton thought her tracksuit bottoms were too tight for her generous backside. An old man still dressed in his blue shorts and grey vest was resting on another table with his sweat-soiled towel draped over his shoulders. He was very still and his eyes were staring longingly at the drinks display. Brenton wondered if he would make it to the counter to order a drink. The smell of chlorine from the swimming pool was hard to ignore and the hum of the air conditioning was irritating him.

Should they be selling crisps and cakes in a sports centre? Brenton thought. I s'pose they gotta make their money … where the fuck is Floyd? He took another gulp from his drink.

Floyd arrived with a victorious smile as Brenton was midway through his second bottle of water.

'You're like a woman, man,' Brenton griped. 'Taking so damn long to get a shower and put your clothes on.'

Dropping his sports bag and his squash racket by Brenton's table, Floyd went to buy two blackcurrant-flavoured energy drinks. A minute later he sat down opposite Brenton, took a generous swig from one of his bottles and smiled again. Brenton kissed his teeth.

'You're a bad loser, man,' Floyd said.

'I've been sick, you know.'

'Sick, my back foot,' Floyd countered. 'You went work Thursday and Friday, didn't you? And you agreed to play. When I lose I don't give no excuses.'

'That's 'cos you don't have excuses … *I'm* a better player.'

'You weren't the better player today. Jah know dat!'

Inhaling slowly to control his irritation, Brenton said, 'I agreed to play with you 'cos I wanted to sweat out what's left of my flu. My energy levels were seriously low today. Believe dat!'

'Fuckery, Brenton. You lost fair, square and rectangle and t'ing.'

'Next week it'll be back to normal. Believe it!'

'Whatever, man. Whatever … Are you gonna go off and sulk and erupt over your teddy bear or you coming around my yard for your dinner?'

'I dunno,' replied Brenton, still wounded by his defeat. 'What's Sharon cooking?'

'Somet'ing better than whatever sad microwave dinner you got in your fridge.'

'Can't you answer a straight question instead of taking the piss?'

'Man! The stepping volcano's inna temper,' laughed Floyd. 'You wanna take your ash cloud away from my direction! I should beat your raas more often and stop letting you win to make you feel sweet. Jah know dat!'

'I'll ask again,' said Brenton, finishing his mineral water. 'What's Sharon cooking?'

'Mutton, rice and peas.'

Brenton was unable to suppress his smile.

'I know you can't resist dat!' chuckled Floyd. 'So stop your damn sulking, deal wid your loss like a man and admit I'm the better player.'

'Fuck you!'

'Brenton, man!' Floyd rebuked. 'Mind your ghetto language. There're kids around.'

They both looked at the boy who had been picking his nose. He was now enjoying a Kit Kat bar and melted chocolate covered his fingers.

Half an hour later, Brenton was following Floyd's black Peugeot 206 to his home in Streatham. He could hear Floyd's boosted-up car stereo boom out Black Uhuru's *Plastic Smile*. As he drove up Wellfield Road he reminisced about the days in his youth when they would walk home late at night from the Bali Hai club on Streatham High Road back to their hostel in Camberwell. Man! Brenton recalled. We didn't give a fuck how long we had to trod home. Kids today? They have to get in a damn car to get to the end of the friggin' road!

Brenton parked behind Floyd. 'My tools are at work so I can't do anyt'ing for Sharon today,' he said as he climbed out of his car.

'Stop worrying, man,' Floyd assured. 'Sharon's not gonna ask you to do nutten.'

'Ain't she?'

Floyd opened his front door and Brenton entered behind him. The wooden-tiled hallway had framed cartoonish images of African women pouring water from flower-patterned vases hanging from the walls. Always makes me wanna piss, thought Brenton. The aroma of rice and peas and mutton smacked him in the face and he licked his lips. Man! he said to himself. Good job I did come here 'cos I ain't got a damn t'ing in my fridge. I should've bought them a bottle or somet'ing. Sharon likes her brandy.

The double-roomed lounge was on the left but Floyd led Brenton to the end of the hallway that led to the kitchen. There was a Daffy Duck clock above the fridge and on the pine kitchen table sat a small television set that was silently broadcasting a political interview. Also on the table were Lambeth council papers and files. Brenton thought of all the social workers he had met. *Wankers!* he yelled in his mind. Apart from Sharon of course … and Mr Lewis.

Sharon was wearing a Bob Marley headscarf and a Tweety Pie apron. A few rogue strands of grey hair grew defiantly on her fringe. She stirred the mutton pan and then checked the rice and peas pot before turning around to greet Brenton.

'Alright, Bren,' she greeted. 'Did you win again? Nice of you to reach. If you've got time I want you to look at our bathroom later on.' She turned to Floyd. 'What was the score today?'

'*I* won!' proclaimed Floyd. 'Oh ye of lickle faith and t'ing!'

'Seriously?' Sharon asked, disbelief on her face. 'You won?'

'You see how she stay though,' said Floyd, gesturing with his hands. 'My *own* wife has no belief in me.'

'You shit though,' laughed Brenton. 'And when Sharon came to watch us that day I murdered your backside.'

'Brenton, man!' protested Floyd. 'Don't use dem phrase, man. You murdered my backside? Makes me feel uncomfortable! Rejig your lingo, dread.'

Everybody laughed and sat down at the kitchen table. 'Can I get you a drink, Brenton?' asked Sharon.

'Yes, please. Cold water. Nuff ice.'

'You're not gonna ask me?' complained Floyd.

'No. You know where the fridge is.'

Rising from his seat, Floyd moaned, 'You see what I have to live with?'

'So where's Gregory and Linvall?' Brenton asked.

'Linvall's playing football in the park and Gregory's in his room,' Sharon answered.

'He never comes out of it,' said Floyd. 'Playing games, down-loading music or films or on that damn phone of his. When the internet police come and fine him for downloading every film in Hollywood history he's on his own. Believe dat! He needs to step out of his room and do different t'ings.'

'Leave Gregory alone,' snapped Sharon. 'Does he trouble anybody? No! Is he polite? Yes! So what if he's a bit shy? Trust me, Bren, he's a nice yout'. Not like dem sour mout' boys I see on street. They ain't got no respect for anybody.'

'I didn't say he wasn't nice,' cut in Floyd.

'I'll get your water, Bren,' said Sharon.

While Sharon was pouring Brenton water, Floyd was serving himself a cocktail of Southern Comfort, Coca-Cola, lime juice, lemon juice and four cubes of ice. He mixed it furiously with a teaspoon, gave it a shake and took a sip before adding another drop of Southern Comfort. He then licked his lips and grinned with satisfaction. Brenton watched him and shook his head.

'I want to re-tile the bathroom, Bren,' said Sharon. 'And put a new bath panel on and put in some shelves. I want your advice … maybe you'll give us a hand when you got time?'

Brenton rolled his eyes. 'I'll have a look.'

Sharon served Brenton his water. She sat down at the table and looked at Floyd. 'Your mum called again,' she said. 'I'm sick and tired of being in the middle so why don't you just go and check on her and see what she wants?'

'Didn't she mention anyt'ing?'

'*No*, she didn't mention anyt'ing!' Sharon turned to Brenton. 'This has been going on for untold weeks. Floyd's mum calls, he don't want to chat to her, I end up taking a message and Floyd won't see her.'

'Might be important?' offered Brenton. 'She might be sick. Look what happened to my mum.'

'She ain't sick,' said Floyd. 'You watch her, she'll live longer than Moses.'

'I'm not gonna be in the middle between you two,' insisted

Sharon. 'I'm tired of it, running to her and running to you. *Go* and see her. Today!'

Floyd thought about it. 'Wanna come, Brenton? You haven't seen her for the longest time.'

Brenton, who was wondering what age Moses reached before he finally passed away, was about to answer but Sharon cut in. 'No, leave Brenton out of it. He don't need to hold your hand. Go and see her on your own. It's obviously something serious she wants to chat about.'

'I'll think about it,' said Floyd.

'No you won't think about it,' ordered Sharon. 'Just see what she wants. How many times have you seen her since your dad died last year?'

Floyd glanced at Brenton then looked at the floor. Brenton sipped his water.

Sharon stood up and leaned closer to Floyd. She dropped her tone to almost a whisper. 'See her today, Floyd.'

'She's probably gonna nag about something,' said Floyd. '*Look how long you've been working in school as a mentor! How come you're not a teacher yet! Go back to college! You don't have any ambition.* And blah friggin' blah. All she does is run me down and tell me how my sisters are doing this and that.'

'Might be somet'ing different,' offered Brenton. 'Your old man might've left a will and left you with a hundred grand or somet'ing.'

'Brenton, when I asked you to come around I didn't expect you to take the friggin' piss! My old man leave me money? Are you sick, Brenton? Are you one long bitching cucumber short of a *raas* salad? The man always hated me. Seriously! He would rather give money to the BNP than give me anyt'ing! Fuck the old man's will!'

'Floyd, you damn fool, if it was about the will that would've been settled shortly after his death,' said Sharon.

'Then I wonder what's it all about?' said Brenton. 'Maybe she's going back to Jamaica?'

'Nah, ain't that,' replied Floyd. 'Last time she went there one of my aunties stole some of the clothes out of her suitcase, her brother was vex 'cos she never bring any duty-free cigarettes, she ended up paying for some uncle called Wilbur's funeral and my cousin, Milton, was caught trying to t'ief her passport. Trust me, she ain't returning there, seriously.'

Brenton and Sharon couldn't contain their laughter.

'Ain't funny, man,' Floyd said. 'Mum's blood pressure was going up like thunderbird three to rarted when she got back. Ever since she's been on some serious pills, dread.'

Brenton chased down his dinner with beer. Floyd then entertained him with a selection of modern reggae but Brenton preferred the old-school style. When Sharon saw that he was losing interest she yanked him upstairs where he advised her on how best she could fix up her bathroom and what he was willing to offer in help.

'Don't I have a say?' protested Floyd.

'I'm *not* painting my bathroom black and putting up black tiles,' insisted Sharon. 'I'm not decorating my bathroom so Count Dracula and his wife will be comfortable in it. It ain't happening and Jah knows dat!'

'What's the point of you asking me suggestions about how we gonna do the bathroom and then you just ignore what I say?' argued Floyd.

''Cos what you say don't match,' replied Sharon. 'I know you love black but a black bathroom? If my superiors at work found out they'd think I'm part of some weird freaky cult that kills kids.'

As Brenton tried to stifle his laughter, they all went down the stairs together. 'I'm leaving now, yeah,' said Brenton. 'Thanks for dinner and t'ing.'

'See him out, Floyd and *go* to see your mother,' said Sharon.

'OK, I will,' said Floyd. 'But I ain't staying long.'

Floyd and Brenton walked out of the house together. Floyd climbed into his car, turned the ignition key and the Revolutionaries' *Death in the Arena* blasted from his cranked-up car stereo.

'You'll be alright?' Brenton asked, standing beside Floyd's car.

Turning down the volume, Floyd replied, 'Can you come with me? But if you do, don't tell Sharon.'

'I've got an early start, man,' said Brenton. 'Wanna get some sleep. I've got nuff work to do in the morning. Gotta lay a floor, put some damp-course down, put up some struts for a wall …'

'Brenton, stop going on old.'

'I'm not going on old!'

'Yes you are! You're going on ancient.'

'Fuck you!'

'Then prove that you're not going on like a grey-back pensioner. Stop fretting about your bedtime and step with me to my mum's.'

Brenton kissed his teeth. 'I ain't staying long.'

'Nor am I,' Floyd assured him.

Following Floyd to Tulse Hill estate, Brenton felt no need to switch on his own car stereo. He bopped his head to Yellowman's *Herbman Smuggling* which was booming out of Floyd's Peugeot. Floyd pulled up outside a five-storey block of flats in the middle of the estate. Despite the darkness, they could hear yelps and shrieks from the nearby children's adventure playground. They could make out the silhouettes of a white couple kissing in a doorway. The Stranglers' *Golden Brown* played out from an upstairs flat and from another block they could hear the crying of a baby.

'Pickney should be in their damn bed,' Floyd remarked.

'Haven't been around here for ages,' said Brenton. 'Hasn't changed much up here, has it?'

'Nope,' replied Floyd. 'Apart from those brand spanking new blocks where Dick Shepherd School used to be. You didn't see the gates at the front of it? Burglars will have nuff trouble making a getaway wid their t'ings from there. It's fucked up. You seen the prices for those flats?'

'No?'

'Nearly a hundred grand for a one bedroom, believe dat!' Brenton shook his head.

'Anyway,' said Floyd. 'I hope Mum's awake.'

'Didn't you call her before we left?' asked Brenton.

'No.'

They walked up six flights of concrete steps and then along a balcony. 'What do you think she wants?' asked Floyd.

'I dunno. You're gonna find out now, innit.'

Floyd paused and looked at Brenton before knocking the letter box of his mother's flat. After five seconds he knocked again.

'Patience, man!' Brenton rebuked. 'She is getting on, you know.'

The door opened two inches and Floyd could see his mother's right eye staring at him. 'Oh, it's you, Floyd,' she said. 'I wasn't expecting you this evening.'

She opened the door fully and made way for Floyd and Brenton to enter the flat. 'Evening, Mrs Francis,' greeted Brenton.

Mrs Francis led her son and Brenton into her living room and invited them to sit down on the sofa. 'I was getting ready for bed,' said Mrs Francis. 'It's nearly ten o' clock. I was just about to turn on my bedroom radio and listen to the BBC News.'

'You wanted to see me, Mum,' said Floyd. 'Now's as good a time as any. I wanted to get it over and done with.'

'Yes,' nodded Mrs Francis. 'I wanted to see you … can I get you anyt'ing to eat or drink?'

'No,' answered Floyd. 'I had a good dinner.'

'You, Brenton?'

'I'm OK, Mrs Francis,' he answered, trying to ignore her brown straight-haired wig. It was *so* obviously a wig, he thought. Someone should tell her.

'Before Christmas I saw your niece,' added Mrs Francis. 'Now, what is her name …?'

'Breanna,' smiled Brenton.

'Yes, that is it,' nodded Mrs Francis. 'She was getting on a bus and I remember myself thinking she really look like her uncle Brenton.'

Brenton swapped a fretful glance with Floyd. 'But she's got her mum's eyes,' Brenton said.

'Yes,' Mrs Francis nodded. 'Sometimes that's how it goes. I have a brother who looks more like my uncle Franklin than my father.'

'Mum!' Floyd cut in. 'You said you wanted to see me?'

Mrs Francis took in a breath. 'Yes, sorry for taking the long route around the park.'

'What?' Floyd queried. 'I haven't come here to listen to your sayings, Mum. Just tell me what you have to say.'

Straightening her back in her armchair, Mrs Francis glanced at Brenton before settling her gaze on Floyd. Her eyes were guilty of something, Brenton thought. Eyes of nuff regret and t'ing. My mum gave me the same kinda look when I saw her for the first time all those years ago. And Mrs Francis's front room is similar to the way Mum had hers. The same black-and-white photos on a mantelpiece, Jamaican scroll souvenirs hanging from the walls, a display cabinet full of china and crystal glasses that she probably never uses and the images of a blue-eyed Jesus complete with long, flowing immaculate blonde hair and a white robe cleaner than a washing-powder advert. What a load of fuckery! How is Jesus gonna be a fucking blue-eyed blonde white boy living in the ancient Middle East? Did Jamaican women who came over here in the fifties and sixties all agree to have the same shit in their front rooms?

'*Mum!* I ain't got all night, you know,' Floyd raised his voice, interrupting Brenton's thoughts.

'It's about your father,' Mrs Francis revealed. She closed her eyes and re-opened them.

'What about him?' Floyd pressed. He leaned forward in his chair. Mrs Francis sank back into hers. The lines around her eyes seemed to have instantly doubled.

'That is it,' she said vaguely.

'What is it?' Floyd urged, becoming more frustrated.

Mrs Francis closed her eyes again. 'Your father is not your father.'

''Scuse me?'

Floyd looked at Brenton. Brenton's eyes flicked between Mrs Francis and Floyd as if he was watching tennis.

'What you saying?' Floyd pressed again.

'Your father … he's not your daddy.'

Floyd stood up. He took two paces towards his mother. He loomed over her. Brenton sat up in his chair, ready to jump in between them. He looked at Floyd and saw that his mouth was moving but no words came out. Floyd glared at his mother and emitted a snorting sound. She closed her eyes. He gestured wildly with his arms and hands as his mother re-opened her eyes and stared blankly through him. He then returned to his chair, gently shaking his head.

'I think you two need to chat over t'ings,' said Brenton. 'I'll be stepping.'

'Park your backside down, Brenton,' Floyd ordered, his eyes not diverting from his mother. 'Aren't you interested to know my *real* story. It explains a lot, man. Why *he* hated me. Why *he* fling me out of the yard when I was only fourteen. *Fourteen!*'

Brenton recognised in Mrs Francis the same weary-of-life expression that he had seen in his own mother.

'*Well?*' Floyd urged.

She took in a deep breath again. She looked at the glass fruit bowl on the coffee table as if it had great meaning. 'In 1961 your father ... my husband had to return to Jamaica because his mother passed away. After your sister was born we weren't getting on that well anyway. Whole heap of argument and fussing. That was us. Evening time he would go drinking with his friends before he come home from work. Weekends me never see him at all. Always at the dog track and here and there. So when him go to Jamaica I was relieved.'

'No need to tell me he was a wort'less idiot,' Floyd said.

Mrs Francis ignored the remark and continued. 'He had a best friend, Neville. Mr Neville King. They grew up in a place called Stony Hill, high above Kingston in Jamaica. They went to the same school.'

Brenton noted that Floyd's anger was subsiding and he was as fascinated by Mrs Francis's story as he was. She went on. 'I met my husband and Neville in 1955 and I watched them step on the boat for England a year later. As you know, I joined him seven months later. Neville was a single man. A kind man. He would always say to me husband to pay more attention to his family. Anyway, me husband had to return to Jamaica. He stayed for almost a year. He had some family business and arguments to sort out over land and other t'ings. During that time I was struggling with your sisters on me own. I didn't even know when me husband was going to return. He sent no letter. I became closer to Neville. We started seeing each other ... he's your father.'

Brenton glanced at Floyd to gauge his reaction. Floyd sat back in his chair. He cupped his jaws with both hands and stared at the floor. He took out his cigarette papers to build a joint but then seemed to remember that he had never smoked in his mother's house. He replaced his cigarette papers in his left trouser pocket. He got up and sat back down again. He raised his eyes and looked at his mother. 'Where is Neville now?' he asked calmly.

'He's in New Jersey,' answered Mrs Francis. 'When me husband finally returned I was already... showing. He wouldn't talk to me. He even packed up his bags and tried to move in with Neville. But Neville admitted our affair. My husband beat him up real bad. Neville was inna hospital for a while. My husband disappeared ... I thought he left me again.'

'When did he come back?' Floyd asked, his tone more gentle.

'A week before you was born,' Mrs Francis replied. 'A strange man was me husband. For all his gambling, drinking and fighting he was never into womanising as far as I know. He was pure about that ... he never spoke Neville's name again though.'

'That's when Neville headed for the US?'

'No, he moved to Nottingham first. He met his wife there. They had a baby girl and when she reach four they moved to the States.'

'What was he like?' Floyd wanted to know. 'Apart from being kind.'

'He worked on the railways,' answered Mrs Francis. 'I would always see him in his black donkey jacket but when he wasn't working he was always dressed very well. He'd wear trousers and shirt and you would never see him in jeans or a T-shirt. He smoked long skinny cigars. He always wore a hat but he used to get his hair cut every two weeks without fail. Some friends called him 'barber saloon'. He was a gentleman. He'd open doors for ladies and t'ings like that. He loved music. Louis Jordan, Curtis Mayfield and Ella Fitzgerald. He loved dancing.'

Floyd stood up once more and looked out the window. The headlights of a passing car illuminated the orange curtains. 'Do you regret your mistake, Mum?'

'A mistake?'

'Yes, that's what I was, wasn't I?'

'*No*! My husband said it was a mistake and as the Lord hear me now *he* made me pay.'

'Then why didn't you leave him?' Floyd raised his voice again. 'He made you pay. He made my childhood a friggin' nightmare and he fling me out of the yard at *fourteen*! And what did you do? *Nutten*! While we were cussing each other you just sat all quiet in a friggin' corner.'

'I was scared,' admitted Mrs Francis. 'I don't think I could have made it on my own wid t'ree children to support.'

'Then how do you think I felt? At fourteen, leaving home? Going to some frigged-up children's home?'

'I wish I ...'

'Don't bother say nutten, Mum. It's too late.'

'Yes ... it is.'

There was an uncomfortable silence for a few minutes. Brenton was still thinking of his mother and felt sympathy for Mrs Francis. He glanced at her and she was still staring into space. Consequences, he said to himself. They last a lifetime. Will Mrs Francis's life be cut short by guilt just like it was for Mum? Going by her expression I'll give her another three years at most.

'Was it worth it, Mum?' Floyd asked, sitting down in his chair once again.

Mrs Francis thought about it. 'Yes,' she finally said. 'When I see you with Sharon, Linvall and Gregory. It makes everything worthwhile. All the misery. All the mental torture.'

'If you could rewind history and the same situation came up, would you do it again?'

Mrs Francis didn't hesitate in her answer. 'Yes,' she nodded. 'If I was warned about my husband's mental torture and throwing the affair into my face whenever we were arguing or fussing ... I would *still* have my time with Neville. Yes, those few months ... I am still living on those few months.'

'Would you have had your t'ing with Neville if you knew the kinda childhood I was gonna have?'

About to reply, Mrs Francis dropped her head. She raised it again only to see Floyd's intense glare. 'I … I … '

'Can't answer that, can you?'

'No I can't,' said Mrs Francis. 'But you really think I *meant* to fall for Neville? You really think I planned to have an affair with my husband's best friend?'

'I s'pose not,' replied Floyd. 'But you had a choice. You could've said no.'

'*No!* I had no choice. That's the t'ing. When you fall in love with someone you don't have a choice … it happens. When you decided that Sharon was the girl for you, could you have ordered yourself *not* to love her?'

'No,' Floyd admitted. 'But she's not you. She didn't breed for another man. She didn't just let a husband fling out her own son.'

'Are you always going to throw that at me?'

Floyd thought about it. '*Yes!*'

Brenton saw that Mrs Francis was on the verge of tears. He couldn't help but admire her. She didn't have a choice, he repeated in his head. I didn't have a choice with Juliet. There was *no* way I could've told myself *not* to love her. I can relate. I know exactly what she's talking about. Neville made her life worthwhile. This is deep. Floyd should be gentle with her.

'If you want I can get in touch with Neville?' offered Mrs Francis. 'He would love to see you.'

'Tell him to frig himself,' said Floyd. 'Not interested. Seriously! I never had a proper dad so I don't need no friggin' dad now. What's he gonna do? Buy me a friggin' Action Man for my birthday? Come and watch me play some ball in the park? Check my homework? Will he feel a little better if he sees me? Will that nice up his conscience? And your conscience too? Make you feel sweet and forgiven and t'ing? I ain't doing that for you or him. Frig that! As far as I'm concerned you can drown in your guilt until your white, blondie, Hollywood Jesus takes you. Nah, just tell him that the only way I'll even consider seeing him is if he's got some serious money to give me.'

Mrs Francis dropped her head. Brenton glared at Floyd. Floyd stood up. 'Come, Brenton, I know you wanna get up early in the morning.' Brenton hesitated but finally followed Floyd to the front door. Mrs Francis remained seated. Very still. Staring at the floor. Broken. Floyd offered her one last accusing glare before opening the door. He said nothing until he climbed into his car. 'Hold up, Brenton. Sit in the car, man.'

Brenton checked the time on his mobile phone, kissed his teeth and rolled his eyes before filling the passenger seat next to Floyd.

'You know what?' started Floyd. 'Our parents' generation fucked up big time. When you're growing up they go on like they're sweeter than sweet, telling you don't do this and that and they used to lick you hard if you step outta line. But they are *fucking hypocrites*, man. Seriously. They got nuff to answer for.'

'Floyd,' Brenton said softly. 'Don't hate your mum 'cos …'

'Why shouldn't I hate her? She lied to me all my fucking life.'

'To protect you.'

'What you fucking talking about, Bren? She didn't protect me from shit. She didn't protect me from my so-called daddy licking a whole heap of shit outta me. Didn't protect me from *him* flinging me out. I'm soooo fucking glad I didn't turn up to his funeral. Mum was even telling me I must reach! Can you fucking believe dat? The whole t'ing stinks, dread. Fuck dem all with their going on all innocent and t'ing ways and their secrets … I wonder who else knows?'

'So you're not gonna look for this Neville?' Brenton asked after a while.

'Nope. What good is that gonna do? It'll be all awkward and t'ing. No! He made up his mind to fuck off with his new wife and t'ing to the States. Why should I spend my time meeting him? Fuck him and his wife and their daughter!'

'He's your real dad.'

Floyd turned to Brenton. He gazed at him with an intensity that made Brenton feel uncomfortable. 'Tell me, Bren. Can you say your life was any happier after you met your mum for the first time?'

Brenton thought about it. I was so fucking angry, he recalled. I had so much pain. When I first met with her I spent my time offloading my shit. She would listen patiently, nodding her head at my children's home tales and fucked-up memories. I knew that every memory I had was an injury to her. I knew it was slowly killing her. Death by a thousand childhood nightmares. But I carried on offloading every chance I got. I had to get that shit off my chest. Did it make me happy? No. Fucking no! I wish we had had more time and got to the point where I stopped offloading shit. Only Juliet made me feel truly happy. Mum did make me feel like I belonged to something though. Is that happy? If I never met Mum I would've never met Juliet. And I'm still fucked up about her. I'm still fucking up whatever relationships I have 'cos of her. Is that happy? No it ain't.

'I have to say no,' Brenton finally answered. 'It gave me a sense of belonging but ... no.'

'There you go,' said Floyd. 'Fuck if I'm gonna check out this Neville. Fuck him and his family. I bet his wife don't even know shit about me. That generation love to cover shit up and then tell you how to live your life. Fuck dem!'

'Don't hate your mum, Floyd.'

'What is this, Bren? *Don't hate your mum, Floyd!* What if I do? You think all mothers are so fucking nice and can do no wrong? Fuck dat! You think if I cuss her I'll go to the fucking dark side? I won't be a fucking Jedi no more? I'll turn into a pillar of salt? *Honour thy father and thy mother!* So the fucked-up Bible says. Nowhere in that fucking book does it say honour your kids.'

'It must've been hard for her,' reasoned Brenton. 'Can you imagine every little argument your parents had and Mr Francis is flinging her affair with Neville in her face?'

'She should've stood up to him more.'

'At least your mum kept you. I went into a home 'cos my mum couldn't stand up to her husband.'

'What is it with Jamaican men of that generation? They're full of shit and pride. Nothing can get in the way of their fucked-up manly reputation. They take no part in raising their kids apart from licking them. They're allowed to fuck around but if their women do the same t'ing they bear a grudge for one bitch of a lifetime.'

'Don't think that just goes for Jamaican men,' said Brenton.

'Families,' said Floyd. 'They just end up hurting you. That's why I always said you were wrong to find your mum. Look how that turned out for you. Over twenty years later you're still reeling from that shit. It's why I don't see my mum too many times. It just … upsets me. Too many bad memories. Bad vibes. It's why I say to you to cut your losses. Start fresh, man. Go somewhere new. Have your *own* family and grow your kids like you wanted to be grown.'

Staring out of the windscreen, Brenton couldn't help but think of Mrs Francis and her plight. *I didn't have a choice.* 'Cool off for a while,' he said. 'And then go back to your mum's and chat to her again. Chat to her properly. *Don't* make the same mistake as I did.'

Climbing out of Floyd's car, Brenton glanced upwards to Mrs Francis's flat. He paused for a few seconds and then made his way to his own car. She's probably still in that same position, he guessed. Staring at the floor, her spirit broken. The only thing keeping her going is her memories of that Neville guy. He must've been a serious charmer. That could happen to me. Just living off long-time memories of Juliet. Fuck if I'll let it happen! Maybe Floyd's right? Need to get outta London. Away from her.

Chapter 14

Donation

LOOKING AROUND THE YOUTH CLUB HALL, Juliet noted that every seat was taken. She was sitting in the front row of wooden chairs surrounded by youth club workers, volunteers, fundraisers, suited youth club trustees and members of the public. She spotted a number of young adults standing at the back of the hall and close to the exits. Breanna *should* have been here, she said to herself. Not just for my sake but for Clayton's. Maybe she's still vexed about me not answering her father question. Where the hell did that come from? Anyway, she still should've been here.

She glanced at the bruised walls, the peeling paintwork and the bent basketball hoops at either end of the hall. Can't they put some kind of netting on the hoops? she thought. It takes away the buzz of scoring if the ball doesn't swish through the netting.

Beside Juliet was Clayton who was nervously going over his speech and glancing at the small dais in front of him. A man in a black suit, white shirt and bow tie approached the dais. He was silvering at the temples and owned a generous stomach. He was shuffling papers in his hands as if he was about to make an important news broadcast. Juliet recognised him: Clive Winter, Clayton's long-time friend. He's more nervous than Clayton, she observed. For a moment Juliet visualised herself answering questions at a press conference as Minister for Children. *I'll do whatever I can and whatever is necessary to protect vulnerable children*, she imagined saying. *Those working with children in care will be put through the most stringent checks and there will be help and support for those teenagers who leave care and face a harsh world on the outside. The way a government is truly judged is not on how much the stock market rises but on how they treat and look after their vulnerable people, especially children.*

'The, um, er, proceedings for the evening are nearly over,' Clive started. 'Don't worry, we won't keep you from the refreshments for too much longer! I, er, just have one more special guest to welcome tonight. I've known him for, er, over thirty years and as far as I remember he has always supported Streatham Youth Community Trust – as a boy playing table tennis and as the sucessful businessman he is today. Ladies and gentlemen, may I introduce you to one of our most impotant benefactors, Mr Clayton Hylton.'

A ripple of applause reached a crescendo as Clayton accepted the goodwill and warm response to his introduction.

'Wish me luck,' whispered Clayton to Juliet as he stood up.

'Good luck!' said Juliet. 'Remember, take your time, don't rush your words and don't forget to smile.'

He walked up to the dais and shook Clive's hand. 'Thanks, Clive,' Clayton said. 'I never thought you'd carry out your threat to have me speak. I'll get you back for this!'

'I think it's important,' Clive said. 'Our members, workers and volunteers should know who our major donors are. You should be applauded.'

Glancing at his speech, Clayton then looked at the audience. Juliet saw that he was uneasy and she gestured to him with her hands to take his time and relax.

'I … I first met Clive in this very building when I was about eight or nine years old,' Clayton began. 'It wasn't a good first meeting. He beat me in a game of table tennis. I think the score was about 21–4.'

'21–3,' Clive corrected.

The audience politely laughed and Juliet clapped.

'Since that day we've become very good friends,' Clayton

continued. 'Of course our meeting place was right here. The youth club provided us with something to do on a Tuesday evening. It kept us off the streets getting up to no good. As well as playing table tennis we played badminton, pool, volleyball and of course we always fell out over table football.'

Clive laughed out loud and the audience wondered what the joke was.

'We also enjoyed many residential trips together, going mountain climbing, abseiling, canoeing, camping and all sorts of other things.'

'Are you two gay?' a teenager at the back called out.

Everyone laughed but Clayton composed himself again by clearing his throat.

'Since those days,' Clayton resumed, 'our paths have gone in different directions. Clive remained at the heart of the community, finally becoming general manager of this great club and I went off to university, reading business and finance. Now I work for an investment bank but my heart is still in this community. My heart is still in this youth club.'

A few people at the back cheered and clapped. Juliet smiled proudly.

'It gives me great pleasure to stand here tonight and make a donation to this wonderful organisation,' Clayton smiled. 'This is not just from me but also from my colleagues at the investment bank.'

Applause rippled around the hall.

'To ensure that there will be further residentials in the school holidays, the refurbishment of this sports hall that we now stand in, the addition of an IT room for the youth club and last but not least, for two new table tennis tables, I can announce that our donation will be fifty thousand pounds.'

Roars greeted Clayton's words and half of the audience stood up to give a standing ovation. Clayton nodded, accepting the applause. 'Of course, I wouldn't have been able to be a success in my career without the support of my beautiful wife, Juliet.'

He pointed to Juliet and she stood up once more as the applause echoed around the hall. You're supposed to say you wouldn't be a success without the support of your *family*, Juliet said to herself. Or you could have at least mentioned Breanna's name.

'Don't you think she is the most beautiful woman in Streatham?' Clayton added.

Oh, Christ! Juliet thought. Why did he have to say that? She sat back down to the accompaniment of wolf whistles and hollering.

Twenty minutes later, Juliet wasn't enjoying her glass of red wine and she reckoned the bread in her chicken sandwich was a bit off. She ate it anyway and tried to hide her grimace as she sipped her wine. Clayton had already introduced her to all the staff and volunteers of Streatham Youth Community Trust and now she wanted to go home and soak in the bath. It had been a long day.

'Is that the last one, Clayton?' she asked. 'There are some really good people here. It makes you feel humble.'

'Yep, you've met everybody,' Clayton replied.

'It's been a good evening,' Juliet said. 'I guess that this kind of event doesn't make it into the pages of the *South London Press*.'

'No, it doesn't,' Clayton agreed, munching a cheese and pickle sandwich. 'As you know the fucking media always concentrate on the negative.'

'Clayton, watch your swearing,' Juliet scolded while looking around. 'How much wine have you had? *I'll* be driving home.'

'Sorry, Jules, I had a few glasses to steady my nerves before I made my speech. As for the media it really pisses me off when …'

'Clayton! I sooo respect the offer you just made,' cut in Tom

Reynolds, Juliet's councillor colleague at the Town Hall. He was wearing a blue suit and red tie and his grin was almost as wide as a basketball hoop.

'What brings you down here, Tom?' Juliet asked. 'Your ward is Vassall Road, the other side of the borough.'

'You know me, Juliet,' Tom laughed. 'Always there for a good cause. It's good that the public sees us at these events. It's a good turnout.'

'It's not easy making a speech to the public, is it,' said Clayton. He glanced around to see where the young people serving drinks were. 'Jules gave me a few tips but I still rushed it, don't you think?'

'You were fine, Clayton,' Juliet assured.

'You were brilliant,' added Tom. 'You certainly got the biggest cheer of the night when you mentioned the fifty grand.'

'I think I would've still got a cheer if I was upfront in a bear suit!' chuckled Clayton. 'I think they were cheering the fifty grand more than whatever speech I made.'

'Fifty grand's a lot of money,' said Tom. 'Did you have to threaten to break a few heads for that? Or do you have some dirt on your friends at work?'

'No,' Clayton shook his head. 'What do you take banking for? We usually make a charity donation and I suggested Streatham Youth Community Trust.'

'So all was good,' nodded Tom. 'Maybe you should have got Juliet to speak to them. They would have given even more.'

Juliet shifted weight on her feet. What am I? she said in her mind. A fucking whore! Please get this idiot the fuck away from me!

'I thought you should have addressed the audience this evening,' added Tom, switching his gaze to Juliet. 'You could have spoken about how important it is for the youth of an area to have somewhere to go to and have good facilities. Are there any photographers around?'

'But it's Clayton's evening,' said Juliet. 'The youth club is his passion. I didn't want to make political capital out of …'

'Talking about political capital,' Tom butted in, glancing around. 'I don't see any Tory councillors here. Or Lib Dems for that matter. Shows how much they care about local issues. Fucking hypocrites. Remember this, Juliet. For when you campaign.'

'I haven't made up my mind yet,' said Juliet. Christ! she thought. Can't he just fuck off! 'As I said to you before I have to talk to my family and see how they feel.'

'I'm all for it,' said Clayton, snatching another glass of red wine from a young adult carrying a tray. 'Nothing much to talk about. You're always saying how you want to make a difference. You can only do so much as a councillor for a broke borough.'

'Don't say that too loudly, Clayton,' said Tom, looking around. 'We don't want the natives to know that we can't do too much for them.'

'It's fucking true though,' said Clayton. 'Juliet's wasting her time working in the Town Hall. Especially since the chief executive earns over a hundred and twenty grand a year when the council is almost bankrupt!'

'Clayton!' Juliet rebuked. 'Watch your damn mout'!'

'And you know what, Tom?' Clayton continued. 'You know what? Juliet doesn't even claim one penny of expenses. For all the travelling she does, all the paperwork she prints and all the time she puts in. Not a fucking penny! While that prick of a chief executive sits in his fucking office and creams over a hundred grand a year!'

'Can't disagree with that, Juliet,' nodded Tom. 'He is a bit of a prick. Especially when he wears trainers with his expensive suits.'

'You had lunch with him yesterday!' said Juliet.

'Strategy, Juliet,' replied Tom. 'Strategy. Anyway, who cares about Town Hall politics. We should be talking about Mrs Juliet Hylton, MP for Lambeth.'

It sounded good, Juliet had to admit to herself, Mrs Juliet Hylton, MP for Lambeth. Has a certain ring to it. She glanced at Clayton and decided to drive him home before he said something he'd regret. She politely made her goodbyes, took the car keys from Clayton's trouser pocket and drove home. I hope Breanna's not in a feisty mood, Juliet feared. Can't cope with her tonight.

Arriving home, Juliet made Clayton a mug of strong coffee. He sat at the kitchen table with his head in his hands. '*Drink it!*' Juliet ordered.

Sipping his coffee, Clayton looked up and said, 'Thanks.'

When he had finished, Juliet picked up the mug and washed it.

'It was a brilliant night,' said Clayton. 'Thanks for coming and supporting me.'

'Of course,' said Juliet, drying the mug with a tea towel. 'I know what the youth club means to you.'

Clayton stood up and went towards Juliet. He turned her around to face him. 'Sometimes when I look at you I just can't believe that you're my wife. You chose me! The nerdy guy who couldn't dance to soul music and who thought Winklepicker shoes were cool.'

'Oh, Clayton. Stop being soppy.'

'But it's true though. Wherever we go you're always the most beautiful woman there.'

'Is that the wine talking to me?'

'No, it's not!' said Clayton, framing Juliet's head with his hands. 'You make Halle Berry look like, er, like average. I'm not saying Halle Berry is ugly or anything 'cos she ain't but if you and her stood side by side then everyone would be staring at you … even BNP male voters would look at you … I think they all secretly fancy black women anyway.'

'Not here, Clayton. Let me check if Breanna's home.'

Juliet brushed away Clayton's hands and went upstairs to see if Breanna was there. She returned a minute later. Clayton was sitting at the kitchen table pouring himself a whisky and Coke. 'She's not home,' said Juliet. 'I hope she's still not vexed with me.'

Downing half his glass in one gulp, Clayton said, 'Get used to my world. Breanna's *always* vexed with me.'

'Stop being dramatic.'

'It's true! Doesn't matter what I do we've never been close.'

'She appreciates you. Just doesn't know how to show it.'

'Don't have to patronise me, Jules.'

'I'm not!'

Clayton finished the contents of his glass and he poured more whisky into it. He added Coke and shook it gently. 'Her argument with you,' he said. 'She's got a point.'

'What do you mean she's got a point?'

'You went to a party and you don't know who you had sex with?'

'Oh for fuck's sake! You as well?'

'It don't sound right, Jules. Don't sound like you. I've never quite thought that was … that was, you know, the full story.'

'Are you calling me a fucking liar!'

'No, Jules. I'm just saying it doesn't quite compute that you would do something like that.'

'You are, aren't you? You're calling me a fucking liar! So what do you think? You think a girl with a face like mine can't get stoned? Can't have a good time? Can't be fucked by a stranger? Have I ever claimed to be the fucking Virgin Mary? Why does everyone think because I have *this* face that I'm some kind of goodie goodie, perfect person? I screw up like everybody else. *This* face doesn't make me immune.'

Clayton took a sip from his glass and he spilled a few drops on the kitchen table. 'You're getting very defensive, Jules.'

'I'm *not* getting defensive … I don't like being called a liar.'

'I'm *not* calling you a liar! Just, maybe, what do they call it? Economical with the truth.'

'That's the same as lying.'

'Come on, Jules. You went to a party, got high on weed, went upstairs with some guy that you can't remember and had full sex? Come on. It does sound a bit way out.'

'It sounds way out because *you* put me on this ... this fucking pedestal. I'm not the dream-perfect girl you always said I was. I have fucked up just like so many girls today fuck up. I made bad choices. I was a single mother. *Deal* with it! You knew all that. Why do you always want to build me up as some kind of angel or Madonna?'

'I'm not building you up as a Madonna, Jules. I'm just saying your story ... your story is a bit ... is a bit out there. It just doesn't seem likely. I mean, if you were raped or something at this party I'd understand.'

'I wasn't raped!'

'If you were so out of it then how do you know you weren't raped?'

'What the fuck are you thinking, Clayton? Jesus Christ! I can't believe you said that. I don't know why you and Breanna are bringing this up now. What's got into you two? The fact of the matter is I *don't* know who Breanna's father is and I *don't* like to be called a liar. Now can you just drop it? I don't want to talk about this again, right!'

Placing his glass down, Clayton held his forehead with both hands. 'Sorry, Jules. Didn't mean to upset you.'

Arms folded, Juliet glared at Clayton. She breathed heavily and closed her eyes every now and again to regain her composure.

I hate lying to him, she thought. But what choice do I have?

Her expression softened after a few minutes. She then walked behind him and placed her arms around his neck. 'Why are we arguing about something that happened more than twenty years ago?' She said. 'Makes no sense. Let's go to bed.'

She kissed Clayton on the neck and pulled him to his feet. They went upstairs together and as soon as they reached their bedroom, Clayton tugged at her clothes. Juliet closed her eyes and allowed Clayton to do what he wanted with her body. He kissed her on her neck and her throat and roughly squeezed and pawed at her breasts. He almost ripped off her underwear and placed his right hand against her crotch. She could feel the nails in his other hand dig into her backside.

'At least when he's half drunk he's more passionate,' Juliet thought.

They made love with Juliet facing the mattress and Clayton on top of her. When he had finished he rolled off her, panting heavily and Juliet lay on her side, facing away from Clayton. He sided up to her and started to finger her ear lobe and play with her hair. She felt his breath on her neck. She closed her eyes and thought of Brenton.

Chapter 15
Dreams and Aspirations

THERE WAS NO WAY the characters on screen would have survived
the beatings they inflicted on each other if they had been human.
Malakai and Sean's thumbs and fingers were a blur as they
attempted to get the upper hand on one another. They contorted
their arms and bodies at strange angles as if more pressure on the
hand-held consoles would give an extra powerful kick or punch.

They were sitting in the living room of Sean's mother's flat.
The burgundy carpet was worn by the door and the beige paint
that covered the walls looked tired. A naked bulb hung from the
ceiling. Celebrity and TV magazines were piled on a small coffee
table and the desktop computer sitting in a corner of the room
had disconnected coloured wires hanging out of the exposed
hard drive, waiting to be repaired. Schoolboy photographs of
Sean grinned out from a mantlepiece and a boom box was sitting
in another corner surrounded by naked CDs with black hand-
writing on them. Beside the sofa was a glass ashtray containing
the remains of four skunk spliffs. The aroma of potent cannabis
blended with the smell of leftover chicken bones from two Kentucky Fried chicken cartons beside Sean's feet.

'You're dead!' Sean exclaimed. 'About you wanna come here
and test me! You can't *test* nothing.'

'You get lucky, bredren,' said Malakai.

'Lucky what? I paralysed you, bredren.'

Malakai flung his console on the sofa. 'We always play the
game that you wanna play. Next time I'll bring my urban warrior
t'ing and mash you up. Blatantly.'

'Stop hyping yourself up, Malakai! Bring all your games, I don't care. Just bring it.'

'I *will*.'

Standing up, Malakai prepared to leave.

'So where you going?' asked Sean, unplugging the Playstation wires from the TV.

'Bree's yard.'

'At this time? It's gone half ten. Her mum lets you stay the night?'

'No,' Malakai answered. 'I just wanna see her.'

'Make sure you tell her about my birthday drink-up at the White House in three weeks' time.'

'Are you sure about that?' Malakai paused, zipping up his jacket. 'The White House is well high profile. Brothers go there from all ends.'

'So what you saying?' challenged Sean. 'I can't ever have a drink-up anywhere in the Dirty South? Besides, the White House is near Clapham Common, near Sainsbury's. It's not like I'm having it in the ends. Stop fretting, Malakai. I ain't gonna hot up myself.'

'You told your mum you're having a drink-up?'

Sean took a while to answer. 'No,' he said finally. 'She will just be giving me grief about it. But don't I have to live my life? I've been under a low profile for too long, bredren. I can't function like that, Malakai. Seriously. For weeks and weeks I've been sitting in this damn flat listening to my mum go on and on. I get up in the morning and watch *Lorraine Kelly!* After that I dunno what to do with myself. I've started to read one of Mum's books; some writer called Andrea Smith. That's how bored and sad I've got, bredren. I need to get out more.'

'You do go out,' said Malakai.

'What? Going job centre and going once to Nando's? I mean *proper* out. Go bars and t'ing. Listen to some music. See some chicks. Get their numbers.'

'But your mum don't want you to step out at night.'

'So what do you want me to do? Spend all my time in here with my Playstation getting cuss by Mum if I leave two plates in the sink and spliff butts in the ashtray? Nah, man. I love my mum but I can't take her sometimes. It's not too different from doing bird.'

'Where is she anyway?'

'She does one late shift a week at Subway. She's s'posed to be bringing home the cheese deluxe t'ing for me.'

'So ... a drink-up at the White House? You ain't fretting about that?'

'Stop going on like a pussy, Malakai. Nothing's gonna happen. *Trust*. It's not like I'm gonna broadcast it all over the place. I'll keep it on the low. I've already asked Jazz to come. She's eager, bredren. Trying to find a way to slip her in my yard so I can wok that good. I'm *dying* for a wok that you won't believe, bredren! But you know the way my mum goes on with me bringing chicks to my yard. I mean, it's not like I complained when she had a man and he stayed over.'

'As far as I remember, Sean, the last time your mum had a boyfriend was when we were about nine. *Blatantly!*'

'Don't matter, I didn't complain.'

'Anyway, Jazz. She's Bree's friend, you know. Treat her proper 'cos if you don't it's not gonna look good on me. Blatantly.'

'And? *She* asked for *my* number. Remember that. I'm gonna wok that like caveman discovered pussy for the first time. *Trust!* She's taking me to the cinema next week, bredren. When I lock her down I'm gonna ask her to buy me some new trainers and shit. *Trust*.'

Malakai sat back down on the sofa. 'Seems like you're in there. She's well onto you.'

'You know it,' grinned Sean. 'But I need some folds to fat-up my wallet.'

'How's the job hunt going?' asked Malakai.'

Sean offered Malakai a glare of contempt. He held his expression for more than five seconds to ensure it fully registered. 'No one wants to give me a fucking job, bredren. Seriously. I'm an ex-con. A fucking jailbird. When employers asked why is there a hole in my CV and I explain to them about me doing bird they just switch off, bredren. I might as well be a paedo asking them if I can wok their ten-year-old daughters, bredren. They ain't loving me. Ain't loving me at all. Seriously.'

'Not all of them will treat you like that,' said Malakai.

'What the fuck you talking about, Malakai? It's bad enough that I'm black! Furthermore, it's bad enough that I'm the blacker shade of black. *Trust!* I couldn't even get a job at my mum's place. It's fucked up. They couldn't even trust me to fling some piece of Italian bread into some fucking oven and then fill a roll with cheese, chicken slice and shit. You know how humiliating that is? Do you? For your own mum to try and get you a job making rolls and you get turned down for that shit because some pussy don't trust you? What do they think I'm gonna do? Run off with the mother-fucking onions and salad? T'ief the takings from two fucking salami rolls? And you know what? At my mum's place they employed this Yardie girl who has a weave you can see from Tower Bridge, make-up put on by a Stevie Wonder plasterer and an accent that only tough-toe man from Jamaica can understand! I'm telling you, Malakai, I'm gonna set myself up doing some kinda hustling. I'm gonna shot some weed soon. *Fuck it.* I'm tired of begging for work!'

'Then you might end up doing bird again,' warned Malakai.

'You know what?' chuckled Sean. 'When you're doing bird you get three meals a day, you get a free gym, get to play ball and if your behaviour is all good you even get to play some games, bredren. I even improved my English and you know what I was like in English classes at school. Fuck it! You even get to do some music and shit. Yeah, hustling's a risk. But society don't wanna rehab me. They keep saying they do but they don't mean it. I'm fucked off with my probation officer telling me if I try hard enough and shit I'll get something. No one's gonna give me some fucking job in a bank or anything like that. *Trust*! It ain't gonna happen no matter what the pussyhole probation officer says. They just want me to behave like a nice little yout' and be all happy-clappy and shit when I finally get my job of flinging cheese in Italian rolls. *Fuck that!*'

'So what?' said Malakai. 'You gonna play the badman?'

'Badman?' repeated Sean. 'Don't have to be a badman to shot weed.'

'You have to look after yourself,' said Malakai. 'Nuff shottas get jacked on these ends so they have to carry something to protect themselves or get one of them Oliver Twist dogs with the big head and short legs.'

'I'll be careful, innit.'

'Sean, you ain't no shotta, it ain't you … you ain't no badman.'

'And how the fuck do you know? Were you doing bird with me? Did you see me tested in prison? I had to look after myself, bredren. *Trust!* You think I can't front up to a man who brings it to me? You think that? You're *wrong*, bredren! I've grown up a lot. *Trust!*'

'Why you shouting?'

''Cos you're fucking me off, bredren. You're chatting like you've been with me for the last two years or so.'

'Sean, I ain't dissing you. I just … I just know you.'

'I've changed, bredren. If I can deal with doing bird I can deal with shotting in the ends.'

Malakai shook his head. 'Look, hold it down, yeah, I'm gonna see Bree.'

Pausing before he made his way out of the room, Malakai said, 'Look after yourself, yeah.'

'Yes, bredren … by the way, have you seen Bree's uncle again?'

'Bree's uncle? Uncle Brenton?'

'Yeah,' Sean replied.

'No, haven't seen him. He doesn't live at Bree's yard. Why?'

'Just wondered,' answered Sean. 'Where does he live?'

'Brixton Hill ends, I think.'

'Oh, ok. Say hi to Bree, yeah.'

'Yeah, man. Laters.'

As Malakai made his way out of the flat, Sean plugged in his Playstation and set up another game. Malakai took a 35 bus to Brixton, texted Breanna on the way and then changed for a bus that took him to West Norwood. He arrived at Breanna's house at eleven fifteen p.m.

He rang the bell and Clayton answered it. He looked Malakai up and down. 'Is, er, is Breanna there?' Malakai asked, putting on his best speaking voice.

Clayton checked his watch and studied Malakai once again. 'Yes, she's …'

Before Clayton could finish his sentence, Breanna arrived at the front door. 'It's alright, Dad,' she said.

Clayton went back to reading his papers in the lounge. Breanna led Malakai up the stairs and to her parents' bedroom. She knocked on the door. 'Come in,' said Juliet.

Juliet was typing a letter on her computer. She took her reading glasses off. 'Malakai's just come to say hello,' said Breanna.

'Good evening, Mrs Hylton.'

'Good evening, Malakai.'

Breanna then led Malakai to her room. She closed the door behind her and let out a sigh of relief. 'My parents always want me to introduce any visitors to them. They're funny about that.'

'Blatantly! Your mum was alright but did you see the look your paps gave me?'

'He's alright. Just doesn't realise I'm twenty-one.'

Malakai took off his jacket and sat on the bed. After Breanna cleared two black beauty magazines off the bed, she joined him.

'So,' Breanna smiled. 'Why did you wanna see me tonight?'

Malakai kissed her on the forehead and both cheeks before finding her mouth. Breanna enjoyed the kiss but pulled away after five seconds. 'Mum's next door,' she whispered. 'Behave yourself, Malakai.'

'This is your room, ain't it? You can do what you like … you're twenty-one.'

He went to kiss her. Breanna stood up abruptly. 'Malakai! Behave!'

She inserted Aaliyah's *Try Again* into her mini-stereo. She lay down on her back on the bed staring at the ceiling. Malakai lay next to her. 'How's t'ings at home?' she asked.

'Nothing change,' Malakai answered. 'Mum still cussing every day about this and that. She wants more rent money from me.'

'It's tough for her though,' said Breanna. 'She's still got your younger brother and sister going school.'

'Yeah, I hear that, Bree. But she could do something for herself instead of cussing me and Dad for more money. She's never worked. Even Sean's mum does a little something. She works in Subway's in Bricky.'

'It wasn't her fault your dad walked out for another woman.'

'I hear that too, Bree. But what's she gonna do? Moan and cuss about it for the rest of her days or move on, get a life for herself and rely on herself.'

'Dads should pay for the families they leave behind,' said Breanna.

'Yeah, they should. That should happen in an ideal world. Blatantly. But this ain't an ideal world. It's messed up. This might sound cold but my mum made a choice to stay at home and not work. She just nags everybody and blames everybody but herself for her situation. My dad should be blamed for shit; he's got a lot to answer for. But the present situation isn't helping my little brother and sister, isn't helping her pay the bills. *Blatantly*. I can't tell you how many repossession letters we get and shit.'

'She must be stressed out.'

'She is,' said Malakai. 'The only way out of it is for her to at least do some kinda part-time work. *Blatantly*.'

'Have you seen Precious lately?'

'No, I haven't, you know. I'm gonna reach up to Crystal Palace one of these Sundays … wanna come with me? Meet my paps and t'ing? Listen to him go on about how he used to wear mad safari jackets and a beaver hat back in the day?'

'Yeah, why not?'

'OK, maybe Sunday week if you ain't busy. You can be my chauffeur.'

Breanna picked up one of her pillows and slammed it into Malakai's face. 'You're always resorting to violence,' Malakai laughed. 'You need to see one of them anger management people.'

Breanna hit Malakai again. 'You know, when we're living together I'm gonna sleep with one eye open at all times,' Malakai said. '*Blatantly!* Don't wanna be murdered by my girl in my own bed.'

'Do you mean that?' asked Breanna, letting go of the pillow and siding up to Malakai.

'Mean what?'

'The living together bit.'

'I did mean it until you hit me with the pillow and showed me your violent side.'

'No, seriously, Malakai. No messing about. You think we could live together?'

Malakai thought about it. 'Depends,' he said.

'Depends on what?'

'Can you cook rice and peas? How are you with a mop and

Mr Sheen cloth and t'ing? Not forgetting my toilet bredren, Mr Domestos?'

Breanna threw the pillow at Malakai and he swatted it away. 'Can't you answer my question?' she pleaded.

'OK, I will, but you have to promise you won't hit me.'

'Alright, alright. Do you think, honestly, that we could live together?'

Malakai looked into Breanna's eyes. He kissed her on the forehead and cupped her jaws with his hands. 'Yeah, I do,' he said. 'No messing about. In five years' time we'll have our first kid, I'll take our kid for a walk to the sandpit in Brockwell Park where she or he can fling sand in my face and beat up all the other kids and jack their mobiles. We'll live in one of those new flats overlooking Brockwell Park. We'll have a games room where I can play my Playstation and t'ing and where I can work out. You can have your girly room where you can invite friends over and watch shit like *Sex in the City* and your soaps. We'll have a king-size bed ...'

'A king-size bed? I mean, er, considering your, er, small size, shouldn't it be a pawn-size bed?'

'You feisty Jezebel!'

'Typical man! You can serve it out but you can't take it. Anyway, go on, you were talking about our house?'

'The main lounge,' Malakai resumed. 'It'll have to be big enough for a fifty-inch TV, *blatantly!* And I want one of them easy-chair t'ings, you know, the one's where you can adjust the leg and headrest and t'ing with a remote. I wanna fish tank along the whole side of one wall with those seriously flat skinny fish inside it. You know the ones I'm chatting about?'

Breanna nodded and smiled.

'Yeah, those fish are skinny but they're well colourful,' Malakai continued. 'They're s'posed to be very calming so when you get to your time of the month I'll just sit you in a chair to stare at the fish. It'll calm your moods, man, blatantly. It'll be good for your violent side.'

'Malakai, you wanna leave my house still walking?'

'Ah! Who can't take it now?'

'And how many kids am I gonna have?'

'Three girls.'

'Nah, I'd like two boys and one girl.'

'Nah, man,' Malakai disagreed. 'I want three girls so that if you are sick or somet'ing happen to you and you can't cook, then I have three substitute cooks for my rice and peas, innit. *Blatantly!*'

Breanna punched Malakai on the shoulder.

'What did I say?' laughed Malakai. 'Stop resorting to violence. How's it gonna look when we're living together and I have to report you to the police 'cos you're always banging me up?'

Levering her right arm, Breanna thumped Malakai again. He managed to grip her arms and roll onto her. She could just about detect his body odour but it smelled pleasant to her. She looked into his eyes and kissed him. She then squeezed his lips with her right thumb and forefinger. 'I'm gonna have to control that mouth of yours,' she said. 'It's too damn feisty.'

She kissed him again. 'Malakai,' she said softly. 'Do you think I'm pretty?'

'Excuse me?'

'Seriously, no messing about. Do you think I'm pretty?'

'Why you even asking, Bree?'

'Just answer the question.'

'Course you're pretty! Why would I have first stepped up to you?'

'Who would you compare me to?'

'What do you mean?'

'Compare me to? Any black female celeb?'

'Grace Jones,' answered Malakai. 'She looks as violent as you. I'm surprised you haven't got an Asbo.'

'Malakai!' Breanna pulled back her right fist but decided against another punch. Instead, she ran her fingers over Malakai's head. 'You know, some guys … some guys just wanna fuck a girl, innit. When you saw me you didn't think, yeah, that girl is an easy fuck.'

'Bree, what you talking about? What's brought this on? When I first saw you I thought *raated!* Now I've got to know you I found out you're quite sensitive and well intelligent.'

'But not pretty?'

'Course you're pretty! When we're stepping out together I love it that *you're* my girl. *Blatantly!*'

Breanna couldn't stop herself smiling. She pulled Malakai's bottom lip with her own lips then released. She gazed at him for a long second. 'Do you think my mum's pretty?' she asked.

'What kinda question is that?'

'Do you?'

'Er, course. She looks really good for a woman of her age.'

'You think I'll be as good looking as her when I reach my forties?'

'Better,' replied Malakai. 'Mind you, your knuckles will be worn away by then 'cos of the amount of times you've banged me up, blatantly!'

'Can't you be serious for more than a minute?'

'Nope. Look, Breanna. I love your company, love the way you look. And no! You don't need a perm or a weave to make you look better. *Blatantly!* Too many black girls I know think extensions and shit is the bomb. It ain't! So stop asking me should you change your hair, do you need to lose weight and do you look pretty.'

Unable to suppress a huge grin, Breanna kissed Malakai. She started to pull at his clothes. 'What about your mum?' Malakai asked.

'What about my mum?' Breanna repeated. 'Why you asking that? You want her to join us? For a threesome?'

'No! You idiot! Stop taking the piss! She might.' Malakai sided up his right cheek to Breanna's and then he began to softly kiss her neck. 'She might walk in … even worse your paps …'

Breanna covered Malakai's mouth with her right hand. She then stood up, walked to the door and secured the small latch. She gazed at Malakai provocatively, pulled off her top and whispered, 'Let's see if I can, er, upgrade you to king-size.'

Before she rejoined Malakai on the bed, she turned up the volume on her stereo a notch. Joe's *Life of the Party* rocked from the speakers. Breanna knee-walked onto the bed and into Malakai's embrace. Keep the squealing down,' she said.

'I don't squeal.'

'You do, when you, er … just keep quiet.'

Chapter 16
Settlement

EMERGING OUT onto Brixton High Street from her lawyer's office, Juliet glanced at Brenton and asked, 'You hungry?'

Brenton looked at the traffic. An angry motorist was cursing pedestrians who kept walking across the road despite the traffic lights turning to green. It was after one o'clock in the afternoon. People barged and fought to get on a 109 bus. The nearby Red Records store was playing a Morgan Heritage track that Brenton could not quite name. Hustlers were selling phone cards in shop doorways and a sad-looking man was holding up a sign advertising a new takeaway food brand opposite Brixton tube station. Brenton glanced up at the clear April sky and wondered in what country he would be viewing the heavens in a year's time.

'Yeah,' he finally answered. 'I'm kinda peckish. Why not?'

'Satay Bar?' Juliet suggested.

'Never been there,' replied Brenton. 'Yeah, let me try something different.'

'My treat,' Juliet offered.

'*No!*' insisted Brenton. 'My treat ... I can afford it now.'

'Just let me ...'

'No, Juliet. Let me do this.'

'OK.'

They made their way to the top of the high street and crossed the road to the Ritzy cinema. Idlers were drinking beer and smoking roll-ups on Windrush Square. A young white couple was kissing at the entrance of the Tate library. A taxi driver was sitting in his black cab reading the *Sun* as he smoked a cigarette.

An ambulance screeched into Acre Lane, its sirens blaring. Located behind and to the side of the cinema was the Satay Bar. Brenton found it dim inside. There was a long counter and a variety of local raves and shows were advertised on the lobby walls. It was mostly black guys with neat trims and black women with straight perms and manicured nation-coloured nails that were enjoying the food and cocktails, Brenton noted. WMCB he thought; wannabe middle-class blacks. Then again, at least they're trying to move up from having lunch at Kentucky. He led Juliet to a corner table for two. He picked up and read the menu and Juliet did likewise.

'What is this?' Brenton asked. 'Chinese food?'

'No, I think it's Malaysian,' answered Juliet. 'Or maybe Thai … what you having?'

'Dunno,' Brenton replied. 'Something that I recognise.'

A waitress came over. 'Would you like to order drinks?' she asked.

'I'll have tap water,' Brenton said. 'You do that, don't you? Don't want no fancy mineral water that costs a whole heap. Put some ice in it, please.'

'I'll have your house red wine, please,' said Juliet.

The waitress smiled and went away. Brenton and Juliet looked at each other for a long twenty seconds. Memories swelled in both of them. Brenton reminisced about making love to Juliet; her naked body, her lips, the dark birthmark below her left hip. Juliet remembered his rhythmical snore, stroking the jelly-like flesh of the scar on his neck and falling asleep in his muscled arms. They could both read each other's tension. Juliet was the first to look away. She glanced at the menu again.

'How … how is Breanna?' asked Brenton.

'Oh, she's at war with me at the moment,' Juliet chuckled. 'I'm not exactly her favourite person right now.'

'Oh, why's that?'

'Er, the other night, she came in tipsy from her birthday night out and told me to tell her who her real dad is.'

'Serious? What did you say?'

'I had to keep to my story. I felt I had no choice. She said I was lying.'

'You are lying,' said Brenton bluntly. 'Have you been going on suspicious? None of this would have happened if we were honest from the start.'

Juliet leaned in closer to Brenton and spoke in an angry whisper. 'I know how you feel now but when Breanna was born *you* agreed to this. Remember? At the time didn't I say to go away and think about it? Didn't I say that?'

'Yeah,' Brenton admitted. 'But I wasn't thinking straight. My mind was all over the place 'cos of what happened to me and you. I was young …'

'So was *I*! Don't you think my head was all over the place too? That's what you forget in all this. My daughter thinks I was some kind of role model who could do nothing wrong. So does Clayton. You thought about it for a good few weeks. Mum didn't interfere. You came back to me and said we should keep it just between you, me and Mum. I agreed to that. Both of us didn't quite know what we were doing but we *made* a decision. For good or for bad. You *can't* change the rules somewhere down the line just because we have all become supposedly more mature and wise and you want to play daddy.'

'Your drinks,' said the waitress, placing the glasses on the table.

'I'll have the lamb and rice,' said Brenton.

'And I'll have the same,' smiled Juliet, not even looking at the menu.

'No problem,' said the waitress.

Juliet waited to speak until the waitress was out of earshot. 'I … I really feel bad about lying to her though.'

'Then tell her the truth.'

Juliet held Brenton's gaze for a long five seconds. Her expression hardened. It's so hard not to pity her, Brenton thought. Her nose always does this twitchy thing when she's vexed. So fucking hard not to fancy her. Impossible not to love her.

His stare softened. He thought of Floyd's mother. She had no choice who she fell for, Brenton recalled her saying. Nor did I.

'Have you been listening to me, Brenton?' Juliet snapped him out of his thoughts. 'Do you respect what I'm saying?'

'Yeah, I've been listening. I still think you should tell her the truths and rights of the situation. I reckon she'll take it better than you think.'

'Oh, so now you know Breanna better than me?'

'I'm not saying that. Just be honest with her ... and I *didn't* have a chance to know Breanna as good as you.'

Juliet thought about it. 'I ... I can't, Brenton. The lie's got too big. It's *me* she'll really hate if this comes out. It's *me* she'll never trust again. It's me who'll lose a daughter. Or don't you think about that when you're only thinking about what's good for you?'

Brenton nodded. 'Yeah, you can say that. Mind you, we could have thought up a better story than the get-high-and-screw-somebody-you-don't-know-at-a-party-and-can't-remember shit. That's one big fucked-up story. A whole heap of fuckery that was. Breanna must have grown up thinking you were this drug-taking, free-loving girl who went to nuff orgies and t'ing.'

'Oh thanks!'

'Even *Eastenders* wouldn't have come up with a plot as lame as that, man.'

Suddenly Juliet burst out laughing. She rocked back in her seat and doubled-up. Brenton watched her and didn't know whether he should laugh with her or be shocked.

'It was a bit C-movie, wasn't it?' Juliet remarked. 'What were we thinking?'

'We?' Brenton pointed at himself. 'It was *your* idea.'

'Oh yeah,' Juliet conceded. She sipped her wine. 'It was. But this is what I'm saying. We were young. We didn't think it out properly. I was just thinking of a baby. I wasn't thinking how we would both feel twenty or so years later. I wasn't thinking that the baby would grow up, develop an attitude, cuss my behind and want to know answers.'

'Has she brought it up again?' Brenton asked.

'The father thing? No. But she's still vexed with me.'

'Why?' Brenton wondered.

'Her boyfriend stayed over the other night.'

'That Malakai guy? The one with the back pockets of his jeans kissing his ankles?'

'Yes,' Juliet chuckled. 'I spoke to her in the morning about it, you know, just told her to be careful. Make sure you use protection. That kinda thing. Then she came with a whole trailer-load of attitude. *You're only saying be careful 'cos you don't approve of Malakai and you don't like him and you hate the way he dresses. You just pretend to support brothers like Malakai but in reality you don't give a shit about brothers like him. But one day you're gonna want his vote, innit!* She gave me a full blast. *You're too much of a damn hypocrite and you're too damn stush! And so is Paps.* And you know what, Brenton? I didn't say a damn thing about his baggy jeans!'

'Bloodfire!' Brenton raised his voice. 'She gave you two barrels.'

'She certainly did,' nodded Juliet. She took another sip of wine. 'The funny thing was it was Clayton who was complaining most of the night about Malakai staying over. At one point he got up in the middle of the night and listened by Breanna's door. I told him to get his backside into bed.'

Not only a prick but a fucking perverted prick, thought Brenton. Why the fuck did she ever marry that fucking bounty? Black middle-class, wanna-be-white *motherfucker!*

'He asked me to talk to Breanna and tell her to be careful,' continued Juliet. 'While Breanna was cussing me about the dad issue, *he* kept quiet.'

'Hmm,' Brenton remarked. 'I ain't making no comment. It might be held against me and t'ing.'

The waitress returned with the food. Brenton quite liked his lamb, rice and salad dish. Just a little bit spicy. He asked for another glass of tap water. Juliet watched him and sipped her wine.

'Too spicy for you?' Juliet guessed.

'Yeah.'

'What am I going to do with you?' laughed Juliet. 'It was the same when we went to that Jamaican restaurant and you tried jerk chicken. Remember that? Breanna's sixteenth.'

'Yeah, I remember that. Clayton *insisted* that he paid for my meal. He couldn't get his fat wallet out quick enough.'

'It must be the white in you,' joked Juliet, ignoring Brenton's last comment. 'Not being able to eat heavily seasoned or spiced food.'

Brenton was unable to hold back his laughter. 'You try growing up with bubble and squeak and dried-up toad in the hole and wet dumplings.'

He laughed at his own joke and Juliet laughed with him. To compose himself, he finished his glass of water and let out a satisfying sigh.

'So,' Juliet said. 'What are you going to do with your inheritance? I reckon after tax you'll clear a hundred grand.'

The ideal person to help invest that money is Clayton, Juliet thought, but I won't go there.

Brenton cleared his throat. He gazed at Juliet and then ran his right index finger over the rim of his glass. Juliet watched his finger. 'What you going to do with the money, Brenton?' she pushed again.

'I still think we should share it,' Brenton said.

'We've gone through this already,' said Juliet. 'The argument done as far as I'm concerned. *Finito!* I've made my choice. In fact I made my choice ages ago. If you start a family you're going to need it. You had nothing from Mum for the first eighteen or so years of your life. At least now if you want to have a family you can give your kids a start. Get some good advice. Maybe talk to, er ... put it in a trust fund or something. Give it to them when they're going uni. I don't know? Buy them flash cars for their twenty-first birthdays.'

'But half of it is yours.'

'I'm alright, Brenton. Clayton earns more than enough. If I took even a pound of that money I'd feel too guilty.'

'She was your mum too.'

'But she wasn't a mum to you for *eighteen* years. Brenton, I'm not arguing about this anymore. It done. We've just signed the papers in front of two solicitors.'

'I can look after myself, you know. Say I never start a family?'

'Then that's cool.'

'I'd leave everyt'ing for Breanna,' Brenton said.

Juliet paused for a moment. She gazed into Brenton's eyes and saw Breanna's face. 'That's your choice,' she said. 'Nothing wrong with that.'

'No, there ain't,' nodded Brenton.

'So, any ideas? You going to invest in property? Sell your flat? Upgrade to something bigger?'

'No,' Brenton answered. 'Upgrade to something bigger? It ain't me. Sometimes I think my flat is too big.'

'That's because there's only you in it. When you start a family, trust me, that place you got will feel tiny.'

'I'm thinking ... no, I'm not thinking. I've decided I'm gonna move abroad.'

'Abroad?' Juliet repeated. A forkful of rice was poised before her mouth.

'Yeah, why not? Make a fresh start.'

'Where?' Juliet asked, placing her fork down and sipping her wine.

'Dunno. Ain't really thought about it. I liked Paris but I wanna go somewhere with decent weather. A place where I can hear reggae music. Forget Jamaica, I don't wanna spend my days there living behind some serious metal grille at the front of my yard and see a goat shitting on my gates and chickens walking around like they wanna mug you. Fuck that and the potholes in the road. Maybe the US?'

'When do you think you'll be going?'

'By the end of the year. When I get my papers and t'ing. That shouldn't be too long 'cos they need skilled trades in nuff countries. In a way it's your fault. You're the one who told me to do my City and Guilds certificate all those years ago; it's recognised in nuff countries. I'm gonna step to the American Embassy and make my application.'

'Won't you be, er … won't you be lonely again? You've lived the first part of your life all alone. You always told me how that was the worst thing about living in care, the hardest thing to deal with. Then you found me and Mum and now you want to live alone again? A long way from friends. A long way from … us?'

Brenton thought about it. He ate two mouthfuls of food before answering. He returned Juliet's gaze again. 'Truth of the matter is I've always felt alone. Even when I found you and Mum. The only time … the only time I didn't feel alone is that time, you know, that time we were … we were together. I know I had Mum after that and we did chat about everyt'ing and get on. And me and you were still talking good. But it wasn't like before when we used to chat about everyt'ing. It was a kinda polite talk, you know. How is the weather? Did you see that t'ing on telly last night? Ain't it a bitch that council tax has gone up. How's Breanna doing at school and t'ing. I'd better check my doctor for my flu and shit. But it could never make up for, you know, there was always somet'ing missing. It never … how can I say this? *Felt* right.'

'I … I've missed it too. Obviously our relationship changed and we don't talk like we used to. You're right; we could really talk about … things. We haven't been … together for a long time. But you still have Breanna and me. She's still your niece; I'm still your sister. Niece, uncle, brother, sister. That's still important, isn't it? Isn't that better than being alone in the world?'

Brenton shook his head. 'And I'm still her dad. I'm still … and sometimes, no, most of the time it's not better than being alone in this fucked-up world. It's hard to explain. The more I got to know Mum the angrier I got with her. Because I realised that I should have grown up with her and the reason I didn't was so fucking stupid and fucked up. It could so easily have been avoided if Mum was stronger. It was … it was like someone stole away my young life, you know. It's getting the same with you; the more I see you, the more I – there's no easy way of saying this – resent you.'

Juliet pushed back into her seat. She stiffened and dropped her gaze to the table. 'I can understand that,' she said. 'I know it hasn't been easy for you. In time it might get better.'

'It won't,' Brenton shook his head. 'It's been twenty-odd years and in that time I felt that same loneliness I used to feel when I was young.'

'But you had a better relationship with Mum than a lot of my friends had with their parents. OK, it wasn't perfect but it was something.'

'But, Juliet. That loneliness don't go away. It stays with you. That's a part of me that will never change. Doesn't matter who I'm with, whether it's Lesley or anyone of my exes or anyone in the future. That's me. You know how hard that is to deal with when I'm visiting you or Breanna and I remember how I felt, you know, with, with …'

'Alright, Brenton. I get it. Excuse me for a minute. Just going to the ladies.'

She stood up and made her way to the ladies toilets. She washed her hands in the sink then looked at herself in the mirror above it. God! she thought. What have I done? I've ruined his life. Because of me he can't form any lasting relationship. Because of *me*! Oh fucking hell, Jules! Don't this guilt ever stop? Must sort myself out. Don't let him see you're upset. What are you talking about, Jules? Of course he can see. He knows. Still want him. Why the fuck did you ask him out for lunch? The sensible thing to do is wish him well if he's going abroad. *Don't* make an issue about it. Oh *fuck!* Where will he end up? How am I going to handle not seeing him?

Juliet washed her hands again and splashed a little water over her face. She dried herself with paper towels and took in a few deep breaths. She fixed her hair, took another look at herself in the mirror and played with her wedding ring. Hold it together, girl, she willed herself. She lifted her head and walked out.

Brenton was sipping another glass of water when Juliet returned to their table. He had nearly finished his lunch. She sipped her wine, dabbed her mouth with a serviette and said, 'Maybe you going abroad is a good idea, Brenton. Maybe we need that space between us.'

Brenton nodded.

'You don't have a family yet so why not?' Juliet continued. 'You'll have all kinds of experiences and you'll see a bit of the world.'

'I was thinking the same t'ing,' said Brenton.

'I've got an announcement too,' Juliet said.

'Yeah? What's that?'

'I want to be an MP for this area.'

'An MP?'

'Yep. Been thinking about it for the past few weeks. Next election should be in a year or two. I'm going to go for it.'

Brenton raised his eyebrows. 'You know how I feel about politicians. What did the Gong sing ... *Never let a politician grant you a favour* ... can't remember the rest.'

'You still know your Bob Marley,' Juliet smiled.

'Of course.'

'I think I can do some good.'

'Like what?' asked Brenton.

'Campaign for more and better schools in this area, get respect for single parents, so many people can't get housing but there are so many empty properties around here, help people adjust from leaving care to the outside world. You know that four out of five people who leave care are likely to have drug addiction, alcohol problems and end up in prison? And ...'

'Jeez and crime, Juliet! You sound like one of those politicians already. Be careful, the stats will start to flow out of your arse, man.'

Juliet chuckled. No tact with Brenton, she thought. He tells you straight. No bullshit. Wish the idiots at the Town Hall could be more like that.

'And Floyd hasn't got an alcohol problem,' Brenton resumed. 'OK, he's still on the weed and so am I but he ain't zonked out of his head on crack and he's a good daddy.'

'I'm sure he is,' said Juliet. 'But I want to help those who haven't come out of a care background in the best of shape. Emotionally and mentally.'

'Then be a social worker.'

'I want to draw attention to social issues. Don't think I'd make a good social worker.'

'You did alright with me,' Brenton said.

Juliet didn't know how to respond to Brenton's last retort. She chose to eat another mouthful of rice and lamb.

'I've gotta be stepping,' said Brenton. 'Catch up on my work. Daniel's on his own.'

'OK,' said Juliet. 'I'm going to finish my meal. Maybe I'll have another glass of wine. I'll need it to go back to the Town Hall.'

'Alright then,' said Brenton. 'I'll pay the bill and I'll be off.'

'Just one sec, Brenton. Before you go, you know, abroad to the States or wherever. Can you leave us some pics.'

'Pics? What pics?'

'Pics of you as a kid, a mad teenager. You showed me them once ages ago. Just for memories' sake. Give me a selection and I'll take them to a photo shop or somewhere to make copies. It'll be good for Breanna … and me too, er, you know.'

'Yeah, alright. Don't know why you wanna see me with my mad Afro though but I'll see what I've got.'

'Alright then, take care and get some advice about that money. Maybe you should speak to … someone at your bank. Make an appointment.'

'I will,' said Brenton, looking around for a waitress.

'Don't forget the pics,' reminded Juliet.

'Juliet! You just asked me a couple of seconds ago. I won't forget.'

She watched Brenton leave and ordered another glass of red wine. It was close to three o'clock when she finally made her way back to the Town Hall. She attended a meeting about planned police operations in Brixton to stem the carrying of offensive weapons into bars and nightclubs. It was agreed that every public bar and club in the area had to comply to perform body searches by security staff. Juliet didn't say much during the debate. Instead she doodled in her diary. She drew sketches of matchstick boys with big Afros.

Arriving home just after eight o'clock, she went to the lounge, kicked off her shoes, threw her handbag onto the sofa and called Tessa on her mobile phone.

'Hi, Tess.'

'Jules? To what do I owe the pleasure?'

'When's the last time we played badminton?'

'Badminton? Last summer, I think. I'm still feeling the pain in my legs and my right shoulder has never recovered. Why?'

'Just need a workout,' Juliet answered. 'Friday evening?'

'A workout? Jules, if I know you, you only want to play badminton when you feel like hitting somebody.'

'Can you stop playing psychologist for once?'

'Ouch! Girl, you are touchy this evening. What's happened? Clayton has formally declared that you're the reincarnation of the mum of Jesus and can no longer have sex with you? A bird shit on your new name-brand handbag?'

'Tessa!'

'OK, Jules. Friday night? Think I got something on but I'll try and get out of it … you OK?'

'Yes, I'm fine.'

'Hmm. OK. See you on Friday then. Gotta go, just about to serve dinner.'

'I'll ring you about the time.'

'OK, bye.'

Juliet placed the phone down. I have to talk to someone about Brenton, she thought. At least she won't bullshit me.

She was just about to go to the kitchen to find something to eat when Clayton entered. He smiled when he saw her, and dropped his suitcase on an armchair before joining her on the sofa. He kissed her on the cheek.

'Good day?' she asked.

'Yes, it was actually,' Clayton answered. 'We closed a new deal. The dollar and euro look strong. How about you? Your meeting with Brenton at your lawyer's went well? No last hitches? Changes of mind?'

'No, Clayton. There were no last changes of mind. We signed the papers.'

'You're very generous,' said Clayton. He kissed Juliet again. 'I hope he uses the money well. Did you tell him that I don't mind advising him on how best to invest his money?'

'Er, not quite.'

'Why not? I don't agree with what you did but now he's got it he might as well know the best way to invest it.'

'He's, er, he's already made an appointment with his bank.'

'Made an appointment with his bank? They'll just tell him to put his money in a high interest account which he'll have to pay tax on.'

'What's wrong with that?' asked Juliet. 'That's the safe thing to do, isn't it?'

'But he could make use of that money. I could have advised him to invest in the stock market and other investment opportunities that'll make him money. He needs to split it up and not put it all in one basket.'

'Why all of a sudden are you so interested in how Brenton invests his money?'

'You made your decision,' Clayton said.

He stood up and walked to the kitchen where he switched the kettle on. He took out a mug and put a teaspoonful of coffee in it, a drop of milk and an even smaller drop of brandy. 'I'm just trying to help, Juliet. That's all. Get on the good side of your *socialist* brother. Me and him have never hit it off. He thinks I was born with a silver spoon in my gob and a platinum rattle in my hand.'

'He just thinks that you had all the breaks in life and he didn't,' said Juliet. 'Don't take it personally, Clayton.'

Clayton was looking at the small bubbles developing in the see-through kettle. 'Don't take it personally? In what? Seventeen years I have never had a proper conversation with your brother. We have never gone out for a drink on our own. Never even watched football for God's sake. What is it about me that he hates? And don't give me this socialist, capitalist crap!'

'I'll have a strawberry and mango herbal tea, please,' said Juliet. 'And Brenton doesn't hate you. You're just ... different people.'

'How are we so different?' Clayton asked, watching the bigger bubbles develop. 'Our parents both came from very poor backgrounds in Jamaica, didn't they?'

'Mum did,' agreed Juliet. 'Remember, his dad is white.'

'But our parents' generation came over here so their children could have a better life, right? And I've got that better life now. I worked hard to get my double first at Cambridge. And there's racism in Cambridge just like there was racism on the streets of Brixton or wherever your right-on brother grew up.'

'Why do you care so much what Brenton thinks of you anyhow?'

'Because ... because he's your brother. I know how important he is to you. I just want to get on with him. I don't want him thinking of me as this corporate bank guy who doesn't give a shit about working-class people.'

The kettle boiled and Clayton made his coffee. He then poured the hot water into Juliet's favourite cup and brought her her herbal tea. 'I had this chat with a colleague of mine the other day. He was saying that the working classes are dead against us but they want what we have. They want to earn the money we earn. They want to send their kids to good schools; they *want* their kids to go to the best universities, they want to build trust funds and leave property to their kids. So why do they hate us so much? I had to agree with him.'

'Oh, Clayton, do we have to talk about this now? Why can't you just accept that you and Brenton will never share a shower together after you play squash or something? Don't worry about it.'

Clayton sipped his coffee. 'Maybe you're right,' he said. 'Are we going out for dinner tonight? I want to check out that new Indian place on Crown Point.'

'Yes, why not?' Juliet said. 'I'm sure the working classes would like to check it out too.'

'Now you're being provocative,' Clayton said. 'I don't know. I'm going to give up trying to be friendly to your brother. Anyway, with the money he's got he's middle class now. Who knows? When he finally realises that he might give it all away to charity.'

Juliet almost choked on her herbal tea.

Chapter 17

Issues with Father Christmas

FEELING A DULL ACHE in his right shoulder after sawing and fixing door panels during the afternoon, Brenton lay on his bed. The room was dark save for the LED lights on his stereo. Earl Sixteen's *Trials and Crosses* was playing on a low volume. On his bedside cabinet was a half-smoked spliff in an ashtray and an empty beer bottle. A half-eaten carton of takeaway pasta was on the floor. His sawdust-specked work overalls were in a heap in a corner. The joint was still smoking but Brenton was reluctant to stub it out. He liked the sweet smell of the weed and closed his eyes.

I'm gonna burn this fucking place down one day, he thought. And if I die in the fire that'll give Juliet something to think about. Fuck it! I can hardly move. Not getting any younger. Juliet. She looked so damn good today. As time goes on she looks better and better and I just feel mash up. And it ain't just my body but my brain too. Don't know how much longer I can take this shit of a life. Even if I do stay away from her I'll see her on the fucking telly when she becomes an MP. If she ever turns up on *Question Time* I'll boot in the telly! She seems well happy that I'm planning to move to a different country. Maybe she didn't take me serious? Fuck it! I'll show her! Let's see her reaction when I do it for real. When it comes to it, she won't want me to go. I just know it. I know her. She'll feel it when birthdays and Christmases go by and I'm not around. At least I won't have to sit at her fucking table on Boxing Day anymore while her pussyhole husband slices the damn turkey with his fucked-up, I'm-better-than-you smile. *You're a big man, Brenton. Five big-man slices for you.* Fucking patronising cunt of a coconut! Why does he talk like that? He's s'posed to be black. What does he think he's doing sitting down for Christmas fucking dinner wearing a shirt and tie and polished shoes? Even Mum gave him a funny look last year. He was always so fucking nice to Mum it made me sick. *Mummy* he called her. *You sure you're OK? Can I get anything for you? Is there any particular programme or film you want to watch on TV? Another mince pie? If you want to watch the Queen's Speech that's OK with us. You want me to drive you to the sales in the morning?* Fucking pussyhole bounty arse-licker! He did all that shit just to make me look bad … I'll miss going to Floyd's on Christmas Day though. Meeting up with Coffin Head, Denise, Biscuit, Carol. Burning herb, drinking Baileys and rum, playing dominos, listening to some old-school revive arguing about who was the greatest boxer ever and what's the greatest black film. Don't care what they say: *Coming to America* is the best. *Fuck!* I'll miss that if I go away. But I've been on my own before. And them lot can come and visit me.

Reaching for his spliff, Brenton relit it. He sucked on it hard and exhaled through his nose. He hummed along to Barrington Levy's *Too Poor*. Christmas, he thought. Fuck! I've had some bad ones, man. Fuck me I have. Christmas? What is that all about? People going into the red buying presents for people they don't even like. Mums taking their spoilt kids to see Father fucking Christmas in a store and sit on his lap. What the fuck is that about? On a normal day they wouldn't take their kids to see some old stranger dressed up in mad red garms and putting them on his lap. Are we telling our kids don't trust strangers but it's OK to sit on an old white guy's knee with a paedo beard and wearing crazy red garms? It's all fuckery. When Clayton dressed up as Father Christmas when Breanna was six, I should've just hit him. It's just *wrong*, man. It looks too weird for black men to dress up as a fucking Santa. Birthdays? Hate them too. Just fucked-up reminders of me getting fuck all when I was a kid. Never got a damn t'ing! Fuck birthdays and all Christmases!

He took another toke of the dying spliff and stubbed it out. He exhaled slowly and watched his smoke disappear into the ceiling. He felt a pang of hunger but didn't have the energy to get something to eat. He couldn't be bothered to get ready for bed. He closed his eyes. 'Jeez and crime,' he whispered. 'Floyd gave me a good draw of weed. It's making me seriously drowsy. It's the only t'ing I can rely on in this damn world.'

He couldn't keep his eyes open. He could feel sleep claiming him.

Pinewood Hills Children's Home, Christmas Eve, 1970

Don't go to sleep, the seven-year-old Brenton willed himself. He opened his eyes. The dormitory was dark. All was quiet. No, he thought. He could hear Ian Nuttall's snoring in the corner of the room. Can't he put some cotton wool or something up his nose? Brenton thought. Maybe his ginger hair makes him snore? I'll cut off his hair one night.

He sat up in his bed slowly. He looked around but couldn't make out too much. Only dark shapes in beds and that spooky framed picture of a clown that hung over the bed next to his. I'm gonna take that down and throw it on a bonfire one day, he promised himself. That clown has to die and I wanna hear it scream to make sure it's dying.

He felt a draught of cold around his neck. He secured the top button of his pyjama top. He could smell urine. At least it's not me, he thought. Must be Stephen Kelleher. He's older than me and he pisses the bed? Ten years old! What's wrong with him? Ever since his stupid auntie stopped visiting him he's been pissing the bed. *She* might not check his bed on Christmas Day but if she does he'll get the belt. If he does get it then good! Her arm might be too tired to give me the belt later on for something I might do. And she should stuff the wet sheet into his mouth like she does with me. Yeah, stuff it down far so his throat goes all funny and his eyes go crazy and he starts coughing.

Brenton could hear a distant buzzing sound. Is that the electric, he guessed. No, maybe it's the fridge. No, can't be the fridge, it's not as loud as that. Maybe *she's* still up doing something? Maybe she's making a cake or something with that mixer thing? Please, Saint Mary, let her be in her bed. Let her never wake up. Make her go down to hell where the devil will whip her and stand on her head with his hooves. Yeah, blood coming out of her nose and eyes. Does the devil have hooves? Yeah, he does. I saw it in a book at Sunday school. Hope they're really really big hooves with football studs. And I hope that all the fires and fireworks down there will melt her head and her arms so she can't hit anybody ever again.

He reached down to the floor where he picked up one of his slippers; he disturbed a matchbox car that raced towards the foot of his bed. Within the slipper was Ian Nuttall's watch that Brenton had borrowed. The numbers on the watch were luminous green. For a short second he marvelled at the pretty sight before he whispered the time. 'Quarter to three.'

She has to be in her bed, he wanted to believe. I'm gonna go for it.

He slipped out of his bed. Ian Nuttall was still snoring. He put his slippers on. He made out the dark shape of the chest of drawers. He tiptoed over to it. On the dressing table were combs, brushes, a tub of Vaseline, a *Beano* comic with its front page missing, a set of playing cards, an armless Action Man doll, a soiled tissue and a bicycle headlight. He picked up the headlight and made for the door. The stench of urine coming from Stephen Kelleher's bed almost made him sneeze. He reached the door and gently squeezed the handle. He opened it just enough to poke his head around the door. He looked along the corridor to his left. There were no lights on. The girls' dormitory was at the end of the hallway and *her* room was in the middle to the right. He daren't switch on his light but as far as he could make out, *her* door was closed. Opposite her door was Georgie's bedroom. His door seemed to be closed too. Good! Brenton thought. He should burn in hell too. Yeah, tie him up with no clothes and burn his willy off! And he should keep his stupid Pinkie Floydie music to himself. Don't wanna go to his room and listen to any of his old, stupid music. Why does he keep asking me to come?

He looked towards the stairs. Dark. He couldn't quite make out the banister. The buzzing sound is coming from down there, he guessed. It must be the fridge. Not *her* making her stupid cakes.

He checked behind him. Ian was still snoring. Time to go, he told himself.

He took a step out into the hallway. He grimaced as he closed the door behind him as softly as he could. He was grateful for the carpet that cushioned his feet. He crept to the top of the stairs. He reached out for the banister. It felt cold and smooth. He walked down the first flight of stairs. The middle step creaked. He stopped and checked behind. A painting of a crying child hung above his head. They're still asleep, he thought. He stepped down that bit quicker. He reached the downstairs hallway landing. He turned right and paused. He switched on the head-light. He panicked when he realised he had nearly knocked over a vase that was standing on the table. He shone the light at the ceiling. Balloons and paper chain decorations covered the upper walls and below this were cut-outs of snowmen, angels, reindeers and elves. Must walk softly, he kept telling himself. It took him ten paces to reach the lounge door. He looked behind again. Then he squeezed the door handle. He let go. Maybe *she's* in there in the dark? he feared. Waiting for me. Maybe I should just go to the larder and see where the chocolate flake cakes are?

Brenton paused. He pressed his ear against the door. He didn't hear anything. He squeezed the door handle again. He switched off his light. The door opened. He put his head around it. Darkness. He counted to five then turned on his light again. The angel on top of the Christmas tree was almost kissing the ceiling. Fixed to the other corner of the room with tacks and masking tape was a thin naked branch. Skinnier twigs forked off the main bough. Sellotaped to the branch were dozens and dozens of Christmas cards. Not one of them belonged to Brenton. He shone his light at the foot of the tree. Presents of different sizes were expertly wrapped and neatly placed under the tree and in front of it. They had little cards slotted under pretty red ribbons. Brenton walked over to the gifts and shone his light at the labels on them.

'To Ian from his loving Uncle Pedraig,' he whispered. 'Weird name. To Stephen from his loving aunt. To Christine, to Rita, to Ian again. To Hayley from Granma May. Granma May was a funny one. Wonder what's wrong with her? Last time she came to visit she couldn't walk properly and her breath stank of something. She kept on wanting to play with my hair. Stupid cow! *She* got really angry with her … to Paul, to Edward from Auntie Violet; she was another funny one. Kept on nodding, she did, when she was drinking her tea and eating her biscuits; why do visitors always get the chocolate and custard cream biscuits and we only get the boring ones? Then after she finished her tea she started to jab her own head. Funny lady. Dunno why it was only me who got the belt for laughing at her; Neil was laughing too.'

Placing presents behind him, Brenton grabbed some more and read the labels. 'To Ian again, to Yvonne, to Neil, to Paul again. Nothing for me? Not even one? To Maria, to Linda, to Robert, to Paulette, to Lloyd. Another one for Rita. Another one for Hayley, stupid cow! She don't deserve two! She didn't eat all her rhubarb crumble yesterday. How comes she didn't have to sit there all night like I had to?'

Brenton shone his light on every label of every gift. None were for him. Tears ran down his cheeks. Not even one from Father Holman? he sighed. He said he'd forgiven me. Like how Jesus forgives everybody. He said if I behave then I'd get baby Jesus' blessing. But I ain't got nothing and everybody got something. Ian wet his bed last week and he got four presents. Rita tried to run away and she still got two. Robert got caught nicking Coca-Cola out of the fridge and he's got a present. Paulette ran out of the house when her mum turned up and she still got a present. It's because of *her*. She probably told Father Holman not to get me anything. Hate her! Hate her! Don't care if Jesus gets angry with me. I just hate *her*! Why can't the Romans and Poncy Pilot put her on a cross, bang those metal things in her hands and feet and kill her? Yeah, and put an even bigger metal thing in her fat face and get the long broom from the outhouse to whack her with. Yeah, a broom with spikes.

He shone the light at the presents again and grabbed the biggest one. The label read *To Ian with lots of love*. In a fit of temper, Brenton ripped it open. The torn Christmas wrapping paper revealed a Subbuteo table football game; the World Cup edition, Brenton noted.

He took out the contents of the box. There was a green cloth with a football pitch marked on it. There were advertising hoardings that surrounded the pitch. He picked out two tiny white goals that had white netting. He collected the four corner flags. There was even a scoreboard and two mini footballs. He took out the inch-high plastic players from their polystyrene casing. One team was coloured in blue and the other red. Anger surged through him. He snapped all the blue players in half from the waist down. '*Hate* Chelsea,' he whispered.

Throwing the broken players into a corner of the room he

then decapitated the heads of the red team. 'And I hate Man United!'

He then broke the legs of the goalkeepers, cracked the scoreboard and was about to rip the green cloth when the lounge room light was switched on. Brenton sat motionless. There *she* was. Her hair was in rollers. She was wearing a peach-coloured dressing gown and beige slippers. Her arms were crossed. Her eyes were unblinking. Brenton knew that was a prelude to a beating. He backed away against the Christmas tree.

Miss Hills looked at the torn wrapping paper and then the mutilated plastic football players. Brenton covered his face.

'You animal!' Miss Hills shrieked. 'You animal!'

She rushed towards Brenton flailing her arms, punching and slapping him with all her might. He tried to defend himself with his arms but it was useless.

'You're nothing but an animal! A bloody animal!'

Brenton's left eye was already closing. He sustained a gash to his right eyebrow. His nose was bleeding.

When Georgie came rushing into the lounge, he found Brenton cornered against a bending Christmas tree. Baubles and tinsel were falling to the floor. Presents were scattered. The angel, losing its wings, fell off the top of the Christmas tree and landed on her head.

'Get him out of here!' Miss Hills screamed. 'Get that animal out of here!'

She backed off. Brenton curled up into a ball on the floor. He covered his face. His nose was still bleeding. His blood spotted the carpet and a few presents.

'Get him out of here!' Miss Hills demanded. 'Just look what he's done! Look what he's done!'

Georgie tried to pull Brenton to his feet but he refused to move. He wanted to remain on the floor, curled up as tightly as he could manage.

'He won't move,' said Georgie.

'Get him out of my front room before I kill him!' screamed Miss Hills.

Brenton felt a punch behind his right ear. As he moved his hands to rub his head, he felt himself being lifted. His waist was almost crushed in Georgie's hold. He took him out of the house through the back door. The cold air stroked Brenton's feet and hands and then he felt it on his chest. His eyes began to water. He was dizzy

'Put him in the outhouse,' ordered Miss Hills. 'I just can't believe what that animal has done! Broke the game! He broke the Subbuteo game!'

Deciding not to struggle in Georgie's grip, Brenton could only think why he went downstairs without his dressing gown. He could now feel the cold on his nose and lips. His toes were feeling funny. His head felt heavy, like someone had poured something warm and horrible into the top of his brain.

As Georgie opened the outhouse door, Brenton wondered if he'd ever be allowed out again.

'Let him stay there till breakfast,' said Miss Hills. 'He's gone too far this time. Smashing other kids' presents. Too bloody far! If he wants to behave like an animal then we'll treat him like an animal. Make sure you lock it, Georgie.'

Shoving Brenton inside, Georgie secured the lock.

'That'll teach him,' said Miss Hills. 'Come on, Georgie, I'll make us a pot of tea. I need it. We'll have a couple of mince pies too. It's Christmas Day now. I don't know what we're going to do about the Subbuteo game? I'll have to buy another one to replace it. By the saints! That child will be the ruin of me! I have a good mind to take it out of his clothing allowance. Animal he is. An animal!'

'Shall I get his dressing gown?' Georgie asked. 'It's a bit nippy tonight.'

'*No!*' Miss Hills snapped. 'Let the cold air bite the little black bastard. It might put some sense into him. Honestly, Georgie! What are we going to do with him? He fouled the Father's front door with his own poo and now this. Disgusting he is. *Bloody* disgusting. When the Christmas holiday is over I'll have to talk to the senior social worker at Blue Star House. I'm *not* putting up with this behaviour. I'm not having it, I tell you, Georgie.'

Brenton heard Miss Hills and Georgie walk away. He heard the opening of the back door and the closing of it. He closed his eyes and rubbed the back of his head. He could feel a swelling. He looked at the palm of his right hand and was relieved to find he wasn't bleeding. He stood up and switched on the light: cobwebs in high corners; the old lounge sofa upside down in the middle of the room; a baby's high chair on its side; rusting bike parts and broken prams; biscuit tins full of nuts, screws, bolts and spanners; a chipped rounders bat on a window ledge. He could smell oil and something else that he couldn't quite place. He placed a hand on the wall. It was damp. He took his hand off the wall and his palm was caked in dust. Resting against the same wall was a blackboard. It was detached from its easel. Someone had played noughts and crosses on the blackboard and Brenton rubbed it off with the palm of his right hand. He found a small bit of white chalk on the floor. He picked it up and started to draw something. He sang a song. '*Tie a yellow ribbon around the old oak tree …*' He couldn't remember the rest of the words so he thought of another song. '*We all live in a yellow submarine, a yellow submarine, a yellow submarine …*'

He paused as he looked at what he had sketched. It was a woman with big eyes and a big smile. She had an Afro that was much too large for her head. Underneath the drawing he wrote *Mum*. He smiled.

Chapter 18

Too Pretty

STRUGGLING TO KEEP THE SHUTTLECOCK in play, Tessa lunged and slipped on the badminton court in the sports hall. She slowly got to her feet, rubbed her knees and swept her hair out of her eyes. Tessa looked around to see if anyone had seen her fall. A young Indian boy, walking by in his white vest and shorts, covered his mouth with his hands, trying to stifle his laughter. Tessa, mockingly, bared her teeth at him and raised a fist.

'14–4,' said Juliet, walking to pick up the shuttlecock.

Tessa readied herself to receive Juliet's serve. The subsequent rally lasted seven shots with Juliet winning the point with an overhead smash. '15–4,' she proclaimed.

Breathing heavily, Tessa offered Juliet a long glare before walking off court to find her bottle of water. She threw her racquet on the floor and sat against a wall beside a folded-up trampoline swigging her drink. Her sports top and baggy track-suit bottoms were stained with sweat. She poured a little water over her head before drinking again from her bottle.

'You're not going to play the next set?' asked Juliet.

'Lay off, Jules,' Tessa answered. 'I'm knackered. You might have to carry me into the changing rooms. I think I'm gonna be sick. Either that or I'm dying.'

Joining Tessa by the wall, Juliet sat down beside her and took out a pink towel from her bag. She swabbed the sweat off her face and draped it around her shoulders. Her red sports top was not as wet as Tessa's and her tight black leggings had drawn glances from every man she passed. She took an energy drink from her bag, took a sip and sighed. She could hear the thwack of racquets, the groans and the pounding of feet from the other badminton court. At the other end of the hall, four Chinese men were playing a serious game of table tennis doubles.

'Needed that workout,' Juliet said.

'I didn't,' replied Tessa. 'Why couldn't we do what most forty-odd women do? Go shopping, have lunch somewhere and then enjoy a massage from a fit bloke?'

'Badminton is good for your heart rate.'

'Good to kill me!'

'Stop moaning, Tess. Didn't you say to me that you need someone to drag you out of the house to do more exercise?'

'Yeah, I said it. Doesn't mean I meant it though. Now take a stroll and leave me to die in peace. I'm seeing that white light thing.'

Juliet laughed. 'Oh come on, Tess. Couldn't have been that bad.'

'Do you wanna bet? If Antonio Banderas walked up to me right now, swinging his bits, undressing me with his sword and offering the hottest sex ever, I still couldn't stand up.'

'When you have your shower, Tess, make sure it's a cold one,' laughed Juliet. 'We'll go for a meal when we get out of here. Lounge Bar? At the top of Atlantic Road?'

'It's not a long walk from here, is it? OK, as long as you're willing to carry me there ... Jules, you haven't said anything to me yet about what's nagging you. Don't even think about not telling me! If I've coughed up my guts for nothing I'm gonna kill you.'

'What makes you so sure that something is nagging me?' said Juliet sipping her drink.

The sweat was still pouring from Juliet's forehead. She wiped it with her towel.

'Cos I've never seen you hit that shuttlecock so bloody hard,' answered Tessa. 'I kept on wishing it was Graham's dick! It's obvious you've got issues. Then again, you've always got issues. If you was American you'd have a psycho-what-you-call-it.'

'Psychologist,' Juliet corrected.

'Miss Drama I should call you.'

'Miss Drama? I'm not the one who burned my ex-husband's Crystal Palace football shirts on the barbecue in front of the kids.'

'You was egging me on.'

'No I wasn't,' Juliet chuckled. 'I just, I just couldn't stop laughing.'

'That's nice, Jules. My marriage was going down the plug hole and all you could do was laugh.'

'If you could have seen yourself,' said Juliet. 'The lighter in your hand, your crazy face and the kids looking all confused … it was funny.'

From trying to keep a serious face Tessa suddenly burst out laughing. 'Yeah, I s'pose it was funny. I shoulda burned all his bloody clothes, especially that Bugs Bunny T-shirt that he really loves and his precious Adidas trainers; that was the only thing he ever washed in the washing machine. He didn't worry about the kids' clothes or anything; he would just throw his bloody trainers in the thing and switch the machine on! Shoulda burned his Coldplay and Morrisey CDs an' all, and his World Cup 1990 DVD. Shoulda smashed his Crystal Palace mug an' all. Fucking cheating slag!'

Juliet took another sip of her drink. 'I don't get it,' she said. 'He was one of the good ones, wasn't he? He didn't seem to be the cheating kind. Not as far as I know anyway. Still can't get my head round it, Tess.'

'He's a man,' Tessa stressed. 'Men *cheat*. They can't help it.'

'Not all men cheat, Tess.'

'Don't they?' Tessa chuckled. 'Trust me, if they're given the chance they'll cheat. It's in their DNA. You could get the most devoted husband in the world, married to his lovely wife for twenty-five years. Two point five kids and all that. Living in a nice house with their Boxing Day-sales furniture and widescreen TV. But if Beyonce whispered in his ear, *I'll give you the most mind-blowing night of sex and dirtyness you will never believe and never forget and no one will ever get to know,* he'll take it. And even if he didn't take it he'll agonise over it and then regret not taking it till he's six foot under. Believe me, Jules. Men would fuck as much as they could if they knew they would get away with it.'

'But Graham?' Juliet queried, shaking her head. 'He seemed so ... shy?'

'You think shy men don't wanna fuck around, Jules? What planet are you ringing me from? You think that slag that's with him now woulda been interested in him if he didn't get a promotion? You think that whore woulda fucked up my marriage if Graham was just another one of the lads and wasn't allowed to park in one of the bosses' parking bays? When Graham became general manager that slag started to give him attention. She wasn't fucking interested before, the fucking slut. She saw pound signs and her future slag babies going to some posh fucking nursery. So she made her play for Graham by standing up and pushing her tits in his face every time he went by. And men being men, Graham let his dick do the talking. The both of them are slags. Fuck 'em both.'

'The kids coping OK?'

'Yeah, they are,' Tessa answered. 'And it's bloody annoying. A small part of my head doesn't want them to cope. That same small ... well I said small but if I was honest it's a big part, wants my kids to hate him. I want them to not stand the very sight of him. Am I making sense, Jules?'

'Yes. You're still raging, Tess. Understandable. Don't know what I'd do if Clayton fucked around.'

'Clayton fucking around?' laughed Tessa. 'No danger of that. More chance of Skinny Spice eating a fat hog.'

'Men are men as you say,' argued Juliet. 'Doesn't Clayton think with his dick too?'

'Yes he does,' giggled Tessa. 'But he's gay.'

'Clayton is *not* fucking gay!'

'Yes he is. He's as gay as a cream suit, a yellow handkerchief and light blue flip-flops. He uses the fact that he's married to a beautiful woman as a cover-up.'

'Oh give it a break, Tess!'

'It's true!' argued Tessa. 'Think about it. A man like Clayton. He's not what I call absolutely fuckable with his weird, pear-shaped head and his please-respect-me suits but he's very successful, right? Earns loads of money. Looks don't come into it for a lot of slags. Trust me, Jules, slags must fling themselves at him twenty-four seven. Slags want the easy life, Jules. They wanna live in a nice house and not go to work. They wanna drive their 4×4s and listen to the latest pop crap. They wanna go shopping in the West End but go to the posh part of it. They wanna walk up and down the high street with their Chanel and Harrods bags pouting like Skinny Spice. And they don't care who they have to fuck to get that. Married or not. And because, as I said, men think with their dicks, most slags, if they got a bit up front and a face that they can make look decent with a bit of plaster, live the life they don't fucking deserve.'

'So have they set up home?'

'Yep. Let them stew together. As soon as her tits begin to drop when she pushes out her first sprog and when she can't get away looking decent with her cheap make-up, Graham will lose interest. They haven't got nothing in common. I heard her on her mobile once. All she ever talks about is *Footballers Wives* and *Hollyoaks*. Graham likes watching *Newsnight* in the evening and *Question Time*. The very thought of watching those programmes in bed with him will do her slag brain in. Mark my words, Jules, when Graham gets bored with her she'll be shopping for her slag knickers in Primark again.'

Juliet bent over with laughter. 'She that shallow?'

'A hoodie's spit on a kerb has got more depth than that slag.'

Juliet laughed again and had to place her right hand on her stomach to compose herself.

'How did we get around talking about Graham and his slag?' Tessa asked. 'I want to know what is nagging you.'

Taking in a deep breath and staring at her racquet, Juliet thought of Brenton. She then took another sip of water. 'Brenton,' she answered.

'Brenton?' Tessa repeated. 'Oh for crying out loud! Not that again.'

Juliet nodded.

'What now?' Tessa asked. 'He was running and tripped over and now you wanna put a little plaster on his leg and kiss it better?'

'Tess!'

'Then what is it?'

Juliet took in another breath. 'He's leaving.'

'Leaving? So?'

'He's going to start a new life abroad,' Juliet announced.

'That's a good thing, ain't it?'

Juliet didn't reply. Instead she stared at her racquet again.

'It's about time Brenton had a life without you in it,' Tessa added. 'He needs to be away from you. Maybe find a girl and make sprogs of his own. Let's hope none of his own sprogs get biblical with each other!'

'I don't know if he can form a stable relationship,' said Juliet.

'Why not? He functions, doesn't he? Everything's in … working order?'

'Yes, but …'

'But what?'

'I've ruined him, Tess.'

'What do you mean you've ruined him?'

'He's still carrying something for me. He still can't get over …'

'Twaddle!' laughed Tessa. 'He's a grown man, for God's sake. He runs his own business. All that fiddling abuse stuff happened years ago …'

'Tess! How many times do I have to tell you? He wasn't fiddled with. He was physically abused.'

'Yeah, yeah. If you prefer it that way. Anyway, he should've got over that by now. And besides, he's *not* your responsibility. No one gave you a job to make your half-brother happy in his private life.'

'But I can't help feeling … it's all my fault. Like I really fucked up his life because, er, what we had.'

'That's long gone, Jules,' said Tessa shaking her head. 'He's gotta find his own way now. What's with you and this guilt thing? I'd understand if you were Catholic but you ain't. Listen to me, Jules. It's best that you just let him go. Who knows? In a couple of years' time you might get a letter from him from Jamaica or wherever telling you he's married and got a sprog on the way.'

'Brenton married,' Juliet said, now staring at her racquet again.

'Yes, married,' repeated Tessa. 'You know? That age-old excuse to buy a white dress and eat a cake with too much icing? And then your husband can't keep his dick in his trousers when a slag winks at him at the reception.'

Juliet thought of Brenton walking down the aisle with someone. He would look so good in a suit, she imagined. How could she just sit there in the front row looking on as he got married? Would she be able to keep her emotions in check? She'd have to.

'Jules?' Tessa called. 'You don't like the idea of Brenton marrying, do you?'

'Of course I do,' Juliet insisted. 'I want him to be happy.'

'Total twaddle!' Tessa raised her voice.

Juliet looked around the hall to see if anyone overheard.

'Jules, my girl,' Tessa continued. 'I'm about to give you a few reality checks.'

'I need reality checking?'

'Yes, you bloody do! Someone's gotta do it so it might as well come from me.'

Juliet picked up her racquet and twirled it around in her fingers. She stared into space. Tessa finished the rest of her drink and looked at Juliet.

'Things have been so cosy for you,' Tessa started. 'Keeping the secret of Breanna's dad, Brenton not living far from you. Whenever he's sick you going around to his gaff to make sure he's alright, tucking him up in bed and all that twaddle. You helping out with his taxes and advising him when he started his business. For crying out loud, you even told him what colour scheme to have in his flat!'

'What's wrong with that?' asked Juliet.

'You shoulda let him stand on his own two feet! And when he was sick it wasn't your job to go around there and give him his medicine. He had a mother. And it wasn't *you!* But I s'pose it eased your guilt looking after him and helping him. It probably made you feel all good by helping him out. Felt all good inside, did you?'

'I didn't do it for my guilt,' Juliet argued, still spinning the racquet in her hands. 'After all he's been through he needed my help, encouragement.'

'Up to a certain point, Jules! Whatever happened in his past is not your responsibility to put right, for crying out loud.'

'Mum's gone,' Juliet said, now looking at the floor. 'I'm all he's got.'

'Twaddle!' Tessa said. 'He's got his mates, he's got his business and he's got his own life. At least he should have his own life. He's a grown man now. Grief! He ain't that sixteen- or seven-teen-year-old who turned up at your gaff with a sob story and a crappy violin.'

'It *wasn't* a sob story, Tess.'

'It doesn't matter what it was,' said Tessa. 'You've got to let him go. Let him have his own space. Allow him to make his own mistakes, his own fuck-ups. That's what grown people do, Jules.'

Juliet dropped the racquet. She sipped her energy drink again and stared vacantly ahead.

'You won't let it go, will you?' said Tessa. 'I can see it in your eyes.'

'Yes I will,' insisted Juliet. 'For his sake.'

'No you won't,' argued Tessa. 'Wherever he goes you will have to follow him.'

'You can't read my mind, Tess.'

'Yes I can, Jules,' said Tessa softly. 'I know you. I know you better than you know yourself. You're used to getting what you want. And you *don't* want Brenton out of your life. You have to be in control of things. You're a control freak. You like it how it is. In fact, since I've known you, you have fascinated me. You're just different. Half the reason why we're still mates is 'cos I'm trying to work out what makes you tick. And I've finally got it.'

'Now who's talking twaddle?' chuckled Juliet.

'There's a lot of twaddle been spoken but it ain't by me,' said Tessa, her expression serious. 'You would like things to be the same. Brenton living nearby, you checking up on him to see if he's OK to satisfy your guilt, your secret all tucked away. All nice and cosy ...'

'You make it sound like I'm a cynical bitch.'

'You said it,' nodded Tessa.

'What's this?' asked Juliet, becoming angry. 'You're rubbishing my character now?'

'No, just giving you a reality check. Come on, Jules, I've known you for well over twenty years. Listen to me. You had an affair with your half-brother. You had Breanna together. And now you're crying to me that he's leaving to make a new life abroad? Something is kinda wrong with that scenario, don't you think?'

'I wasn't crying, Tess. Just stating a fact.'

'No! You wanted me to feel sorry for you. Well I ain't gonna feel sorry for you. I ain't gonna be all huggy with you and say how much I understand and all that twaddle. You brought this on yourself 'cos you're spoilt.'

'Oh! I'm spoilt now? That's nice, Tess! Coming from my supposedly best friend. What else have you got? I'm already a cynical bitch.'

Tessa's eyes wandered for a few seconds. She glanced at the ceiling, looked at the Chinese table tennis players and briefly watched the badminton game in front of her before returning her gaze to Juliet. 'Yes,' she finally said. 'Most too-pretty girls are spoilt. Most of 'em don't even know they're spoilt.'

'Oh and how do you work that one out?' asked Juliet, throwing her racquet on the floor and crossing her arms.

'It's all too easy for very pretty girls,' said Tessa. 'At school they don't have to work hard to make friends like us normal-looking kids. As for the ugly ones, well, they really have to make an effort. Why the fuck do you think they're so many ugly comedians? Anyway, pretty kids are just popular 'cos of the way they look. Everyone is that little bit more polite to them 'cos of the way they look. They get jobs that bit easier 'cos of the way they look. And you know why? 'Cos male bosses think if they hire a pretty girl there might be a very slight chance of fucking them.'

'Come on, Tess!'

'It's true,' insisted Tessa. 'Remember, Jules, your first job? I was there, remember. I looked at all the CVs. We got over forty. And believe me, Jules; most of the girls going for your job were much better qualified than you. Some of them even had degrees.'

'But I showed ambition and a willingness to learn.'

'So did the other girls who came for an interview,' said Tessa. 'But what swung it for you was the fact Baldie fancied you. For crying out loud, Jules, *everybody* fancied you. They still do. Now, Baldie, even though he was polite, happily married an' all, he was probably thinking in the back of his bald head, that there might, just might, be a very slight chance of fucking you. Call it male fantasy or what you like ... but it's true. He probably wanked in the toilets over you.'

'Didn't Baldie hit on you?'

'Yeah, he did,' answered Tessa. 'Only because he reckoned he had a little bit more chance of fucking me than you. That's how men work, Jules. Baldie didn't want to be totally rejected by you but with me, he reckoned he had a chance. Obviously I told him to fuck himself.'

Picking up her racquet once more, she twirled it in her hands again. 'How comes you never said anything to me about this before?' asked Juliet.

'I was going to when I found out you got the job,' replied Tessa. 'But you were alright. You weren't stuck up. I liked you. Grief! That bank could've done with a bit of colour working for it. It was sooo white.'

'So how does all this make me spoilt?' Juliet wanted to know.

'Because you're so pretty you're used to getting what you want. People give you what you want 'cos everyone wants to be next to beauty. Have you ever had to try really hard to get a job?'

'No,' admitted Juliet.

'Then there you go,' nodded Tessa. 'You were a single mother with your brother's baby, yet you end up marrying a fucking banker! Talk about landing on a pile of shit and somehow coming out clean. And now you live in a house worth, I dunno? Four hundred grand? I grew up in Bermondsey and believe me, Jules, Bermondsey has its fair share of single mothers, just like Lambeth, Peckham or wherever. You're the only one I know, Jules, who landed a husband earning a six-figure salary and is going to be a fucking MP. *Don't* tell me your looks had nothing do with all that. Pretty people are used to getting what they want. You think some fat, ugly, single mum living in some tower block in Rotherhithe will ever end up with a banker husband? No fucking chance. Ain't gonna happen.'

'But I've worked hard for my community,' reasoned Juliet. 'I've campaigned for loads of things and got people's support.'

'You still don't get it, do you?' asked Tessa. 'Look at when we arrived at the leisure centre. That assistant took one look at you and almost tripped himself up to set up the net for our game. He was so eager to please and he made it so obvious he was think-ing of his dick. You think if you were a fat ugly slag he would've jumped to attention and been so helpful? Fuck no!'

'That's his job, Tess,' reasoned Juliet. 'He was just being polite.'

'*No he wasn't!* At the back of his head he was thinking if he was really nice to you he might, just might, if he played his cards right, get to fuck a very beautiful girl. He hardly noticed me! Let me give you one more example. Newsreaders.'

'What about newsreaders?' asked Juliet, now holding her cheeks within her palms. 'They're all spoilt too?'

'When it comes to a woman newsreader,' said Tessa. 'Have you ever seen a really ugly, fat one? Seriously? And not just in this country but abroad?'

'Er, don't think …'

'Course you haven't! Now you can't tell me that somewhere out there in the wide world there ain't some really fat bird who can't read the fucking news. There's gotta be at least one. But do they get a job on *News At Ten*? On Sky? Fuck no! They probably have the right speaking voice, degrees and everything but they don't get the job 'cos they're too fucking fat and ugly.'

'I get your point, Tess,' said Juliet. She stood up to stretch her arms and legs. 'No need to go on about it. It's not my fault I look this way.'

Juliet sensed Tessa studying her as she performed her warm-down exercises. She touched her toes, stretched her hamstrings and bent her back. She then did a few knee bends before finishing by moving her head from side to side.

'In a way,' Tessa said. 'I feel sorry for Brenton and Clayton. I mean, look at you! Over forty and you're still gorgeous. Makes me sick! But seriously you have to let Brenton go. Make sure he knows there is absolutely *no* way that there's a chance of you two ever getting together again.'

'He knows that,' said Juliet. 'It has been over twenty years. We have coped with not making love on the spot every time we see each other since then, Tess.'

'You sure? I saw the way he looked at you at your mum's funeral. He's a jailbird to your beauty just like the leisure centre assistant. Let him go, Jules. Maybe write the odd letter, send him a birthday card if you have to with a badge on it. But don't visit him wherever he goes. For his own good.'

Juliet picked up her racquet and started to tap it on the floor. She stared into space and considered life without Brenton's presence in it. Tess is right, she concluded. But never see him again? I don't think I can do that. He's part of me. My brother. He's had such a shit life. If I don't look out for him then who will? I'll keep my distance but every now and again I'll have to see how he is. Isn't that what Mum would like me to do? He's still got a few issues he needs to work on.

'I can read you, Jules,' said Tess. 'I just know you. If he goes somewhere sooner or later you're gonna have this urge to go to him. *Don't* give in to it, Jules. Him going away to another country could be his last chance of building his own life; and I mean the personal part of his life. Don't mess it up for him, Jules. Stay away from him. If you don't, you might destroy him, fuck up his mind completely. Accept that with this thing you can't have what you want; you'll have to deal with that guilt of yours in a different way.'

'Don't worry, Tess,' said Juliet. 'I'll stay away from him … you're right.'

'Course I'm right,' grinned Tessa. 'I'll hold you to this. I'm not having you come to me a few months down the line telling me you have to see him because of all that, what is it? Genetic what-you-call-it?'

'Genetic Sexual Attraction, Tess.'

'It's a fancy word but it's total fucking twaddle. Who makes up that kinda bollocks? I'm warning, you, Jules. When he goes, stay away.'

Juliet stared at the ground beneath her and nodded.

The two friends said nothing to each other for the next few minutes. Instead they finished their drinks and watched the badminton game taking place to their left.

'You should've played one of them, Jules,' remarked Tessa. 'They're miles better than me.'

'I ain't that good.'

'Jules,' Tessa called, her eyes now closed.

'What is it, Tess?'

'The kids … the kids really miss their dad … what am I gonna do? I … I miss him too.'

Juliet embraced Tessa and Tessa's eyes started to water. 'Take it day by day,' said Juliet.

'I've been trying to,' said Tessa. 'But I feel so … *ugly.*'

Juliet gave Tessa a reassuring squeeze. 'You're not ugly, Tess.' She wondered who would hug her and reassure her when Brenton finally left. Her tears for him would have to be in isolation, just like they always were. Alone with her torment.

'Come on, Tess,' Juliet said. 'Let's get out of here and cheer ourselves up with something that bubbles in a glass.'

'Yeah, OK,' laughed Tessa. 'Get your arms off me! Don't want the guys around here thinking I'm a lesbo! Might harm my chances.'

Chapter 19

Going Greek with Bob Marley

LYING IN BREANNA'S BED, Malakai watched her sitting in front of her dressing table mirror in just her red bra and red panties. She was carefully applying her eye make-up and she spotted Malakai staring at her. She smiled. Finished with her eyes, Breanna applied a touch of lavender oil onto her hands and arms. She sniffed at it and grinned again as she caught Malakai's gaze in the mirror. 'What sweet you?' she asked.

'You do,' Malakai replied.

'Come on, man,' Breanna urged. 'Get your shower. We're s'posed to be meeting Sean and Jazz in what? Forty-five minutes. It's quarter past eight.'

'Do we have to go?' asked Malakai. He got out of bed and went to Breanna. 'Can't we set up base camp for the night?'

She looked at his naked body in the mirror and couldn't help giggling.

'What's so funny?' he asked. 'Man is kinda feeling inadequate when you're laughing like that.'

'Nothing,' chuckled Breanna.

Wrapping his arms around Breanna's neck, Malakai kissed her on her left cheek and they both looked at their reflections in the mirror. He helped Breanna to her feet. He kissed her throat then worked his way down to her breasts. He unclipped her bra and slid his right hand under her panties to squeeze her backside. 'Let me call Sean and tell him I'm sick. Or I'll tell him that you're sick and you need some TLC. Toe-knocking lovemaking and cuddling.'

'Malakai!' protested Breanna. 'He's your bredren! Besides, I can't let Jazz down. She just texted me half an hour ago. She wanted to know what I was wearing.'

Dropping down to his knees, Malakai started to kiss Breanna's navel. He turned her around and gave her lower back the same treatment.

'Malakai!'

'Say you're not feeling it,' said Malakai as he continued to kiss Breanna all over. 'Say you're not feeling it.'

Grabbing his manhood and twisting it, Breanna laughed. 'Are you feeling that? Go and get your shower before I pull this *inadequate* thing off!'

'What? Naked? You want me to go out into your hallway like this?'

'*Malakai!*'

'Alright, I'm going … you sure your paps and mum ain't here?'

'Yes, I'm sure. Did you hear the door open and close?'

'No … but we were kinda … knocking toes and kneecaps. I wasn't exactly concentrating on the front door.'

'They're not here,' said Breanna. 'As I said they went down to some local Labour party meeting; they're welcoming new members or something, well boring. So grab a towel from the top of my wardrobe and get your damn shower.'

Breanna started to fix her hair and Malakai found a purple towel and wrapped it around himself.

'Are you serious about the holiday?' Breanna asked, a tub of hair oil poised in her left hand. She watched Malakai's body language in the mirror.

'Blatantly!' replied Malakai. 'It'll be all nice. Waking up in the morning and not having to worry about your paps slicing my t'ings when I'm having my toast and Coco Pops. Yeah, man. Let's go somewhere hot and quiet. The sea is a *must*. And the hotel has to have a seriously sturdy bed so we can get medieval with each other and knock toes till they get bruised. *Blatantly!* You know that!'

Breanna couldn't stop smiling. 'So where? Where do you wanna go?'

'Like I said, somewhere quiet by the sea ... an island.'

'An island?' Breanna repeated. 'I'm feeling that. Somewhere in the Med.'

'Yeah, one of the Greek islands, *blatantly.* Where man could just go down to the beach, step into one of them wooden boats, give his girl the paddles, whip her so she starts rowing, catch two fish, drink two glass of local wine, nibble nuff olives, swallow untold grapes, burn a spliff and have medieval sex like a gladiator before he has a fight to the death.'

'*You* can do the paddling!'

'And we can sing that Bob Marley tune. *We'll be together, with a roof right over our head, we'll share the shelter, of our single bed, is this love, is this love, is this love that I'm feeling!*'

'Malakai,' called Breanna.

'Yeah, Bree. You feeling what I'm feeling? My mum's always singing this; *I want to love you! Every day and every night, we'll be together ...*'

'No ... just please *don't* sing. You make the tune sound bad.'

Twenty minute later, Malakai was pulling on his jeans. Breanna was styling a kiss-curl over her right cheek. She had chosen to wear black slacks, a white top and a brown half-sleeve leather jacket. A variety of wooden bangles were on her wrists and she wore wooden Nefertiti earrings.

'I'm gonna have to use your deodorant, Bree,' said Malakai. 'Mine's at home. Hope peeps who sniff me don't think I'm going on like a girl.'

'Stop being stupid! Most people can't tell the difference.'

'So Sean's twenty-two today,' said Malakai. 'To tell you the truth he needs a night out. *Blatantly.* I wouldn't like to be stuck up in his flat with his mum. She can go on a bit.'

'He hasn't invited too many peeps, has he?' asked Breanna. 'It should be a low-profile t'ing. Considering his situation.'

'No, but I saw him yesterday and Jazz was texting nuff people about this t'ing at the White House. And Sean told one of the DJs so they can send out a special request for him.'

'Jazz is Miss Gossip,' laughed Breanna. 'Last night she called me and told me that Sean made a move on her. *Lord!* She went into so much detail I thought he was making a move on me!'

'Ha ha, yeah,' laughed Malakai. 'She can chat.'

Patting down her hair, Breanna gazed into the mirror and asked, 'So? What do you think?'

'I think it's gonna be a *sick* evening,' replied Malakai. 'Don't wanna stay too long though. I got my return ticket for here.'

'*Not* about the evening, about the way I look?'

'You're alright.'

'Alright?' Breanna turned around. Her hands were on her hips. She glared at Malakai. 'Just alright? You know how long I've been sitting here nicing up my face and you say I'm only *alright?*

Pulling on his denim top, Malakai walked over to Breanna. He bent down on both knees and held her face within his palms. He kissed her on the forehead then kissed her delicately on her mouth. Breanna smiled.

'What's that tune your mum was playing the other day?' Malakai asked.

'Last Sunday afternoon when she was playing her old-school disco while she was cooking?'

'Yeah.'

'Barry White?'

'Yeah. What was it called? *My First, My Last, My Everything.* Yeah, that's it. Says it all. *Blatantly.*'

Breanna grinned again and returned the kisses with interest.

'After the holiday,' said Breanna, 'if we both start saving, we could have our own place in a couple of years' time? What do you say?'

'I feel that,' replied Malakai as he laced up his white trainers. 'Can't wait to get out of my place. It might buck up Mum's ideas and force her to get a job. Yeah, I'm feeling that. Can you cook though? And a washing machine is not like an alien to you? You know where the *on* button is?'

'Malakai!'

It was twenty past nine when Breanna was driving west along Acre Lane. Brandy's *It's Not Worth It* shrieked from the car stereo. Malakai was nodding his head. Breanna was concentrating on the road ahead but when she stopped at traffic lights she was checking her face in the rear-view mirror.

'Do you think Jazz is pretty?' she asked.

'What?'

'Do you think Jazz is pretty?' Breanna repeated.

'Why you asking me that?'

'Just wondered,' replied Breanna shrugging her shoulders.

'She's alright,' Malakai answered. 'What do you expect me to say?'

Breanna turned into Clapham Park Road. 'Just wondered that's all.'

'Yeah, she's kinda pretty,' Malakai said.

'Prettier than me?' Breanna wanted to know. She glanced at Malakai, expecting an answer.

'Bree, I shouldn't even have to answer that, *blatantly!* Remember, you're the first, last, *everyt'ing!* What more do I have to do to show you? We got somet'ing good going on. And I'm not going anywhere and I ain't looking at anyone else. You get me?'

'Sorry, Malakai,' apologised Breanna shaking her head. 'It's just that … sometimes … sometimes I feel that someone really good looking is gonna take you away. You know, someone with breasts up to her throat, a backside you can roll a spliff on and wearing a weave as long as the red carpet outside the Oscars.'

'Turn left into Notre Dame estate,' said Malakai pointing a finger. 'You'll find parking space in there; you can't be too careful with those wardens about. Them bastards work well late.'

Breanna did as she was told. Did that come across too needy? she thought. Is he gonna think I'm really insecure now? He must've noticed it already. Get a hold of yourself, girl! Why you messing up a good night? But isn't it best to tell him how you feel? 'Cos maybe one day some better looking bitch than myself *will* take him away. *Stop* going on negative, Bree! Why can't you just enjoy the night? *Stop* bringing up your issues! Wish I was as good looking as Mum. *Stop* thinking that! You're OK. And Malakai's sitting beside you. He's *not* sitting beside any other girl but *you!* Maybe we shoulda stayed at my place and chill in bed? He might take a fancy to one of the girls at this White House place tonight? If he does I'm gonna maul his fucking balls like a fucked-off lion!

Climbing out of the car, Breanna saw some boys playing football under the streetlights. Two teenage girls were watching from a second-floor window. Somewhere on the third floor, a child was laughing out loud. Below, a white vest-wearing teenager was straining to hold on to the leash of his bull terrier and two black guys were talking to each other in their parked cars. A black cat was watching over everything from a wall overlooking the large communal dustbins.

Malakai walked around the front of Breanna's car and reached out to her. He interlocked his fingers with hers and gazed at her. 'Bree, I ain't going nowhere and I ain't looking at no one. There's just you and your skills in paddling and in the kitchen. *Blatantly!* So stop fretting.'

Holding hands, Breanna and Malakai walked out of the estate. It was a mild night and they could hear rap music from somewhere above back-dropped by the hum of traffic on Clapham Park Road. They crossed the road at the lights and could see late-evening shoppers emerging out of the supermarket car park. They felt the wind of a passing number 37 bus. About thirty yards away many young people were queuing up to gain entry to the White House nightclub. Two boys on small bicycles were performing wheelies and spins on the pavement. Three white kids were sitting on a nearby low wall smoking cigarettes and drinking beer. Two bouncers at the nightclub door were keeping the queue in order. Breanna heard the *thump, thump, thump* of an R&B track she couldn't quite name. She squeezed Malakai's hand. He kissed her on her left cheek.

'Bree!' Jazz called. 'Bree!'

Joining the queue from a bus stop was Sean and Jazz. Performing a strut, Sean bounced up to Malakai and touched fists. 'Yes, bredren,' Sean greeted. 'You reach. We're both kinda late though but I'm ready to get my Clap Town dance on.'

'Hi, sis,' Jazz greeted Breanna. 'Sophie's inside already, she just texted me. Cerise is on her way and Joanna just texted me a few minutes ago telling me she can't reach. She's lame, man, always letting me down at the last minute. Fuck knows where Venetia is. Tried to call her but her phone's on voicemail.'

'Joanna has got Jerome to look after,' said Breanna. 'Maybe she couldn't get a babysitter? As for Venetia, she's got issues with Cerise.'

The bouncers were checking and patting everybody as they entered the club.

'It's gonna be ram, man,' said Sean. He performed a dance step. 'Yeah, bredren, I'm gonna get my Clap Town dance on.'

Suddenly, a shot was fired. Heads turned in the direction of the bang. People screamed. Some dropped to the floor. One girl looked to the road, thinking she heard an exploding tyre. Three guys and one girl ran in different directions. The bullet grazed

Sean's left arm. The boys on the bikes pedalled away keeping their heads as low as possible. Seven people ran into the club. The bouncers closed the doors. Malakai shoved Breanna to the ground. He turned around. He saw a man with a gun. He was wearing a balaclava and black leather gloves. His jeans seemed to be falling from his waist. His arm, shaking slightly, was outstretched. The gun was smoking from the first shot. He was aiming at Sean. Sean held on to a screaming Jazz. He shoved her between the gunman and himself. People were still running. The music inside stopped. Someone was banging the inside of the club's doors. Malakai moved towards the gunman. The gunman was trying to get a fix on Sean's head. Jazz wriggled and squirmed out of Sean's hold. She tried to run but tripped over in her heels. She fell over and scraped her head on the pavement. Malakai was only a few feet away from the gunman. The gunman turned around. He saw Malakai. He closed his eyes. He squeezed the trigger. Sean ran towards Acre Lane. Screams rang out again. Malakai was shot in the head. The bullet entered just below his right ear. He was dead before he dropped to the ground. A number 35 bus braked sharply. A man came out of his car to have a look. The gunman hot-stepped it towards Clapham Common tube station. Girls were still shrieking. Men were panicking. Malakai's blood stained the pavement. Breanna opened her eyes. She turned her head this way and that. She saw Malakai. She saw he wasn't moving. She saw the gaping exit wound that had exploded his right cheek. She saw his blood. She crawled over to him. She heard people crying and shrieking. She reached Malakai. She held his head. Blood seeped onto her hands. She could feel her heartbeat vibrate in her throat. Malakai's eyes were closed. She gently placed her forehead on top of his. Her palms supported the back of his head. She heard people shouting and cursing. She paid them no mind. She could only look at Malakai. His peaceful face.

'Oh God!' Jazz screamed as she saw Malakai. 'Oh God! Please somebody. Somebody. Oh Jesus Christ. Oh fucking Lord!'

Somebody took hold of Jazz. They took her away. Breanna held onto Malakai's head. Her vision was blurred with tears but she heard people moving around her. She lost all sense of time. She heard sirens. The next thing she remembered was someone helping her to her feet. She couldn't recall if it was a policeman or a paramedic. Then these policemen in strange white jump-suits, medical gloves and face masks arrived. She watched them from a police car and it occurred to her that they looked like they were dressed for skiing. She recalled the opening credits of a James Bond film. What was it? She asked herself. *The Living Day-lights?* No, don't think so. *The Spy Who Loved Me?* Can't fucking remember. I know Roger Moore was in it. Malakai could've been an actor. Yeah, why not? He could've been James Bond.

Clapham Park Road was cordoned off with police tape. The men in the white jumpsuits were on their knees on the pave-ment. In their hands, Breanna noticed, were little brushes. I never asked Malakai if he could paint, thought Breanna. He had nice, delicate hands. Tender. So maybe he could've been a good painter. Or a good designer. Maybe he could have drawn a por-trait of me? That would've been so nice. Blatantly. He could've used his hands to massage me on holiday, hold my face, make love to me. Yeah, on one of those Greek islands. '*With a roof right over our head, we'll share the shelter, of my single bed ...*'

Chapter 20

Apology Not Accepted

Eleven days later

SITTING IN FRONT OF HER MIRROR, Breanna stared blankly into it. The memory of Malakai's coffin being lowered into the ground was still fresh. So was the smell of dried earth. The silence of Malakai's mother and her harsh gaze were impossible to erase from her mind. Also hard to forget was the endless black. Hats, suits, ties, skirts, shoes and even gloves. Malakai never dressed in black, she recalled. He liked bright colours, living colours.

All those fake smiles, Breanna reflected. People being nice to me, people being nice to Malakai's mum. I wonder how long that will last. I overheard one woman whispering how Malakai's mum is a benefit queen and this was coming to her because she was a rubbish mother. People always act at funerals. It was all so unreal. So fucking unfair. Does God just take all the good ones early and let the bad ones live out their selfish lives here? Does he take the good ones away so the rest of us try and struggle to be as good as them? But God knows we can't be like them so he lets us live. And all of us left living know we can never be as good as the good ones that He takes away from us. Hell isn't somewhere where bad people go to when they die. Hell is here. Hell is trying to deal with someone taken away who you've grown to love. *Fucking bastards!* I don't care what the fuck the churchman said about a compassionate God and Malakai is in His arms now. *Fuck that! He* took away my Malakai.

'It wasn't your time,' she whispered. 'It just wasn't your time.

But God still took you anyway. That fucking cruel God took you anyway. You fucked up big time!'

Why? She thought again. What fucking idiot just fires into a crowd? Doesn't he respect life at all? Why couldn't the fucking killer wait to get Sean on his own? Don't these fucking people have a brain? Don't they think? He probably thinks he's so bad now. *I'm the man!* he's probably saying to himself. He's probably boasting to his crew right now. Probably waiting for next Friday so he can read about himself in the *South London Press*. He's probably writing about it on his fucking MySpace page. I bet he's got a pic of him on his site doing some bullshit macho pose. What is wrong with these idiots? Don't they have parents who bring them up right? His bredrens are probably saying, yeah, you're a soldier. *A fucking soldier!* Is that all they live for? To be called a soldier by their wasteman crew? Don't these people have a fucking conscience? They shot the wrong man! They know it! But don't want to talk. Don't want to come forward to the police or even make an anonymous phone call. Fucking cowards they are. *Cowards!* Fuck them! Fuck them all! I swear if I had a gun myself. *I swear!* I'd kill all the wastemen out there. Kill them all.

Tears ran down Breanna's face. They weren't tears of loss. Tears of anger. *Why?* she repeated in her mind. Some childish fucking feud probably. Sean talked so they just have to try and kill him. They'd do anything to keep up their badmen status. So fucking childish. *Why?* They make me sick. They all make me sick. Protecting their ends, protecting their hoods, protecting their soldiers! Fuck them! All of them!

There was a knock on the bedroom door.

'Who is it?' asked Breanna.

'It's Mum, Breanna. Can I come in?'

'Yeah.'

Juliet entered the bedroom. She paused and looked at her daughter before embracing her. 'You OK?' she asked.

'Yes, Mum,' replied Breanna without turning around.

'Sean is downstairs to see you,' Juliet revealed. 'He's there with a couple of police officers. He's under protection. He said he has to talk to you. I told him I'd have to ask you first. You don't have to if you don't want to.'

Still gazing at her reflection in the mirror, Breanna calmly replied, 'Yeah, I'll see him. I'll be down in a sec.'

Juliet wiped away Breanna's tears with her right hand. She then held her shoulders, gave her a look that mothers reserve for their children and hugged her. 'You sure?'

'I'm sure, Mum.'

Breanna paused at the top of the stairs. 'Mum, hold up.'

'What is it, Breanna?'

'Just want to say thank you.'

'That's alright, Breanna.'

'No, seriously,' said Breanna. 'You've been brilliant. Helping with the funeral, talking to the police, preparing that statement for them and even helping with that BBC London thing. You were brilliant, Mum. Malakai's mum is so grateful.'

'Yes, she thanked me,' said Juliet.

'She wasn't in no state to talk to those news people,' said Breanna. 'Nor was I. Thanks for looking after all that … I just hope someone comes forward soon.'

'Come on, Breanna,' smiled Juliet. 'Sean is waiting. He's suffered a terrible loss too. Be gentle.'

Breanna's gaze hardened and she squeezed her left thumb.

Juliet led Breanna down to the lounge. Clayton was making cups of tea for the police officers in the kitchen. Sean was sitting in an armchair. He was nervously rubbing his hands together and he couldn't keep his feet still. His eyes were shifting. He was playing about with his mobile phone. When he saw Breanna he stood up. 'Do you …?' Juliet offered, 'do you want me to give you some privacy?'

'No, Mum,' Breanna answered calmly. She looked at Sean. 'Sit down.'

'I'm really sorry,' said Sean, shaking his head. 'So sorry.'

His eyes were reddened from anxiety and exhaustion. Breanna guessed he had hardly slept since that ... when greedy God took Malakai away. Sean looks like a little boy lost, she observed. Pathetic! Look at him all nervous. He can hardly stand up. Fucking wasteman! What's he doing here? If he thinks he can just say sorry then he's got something coming to him.

'Can I get you a drink?' offered Breanna. 'Sit down, man. I'm not the queen.'

'No, no,' said Sean taking his seat again. 'I ... I don't wanna drink. I just wanted to see you. Tell you how I'm sorry. *Trust!* Malakai was one of the good ones. Much better man than me. I was well lucky to have him as a bredren. *Trust!* He was always telling me I must fix up. I know you're probably blaming me but ...'

'Yes,' Breanna interrupted. 'He was a much better man than you.'

Juliet glanced at Breanna and could hardly comprehend how she seemed so composed and in control of herself.

'Yes, I am blaming you,' continued Breanna. She folded her arms and glanced at her mother. She then began to walk around the room. Sean's eyes followed her. He started to rub his hands again. The polite conversation drifting over from the kitchen paused.

'Me and Malakai talked about you a lot,' said Breanna, now glaring at Sean. 'Yeah, we talked about everything. We talked about how you wanted to start shotting weed. How you wanted to be a badman. How you wanted *respect* from man on road ...'

'Breanna, is this the right ...' Juliet butted in.

'He needs to hear this, Mum,' Breanna said, still staring at Sean. 'But Malakai knew you. He said you were always fronting up, pretending you're this and that but you couldn't be a badman 'cos deep inside you don't have manness inside you. Manness, yes, Malakai's word. He was good at making up new words. He could've been a writer. He could've been anything … He told me how you would always run away from fights. Yeah, *manness*. Malakai had that. He had a shit upbringing just like you. But he didn't want to be no badman. He didn't want to be part of some fucked-up crew that traded in showing how bad they were. He didn't want to be no fucking soldier. He was man enough to try something different. Man enough to do something positive with his plumbing training and stuff. But *you …*'

'But Bree if I can just …'

'Shut the fuck up and listen!' Breanna raised her voice. Juliet was about to say something but decided not to. Clayton entered the room with half a mug of tea. He stood in the doorway and looked at Breanna. She didn't notice him.

'And he wasn't wrong, was he?' Breanna added. 'Malakai tried to protect us and you *ran*. Before that you even put Jazz in front of you. What were you thinking? That some stinking wasteman with a gun would give a shit about shooting women? They don't give a fuck who they shoot. You should know, you're always around wastemen on road and want their respect.'

'I'm, I'm not,' Sean stuttered. '*T-trust!*'

'No manness,' affirmed Breanna. 'Listen good, Sean, 'cos after this I don't want to see your backside again … you're a walking stereotype. A wasteman. You're nothing. You ain't going no place and you ain't going nowhere. You give positive young black guys like Malakai a bad name. You haven't got anything to offer the world, no ambition, no thinking of trying to make yourself better. *Nothing! You're fuck all!*'

'Breanna!' Juliet remonstrated.

Breanna ignored her. Clayton glanced from Juliet to Breanna. 'The only thing you have to offer is to show your crew how bad you are. Show them how street you are. Show them how much of a fucking soldier you are. That's all you live for, innit? To get your *respect* from other wasteman on road. And at the end of the day, you couldn't even get that. That's why they tried to kill you. I saw for myself. You're a mouse. You're a fucking coward! They should throw yellow paint on your backside wherever you go or mark it on your forehead with that stuff that doesn't come off.'

'But, Bree …'

'Don't even call my name!' shouted Breanna. 'And don't even try to call Jazz. She don't want to see you again either. If you try texting her or even messaging her on Hotmail I will *fuck* you up myself! And trust me, I mean that!'

Clayton's eyes widened. Juliet's mouth opened.

'You're nothing,' added Breanna. Her eyes were now full of tears. She swabbed her face and continued. 'You wanted to come here, didn't you? Tell me you're all sorry. Tell me you're suffering. That way you won't feel so guilty. And it'll be no problem, you probably thought. Not from Bree. She's just Malakai's stush girlfriend. Nice laid-back Bree! She talks all nice and she comes from a decent family. She'll understand. She'll know how sorry I am. She'll forgive everything. Yeah, Malakai told me how you thought I was stush and stuck up. Didn't quite go to plan, did it? So, Sean, I want you to take your backside off my mum's armchair AND GET THE FUCK OUT OF MY HOUSE!'

Turning her back on Sean, Breanna marched out of the room and stomped her way upstairs. Clayton and Juliet exchanged glances. Sean dropped his head.

'I'll … I'll see if she's OK,' said Clayton.

Clayton followed Breanna. Juliet sat down opposite Sean as he covered his face with his hands. He started to sob.

'I'm, I'm really sorry, Mrs Hylton … I didn't mean any of this to happen. *Trust!* Seriously I didn't …'

'I know,' said Juliet. 'But you can still help Breanna and Malakai.'

'How?'

'By trying to think who did this to Malakai.'

'I've been trying, Mrs Hylton. He was wearing a mask. He didn't say anything.'

'You *must* try,' insisted Juliet. 'Maybe there was something familiar about his body shape?'

'I ... I don't know,' said Sean. He was still covering his face with his hands.

'Sean,' Juliet said softly. 'Malakai's dead. You saw at the funeral how much that affected and still affects his family and friends. You *must* try.'

'I'll try.'

'OK then,' nodded Juliet. 'I'll see you out.'

'There's just one more thing, Mrs Hylton,' said Sean, now taking his hands away from his face.

'What's that?'

'I wanna change myself. Learn something. *Trust!* Get a job. I know you've got a brother who's a builder, right?'

'Yes, Brenton.'

'I just wanna learn, you know, pick things up. I don't mind if it's just a few hours a week. I don't mind if I'm just sweeping up and stuff ...'

'OK, Sean,' Juliet nodded. 'I'll let him know.'

Sean stood up. 'Tell Bree I'm sorry ... really sorry. I know it's all my ...'

'Just give her time,' Juliet said. 'Right now she's crushed. I really don't know how long it'll take her to get over it. We'll all have to help her through it.'

The two police officers were waiting in the hallway and one of them went outside first to check that everything was safe. When he gave the all-clear, Sean was quickly bundled into the police car. With her arms folded, Juliet watched until the car had disappeared from view. She then went inside and thought it best if Breanna spent a little time with Clayton. It'll be good for their relationship if Clayton can help her get over all this. But Christ! she thought. She has Brenton's cold temper. The way her eyes bored into him! I thought the poor boy was going to shrink. She'll never be the same. How is she going to come out the other side of all this?

Chapter 21

Shadow of the Past

Three weeks later

WALKING ALONG ENDYMION ROAD that led off Brixton Hill, Sean admired the houses on the street as he checked the numbers. He also looked inside the interior of a 4x4 Honda and was impressed. 'If my paps never died my fam coulda lived in a street like this,' he whispered to himself. 'Yeah, Mum woulda liked living here. She might've been driving a car like this listening to her old-school soul.'

The short rain shower had stopped but daylight was fading. High above, a plane, blinking red, disappeared above a roof of grey cloud. There was an event at the nearby church but Sean didn't notice the people congregating about the entrance of the building. He felt sweaty in his thin anorak and he shook off his hood. He wiped his forehead. He paid no attention to the barking of a Rottweiler dog across the road that was being led by a young white guy.

He finally arrived at the number he was looking for. He pressed the intercom buzzer for the top flat. He slipped his hand inside his anorak and felt the bread knife he had taken from his mother's kitchen. He wiped his forehead again then let out a sigh. He tried to compose himself and control his breathing. 'You can do this, Sean,' he said to himself. 'You ain't no fucking coward. I'm as brave as a next man. Don't care what Breanna or what Malakai used to say. You can do this. *Trust!*'

'Is that you, Sean?' said Brenton through the crackly intercom.

'Yes, bredren,' Sean answered. 'It's me.'

There was another buzzing sound and Sean pushed the door open. He wiped his feet on the doormat inside, palmed away the sweat that was building on his temples and exhaled. He felt for his knife again before he set off climbing five flights of carpeted stairs. He reached Brenton's front door and found it open. He paused before entering. He slowed his breathing. He closed his eyes for a short second before taking a stride inside.

'Is that you?' Brenton called from the kitchen. 'I'm just washing up a few t'ings. Sit down in the front room, man. I'll be with you in a sec.'

Sitting down at the dinner table in the lounge, Sean slowly took in his surroundings. He looked at a framed photo of a sixteen-year-old Breanna that was staring out from the glass cabinet. So innocent, he thought. Little did she know back then that her future man would be shot down by a bullet meant for me. Oh *fuck*.

He could hear the sound of running water and the chink and clatter of cutlery being thrown onto a draining board. He could feel his T-shirt sticking to his chest and back. His sweaty boxers felt uncomfortable against his crotch and his backside. He felt for his knife again.

Drying his hands with a tea towel, Brenton sat opposite Sean. 'Oh, I forgot,' he said. 'You want somet'ing to drink? I've got a brew in the fridge.'

'No, thanks,' replied Sean. His right hand was still inside his jacket.

'Do you wanna take your jacket off?'

'Nah, nah. I'm good. I can't stay too long.'

'You wanna towel to dry off the rain?'

'I'll be alright,' said Sean.

'OK,' said Brenton. He looked Sean over for a long second. 'My sister Juliet tells me you're hunting work.'

'Yeah, I am,' answered Sean. 'Malakai, may he rest in peace, always said I shouldn't stop looking and asking. *Trust.* So I'm asking you.'

'You have any kinda experience? Like you ever fixed on a lock into a door or even hung a door?'

'No.'

'You ever helped putting down wooden flooring or somet'ing like that?'

'Er, no. But I can learn, innit?'

Brenton took a long hard look at Sean. He's obviously nervous, he observed. Why's he sweating? Ain't that hot in here. Must want a job bad. Good! He should want a job bad. Seems like he wants to turn his life around. What will Breanna say if I give him a little somet'ing? I wonder if she still isn't chatting to him? Hope it'll be alright with her.

'I can't give you anyt'ing full-time, you understand?'

'Yeah,' Sean nodded.

'But maybe I can give you like, sixteen, maybe twenty hours a week. Some overtime when it's needed. I've got nuff work coming up but I need someone reliable.'

'Yeah,' Sean nodded again. 'Course you do. *Trust!*'

'I want someone on serious time, someone who doesn't ding me at the last minute and say they can't make it. That ain't no fucking good to me, you understand?'

'Yes, bredren.'

'You ain't my bredren,' rebuked Brenton. 'Call me by my name. Brenton or Mr Brown. I ain't your friend on street. I'm your employer. Remember that.'

'Yeah, I will.'

'And if you're gonna work with me I don't wanna see you chatting on your mobile all day,' stressed Brenton. 'Them t'ings really fuck me off. If your mum's on the way to hospital then yeah, I can allow that but if a friend is dinging you about some fit girl he saw in Tesco's then I'm *not* allowing that, y'understand?'

'Yeah I hear you,' said Sean. 'Man s'posed to be working, innit. It's a big disrespect if man's chatting on his mobile all day. I know that. For real.'

'Whatever I do at work I'll show you how to do it,' explained Brenton. 'Use your initiative, watch and learn closely.'

'That's a given, man … er, I mean, Brenton.'

'On most of my jobs I work with a painter and decorator,' informed Brenton. 'His name is Daniel. White guy. Sometimes you might have to give him a hand.'

'That's all sweet,' nodded Sean.

'I have to tell you one t'ing though,' said Brenton. 'Be honest with you and t'ing.'

'What's that?'

'I'm leaving this country by the end of the year,' revealed Brenton. 'So that gives you what? Six months and a bit working for me, if you like. I'd well understand if some other job came up though and you wanted to step to it.'

Sean nodded. 'Yeah, I hear that. But man out there don't wanna give a job to someone like me who done bird. So I don't think I'll be getting too many offers. *Trust!*'

'But in the time we've got,' added Brenton, 'I'll try and teach you everyt'ing I know. It's up to you after that.'

'I'm on that,' nodded Sean again.

'Most of the time I'm working on people's property,' explained Brenton. 'And when you're working inside people's property you have to respect that. Seriously. So if the owner's there and you wanna piss then you ask permission to use his or her piss pot, you understand? If you wanna use a mug and make a cup of coffee then you ask permission to pick up that mug, you understand? If it's one bitch of a hot day and you find a Cornetto ice cream in someone's fridge, *don't* trouble it, you understand? You get my drift? If there's a mat outside the door then use it and always be polite. Use Mr this and Mrs that or Miss whatever.'

'Yeah, yeah, I'm on that.'

'*Good!*'

Brenton smiled. He slapped Sean on his right shoulder in a gesture of welcome. Sean felt his knife jump and move an inch before it settled down. He palmed away the sweat on his forehead once more and then pulled up his anorak zip close to his throat.

'I've got some chicken patties in the fridge,' said Brenton standing up. 'I was gonna put two in the microwave for myself. You want one?'

'Er, chicken pattie? Yeah. Why not. Kinda hungry.'

Brenton went to the kitchen. Sean closed his eyes and then reopened them again. He took in a deep breath. He pulled down his jacket zip a few inches. He felt for the handle of the bread knife. His hand was clammy. He exhaled. He heard Brenton clattering about in his freezer. He wiped the sweat of his palms onto his jeans. He stood up and looked into the kitchen. He saw Brenton kneeling down, looking for the frozen chicken patties. He took two paces towards him. He stopped. He groped for his knife. His right thumb and forefinger rested on top of the handle. He walked the rest of the way to the kitchen. Brenton was still searching for the patties. With his left hand Sean swabbed away the sweat from his face. He could feel perspiration dripping from his armpits onto his ribs.

Coward, Sean thought to himself. Breanna called me a *coward*. She said I was nothing. I won't be nothing if I merk him. No one can call me a pussy if I shank him. But he's offering me a job. Giving me a chance. No one's given me a proper chance before. Except Malakai. He always thought I could do something. Rest in peace, bredren.

Turning around, Brenton was alarmed to see Sean so close. 'Found them!' Brenton said, smiling big. 'Gotta sort out that fridge, man. It's a mess. Did you want somet'ing?'

'Yeah, yeah,' said Sean, bringing his hands down to his sides. 'I do wanna drink. Not a brew though, water will do. Cold water. Ice if you got it. I'm feeling kinda hot.'

'Yeah I can see that,' laughed Brenton. 'Water is all I've got. Ain't got no soft drinks, juice or anyt'ing. Sit down and rest up, man. I'll get it.'

Brenton went to fetch a glass of water. Sean watched him bang the ice cubes out of their tray. He placed five cubes in Sean's glass. He offered the drink to Sean.

'Thanks,' said Sean. He took it and returned to the dinner table. He drank half of it in one go.

Two minutes later the microwave beeped and Brenton served Sean with a hot chicken pattie. 'Thanks,' said Sean once again.

'I'm just going to the piss pot,' said Brenton. 'Soon come.'

Brenton disappeared into the hallway. Sean took a sip of cold water. He nibbled on his chicken pattie and took another sip of water. He felt for his knife. He grabbed the handle. He took it out from his jacket. He studied the blade. He ran his finger over the cutting edge. He imagined blood running down its length. He visualised the knife sticking out of Brenton's chest. The man fucked up Mum's life, thought Sean. Fucked up my life too. Even if I do bird again no one can call me a pussy. And bird ain't too bad. At least I can do my weights there, play b-ball and play five a side on the AstroTurf. Food ain't bad either. Three meals a day. If I do go down then I hope they don't send me too far away. I hope they send me to a place that Mum can reach. If I shank him no one can call me a coward. Not if I shank a proper Brixton badman. He's old school but he's still a bonafide badman. Nuff old peeps still chat about him. The *steppin' volcano*. My paps was a G and people were scared of him. They'll be scared of me if I shank *him*. Yeah, at least I'll get some respect ... but he offered me work. Ain't no one out there who's offered me shit.

The sound of a toilet flushing and a latch being pulled prompted Sean to hurriedly put the knife back inside his jacket.

He took a generous gulp of water and then bit off a sizable chunk of chicken pattie. Brenton emerged just as the microwave beeped again. He went to the kitchen and took out his two chicken patties. He took a bottled beer from the fridge and joined Sean at the dinner table.

Sean continued eating. He took another sip of water. He looked up and saw Brenton staring at him. 'I've got to tell you something,' Sean said.

'Tell me what?' asked Brenton. 'Oh, by the way. When you start, make sure you remember to give me your national insurance number. You alright to start next Monday? Oh, give me your shoe size too. So I can get you a pair of safety boots. You wouldn't believe the tribulation I would get if you stepped on a raas piece of nail in your trainers on your first day. I need to get you some safety glasses for when you drill and t'ing. I've got a spare helmet. It should fit 'cos you ain't got a 'fro. It's all about the safety these days, believe me.'

'I have to tell you something,' repeated Sean. He was now fiddling with his thumbs and looking at the table.

'Tell me what?' Brenton wanted to know. He was watching Sean's hands.

'You, er ...'

'I what?'

'You knew my paps.'

'Yeah? What was his name?'

Sean pressed his palms together and interlocked his fingers. He sensed sweat dripping down his chin. He felt his heart pump faster. He glanced at Brenton. He quickly looked away.

'Chat to me, man,' urged Brenton. 'What's troubling you?'

'Er, Terry ... Terry Flynn ... you killed him.'

Not moving in his chair, Brenton just stared at Sean. He studied his forehead and his eyes. His mind rewound back to 1980. The images and sounds were at first blurry but they were becoming clear. Brixton tube station. The hum of the escalator. The fight with Flynn on the platform. Flynn biting into his shoulder. Flynn spitting out a mouthful of skin and flesh. The agonising pain. The blood. The crackle of the live rail. The gust of wind. The headlights of the tube train. Flynn trying to reach his knife. Flynn's scream. Flynn's body being dragged by the train. Flynn's arm tearing off. The shrieks. The fainting woman. The silence from Flynn after his wailing. His still body. The blood. The mess. The mangled arm. The stench. People running. People staring. A lone voice shouting. His adrenaline racing. Trying to catch his breath.

Standing up, Brenton turned his back on Sean and walked towards the glass cabinet where he paused. 'He tried to kill me, Sean,' he finally said. 'We tried to kill each other. I was the one who got lucky.'

'Mum tries to give me the story that Paps was alright,' said Sean. 'You know, a man trying to do his best. But some old-school Bricky man tell me he was a proper G. A lineman. I heard he jacked and shanked nuff nigg ... er, I mean brothers.'

Brenton nodded. He was now staring at a framed photo of Juliet in his glass cabinet.

'Mum always blamed you,' continued Sean. 'She reckons that if he lived Paps and her woulda made a go of t'ings.'

'Maybe they would have,' admitted Brenton. He turned around and faced Sean. 'Those were mad days. Me and your paps had this beef ...'

'Yeah, I know,' said Sean. 'They called you the steppin' volcano right?'

Brenton nodded.

Sean took another two bites from his chicken pattie and finished his water. Brenton watched him but in his mind he saw something quite different. He was back in 1980. Outside Brixton tube station. In excruciating pain he jumped on a Routemaster bus. He had to see Juliet. Passengers moved out of his way. He couldn't stop his own bleeding. He felt dizzy. Had to see Juliet, he remembered. Just had to see her. Blood was spotting the floor of the top deck on the bus. For some reason he tried to stamp it out with his feet. What was he thinking? What a fucked-up day that was, he recalled. Almost dead and found out Juliet was pregnant. Seems like yesterday …

'Mr Brown!' called Sean. 'Mr Brown. You alright?'

'What? Yes, sorry. Give me a sec.'

Brenton returned to the kitchen. He filled a glass with cold water and drank it in one go. He stared into the sink. He felt his face getting warm so he sprinkled water on the top of his head. He closed his eyes, took in a deep breath and exhaled. Son of Terror Flynn! He thought. Badman Terror Flynn. He terrorised nuff people, jacked a trailerload of man back in the day. Floyd ain't gonna believe this. Jesus on a fucking moped! Christ on a raas claat bike! Life sometimes funny. What do I do? I can't take away the job I've just given him. That would be fucked-up and bad-mind. Son of Terror Flynn? Boy! What a palaver. He ain't looking for revenge, is he? He might wanna kill my backside.

Taking in one more deep breath, Brenton returned to the lounge. Sean watched him all the way. Brenton slowly sat down. 'I didn't kill him,' he said. 'Yeah, we were going to war on each other. We had this mad blood feud going on. But the tube train killed him.'

Sean studied Brenton's face as if he had to write an essay about it. He said nothing for the next few minutes. Brenton started eating his patties again. He drank his beer. Only when he finished did Sean speak again. 'One of my paps old-time bredrens said you was a proper warrior, not scared of nothing.'

'Not scared of nothing?' repeated Brenton. 'That ain't true.'

'But you weren't scared of my paps rep or anybody else.'

'I was scared of everyt'ing,' said Brenton. 'Your paps scared the living backside outta me. I knew he was after me. I couldn't sleep at night. Could hardly walk on street without looking over my shoulder.'

'But you still went to war with him,' interrupted Sean. 'Why?'

Brenton thought about it. 'I'm not sure. I think I was a bit cuckoo, you know, crazy. I was reckless. I didn't have nothing to lose. But I was still scared. I think I couldn't stand the fact that he was looking for me. It seriously stressed me out so I thought what the fuck? I might as well look for him.'

Sean leaned forward in his chair. He searched Brenton's eyes. 'What? What makes you brave? What makes a man brave? What makes them stand up and fight when a next man is thinking of running away?'

Brenton scratched behind his right ear. He was about to say something but paused. He gazed at Sean. 'Depends on what you think is brave,' he finally said. 'It's not all about going to war with a man. Some people are not cut out for that shit. Some are. But whether you are or not it don't mean that you're all brave. Sometimes being brave is about doing something positive when your own bredrens are laughing at you. That's brave.'

'What do you mean?' asked Sean.

'I used to know a rapper,' Brenton answered. 'In my day we used to call them toasters. He wanted to be the best so everywhere he went he took his notepad with him, seriously. He would write his lyrics down and nuff yout's did laugh at him. Back in my day no rapper trod street with a pencil and paper, y'understand? Anyway, this rapper used to have this small dictionary, you know, one of them pocket-sized t'ings. He used to go to the library and read nuff books, you understand? Man and man would laugh at him, take the piss outta him, kick all his books outta his hands. But he left Brixton to go Jamaica and become massive.'

'What was his name?' Sean asked.

'Ranking T-saurus,' replied Brenton. 'He could chat lyrics all night. He got a recording contract with some American label and now he's living in style in Atlanta. Believe me! But my point is when man and man was laughing at him, it was seriously brave to keep doing what he did, y'understand?'

Sean nodded.

'I've got a brother-in-law,' continued Brenton. 'Clayton. To tell you the trut' I've never got on with him. Clash of personality and t'ing. Trust me. Me and him can never agree. He goes on all superior and t'ing. He gets on my damn nerves with all that shit. But I respect him though 'cos he went to uni where there was whole heap of white people; I think he was the only black brother in his class. Yeah, Juliet told me all about the shit he had to deal with. I think he was the only brother in the whole damn uni. Anyway, he took all their fuckery, all their fucked-up whispers, all their racism and t'ing and got what he wanted, y'understand. That's *brave.*'

'I hear that,' nodded Sean.

'So even you,' resumed Brenton, 'coming to my yard today. Juliet told me a little about your life, how you got involved with a madness, went prison and t'ing. But you stepped to my yard. You wanna change. Respect due! That's brave. With Malakai passing away and t'ing you coulda gone to war with them other yout's, y'understand? There might've been pressure dropping on your head from the street to get your revenge, you know. Malakai was your best friend and t'ing. But nah, you stepped to my yard looking work. Respect due for that. That's brave. Y'understand what I'm trying to say?'

'Yeah. I see what you mean.'

Brenton nodded. 'I'm sorry for what happened with your daddy but it was a long time ago. It was a me-and-him situation, a last-man-standing kinda fucked-up t'ing. I could understand if you didn't wanna work with me but the offer's still there.'

Sean looked at the table then glanced at Brenton. 'Yeah, it was a long time. Man wants to move on now. I wanna make something outta my life. Malakai thought I could. So I owe him at least a try. *Trust!*'

Offering his right hand to shake, Brenton looked into Sean's eyes. Sean studied Brenton's hand. He then swapped glances with Brenton and shook his hand.

'Next Monday morning,' said Brenton. 'Reach my yard at seven thirty in the morning.'

'Yeah, I'm up for that,' said Sean.

Five hours later, Brenton was naked staring at himself in his bathroom mirror. Johnny Clarke's *Jah Love Is With I* was playing from his bedroom. He studied the scars on his neck, his shoulder, his chest and on his legs. 'You're lucky to still be here,' said Brenton to himself. 'Damn fucking lucky.'

He picked up a jar of moisturising cream and started to rub it on. His landline phone rang. Brenton went to answer it in the lounge.

'Hello,' he greeted.

'Hi, it's Juliet.'

'Bit late, innit?'

'I just wanted to find out how your meeting with Sean went?'

'Went alright,' answered Brenton.

'Just alright? Did you offer him something?'

'Yeah, a part-time kinda t'ing. He's starting with me next Monday.'

'That's brilliant, Brenton!'

'No worries, just trying to set a man back on the road, y'understand?'

'Thanks for doing this, Brenton.'

'You sure it'll be alright with Breanna?'

There was a pause.

'She's still vex about him.'

'That'll pass,' said Brenton.

'She might need counselling, Brenton. She's still very upset. She never leaves her room. Always crying …'

'What do you expect, Juliet? She just lost her man. Course she's gonna still be upset.'

'But she's saying she wants to quit her job and do some voluntary youth work.'

'What's wrong with that?' asked Brenton.

'She's throwing away her career.'

'She might not like her so-called career,' argued Brenton.

'I told her not to do anything drastic,' said Juliet. 'She's still grieving. I told her to give herself time.'

'She's old enough to make her own decisions, Juliet.'

'But she's not thinking straight. She swore at Clayton tonight and all he was trying to do was to tell her to take time out and think things over. She's been feisty like any other young girl at her parents but, Brenton, I've never heard her swear at one of us before.'

'Juliet, what do you expect? She saw her man get gunned down on the street for fuck's sake …'

'And I'm trying to see her through it …'

'No, Juliet. Breanna needs to go through it in her own way. Let her do what she wants to do. What's so wrong with doing youth work anyway? You and Clayton should let her do it if that's what she wants to do.'

'Brenton, she needs help,' said Juliet. 'Maybe I should arrange for her to see a counsellor or someone?'

'Did she ask to see a fucking counsellor?' asked Brenton. 'Leave it alone until she wants to see one of them people.'

'I'm worried for her, Brenton. Really worried.'

'She'll come through, man. It's only been what? A month or so? Give her time, man. The shock is still in her.'

'Brenton, with all that's going on …'

'With all what's going on?'

'I just think,' stuttered Juliet, 'I just think that we should all be there for her, you know.'

'We are all there for her,' said Brenton. 'What do you mean?'

'Your plans.'

'What plans?' asked Brenton.

'Your plans to leave.'

'What about it?'

'Don't you think you should put them on hold?' said Juliet. 'Breanna needs all of us right now …'

'I'm not leaving tomorrow, for fuck's sake!'

'Yes, but how do we know if Breanna's going to pull through all this? We don't know. She needs you here.'

'Juliet, I'm not going nowhere for months. Not at least till November. Breanna will be alright by then, believe it.'

'Say she's not?'

'Oh for fuck's sake, Juliet! Think positive. Look, I'm not changing my plans. The paperwork's gone through already. What happened with Malakai was a tragedy and t'ing. Breanna will get back her life.'

'Why you so sure?'

'Wherever I am in six months' time she's free to visit. The same goes for you.'

There was a long pause.

'Would you come and visit, Juliet?'

'I … I just think you shouldn't go when Breanna is going through all this stress.'

'You didn't answer my question, Juliet?'

'I … I don't know,' answered Juliet. 'All I can think of now is Breanna.'

'Yeah, of course,' said Brenton. 'She'll be alright. As I said just give her time.'

'You're right,' said Juliet. 'Sorry to call you so late. I was just, you know, so worried about her.'

'That's alright. You don't have to apologise and t'ing.'

'Sorry, I just feel a bit ... helpless. Do you realise that when you go to America you have to have health insurance and all that? If you haven't got it they can turn you away from the hospital. Did you know that?'

'Stop fretting, Juliet,' said Brenton. 'I've looked into all that. I'm on the case. My eyes are wide open. Believe me ... is there anything else?'

'No ... sorry again for calling so late.'

'No worries.'

'OK, Brenton. Good ... goodnight.'

'Goodnight, Juliet ... tell Breanna I'm thinking of her.'

'I will.'

Chapter 22
Exile

Six months later – December 2002

'WHERE YOU GONNA SMOKE a spliff in Miami?' asked Floyd, draining a glass of beer. 'Police in the States don't ramp, you know, especially in Florida. Dat's George Bush's brother state. Major worries! They'll fuck you up without no apology. You know that their truncheons are about three-foot long. The redneck police have spikes on their truncheons and it has this homing t'ing on it that beeps when it's close to a black man. It might be best to step where the crocodiles coch so you can burn a zoot in peace, dread.'

'Serious t'ing,' laughed Coffin Head.

Coffin Head was standing up, glancing through the large windows at Brixton Town Hall from his vantage point three floors up in the Ritzy bar. Christmas lights lit the lone tree in Windrush Square and festive illuminations were threaded through the branches on the trees that surrounded St Matthew's Church. Within the grounds of the church, despite the snarling wind and biting cold, idlers, the homeless and the confused drank their drinks straight from the bottle and hunted for cigarette butts to make roll-ups. They watched a lone dog snout for a late supper in an overflowing bin. Coffin Head looked to his right towards the High Street and he saw a 159 bus brake sharply to avoid a reeling woman. Young black men congregated outside the Kentucky takeaway as outside the restaurant a black-cab taxi driver refused the custom of a dreadlocked, shoeless white guy. Dancehall music was earth-quaking out of a jeep that had stopped at the traffic lights beside the Ritzy cinema. Coffin Head looked to his left where next door to the Town Hall bouncers from the Fridge nightclub were storm-trooping a cursing raver out onto the street and apparently starting to kick him. Just below the Ritzy a well-dressed teenage girl was sitting on the kerb with her head in her hands. She was sobbing as a police siren rang out in the distance. Coffin Head shook his head and muttered, 'Different people may come and go but nutten change inna Brixton.'

Inside the Ritzy bar, Luciano's *It's Me Again Jah* was sounding out from the stereo system. The clientele included moviegoers who had come up from the Ritzy cinema downstairs. The walls were covered in classic film posters. The coffee machine at the bar seemed to be forever buzzing and crammed into a corner members of a black book group were having a heated debate about Eldridge Cleaver's *Soul on Ice*.

Brenton's party included Floyd, Coffin Head and Biscuit. Their table was covered with empty and half-full glasses of beer and cocktails.

'You're not gonna take one last look, Brenton?' said Coffin Head. 'Brixton in all its fucked-up glory! Some yout's call it the Dirty South. What did we call it back in the day? The ghetto, I think. What age did you come to Brixton?'

'Sixteen,' answered Floyd. 'And when I first saw him I said to myself who the blouse and skirt is this idiot with the mad grey Afro and white people clothes!'

Brenton chuckled. 'To be honest,' he said. 'I could hardly understand a word you were saying, dread.'

'I never met a yout' like that before,' said Floyd. 'His accent! There was some kinda BBC, Surrey fuckery going on with his accent. I thought he went to some posh school where they wear dem black square t'ings on their head-tops and dem vampire garms.'

'Nah,' said Biscuit shaking his head. 'I could tolerate his accent.

Didn't bother me. What freaked me out was his walk. When I sight Brenton for the first time I just couldn't stop laughing at his walk. I mean, where the fuck did you get that walk from? That was some farmer, cow-nibbling, sore-bunion, straw-yamming, country-bumpkin kinda walk, dread. Man! I laughed!'

'I had to teach him to walk like a Brixtonian,' said Floyd. 'You know how stressful that was? You see dem programme about a greyback granny learning to drive? You see how stressed out the instructor gets when the greyback can't even remember how to start the car? Well quadruple that shit and you might get near to how Brenton stressed me out with me teaching him how to walk street like a black man. He had no riddim, man. No bounce.'

Everybody laughed.

'And then I tried to teach him how to crub with a girl,' continued Floyd.

'Yeah, I remember that,' said Coffin Head. 'Serious t'ing. That girl in Clouds.'

'What girl in Clouds?' Biscuit asked. 'Was I there?'

'No you weren't there,' recalled Brenton. 'Your mum wouldn't let you go.'

'That's cold, Brenton,' chuckled Biscuit. 'Did you have to remind me of that? Can someone tell me the runnings of what happened with Brenton and this girl at Clouds?'

Floyd began laughing. Coffin Head joined in and Brenton wasn't impressed.

'Stop the skinning the teet' man,' complained Biscuit. 'Tell me the story nuh!'

Composing himself for a couple of seconds, Floyd burst out laughing yet again.

'For Jesus in a fucking jeep!' moaned Brenton. 'Can we move on from this fuckery?'

'No, no,' said Floyd. 'I'll tell the story.'

'Go on then!' urged Biscuit. 'And stop fucking about.'

'Alright, alright,' said Floyd catching his breath. 'Here's the SP. For one long bitching week I was trying to teach Brenton how to crub with girl, y'understand? Man! It was like teaching Prince Charles how to roll a five-paper spliff.'

'What?' queried Coffin Head. 'You was crubbing with Brenton? Fuck my living days, dread! I always wondered what you two got up to in that hostel. That is just fucked-up nastiness, dread. Two man crubbing? Did the both of you get a Thunderbird One erection? All juices are go? Full blast and t'ing?'

'Coffin Head,' called Floyd. 'Will you keep your beak quiet while I tell my tale.'

'Tell your tale then but I don't wanna hear no battyman runnings. My earlobes don't like dem t'ing there.'

'Anyway,' resumed Floyd, offering Coffin Head a mean eye pass. 'I was showing him the movements, you know, one step, two step, figure eight, double dip, rookumbind, bruise pussy and all the rest. He seemed to get the hang of it when he was dancing by himself …'

'I'm getting a fucked-up image of Brenton doing this figure eight on his own,' laughed Coffin Head.

'Coffin Head!' called Floyd again. 'Can you please staple, superglue and double-lock your beak, man. I'm trying to tell the story! Fuck my rasta lying flat on a fucking road ramp!'

'OK, OK,' said Coffin Head. 'Carry on and t'ing. I won't interrupt.'

Floyd offered Coffin Head another brutal eye pass. Brenton rolled his eyes and Biscuit kissed his teeth.

'So after the training,' Floyd resumed. 'I took my man to Clouds. I had to lend him some of my garms and tell him to fix up himself 'cos I wasn't stepping into Clouds with Brenton dressed in his white country-bumpkin clothes and his fucked-up Afro. Lord Jesus! Brenton's hair was dry! I should've sent him to one of dem Arab countries to dip his head in an oil well!

The Afro was a fire hazard, nuff danger and t'ing! Anyway, he also had his fucked-up side-burned farmer trod and his plastic shoes. When he put those t'ings on his feet I called him the PVC Kid. Man! You could hear the squeak of his shoes from the bins behind Cowley estate, dread! He didn't know nutten about fashion. He was lucky there wasn't a heat wave going on 'cos his feet woulda come like a whole heap of chocolate button on a firing barbecue, serious.'

'Get on with it, man,' said Brenton.

'Nuff girl was there,' continued Floyd. 'Nuff Vauxhall Manor School girls there, Dick Shepherd, Priory Park, St Martin's, basically a whole heap of girl. Brenton was kinda nervous and he was sweating like an old man with nuff heart worries inna whorehouse. I pulled this girl. Brenton watched. When I finished crubbing her I told Brenton to pull her friend.'

'Her friend was a trog, man!' protested Brenton.

'Yeah, she was a bit serious train accident disaster and t'ing but man have to start somewhere, right?' said Floyd. 'Anyway, at first Brenton wouldn't pull the girl. I was getting pure frustration 'cos of the amount of time of training I put in. I told Brenton that if he don't pull the trog I'm stepping home.'

'No,' argued Brenton again. 'You wanted to step home 'cos that girl you was crubbing with didn't give you her digits.'

'Anyway,' Floyd went on. 'Brenton pulled the trog. They started crubbing. Lord on a fucking lilo! I don't know what the fuck Brenton was doing.'

Everyone laughed again, even Brenton.

'I think Brenton was trying to do the two-step,' Floyd resumed. 'But he was going waaaay too fast, bredren. You know like how white men with no riddim do that old-school locomotion dance? Brenton was looking down at his feet and the trog started to get vex, and man, she looked even more ugly when she got vex. The next t'ing I know, they both drop.'

'Right in the middle of the dance floor?' asked Biscuit.

'Yep,' Floyd answered. 'Slap bang, golden bolt, Crafty Cockney bullseye and t'ing. Everyone stopped crubbing and looked at Brenton and the trog. It was embarrassing. The trog started cussing Brenton. Brenton just kinda stood there. He had to take all her Brixton fishwife, ghetto-drain cussing. He didn't know what the fuck to do or say. It was embarrassing, dread. I had to step away. I could hardly look and t'ing.'

Everyone collapsed into giggles and Brenton could only shake his head and join the laughter.

Ten minutes later, Coffin Head was composed enough to ask, 'Why you really going, Brenton? Florida's a long way, bredren. You ain't gonna miss us?'

Brenton thought about it. 'I want what you have,' he finally answered. 'All of you got your families and t'ing. Got kids and t'ing. I haven't got that yet. Believe it! I've tried but it's never worked out with anyone.'

'What happened to Lesley?' asked Biscuit. 'She looked alright. Fit for her age and t'ing. Good mum, well educated. She had her own hair. And her cooking weren't too bad.'

Brenton shook his head. 'T''ings just didn't, you know, work out.'

'So you think it might work out with some American girl?' asked Coffin Head.

'You never know,' replied Brenton. 'I just wanna change, dread. Been in Brixton for how long? Twenty-five years or thereabouts. Wanna coch in another corner of the world.'

'Yeah and when you settle we're gonna come over,' laughed Biscuit. 'We're gonna piss in your pool, shit in the sea, jack Mickey Mouse, rape Barney Rubble's wife, burn a fat spliff in the magical kingdom, drug up Coffin Head and push him in alligator pond.'

'Rape Barney Rubble's wife!' repeated Coffin Head, disgusted. 'Biscuit, dread, you've got issues with your female characters in toons, dread. Serious t'ing. You're fucked up. You're seriously fucked up.'

'What's a matter with you, Coff?' asked Biscuit. 'Brenton knows I'm joking. How the living fuck am I gonna rape a cartoon character? Christ in a crackhouse! I'm just saying that we'll all visit him and t'ing when he's settled.'

'That'll be sweet, dread,' said Brenton. 'And I'm gonna try and come over here at least once a year ... by the way, who's gonna put me up?'

'Not me,' said Floyd. 'You poop too much. I remember his poops from the time I lived with him in the hostel. Brenton's poops are seriously dangerous, weapon of mass destruction and t'ing. You ain't stinkin' out my yard, you know how Sharon stays about that kinda t'ing.'

'See how your best bredren treats you though,' said Coffin Head. 'You can stay with me and Denise. We got a spare room and t'ing.'

'I'll hold you to that, Coffin Head,' said Brenton.

'No worries, dread,' replied Coffin Head. 'Just let us know in advance so we got nuff time to buy some serious air freshener, incense sticks and t'ing.'

Everybody laughed again. Brenton finished his drink and as he did so he took a long look at his friends and wondered how his life would have been different if he hadn't met them.

'Gotta step now,' Brenton said. 'Gotta be at the airport by half seven but before I hit my bed I have to drop something off at Juliet's yard.'

'Alright then,' said Floyd. 'Coff, how much liquor you had tonight?'

'Just the one, man!' Coffin Head replied. 'What do you take me for?'

'Alright, alright,' said Floyd. 'No need to burst no blood vessel and t'ing. Just checking.'

'Come on, man,' said Biscuit. 'Let's step to Coff's BMW. You know what? This is the first time I've been in his BM and he's had it for what? Seven months now?'

'It's gonna be the only time,' insisted Coffin Head. 'There's custard cream crumbs all over the passenger seat, man. Serious t'ing! And you ain't cleaning it up.'

'Oh for fucking Buddha on a bouncy castle!' Biscuit said. 'Stop bitching, Coff!'

As Brenton heard the banter of his friends, he realised how much he would miss just listening to them. It was a joy to hear their jesting and he reckoned he had no need to fork out and watch a play for entertainment like Juliet had always encouraged him to do. But would he be able to make new friends in Florida? he wondered. Probably not. And if I did they'd be nowhere near as good or funny as Floyd, Biscuit and Coffin Head. Maybe it's easier for me to discover and live in another place? My roots are not in south London. Not like it is with them. They belong here. This place has defined the way they walk, talk and carry themselves. They're at ease here. If I was honest with myself I'm not at ease here. Not at all. Serious. Maybe I'm not at ease anywhere. But I'll be alright. Been on my own before.

The image of the outhouse where Brenton was locked in for so many hours as a child grew large in his mind.

Coffin Head led Brenton and the others to his BMW. When Brenton climbed inside he could smell a strong mint air freshener. The interior was pristine clean and Brenton found no crumbs on the front passenger seat. He spotted a small battery-operated hoover on the shelf behind the rear seats. Coffin Head started the car, the Chantells' *Waiting in the Park* harmonised from the stereo and Brenton smiled as Coffin Head drove around the one-way system and up Tulse Hill.

Pulling up outside Juliet's house, Coffin Head shook Brenton's hand. 'Keep in touch, man,' he said. 'And let me know when me and Denise can reach.'

'Same goes for me and Carol,' said Biscuit. 'Don't take too long, you know! Have a safe flight and t'ing and don't burn no herb on the plane.'

Picking up a plastic bag from the glove compartment, Brenton turned to Floyd. 'Make sure you get to my yard on time, you know.'

'Stop fretting, dread,' Floyd replied. 'Six a.m. on the black dot and t'ing. You just make sure you're ready when I ding you.'

Brenton climbed out of the car. He took one last look at his friends before Coffin Head found first gear and pulled away. He tooted his horn twice. Brenton watched them disappear into the next left-hand turning. He checked his watch. Ten forty-five p.m. He walked up to Juliet's front door and pressed the doorbell.

He shuffled his feet nervously and rubbed his hands together. He scratched behind his right ear. Juliet opened the door. She was wearing black slacks, a T-shirt and a black cardigan. She smiled as she greeted her brother. 'I was surprised to get your call that you're coming this evening.'

'Yeah, er, sorry I'm a bit late,' said Brenton. 'We was in the Ritzy, you know, saying goodbye and t'ing.'

Juliet led Brenton to the lounge. Brenton sat in an armchair. He unbuttoned his leather jacket.

'Do ... do you want a coffee?' Juliet asked.

'No, no,' answered Brenton. 'Trying to keep off coffee and t'ing till I fly off. It makes me wanna piss quick time and I hate using plane toilets, man.'

'You want anything to eat?'

'Nah, nah. Had something earlier. We went to that place on Acre Lane, the Jamaican restaurant. Bam ... something. Biscuit chose the place.'

'Bamboula,' corrected Juliet. 'Food there is alright I s'pose but they make their rice and peas too sweet.'

'I ... I just come to drop off the photos and t'ing,' said Brenton.

'You remembered?'

'Yeah, no worries. I went to that photo shop place and some of the old ones, me as a toddler and t'ing, they cleaned up, made it look better.'

'Thanks, Brenton.'

'No worries, man.'

'Am I still driving you to the airport?'

'Er, no. Floyd said he'll take me. He got a little vex that I didn't ask him first. Well, not a little vex. He got big-time vex. You know how he stays.'

'I understand,' said Juliet.

'No Clayton? No Breanna?'

'Breanna is out clubbing with her mates,' said Juliet. 'Clayton's on his way back from Paris. His train gets in about now.'

'Can ... can you drop me home then?' asked Brenton.

'Course ... now?'

'Yeah, I wanna put in a good night's sleep before I leave.'

'Alright, let me get my coat.'

Waiting in the hallway, Brenton wondered if he'd ever stand in it again. He recalled the first time he set eyes on his sister at his mother's house. Mum had a similar hallway, he remembered. The white Jesus pic, the velvet scroll of Jamaican icons and a painting of a Jamaican bus. Jamaican buses! Man! They should be a ride in Alton Towers. That'll scare the kids.

'Come on then,' said Juliet, placing a woolly hat on her head.

Brenton followed her to her car. She unlocked the doors with a mechanism on her key ring. Brenton climbed into the front passenger seat. This smells even better than Coffin Head's car, he thought.

Juliet climbed in beside him. She switched on the ignition

and cranked the heating up. Brenton gazed at Juliet. She held his gaze for more than a few seconds. She then indicated right and switched her attention to the road. Neither of them spoke.

Brenton broke the silence. 'So how's Breanna doing at the youth club?'

'She's loving it,' said Juliet. 'She's going on a residential at the end of February during half term. Wales, I think. They're going on this obstacle course, doing a bit of canoeing and rafting. A bit of climbing and abseiling. She's always talking about the kids she works with.'

'That's good, man,' Brenton nodded.

'She wanted to come with me to drop you off at the airport in the morning.'

'Oh, sorry about that.'

'It's alright.'

'Will Sean be alright?' she asked.

'Yeah, he started work two weeks ago for another firm,' Brenton answered. 'I gave him a reference. I'm kinda proud of him. He never missed a day's work when I wanted him and he learned a lot. Daniel's now setting himself up on his own. He'll do good.'

'You're proud of him,' said Juliet. 'I'm proud of you, taking him on when nobody else would.'

'I know what it's like to be in his position, Juliet. At one time everybody wrote me off. No one wanted to give me a chance.'

'I did,' said Juliet. 'First time I saw you I knew you had a softer side, a vulnerable side. You weren't this crazy street boy who wanted to fight everybody. You just wanted to be ... liked.'

Brenton thought about it and nodded. He had a flashback of sitting in a police interview room. He was sixteen. A police sergeant was leaning towards him. His sleeves were rolled up. He had a bad moustache. He stank of cigarettes and a sweaty shirt. 'Are you a fucking psycho, Brown?' he shouted into his face.

Brenton remembered how frightened he was. How he thought he might get beaten up at any minute. But he still replied, 'Fuck you and your mum, you dirty cunt!'

'So this is it!' Juliet said, jolting Brenton out of his memories. 'Are you going to write me? E-mail me?'

'Are you gonna visit me?'

Brother and sister gazed into each other's eyes again.

'I really don't know when I'll be able to,' replied Juliet. 'Breanna wants to visit you though, as soon as you're up and running. She's probably bought her beach stuff already.'

Brenton laughed. Juliet leant in towards Brenton and kissed him on his cheek. Her lips lingered on his skin. She pulled away two inches and then kissed him on the other cheek. 'Take care of yourself,' she said. 'Stay in touch.'

Brenton returned the kiss on Juliet's cheek. He then kissed her on her chin. He pulled away. He looked into her eyes and kissed her again just below her mouth. Juliet found her right hand riding up Brenton's left shoulder. She pulled away, adjusted her coat and looked through the windscreen. 'Bye, Brenton. Call me or text me when you land. Let me know you're safe.'

'Yeah … yeah, course.'

'Don't forget.'

'I won't.'

Brenton climbed out of the car. Juliet gripped the steering wheel with both hands. Her eyes were fixed on the road ahead. She was reluctant to pull away until Brenton went inside but he stood there, watching her.

Finally, Juliet found first gear, indicated right and pulled away. As soon as she turned into the next corner she pulled up again. She applied the handbrake and dropped her head into her hands. Juliet sat herself up. She wiped the tears off her face and stared vacantly through the windscreen.

Ten hours later, Clayton was running down the stairs adjusting his cufflinks. He went to the kitchen where he poured himself a glass of apple juice. He downed it in three takes, and poured himself a little more. He searched his trouser pockets for a chewing mint and popped it into his mouth. He then checked his appearance in a hallway mirror before going into the front room. He was about to pick up a newspaper that he had asked Juliet to buy for him the day before but something else caught his eye. On the coffee table was Brenton's photo shop bag. Clayton picked it up and looked inside. He took out the photographs of a young Brenton and placed them on the coffee table. He concentrated on the images where Brenton was very young. He picked one photo up and brought it closer to his eyes. He squinted. 'I knew it,' he whispered. 'Just fucking knew it.'

He switched on the light and studied the photo again. He then bull-frogged upstairs and into his bedroom. He opened Juliet's wardrobe. On her top shelf, where she kept her hats, were the photo albums. He took five of them down and dropped them on the bed. He locked the bedroom door and returned to the photo albums. He placed the picture of a very young Brenton on the bed and began to leaf through photographs of a young Breanna. He stopped when he found a portrait picture of Breanna when she was four years old. He placed Brenton's photograph beside it. He opened his mouth and then covered it with his left hand. '*Shit!*' he uttered. '*Oh my God!* So alike! That's it! Always knew it! Should I go to her about it? No! She'll deny it. Anyway the dumb prick is leaving this morning. About fucking time.'

He carefully replaced the photo albums in Juliet's wardrobe and then unlocked the bedroom door. He checked the hallway before going back downstairs with Brenton's photo. Before he put the photograph back in the bag he took a last look at it. '*Him,* Juliet?' he whispered to himself. 'Of all the people in the world why the fuck *him!*'

Chapter 23

Heathrow to Streatham

Three years later, April 2005

LIFTING BREANNA'S SUITCASE into her car boot, Juliet said, 'Are you sure you didn't have to pay extra for your baggage weight? It's twice as bloody heavy from when you left.'

'What do you expect, Mum,' said Breanna, placing her travel bag and her duty-free shopping on the back seat. 'I bought a lot of clothes and three of my friends wanted some perfume; it's proper cheap over there and I've got some rum, vodka and Baileys.'

'You didn't have to buy the drink, Breanna,' said Juliet slamming the boot closed.

'It's cheaper in duty free,' said Breanna throwing up her arms. 'Besides, waiting in the departure lounge is boring. You might as well spend some dollars while you're waiting for your plane.'

Breanna climbed into the front passenger seat. She crossed her arms, let out a sigh and closed her eyes. Juliet started the car, reversed out of her parking bay and headed out of the airport complex. The traffic was slow towards London and Juliet tuned the radio to Choice FM. It wasn't until she was on the A4 driving towards west London that Juliet spoke again. Her eyes remained fixed on the road ahead as she asked. 'How is he?'

Breanna opened her eyes. She squinted at the brightness of the sun. 'Why don't you ask him yourself, Mum? When's the last time you called him?'

'I called him two and a half weeks ago on the day you left.'

'So you should know how he is then, innit.'

'Breanna! I just asked you an everyday question. Call it polite conversation. Why you have to be so damn awkward? Does he look OK? Is his job working out? Do you think he's happy?'

'Uncle Brenton's safe,' Breanna answered. She felt the cold breeze against her face so she wound up her window. 'He's got used to Miami. Work is going alright for him. There's all these new places being built on the way to the Keys and he's working there.'

'Was that so hard?' Juliet asked.

'*You* should go and see him yourself.'

'Breanna, you know I've been so busy with the election campaign and trying to get other things done. I can't just drop everything and fly off to Miami.'

'Why not? You could've gone last year ... and the year before that. He's been out there for three years and you haven't seen him once. Why, Mum? What did he ever do to you? You're always going on about how he had a messed-up life when he was a kid and how unlucky he was. You always used to say how he grew up alone. But you can't even be bothered to see him. I don't care. That's blatantly *bad-mind!*'

'Breanna! Sometimes you're so much like your ...'

'So much like what, Mum? Let me answer your question fully. Yeah, Uncle Brenton is alright. He's got a nice place. His standard of living has gone up; he's earning some decent dollars. But he hasn't got many friends out there. There's some Cuban guy he works with and who comes round to his place now and again, but he don't speak good English. There's also some Guatemalan guy too and he don't speak English too good either. That girl he was seeing last year, he broke up with her. Saw a picture of her on Uncle Brenton's computer. Real pretty Nicaraguan girl. I think she was in her mid-twenties. Shame they broke up ... I think she was his only girlfriend since he's been out there. He's a bit lonely now.'

'I didn't force him to leave, Breanna,' Juliet raised her voice. 'I didn't push him on a plane ...'

'You know what, Mum?' interrupted Breanna. 'Most days he goes to work. He comes back and only 'cos I was there he would cook something. He goes to his garden, eats his dinner. He watches the BBC World News and then he listens to one of the reggae radio stations. Then he goes to bed.'

'Most people do that in this world, Breanna. I do the same. I wish I had time to socialise when I come home from work but I haven't got the time or I'm tired. Brenton's probably the same.'

'No he's not,' argued Breanna. 'You're being flippant! He's lonely. When he gets home he can't just call up a friend because his best friends are over here.'

Juliet turned off the A4 and headed towards Kew Gardens. She checked her reflection in the rear-view mirror and now wished she had asked Clayton to pick Breanna up from the airport.

'At least his friends made the effort to see him,' continued Breanna. 'Or call him. Floyd calls him every other Sunday. Everton and Denise went over last November. Lincoln and Carol saw him last summer. Floyd and Sharon have been over twice. But you! You're s'posed to be his sister, for fuck's sake! *That's* a joke.'

'Breanna! Ever since …'

'Ever since what? Every since Malakai died I speak my mind? And I don't care who I'm speaking to? Deal with it, Mum. Sorry for swearing, but it's true. I've heard you arguing with Dad. Especially that time after Gran died. *Uncle Brenton never had anybody* you were saying. *Uncle Brenton deserves everything that Gran left because he never had her love growing up. You had all of Mum's attention and Uncle Brenton was left to rot.* I remember you saying all that. But now? Don't you fucking care anymore, Mum? Or you're too busy wanting to be an MP? Are you too fucking ambitious? Going to see Uncle Brenton is too much of an inconvenience for you. You know, over the years I've always respected the way you treated Uncle Brenton. But these last few years? It's like he's dead to you.'

Juliet offered Breanna a cold glare. She then concentrated on the road ahead but her angled eyebrows and her protruding lip betrayed her fury. 'You might be twenty-four but *don't* you think you're not old enough for me to stop this car and give you a box! You're not talking to me like that!'

'And what?'

'Sometimes, Breanna, you are so immature.'

'I'm immature! Me? You're the one who won't see your brother! Makes me laugh! All the newspapers think you're so good. *Juliet Hylton says that despite campaigning to be the first black MP representing the Brixton area, her family is the most important thing to her.* Did you really say that, Mum?'

Juliet nodded. 'And I meant *every* word,' she insisted.

'You know what, Mum?'

'What, Breanna? You've come up with a new way of insulting me? That's all you do to me these days, isn't it.'

'Don't expect me at your election count,' Breanna snapped. 'I'm sick and tired of playing happy families. Fuck it! I won't be there. I'm not going be a hypocrite, pretending everything is all rosy ... and *don't* even think about getting your election manager or whatever he calls himself to change my mind. I can't believe you gave that idiot my mobile number! If he calls I'm going tell him to fuck himself.'

'Maybe I should tell him to call you to teach you good language!'

'You're so funny, Mum.'

Twenty minutes later, Juliet reached the South Circular Road. Breanna's eyes were flickering but she opened them fully when Juliet drove over a road ramp in Putney.

'It might be a bit late to ask but did you enjoy yourself?' asked Juliet.

Breanna sat up a bit in her seat and thought of a holiday memory. 'Yeah, I did,' she answered calmly. 'Uncle Brenton took me everywhere I asked him to. Took me one Sunday to see the alligators even though he hates them. He was proper jumpy even with the baby ones at the alligator farm. He didn't want me spending my own money. As you know, he drove me up to Orlando. We went to Disneyworld for three days. Went to Universal Studios and … what's it called? The, er … Epcot Center. I think that's what it's called. He drove me down to the Keys. The way he goes on about the Keys and the little beaches there I think that's his favourite place. But you wouldn't know that, Mum. Would you? It's a long drive though. He said it's near Cuba.'

'So you had a great time?' Juliet asked, her eyes still fixed on the road ahead.

'Yeah, I did,' answered Breanna. 'I kind of got to know Uncle Brenton. We talked a lot.'

'What about?' Juliet wanted to know.

'About life. He was saying that if I get a chance at happiness then I must take it. Don't stall, he said. You only get the one life, he kept on saying. Remember the times you had with Malakai, he said. But don't let that define the rest of your life.'

'He said that?' said Juliet, glancing at Breanna.

'Yeah, he did. When he was talking I noticed something real sad about him. Can't put my finger on it. Something? I don't know.'

'His childhood,' suggested Juliet. 'He had a shitty childhood.'

'I know,' nodded Breanna. 'He talked about that. How he was so alone and all that. But he was alright talking about that stuff. He wasn't crying or anything. There's something else. Sometimes when he didn't realise I was watching him I could see it in his face. Some proper sadness. Like he had a loss just like me.'

'No, it's not that,' said Juliet. 'He's survived a shit of a childhood but some internal scars will never heal. Some bad memories never go away.'

'No they don't,' nodded Breanna. She was thinking of Malakai.

Passing through Wandsworth, Juliet turned towards Streatham. Breanna watched her. She admired her mother's beauty. She was happy she came and picked her up but still mad with her over Uncle Brenton. She was relieved Juliet didn't flip when she was swearing at her. She must be sick and tired of telling me off about it. She thought of Uncle Brenton. A lasting image appeared in her head. All alone. Hands on hips. Very still. Staring vacantly into the endless blue. The vast Atlantic. The sea rippling around his ankles. The hot Florida sun shining off his almost-bald head. Thinking of something that made him feel sad.

'Mum,' Breanna called softly.

'Yes, Breanna?'

'Go see him, *blatantly*. He's lonely.'

Chapter 24

It's All Red on the Night

Five days later

NERVOUSLY LOOKING AT THE TV CREW in the corner of the assembly room within Brixton Town Hall, Juliet adjusted her Nefertiti earrings. She was wearing a smart burgundy-coloured business suit and a red rosette covered half her chest. She was sporting red shoes with three-inch heels; she didn't want to look like a midget standing beside the very tall Tory candidate who was an Oxford-educated black guy and spoke like he was raised in Windsor. Juliet compared him to the characters Sidney Poitier played in films in the 1950s and 60s; a perfect unthreatening black man who always wore a suit and tie, always had his top button secured, had the look of a recent haircut and was more polite than a Buckingham Palace servant. Brenton would have really taken the piss out of him, she thought. She turned to Clayton. 'What's the time?' she asked.

'You just asked me that,' replied Clayton. 'It's quarter to five. Try and relax. It's in the bag.'

Juliet glanced at the television people again. There was another TV news team outside in the lobby. Inside the hall, endless tables were put together in long rows with large black metal boxes on them. Grim-faced election workers were frantically counting votes. Some of them were sipping from teas and coffees in polystyrene cups while others had their own flasks on the tables. A few nibbled on sandwiches that were wrapped in kitchen foil and there was a steady stream of smokers going outside for a cigarette. Microphones were set up on the stage and the constant drone of conversation floated around the wood-panelled room. Men in suits and women in conservative dresses walked by on the polished wooden floor as if they were important and the mayor of Lambeth plastic-smiled and backslapped everyone she met. Half of the people in the hall were talking into their mobile phones.

Where do they get those vote counters from? wondered Juliet. She glanced at the TV crew. I wish they would stop pointing that fucking camera at me! she screamed in her head.

'Stop fretting, Mum,' said Breanna, observing Juliet's anxiety. 'It's a done deal.'

'I'm not worried about the result,' said Juliet. 'I'm worried about the TV people. I should have done more work on my speech.'

'Just say what you feel,' said Breanna.

'She's right,' said Clayton. 'You're best that way.'

Tom Reynolds, Juliet's campaign manager, walked purposefully over to Juliet with a massive grin on his face. He was wearing a blue suit, a fat red tie, a red rosette that was even bigger than Juliet's and Italian-made shoes. He also had a polystyrene cup in his hand but he was drinking something much stronger than coffee, Juliet noted. Rum and Coke, she guessed, with a hint of tequila. He greeted Breanna and Clayton with an over-smiling nod before addressing Juliet. 'It's an IM,' he hailed. 'A massive IM.'

'What's an IM?' asked Juliet, glancing over at the TV crew who were now animated; the presenter was preparing herself for broadcast.

'Increased majority,' explained Tom. 'The Tories nearly lost their deposit. I still can't believe they put up a black guy who knows more about Frankenstein farming than urban shotting. What a traitor! The Respect party only got a BIG disrespect as they say around here and as for the Liberals. What can I say about the fucking Liberals? Fucking yellow surrender monkeys!

The Greens did alright but fuck them too and their veggie diets. If they had it their way we'd be having the count in Brockwell Park with a scout fire and eating lettuce and drinking from the pond. Fucking idiots!'

'Tom!' Juliet rebuked.

'Why the worried face, Jules?' asked Tom. 'You're about to be the first-ever black MP representing Lambeth. You're going to be the face of Brixton. The *Guardian* and *Independent* will love it. You'll get so much attention the PM will have to give you a junior minister job. My advice is don't go into the Home Office. Poisoned chalice that. All it takes is for some nutjob to go on the rampage in the Shires and kill a few people and the Tory media will want to blame you. Worse than that if there's a paedo on the loose who has molested posh kids in Berkshire or somewhere then you'll get the blame for that crap too. Banana skins all over ...'

'Slow down, Tom,' said Juliet. 'They haven't even called it.'

'The so-called TV experts are getting ready to call it now though,' said Tom. 'Looks like we're going to have a majority of around thirty, forty seats. I really can't wait to see Paxman grilling the Tory top brass to explain their defeat. He shouldn't even bother to interview the Liberal tossers. I better phone home and make sure that gets recorded. *Mullered,* they were, the Tory cunts. Absolutely *mullered!* Especially in London.'

'Keep your voice down!' said Juliet. 'Who knows if the TV people haven't got mics all over the place? And it's not good to gloat. Make sure you wipe the smile off your face when I'm making my speech.'

'Not in public it doesn't, Jules,' nodded Tom. He drank from his cup again. 'But in private? It's party time, man!'

Slapping Clayton on the shoulder, Tom went off to the back of the hall where more Labour supporters were congregated.

'I don't know why you ever agreed to work with him,' remarked Clayton. 'The man's a hooligan!'

'Yeah, he is,' nodded Juliet. 'But he's bloody good at what he does. I have to admit he ran the campaign like clockwork. He exposed the opposition for what they were and that idea of having me campaign outside new gated estates where schools used to be worked a treat.'

Twenty minutes later, Juliet found herself on the stage along with the other candidates. As the returning officer read the results, she thought of her mother. She remembered the early mornings her mother had to get up for work. She recalled the kisses on her forehead before she departed at five thirty a.m. on the dot; she had to catch the first bus. Should have been here, Mum, Juliet said to herself. You should have been here.

'… for Mrs Juliet Lana Hylton,' the returning officer announced, '34,751 votes.'

Roars and whistles echoed around the hall. Red balloons were loosed. Everyone applauded, including Tory, Liberal and Green party supporters. Juliet spotted Tom jumping up and down and clenching his fist and baring his teeth at the Tory delegation. She saw Clayton hugging Breanna. Oh my Lord, she thought. Clayton's going to cry. Stupid fool. Not now! You'll have me going. Not now, Clayton. Oh shit! Tom looks like he's going to hit someone. Calm down, you idiot. Calm down.

Striding towards the microphone, Juliet composed herself and looked around the hall before she addressed everybody. 'I just,' she managed. 'I just want …'

Shouts sounded out again. Wilder applauding. The bright television lights forced Juliet to squint. 'I just want to thank all the candidates who are standing here this morning for the way they conducted themselves at this election,' Juliet resumed. 'The whole campaign was fought fairly and with respect for each candidate.'

A few of the Tory delegation glared at Tom. In response Tom gave them a V sign and then his middle finger.

'Before I go on,' continued Juliet. 'I really have to thank my campaign manager, Mr Tom Reynolds, who three years ago made me believe this night and early morning could be made possible. He has worked twenty-hour days for many weeks and I'll be forever grateful.'

Tom pumped his fists, lapped up the applause and smiled cheekily at Tory supporters. Clayton rolled his eyes.

'And I really want to thank all the hard-working Labour members who knocked on so many doors in all weather, handed out leaflets in front of supermarkets, train stations and so many other locations. Your names are too many to mention but you know who you are. This victory is yours as much as mine. I don't want to go on forever because it's been a long night but I really must thank my family. My patient husband, Clayton, who has supported me all the way and, in my absence, has learned to cook a wicked curried goat. And of course my daughter, Breanna, who now has to paint her room red.'

'Can't it be pinkish?' shouted Breanna.

'No,' laughed Juliet. 'You said if I win you'll paint it red! I'll let you all go to bed very soon but I just want to say this. I will do everything I can to keep my campaign pledges. I will fight to improve schools and to keep them open in the borough. It's a scandal that so many of our children have to travel to another borough just to get an education. An absolute *scandal!* There is no reason why a child attending, say, Charles Edward Brooke School, cannot be the next Prime Minister or the next chief executive officer of Shell. I will fight to open more youth clubs and facilities. I will fight for improved housing. Why are there so many vacant properties and so many homeless? I will fight to help ordinary hard-working families, for ordinary families are the backbones of communities. I will fight for everything I have pledged for. That's a promise from someone who grew up in these streets, someone who knows the concerns of the community and someone who loves and is a part of that community. I now *serve* all of you. Thank you very much.'

Stepping off the stage accompanied by roars of approval and wolf whistles, Juliet thought of Brenton and wondered if he'd be watching the BBC World News in Miami to see if she had won. In her left pocket her mobile phone vibrated. She picked it up and answered it.

'Hi, Tessa,' Juliet greeted.

'Congratulations, Jules!' yelled Tessa. 'You did it! I can't believe my best mate is a fucking MP!'

'You better believe it!'

'I've just seen you on the BBC!' revealed Tessa. 'Why you wearing that boring burgundy trouser suit? You should've worn a figure-hugging dress or something. Show off that figure of yours. You should've got your tits out a bit more, wear something low-cut, give all those boring men in boring suits on TV yabbering about the election something to drool over.'

'Tess!'

'Seriously, Jules, congratulations, girl. You deserve all of it. I was waiting for your speech all fucking night! Why can't Lambeth be like that place in Birmingham that declares their result just after half past eleven? Don't those people who count the votes have any consideration for people who wanna see the results? I had to put up with all these fucking projections, opinion polls and all the other twaddle.'

'Hope it was worth it,' said Juliet.

'It was,' said Tessa. 'But I'm off to bed now, I'm knackered!'

'Good night, Tess.'

'What do you mean good night? It's morning!'

'OK,' laughed Juliet. 'Good morning. We'll catch up at the weekend.'

'I knew you'd win,' said Tessa. 'From the day you said you wanted to be an MP. I knew this night would happen.'

'How did you know?' asked Juliet.

''Cos you always get what you want,' answered Tessa. 'Ever since I've known you you've been like that. And good for you!'

'Not *everything* I want,' said Juliet.

'Anyway, bye then,' said Tessa. 'Now get off the fucking phone. I'm going to my bed.'

Before Juliet could leave the Town Hall she had to conduct further live interviews with local and national television and media. Clayton drove Breanna home but he returned for Juliet. It wasn't until half past six that Juliet collapsed into the front passenger seat of Clayton's new Audi sports car.

'I am so tired,' said Juliet. 'Did you hear some of the questions they asked me? *Now you'll be taking your seat in the House of Commons does that mean your husband will have to learn to cook more than curried goat?* I mean, everything is so trivial to them. No one asked me about my schools, families and youth club initiatives.'

'That's how they are,' said Clayton. 'You better get used to it.'

'You'll have to get used to it too,' laughed Juliet. 'I bet they'll ask you to appear on one of them celebrity cook programmes!'

'No fucking way,' said Clayton. 'Mind you, the media might come in useful to promote the youth club. Me and Breanna were talking about it when I drove her home. It'll be good for her. They need all the publicity they can get.'

'You're asking me to abuse my position, Mr Hylton?'

'No, just a little nudge in the right direction.'

'Oh, Clayton, I'm so tired. At least I'll have a few weeks off in the summer. I was thinking …'

'Thinking what?'

'I'm thinking of going to see Brenton.'

'Brenton? Why now? What brought this on?'

'Since he's settled in Miami I haven't seen him.'

'Breanna says he's happy,' said Clayton. 'I thought you would use the summer recess to get to know your constituents.'

'I know a lot of them already,' reasoned Juliet. 'I've been in the face of constituents too much lately. They're probably sick and tired of seeing me ... I need to see Brenton.'

'Why do you need to see him? He's a big boy now. He's got a nice house, good job. He's doing alright. He doesn't need you to look out for him anymore.'

'He's my brother, Clayton.'

'And I'm your husband! In the last few weeks I have hardly seen you! I was thinking of a holiday myself. Me and you. Go to somewhere quiet. I was thinking of St Lucia. Maybe a cruise?'

'We can do that,' said Juliet. 'But later. In the summer I need to see my brother.'

'You can call him to see if he's alright. I really don't mind the phone bill. Or e-mail him. Talk to him on your laptop.'

'*Clayton!*'

Clayton was silent driving up Leigham Court Road. Juliet checked his expression in the rear-view mirror. His eyes were hard. His lips were tense. Why's he getting so vex about me seeing Brenton? she asked herself. I haven't seen Brenton for three years. We can always go St Lucia. Clayton's been really understanding during the campaign though. But Breanna's right. I have to see Brenton.

Clayton didn't say another word until he opened his front door. 'So, er,' he began. His tone was softer. 'When are you thinking of going?'

'The week after school breaks up,' said Juliet.

'For how long?'

'Two weeks. So if you want we can go somewhere when I get back.'

'Yes, we could,' nodded Clayton. 'I'll think of somewhere.'

Kicking off her shoes, Juliet picked them up and walked up the stairs. 'I'm going to my bed,' she said. 'Thanks for understanding about me going to Miami.'

'That's alright,' said Clayton. 'I was being a bit selfish. It's just that I haven't seen much of you lately. I've missed you. You go and see Brenton … I'll be up in a sec, I've just got to check something on my computer.'

'See you in bed then,' said Juliet.

'Alright.'

Juliet disappeared upstairs. Clayton went to the front room. He sat down in an armchair and stared vacantly at the floor. He then stood up and almost ripped off his tie. He took off his jacket and rolled up his sleeves. He picked up his laptop from the coffee table and switched it on. He logged onto the internet and typed Virgin Atlantic into the search engine. He browsed business class flights from late July to early August. He then did a search for Miami hotels. He stood up again and went upstairs. Juliet was lying down on the bed still in her clothes. Her eyes were closed. Clayton picked up his diary from his bedside cabinet. He returned downstairs and flicked through it.

'*Shit!*' he whispered to himself. 'If she leaves for Miami just after the schools break up I won't be able to follow her for maybe five or six days. I'll follow her anyway and surprise her. Yes, surprise her with a cruise or something. No way I'm leaving her with *him*. Can't do that. *Fuck* that.'

He went to the kitchen and poured himself a tequila and Coke cocktail. He squeezed in drops of lime juice and opened a packet of cheese and onion crisps. He returned to the lounge and browsed for Miami hotels four-star or better. He glanced to the ceiling, took a sip of his drink, grimaced and continued his search.

Chapter 25

South Miami Heights

Three months later

THE FLIGHT HAD BEEN NINE HOURS LONG and Juliet was waiting outside Miami International airport on a sidewalk in an under-pass in her beige three-quarter-length slacks and sky-blue top. The humidity and the exhaust fumes were making her feel nau-seous and she looked for somewhere to sit down. She couldn't find any bench or seat so she sat down on the pavement. She took off her sandals to air her feet and flex her toes then put them back on again. She watched a Spanish-speaking family trying to fit their suitcases into two taxi cabs. A few yards away an old man was sitting in a wheelchair smoking a cigarette. They exchanged weary glances. Juliet recognised a black guy who had been on her flight. He was greeted with hugs and kisses by family members who relieved him of his luggage and led him away.

Where the *fuck* is Brenton? Juliet said to herself. She wiped her forehead with a handkerchief and took a swig from her bottle of mineral water. She noticed that most of the cars that went by were big-wheeled 4x4s and the sound of their engines amplified and echoed around her. She took out her mobile phone, remembered not to dial the international dialling code and called Brenton. 'Where are you? I'm dying a death out here!'

'I'm here, man,' Brenton answered. 'Just coming around. I'm in a pick-up truck. I'll be with you in a sec.'

'A pick-up truck? Hurry up! It's so steamy here. I feel like I'm going to faint.'

Juliet snapped her mobile phone closed and just as she took a long gulp from her bottle, Brenton appeared in his mud-splattered Ford pick-up truck tooting his horn. Juliet smiled with relief. Trust Brenton to drive the dirtiest car I've seen today, she observed. Thank God he's here though.

A nearby motorist wasn't happy at the way Brenton cut in on him. Brenton ignored the cursing driver and parked his truck at an angle. He jumped out and bear-hugged his sister, kissing her on the left cheek. Juliet gasped for air. He was wearing a white vest, lime-green khaki shorts, open-toed sandals and his sunglasses were balanced on the top of his shaved head.

'About time!' she said. 'I thought you were going to meet me in arrivals.'

'Do you know how expensive it is to park a pick-up at the airport?'

'You cheapo! I could've got lost in there!'

Brenton picked up Juliet's sky-blue coloured luggage and dropped it into the back of his truck amongst various building materials and power tools. He noticed that even her handbag was sky-blue.

'Don't be so rough with the luggage, man,' Juliet complained. 'That's all new. You know how much that cost me? And what if it rains?'

'Man! You're seriously grumpy. I've got a plastic cover in the back if it rains. Bad flight?'

'As it goes, *yes!* I didn't have a window position and I was stuck in the middle seats beside this overweight woman who had a cough.'

Brenton laughed. 'Breanna had the same problem when she came over. I thought you woulda booked first class and t'ing, you know, with you being an MP and t'ing.'

'I can't fly first class,' Juliet said. 'I'm an MP representing Lambeth. How will it look if I'm seen flying first class?'

Brenton shook his head. 'Anyway, you're here now,' he said. 'Get in. We've got about a forty-five-minute drive to my place.'

Juliet stepped inside Brenton's cab. Brenton ran around the other side and climbed into the driver's seat. He closed the tinted windows and switched on the air conditioning. Alpha's *Can't Get Over You* chirped from the truck stereo. He kissed Juliet again on the cheek then he signalled left and pulled away. As they emerged from the underpass Juliet had to put her sunglasses on to shield her eyes from the sun's fierce glare.

'I was hoping you'd get in a bit earlier,' said Brenton. 'From three o'clock the traffic really starts to build up.'

'Customs took forever,' she said. 'They took my fingerprints and asked me to look in this camera thing. Then they asked me to empty my flight bag.'

'So that's why you're so fucked off,' Brenton reasoned. 'They don't mess about with security here. And you being an MP doesn't matter a shit. No one over here cares a damn about what happens in England. Most people here didn't even realise there was an election in the UK this year.'

Looking at the palm trees that lined the road, Juliet sighed and enjoyed the sensation of the air conditioning cooling her body. 'You don't get any little Ford Fiestas or Vauxhall Corsas here, do you. Most of the cars are so big.'

'Yep,' Brenton nodded. 'Americans love their cars. Mind you, you need your car in Miami. Public transport is shit. Not like London.'

'So how did you cope without a car when you first come here?'

'I had to take a taxi to work,' said Brenton. 'It cost me nuff dollars but I soon got myself a second-hand ride.'

'A second-hand *ride*?' Juliet laughed. 'You're starting to chat like an American.'

'Ride. That's what they call it out here. You want me to stop for anyt'ing? I haven't had time to do any shopping and there's not a damn t'ing in my fridge. I thought you wouldn't mind if I took you some place for dinner. What you saying?'

'Yeah,' agreed Juliet. 'We could do that. I need a shower though and a change of clothes.'

'Alright,' said Brenton. 'Just got to get myself on US One and it's more or less a straight drive once we're on it.'

'US One?' queried Juliet.

'The South Dixie Highway. Like the main road through this part of Florida. It was well confusing when I first came over. Got lost nuff times and it took me ages to get used to driving on the right. When I came up on the junction I was always looking the wrong way. I always looked right when I should've been looking left. I do it automatically now though. Seriously, I'm all safe and t'ing.'

Juliet looked out of the window. All the roads seemed to be in straight lines, she observed. No hills and hardly any curves.

She glanced at Brenton and thought he looked really well. His skin looks so much better. Nice and toned. There's a bit more definition in his muscles; especially on his arms. He's a bit darker than the last time I saw him. He's still got his square jaw. Not a pinch of fat on that. His abs looking kind of alright too. How old is he now? What? Forty-one? Forty-two? Jules, you're getting old, girl. Can't even remember how old Brenton is. Two years younger than me. Yeah, he's forty-two. Anyway, he's looking good. Working in this weather must keep him fit. And his eyes. Breanna's definitely got his eyes.

'So what have you got planned for me?' asked Juliet.

'I live close to the zoo,' said Brenton. 'Gonna take you there tomorrow. We're gonna share a bike and look at some animals, ride on a giant turtle's back and tickle a lion's mane and t'ing.'

'Share a bike?' wondered Juliet.

'Yeah. They got these tandem bike things. Much easier getting around the zoo on them. It's a big space. Me and Breanna were tearing around the place on one. You up for it?'

'Er, yeah, why not?'

'On Sunday I'm gonna take you down to the Keys,' continued Brenton. 'The drive down there is wicked, going over all these bridges over the sea. There's a nice beach at Big Pine Key. I go down there every few weeks or so. Really nice. They say on a good day you can see the tip of Cuba. I've been there nuff times and I couldn't see shit but you get my drift; the view is wicked and t'ing. Biscuit and Carol loved it there and Floyd and Sharon. Oh, that reminds me. I'd better pick up some t'ings to eat and drink for the drive to the Keys.'

'I'll come with you,' offered Juliet.

'No, no! You're gonna be tired from jet lag and t'ing in the morning. You sleep in.'

Juliet peered through the window again. The palm trees looked so much taller seeing them live than in the photographs that Breanna brought back home, she thought. Every couple of miles or so there was a shopping mall or a fast-food restaurant, Juliet observed. No corner shops or newsagents here. She glanced up at the traffic lights that seemed to be held up by thick wires and slim poles. 'Is it hurricane season yet?' she asked.

'Just coming into it,' answered Brenton. 'Didn't get no serious breeze last year though.'

'What happens to the traffic lights when you get a storm?'

'They blow about a bit,' Brenton replied casually.

Fifty minutes later, Brenton turned into a short drive and pulled up outside his bungalow in South Miami Heights. Juliet climbed out of the cab. She could feel the intensity of the late-afternoon Miami sun but she could only admire his house. Brenton had landscaped a small front garden where he installed a little oval-shaped pond. Bright flowers fronted the garden; Juliet couldn't guess what they were called but she was quite taken aback that Brenton of all people would plant flowers in front of his house. The stonework of the building was painted peach and the arched light-brown roof tiles complemented the peach nicely. The pathway that led to the front door was lined with round white stones the size of footballs. The windows were covered in mosquito grilles and French-style wooden shutters. She noticed American flags fluttering in a few front gardens in Brenton's street and she wondered what the neighbours would say if Brenton strung up a Lion of Judah flag. They'd probably think he's a terrorist, she chuckled.

Collecting Juliet's luggage, Brenton led her to his front door. He turned the key, pushed the door open and ushered Juliet inside. She walked into the light-brown ceramic-tiled reception area and staring at her from the opposite wall was a framed image of a young denim-clad Bob Marley strumming his Gibson guitar. To the left of the reception were the kitchen and the laundry room. Through a door beside the Bob Marley picture was the lounge and to the right was a hallway that led to the three bedrooms. There was a small teak coffee table in the reception area and resting on it was a glass vase of orchid lilies; Juliet closed her eyes and breathed in their fragrance.

'This is *really* nice,' she remarked. 'I love how you've used the colours here. *Really* nice.'

'To be honest when Sharon and Floyd first came out here,' Brenton explained, 'Sharon kinda advised me on the colour t'ing. She's good at all that kinda t'ing.'

'She is,' Juliet nodded.

'Let me show you your room,' said Brenton.

He led Juliet along the hallway and she looked at the framed photographs of legendary footballers, Pele and Maradona, hanging from the walls and there was one of the cricketer, Sir Vivian Richards. Brenton turned right and showed Juliet the bedroom that overlooked the front garden.

'It's all clean and t'ing,' said Brenton putting down the luggage. 'Breanna slept in here. I hoovered it out last night and Ajaxed it and t'ing. The ceiling fan wasn't working but it's sorted. The

TV remote is on the bedside cabinet. I was gonna buy you some magazines but I haven't a clue what you like.'

Suitably impressed and sniffing in the scent of red and orange roses in a vase on the dressing table, Juliet put her handbag on the bed and sat down in a chair next to the window. 'Since when have you been interested in flowers?' she asked.

'Oh, that was probably Shyanza's influence.'

'Shyanza? You never told me about her?'

'She was a girl I was seeing.'

'Was? What happened?' Juliet asked, opening her handbag and taking out a mint.

'T'ings didn't work out. She came from a big Nicaraguan family and she had all these *married* older sisters. I think her main ambition in life was to become a married sister and that's all she ever went on about … apart from flowers. With that and the fact she was so damn Catholic, t'ings didn't work out.'

'Sorry to hear,' said Juliet.

'She could really whine up her hips and dance though,' Brenton revealed, a nice memory forming itself in his mind. 'And as I said she loved flowers. On Sundays she would stick a flower in her hair before she went to church. She looked real … Every week or so she would get me to buy flowers and put them in the kitchen, in the reception area and in the front room. I just kinda carried on the habit and I thought it would be nice if I put some flowers in your room … if you don't like them …'

'No, no. It's a nice touch. And I'm sure she looked really *pretty* with the flower in her hair.'

Brenton opened the wardrobe. 'There're towels and flannels on the top shelf,' he said. 'Do you wanna cold drink? I've got some mango and grape juice in the fridge. My ice machine is bruk; meant to call someone out about that but there's ice in the freezer. Haven't got any wine. Have to get some later. I know you love off your wine.'

'I'll have mango, please,' said Juliet kicking off her sandals.

Brenton went to the kitchen. Juliet looked around her surroundings. She placed her feet down on the ceramic tiling, kicked off her sandals and enjoyed the cool sensation on her naked soles. She let herself drop on to the bed and closed her eyes. She opened them again and stared at the three-rotored ceiling fan. She recalled the first time she made love to Brenton. She smiled. A street kid back then, she thought. But look at him now.

Brenton returned with Juliet's drink. Juliet chuckled as she could see about ten ice cubes in the glass. 'I'm going to take a shower,' she said. 'Got to get out of these clothes. I must stink.'

'Alright then,' said Brenton. 'You're next to the shower. Holler if you want something. I'm, er, I'll just be in my room. It's the end bedroom.'

Juliet watched Brenton depart before she opened her suitcase to find her shower bag and toiletries. She decided on her beige three-quarter length cheesecloth trousers and a white T-shirt to wear afterwards and she wondered where Brenton would take her for dinner.

After showering, Juliet wrapped her pink, full-length towel around her and put on her pink flip-flops. She came out of the bathroom and into the hallway. 'Brenton!' she called. 'Brenton! Do you have a laundry basket? Somewhere to put my dirty clothes?'

Emerging into the hallway, Brenton had his mobile phone pressed to his left ear. He took a long look at Juliet standing opposite him. 'I'll call you back later,' he said into the phone. 'My sister's just come in from London. I might come in on Monday to check the foundations and shuttering.'

Walking slowly towards Brenton, Juliet took the phone out of his hand, led him by the other hand to her room, placed the phone on the dressing table and kissed him on the lips.

'Juli–'

She placed her arms around his neck, gazed into his eyes and kissed him again on the forehead. 'No point me kidding myself anymore,' she said.

They stood there kissing each other softly, looking at each other, stroking each other's cheeks and foreheads, and smiling. Juliet arched back her neck. Brenton kissed her throat and the entire length of her collarbone. He unwrapped her towel. It fell to the floor in a heap. Brenton pulled off his vest. Juliet helped him.

'You're gonna need another shower,' he joked.

Juliet laughed out loud. She pulled down his khaki shorts. They fell onto the bed. Juliet hit her head on her handbag. Brenton massaged and kissed it better. He pulled off his boxers. As she lay on her stomach Brenton kissed her from the nape of her neck to the base of her spine. He delighted in watching the tiny pimples of her skin. They took their time getting to know one another's bodies once more. They did not speak in fear of spoiling the vibe. They spoke with their eyes as they pressed their cheeks and foreheads hard together. He moved down and circled her nipples with his tongue before sucking them. She could feel his hard muscled stomach rubbing against her and she arched her neck again, raising her knees. She caressed his shoulder blades and she could feel his longing in every movement. Brenton kissed and licked further down her chest and stomach and she could now sense his growing energy and excitement. The kissing became harder, almost violent. The hand that had caressed her inner thighs was now pressing down. She felt her legs being spread apart. She wanted him to enter her at that moment but he was wildly pawing and squeezing her backside and kissing and licking her. She glanced at the top of his perspiring head. She opened her legs wider, inviting him to enter her. He came back up and started to kiss her throat once more. He nibbled her ears as his fingers stroked her cheeks. She could feel his manhood pressing on her stomach. She slid further up the bed, opened her legs even wider before linking them around his back. Brenton entered her but after two minutes or so, turned her over on to her stomach and entered her again. He cupped her breasts as he made love to her and she could feel his perspiring temples against her neck.

Afterwards, Juliet lay on top of Brenton, resting her head on his chest. Brenton was stroking the top of her head. 'I was thinking on the plane about the possibility of this happening,' admitted Juliet.

'I've always thought about the possibility of it happening,' laughed Brenton. '*Every* day. Since … since … you know. Nothing changes, does it? After what? Twenty-four years?'

'Twenty-five,' corrected Juliet. 'And four months.'

'You're an MP. I'm out here. We're meant to be what? Wiser? And here we are. The best feeling in the world!'

'I know … what are we going to do?'

'If … if you come over here,' said Brenton. 'Then as far as I'm concerned you're not with *him*.'

'He's my husband, Brenton.'

'Is he your husband now?'

Juliet thought about it. She looked at Brenton's naked body. She looked at her own. She observed how blissfully happy he was. She finally shook her head.

'You coming over every year,' said Brenton. 'Or whenever you can. I can live with that.'

Kissing Brenton on the forehead, Juliet cradled his jaw with her palms. 'I'll come over whenever I can … but …'

'But what?'

'What if Breanna comes with me?'

'Then we go back to brother and sister.'

Juliet thought about it again and then nodded.

'Don't ever bring *him* over here though,' said Brenton. 'I don't think I could stand that. Back in the UK the jealousy t'ing was slowly killing me.'

Juliet nodded again.

'Oh, by the way,' said Brenton.

'What is it?'

'The laundry basket is in the laundry room next door to the kitchen.'

Juliet burst out laughing and picked up a pillow and smashed it against Brenton's head. They started a play-fight with Juliet winning, two submissions to one.

Brenton watched Juliet stretching out on the bed. 'You're still gone clear,' he said.

'Gone clear? What does that mean?'

'Something Floyd used to say about really pretty girls. *Gone clear!*'

'It can be a bitch too,' said Juliet. 'Looking like this.'

'What do you mean?'

'If you've noticed, I haven't got many close friends. Only Tessa.'

'Join the club,' said Brenton. 'I've only got Floyd who I can be real with.'

Juliet gazed at the ceiling. Brenton kissed her on her forehead but he detected sadness in her eyes. 'I was real popular at school,' she said. 'But as I got older and friends started dating, they were different to me. They wouldn't trust me. If I said hi to any of their boyfriends they'd automatically think I was trying to steal him from them.'

'Their boyfriends probably fancied you,' suggested Brenton.

'That was the problem,' said Juliet, still staring at the ceiling. 'A few of them did. I didn't lead any of them on but two of them asked me out while they were still going with my friends. Did my friends believe me? Oh no! I was labelled a relationship breaker, a fucking bitch. They reckoned I thought I was *too pretty* and all that and I would go for any man I wanted and not give a shit. One of them threatened to scar my face.'

'Must have been rough,' said Brenton.

'It was. At the time I met you, friends were just drifting away from me. I didn't do anything wrong.'

'Their loss,' said Brenton. 'You're with me now. Fuck them.'

Brenton kissed her again on the cheek and gave her a reassuring hug.

She fell asleep in Brenton's arms for two hours and when she woke up they made love again. They showered together before leaving for a South American steak restaurant. Following their meal they departed holding hands and shared a kiss before Brenton switched the ignition on.

'How is Breanna?' asked Brenton.

'Opinionated,' answered Juliet. 'Headstrong. Ever since Malakai passed away she's become more confident, outgoing. We should always be thankful to him. She doesn't worry so much about her looks anymore. Finally she likes herself. She's comfortable in her own skin.'

'That's good.'

'Yes, it is, but she argues with me over everything.'

'How's her job?'

'She loves it. She's just done a course about identifying children's behavior that could mean problems within the home and she's taken over the youth club's homework sessions. Clayton's a patron of the organisation so sometimes we drop in to where Breanna works. I tell you what; she's much more patient with kids than I ever was.'

'Yeah, I hear that,' said Brenton. 'When she was over here all she would talk about is the kids she works with. How she likes making some kind of difference to them. I'm seriously proud of her.'

'Me too,' nodded Juliet.

'Any boyfriends on the scene?' asked Brenton.

'Not that I know of,' answered Juliet. 'It doesn't bother her that she hasn't got a man like other girls of her age I know.'

'She might as well wait for a good one.'

'Yeah … by the way, I bumped into Sean the other day.'

'How's he doing?'

'He's working and going to college,' said Juliet. 'You know you were great for him.'

'He wasn't that bad, you know,' said Brenton. 'Just made some wrong choices. He just needed someone to tell him that yeah, he's OK; he can do shit and get a good job. He can be a part of society. I just gave him stuff to do. I was strict about him turning up on time and I wouldn't take any fuckery. He soon learned that I wouldn't take his chatting on his mobile every minute. One time I told him to give me his phone first t'ing in the morning and I gave it back before he went home. He got used to my ways.'

Juliet leant over to her left and kissed Brenton on the cheek.

'Wasn't I the same?' asked Brenton. 'I wasn't any different. But you came along. Remember that first time I saw you?'

Juliet nodded. She smiled.

'You told me I could do shit,' resumed Brenton. 'What was it? You told me to get my backside to college and ask about courses.'

Juliet grinned at the memory. Brenton glanced at her before concentrating on the road again.

They arrived home and Brenton helped carry Juliet's luggage into his room. They made love again before getting up together in the middle of the night to share chocolate ice cream and Dominican rum in the lounge beneath a large framed photo of Charlie Chaplin and a very young Jackie Coogan in a still from their silent movie *The Kid*. Hanging from the opposite wall was a poster from the classic musical *Oliver!*

Juliet was lying on her back on the leather sofa as Brenton fed her the ice cream. He was making her laugh and the ice cream didn't go where it was meant to go. Brenton kissed the chocolate off her face.

The next day they toured around Miami Metrozoo in a tandem and Brenton accused Juliet of not doing her share of the pedalling. In the afternoon they drove to Southridge Park where they picnicked, massaged each other and lazed under the hot Miami sun. They went home and started to make love in the shower before finishing in the bedroom. They fell asleep naked on top of the bed, spooned together. A lovers' rock CD was playing on a loop.

They both rose in the early hours, not bothering to put on any clothes. They snacked on mango and melon chunks and finished off the Dominican rum.

Driving down to the Keys the following day, Juliet was dressed in a black bikini, a wide-brimmed straw hat and a rainbow-coloured sarong. Brenton decided to drive with the windows open and while Juliet was marvelling at the views of the blue Atlantic on either side of her, Brenton was admiring her body. Her wraparound sunglasses perched on the top of her head, she was sipping from a carton of guava juice and eating a bunch of red seedless grapes. The trailing wind messed up her hair but she had no thought about that. She glanced up at the cloudless sky and then to Brenton. *You always get what you want*, she recalled Tessa telling her. Why shouldn't I get what I want, she said in her mind. Just for a little while. Two weeks of the year. Why not? Brenton knows my situation. He's OK with it. He's more than happy that I'm with him. What Clayton doesn't know can't hurt him or anybody else for that matter. So much for this being a sin. *Fuck it!* If there is an all-powerful God then He made me fall in love with Brenton. I can't choose not to love him. Nothing will stop me from seeing him. *Nothing*!

'So what's it like being an MP?' Brenton asked, interrupting Juliet's thinking.

'Frustrating,' she said. 'We've just been re-elected but instead of getting on with what we should be doing, the talk and memos are all about how we must appeal to the public, how we must come across on TV and forums. Even now they're thinking of how they're going to get re-elected in the next election. Can you believe that?'

'So not how you thought it would be?'

'Not really. The whips go on like they're enforcers ...'

'Whips? Who the fuck are the whips? Brothel madams and t'ing? I always knew MPs were kinky.'

Juliet laughed. 'They're just people in the parliamentary party who try and tell you what to vote for, toe the party line, what to say and all that. They walk around Westminster like they're your parents.'

Brenton glanced at Juliet. 'And you put up with that?'

'Fuck no!' Juliet answered. 'I tell them what to do with themselves. I won't let them intimidate me.'

'So how is it working at the ... what is it? Where do you work?'

'I'm a junior minister at Works and Pension. I was offered a junior ministry at Health and the Home Office but I turned it down. I really wanted the Children's minister job.'

'So what's it like then?'

'To tell you the truth all of us new junior ministers and the so-called ministers of state didn't have a clue the way the whole thing worked. We're so reliant on the civil service. Trust me; it's them who really run the country. MPs might pretend they know what they're doing but we haven't got a clue. One ex education minister told me he was in the job for four years and still didn't totally know what he was doing. After five years he had a little idea but then there was a reshuffle and he got sacked. Now he's saying what he always wanted to say from the backbenches while the new education minister sits in his office all confused. At the end of the day it's all about jobs for the boys from Oxbridge. Most of them don't care about people. They only care about who might be the next Foreign Secretary or Chancellor or who gets to chair some jumped-up select committee or what City job might fall into their laps when they leave office. Now and again they might give a woman the Home Office or Health just to make it look like they're not sexist. But really, it's a boys' club, looking after themselves.'

'Sounds like a lot of fuckery,' remarked Brenton.

'I will serve out my time and then maybe do something else. Maybe work for a children's charity or something.'

'Enough about politics,' said Brenton. 'Sometimes I don't know half the fuck of what you're going on about.'

Juliet burst out laughing.

'You're seriously going to love this beach,' he added.

An hour later, Brenton pulled up within walking distance of Big Pine Key beach. He walked hand in hand with Juliet across the sand towards the curved shoreline. The ocean shimmered in tones of blue; the darker the further they looked out. Brown seaweed rode on the gently breaking frothy waves. The smell of salt filled their nostrils. The sea was calm. Juliet found it hard to believe that hurricanes ripped through these beaches on a regular basis. She looked out to the ocean. Quiet, still vessels skirted the wavy horizon. Excited shouts from children playing with lilos and rubber rings broke the serenity. Sunbathers on long towels glanced up at the only black couple on the beach.

Finding a clear spot, Brenton and Juliet rolled out their towels. Juliet lay down looking at the sea and Brenton took out his bottle of lavender oil and started to massage it into her shoulders. She closed her eyes.

'I'm only doing this for ten minutes,' said Brenton. 'Then I'm going for a dip.'

'One hour then you got a deal,' said Juliet.

'Half an hour.'

'Forty-five minutes.'

'Forty minutes,' chuckled Brenton. 'But a break after twenty.'

'Deal,' laughed Juliet. 'But you have to make up the hour when we get home.'

'Deal!'

Three days later

Checking in at the Blue Moon Hotel that overlooked Miami South Beach, Clayton asked the receptionist if she could arrange for his rental car to be ready and waiting in two hours.

He went up to his room and showered, changed his clothes and had a light meal. He then checked his messages on his laptop computer but every now and again he took out a scrap of paper and read the address written on it. Before leaving his room he took out his wallet from his back pocket and looked at the image he always kept in there; a photograph of a three-year-old Breanna, Juliet and himself. Carefully he placed it back in his wallet and made his way to the hotel's reception. He picked up his rental car keys along with a flyer advertising the hotel's spa swimming pool. He made a mental note to check out the fountains and waterfall feature of the hotel and thought Juliet would enjoy seeing it ... if she returned with him.

Stepping outside he was hit by the heat of the afternoon sun and he quickly climbed into the car and adjusted the rear mirror. He took out the address from his back pocket and keyed it into the satellite navigation system. He turned the ignition, switched on the air conditioning but before he pulled away, he looked at his reflection in the rear-view mirror. 'Juliet,' he whispered. 'Don't let this be true.'

He drove out of the hotel car park and made his way to the

South Dixie Highway – US One. He glanced at the graphics on the satellite navigation system and it read *South Miami Heights*. He checked the time on his watch. Three twenty p.m.

'You're not getting dressed?' shouted Brenton from his kitchen. 'You'll have to get ready sooner or later. I wanna leave here by five. It's half past three already.'

'Do we have to go out this evening?' said Juliet, dressed only in one of Brenton's old T-shirts. 'Can't we stay in?'

'I've already told Ramirez about you,' replied Brenton. He turned over four rashers of turkey bacon in the frying pan. 'He wants to meet my sister. His wife is cooking something for us.'

'Can't we see him tomorrow?'

'I have to work tomorrow,' said Brenton.

'I'm tired,' argued Juliet.

'You can sleep tonight.'

'I would sleep but you won't let me! I've hardly slept since I've been here.'

Satisfied that the turkey bacon was cooked, Brenton placed two rashers on each plate to complete a meal with scrambled eggs and toast. He placed Juliet's plate on a tray and brought it to her.

Sitting up in bed, Juliet was flicking through the TV channels. 'I can't watch American TV,' she remarked. 'Too many adverts.'

'That's why I don't bother,' said Brenton. He presented the tray to Juliet. 'I just listen to the radio or play my music.'

'Thanks, Brenton,' said Juliet accepting the tray. 'I have to see if I can find this turkey bacon in England. This is bad. Having breakfast after three o'clock?'

'Don't worry about it. You're on holiday.'

'Don't worry about it,' Juliet repeated. 'If that's the case, let me eat this and have a nap afterwards. I really need to catch up on sleep. Can't you call Ramirez and tell him we're going to be a bit late?'

Brenton kissed Juliet on the forehead and said, 'Yeah, OK. No worries.'

'Looking forward to going to Orlando at the weekend,' said Juliet.

'Yep, you're gonna love it.'

'I want to check out the Epcot Center. How long does it take to get there?'

'About four hours. It's one straight drive.'

'And we're spending the weekend there?'

'Yep. One day at the Epcot place and the next day at Universal or Disneyland. Your choice.'

'I'll sleep on it and look at the leaflets again,' said Juliet.

'OK, I'm going to eat in the front room; got to catch up on my taxes and t'ing. Oh, and I got to reply to Floyd's e-mail.'

'OK,' said Juliet. 'Don't be too long and join me when you're finished.

Fifty minutes later Brenton's doorbell rang. He got up from his computer desk in the lounge to answer it. He pulled the door open and saw Clayton in front of him. He reeled back slightly. He blinked and re-focused his eyes. Before Brenton could react or say anything, Clayton walked into the reception area. 'I thought I'd surprise, Juliet,' he said. 'I've lined up a Caribbean cruise. Where is she?'

Still standing by the front door with his hand on the door-handle, Brenton stuttered and couldn't get any words out. Clayton offered him a suspicious glare before turning right into the hallway. 'Juliet!' he called. 'Juliet!'

Something within Brenton allowed Clayton to look for her. He remained in the reception area. Shock was written on his face.

Clayton checked the first bedroom. He quickly walked into the second. As he was coming out into the hallway he met Juliet under the doorframe of Brenton's bedroom. She was wearing a pair of Brenton's tracksuit bottoms and Brenton's T-shirt. Clayton scanned the room. He noticed the untidy bed. He saw Juliet's suitcase. Her toiletries. His deodorant. Her make-up. His shaving cream. Her slippers. His sandals. Her underwear. His socks. Juliet's long pink towel was covering the foot of the bed. One of Brenton's towels was draped over a chair. Juliet retreated until her legs hit the bed. She sat down. Clayton followed her every move. Something stopped him from entering the bedroom. Juliet could hear Brenton's naked feet padding along the hallway. Clayton still glared at her. He turned away. Brenton walked towards him. He stopped.

'I always had a thought in the back of my head,' Clayton said calmly. 'Even before Ms Massey passed away. I didn't want to think ...' Clayton spun around again. He searched Juliet's eyes. 'For years I was praying it wasn't true.'

His black shoes echoing off the ceramic tiles, Clayton about-turned and brushed past Brenton. Juliet remained on the bed motionless. She gazed into the palm of her right hand. Brenton stared at her. Clayton reached the reception area. 'Breanna will find this interesting!' he shouted.

Juliet and Brenton stared at each other. For a long moment they couldn't move. Juliet finally found her voice. 'He can't tell Breanna!'

Frantically searching for his truck keys, Brenton found them on the bedside cabinet. He ran along the hallway and out of the house. Clayton had just pulled away. Brenton jumped into his cab and fired the ignition. He screeched into reverse and chased after Clayton. Clayton turned left at the next junction. Brenton changed gears and signalled left. He looked right for oncoming traffic. He didn't see the big truck speeding from the left. It smashed into his cab with such power that what was left of Brenton's small pick-up truck spun five times before it came to a standstill. Brenton was killed instantly on impact.

Hearing the crash behind him, Clayton pulled up and leaped out of his rental car to take a look. He climbed back in and performed a u-turn to take a better view. He saw Brenton's mutilated body protruding out of the windscreen; he wasn't wearing a seat belt.

Holding his head in his hands, Clayton closed his eyes. 'Oh my God!' he whispered. 'Oh my God! Oh my God!'

He composed himself enough to dial 911 on his mobile and he checked on the driver of the large truck; he was in shock but had only superficial cuts and bruises. Other motorists were stopping and coming out of their cars.

Taking in a deep breath, Clayton returned to his car and drove the three hundred yards to Brenton's house. He saw Juliet walking towards him with her arms folded. He parked the car and waited for her. Residents were emerging from their homes to see what had happened.

Juliet reached Clayton. 'I'm, I'm so sorry,' he said.

Juliet didn't seem to have heard him. Staring ahead she could see the back end of Brenton's pick-up truck pointing towards the pavement. Her steps were measured and calm. Her gaze didn't falter.

'I'll, I'll drive you the rest of the way,' Clayton offered.

Ignoring Clayton's offer, Juliet walked straight ahead, arms folded and staring vacantly in front of her. It was as if she knew already that Brenton had passed. The further she walked the more she could see of the devastation. By the time she reached the crash scene, sirens were sounding in the distance. Clayton tried to comfort her the best way he could as ambulance men cut Brenton's body free of the wreckage. Juliet watched calmly. She didn't listen to anything that was being said.

When Brenton's body was finally laid on a stretcher in a black body bag, Juliet walked up to him. 'I'm his sister,' she said to the medics.

She unzipped the body bag to reveal Brenton's bloodied head. His eyes were now closed. She knelt down and placed her left palm on his cheek. She kissed him on the forehead. The medics looked at her. She unzipped the body bag further and took out Brenton's left hand. She brought it to her left cheek and closed her eyes. She opened them again before carefully replacing the hand. Clayton looked on. She kissed Brenton on the forehead and then the lips. She wiped something from his nose. She traced her right finger over the contours of his face. She ran her fingers over his head before kissing it. She dropped her head as she zipped up the body bag. She stood up. Brenton's blood was on her face and her hands. 'OK,' she said, still gazing at the body bag.

The medics wheeled Brenton into the waiting ambulance. Juliet stood watching as the police interviewed witnesses. Clayton went to comfort her but she didn't acknowledge him.

It was Clayton who arranged for Brenton's body to be flown back to London. He and Juliet didn't exchange a word until they were flying halfway across the Atlantic. Climbing out of his business class seat, Clayton walked down to where Juliet was sitting in economy class. She was staring vacantly out the window. 'If you are ... ' he said in a whisper. 'If you are worried then don't be. I will never tell Breanna. She doesn't deserve that.'

Juliet kept on gazing out the window.

'As for us,' Clayton resumed. 'I'll ... I'll leave any talk of divorce for now. I don't want the media saying I'm a heartless bastard for filing for divorce when you have just buried your brother.'

Juliet didn't respond.

'But we'll have to deal with that eventually,' Clayton continued. 'At the end of the day I want someone to, er, feel for me the way you ... you felt for him. I want to be with someone like that. You understand?'

'Of course you do,' said Juliet. She still stared out of the window. 'I'm sorry that someone couldn't have been me … real sorry.'

'Yes.'

At last Juliet turned around to face Clayton. 'Thanks for everything. I was in no state to …'

'I know,' said Clayton. 'I'm, I'm going back to my seat now. We'll talk when we land … I still don't understand why you wanted to fly economy class?'

Juliet nodded and offered a weak smile.

Epilogue

ARRIVING HOME FROM BRENTON'S FUNERAL, Floyd went to his kitchen, took a bottle of whisky from a cupboard, poured it into a glass and mixed it with Coca-Cola. He dropped in three ice cubes and took his drink upstairs to his bedroom. He sat down on the chair facing his computer screen, put his glass down on a mouse pad and loosened his black tie. He took a sip of his drink, recoiled slightly as the whisky hit the back of his throat and stared into the blank computer screen. 'Too much whisky,' he whispered to himself.

As he took a second sip, his wife, Sharon, entered the bedroom. She took off her jacket, draped it over a chair and threw her handbag on to the bed. She walked over to Floyd, cupped his jaw and kissed him on the forehead. She then sat down on the bed, propped up by a family of pillows. Floyd switched on his computer.

'I was crying more than everybody,' Floyd admitted. 'Just couldn't keep it in.'

'Most of us felt like that,' Sharon replied. 'Breanna was in bits. But Juliet? She seemed like she was in a different world. She didn't say a word to me or anyone. She was all calm-like. Too calm. It was weird. It was like she was there but not there.'

'Did I tell you?' Floyd said, ignoring Sharon's remarks. The computer screen flickered into life. Using the mouse he clicked on to Hotmail. He took another sip from his drink. 'Brenton sent me an e-mail on the day of the crash.'

'No, you didn't tell me,' said Sharon. 'What did he say?'

'I'll read it to you. I didn't see it till yesterday but here it goes. *Yo, Floyd. I know people say it's wrong but it just feels right. In fact it feels perfect. It was unbelievable last time and even better this time. It's like God made her for me. Serious. Nuff years have gone by but the way we feel hasn't changed a damn thing. I can't really put it into words but I feel so good right now. It's like we have no say about the way we want each other. There hasn't been a day when I haven't thought about her, you know, being with her. It's like fate. Serious. How can that be so wrong? It's like God wanted it this way. There's only her. Gonna drive her to Disneyland in a couple of days. I just enjoy being with her, you know, listening to her. It's not all about the sex as you once said it was. Just watching her eating my cooking gives me a buzz. Anyway, laters for now. I hope you can reach in the new year. Oh, by the way, say hello to your mum for me and everybody else. Laters.'*

'Hmm,' Sharon replied.

'What do you mean hmm?'

'Since you told me about Brenton and Juliet you've always told me about this *they had no choice* t'ing. They were *fated* to be together and all that.'

'Yeah,' nodded Floyd. 'I believe that. Them two were meant to get together at some point. There was no escaping it.'

'Rubbish!' countered Sharon. 'They had *choice*. Brenton convinced himself that he had some kind of destiny to be with Juliet. He wouldn't consider anything else because he thought that he was fated to be with her. He had choices, Floyd. It didn't have to be that way.'

'He didn't have a choice,' argued Floyd. 'From the day he saw her that was it! *Boom!* He was on her. He was lost on her. And it was the same for her.'

'They were arrogant,' said Sharon. 'They thought they could break all the rules. They behaved like they were gods or somet'ing. Say everyone did what they did? The world would be in fucking chaos! Sometimes I fantasise about Denzel Washington but it doesn't mean I would risk everyt'ing and sleep with him! That's what they did! Risked all. They didn't give a fuck about anyone else. It was a fuck-up when they first got together and an even bigger fuck-up to do the same t'ing a whole heap of years later. He could have chosen another life instead of forever waiting for the great beautiful Juliet Hylton to finally go to him. There was Lesley who was perfect for him. He fucked that up. And Shyanza who was real nice and loved him. But no! Brenton wouldn't consider that. Why was he running away from marrying Shyanza? And you know why? 'Cos he had this fucked-up t'ing in his head that there was only Juliet for him. Only her! *That's* the tragedy.'

'But he believed that,' said Floyd. 'That was his reality. He really believed that Juliet was made for him.'

'And I s'pose you're gonna tell me it was the same for her?'

'Yes, it was!'

'*No!* Floyd. They didn't allow anyt'ing else to develop with anybody else. Even Juliet marrying Clayton was a smokescreen. In her mind she still wanted Brenton. You know, think about it. With her looks and t'ing Juliet could've had anybody she wanted. If she wanted some kinda thrill to nice up her sex life she coulda chose someone a bit more discreet. But her *brother*? I've always had serious issues with that. Of all the men in the world she coulda chosen she chose her fucking brother!'

'But don't every woman in the world want to follow their heart and be with the man of their so-called dreams?'

'Yes they do,' answered Sharon. 'But ninety nine point nine per cent of all women accept that they can never have their dream lover, their fantasy man, their Denzel Washington. They look at other options. After they have their teenage crushes on Denzel or Brad Pitt they decide on someone else and learn to love them. That's the way it is for most of us. But no! Not for Juliet. Not for Brenton. Like I said they behaved like gods. They thought there were no rules for them.'

Floyd drank the rest of his whisky and Coke. He placed his

glass down and his eyes misted over. Sharon got off the bed and went to him. She held his left hand, caressed it and kissed it. Tears ran down his face.

'He was like a brother,' he said. 'More than a brother. Brothers I know always have issues with each other. But with Brenton ...'

'I know,' nodded Sharon.

'Even if he lived his life woulda been a torment. You know, without her. It was killing him while he was living here, you know, to see her and Clayton ...'

'It would have been a torment because he convinced himself that he *had* to have her,' said Sharon.

She stood up, walked behind Floyd and placed her arms around his neck.

'That was his fate,' argued Floyd. 'Her fate too. They couldn't escape it. But you know what? Maybe you're right. They did go on like they're gods. What man or woman doesn't want to feel the way they did when they were together?'

Sharon thought about it. 'I have to agree on that,' she said. 'They really went for what they thought would make them happy. But what a price he paid. What a price she's going to pay.'

'But isn't that what it's all about?' asked Floyd. 'What's the point in living if you don't go all out to do what makes you happy?'

THE END

Acknowledgements

I'D LIKE TO SAY THANKS to the usual suspects who have kept me going through this writing lark; my family, Laura Susijn, Courttia Newland, Kolton Lee, Nadifa Mohamed, Mia Morris, Yvonne Archer, Mark Norfolk, Shayne Donnelly, Denise Grossett, Gaverne Bennett, Barbara LeVette and her posse down at the Children's Discovery Centre, numerous public, prison and school librarians and so many more.

A big thank you to my son, Marvin, for the brilliant cover art and a special mention to Jatinder, Jonathan, Katie and the rest of the crew down at Tara Arts who helped me produce my one-man Uprising show which tells the story behind *Brixton Rock* and *Brenton Brown*.

For more information on the good work of Streatham Youth Community Trust please go to: http://streathamyouthandcommunitytrust.org.uk

'The biggest man you ever did see was once a baby,' Bob Marley